LONDON BLUES

Anthony Frewin

LONDON BLUES

> Touch blue
> Your wish will come true.
> – MOTHER GOOSE'S MELODY (*circa* 1765)

NO EXIT PRESS

First published in Great Britain by No Exit Press, 1997.

This edition published in 1997 by No Exit Press,
18 Coleswood Road, Harpenden, Herts, AL5 1EQ, England.

A CIP catalogue record for this book is available from the British
Library.

ISBN 1-874061-73-4 London Blues

9 8 7 6 5 4 3 2

Typography by the author.
Composed in Palatino by Koinonia Ltd, Manchester
and printed and bound in Great Britain.

Part One

1

On Green Dolphin Street

God has a hard-on for paranoids.
– Dan Nordau (*circa* 1968)

IF TIM PURDOM hadn't made all of those black-and-white porno movies in London back in the early 1960s he'd probably still be alive today. I mean *officially* alive … because, of course, nobody can be sure, really sure, that he is dead. They hope he is, but they don't know.

If you're quietly going about shooting blue films with static camera set-ups and too much use of the zoom lens in dingy single rooms at the Hotel Exquisite, Bayswater, featuring a Notting Hill Gate minicab driver flat on his back with one buxom girl astride his loins and another astride his face, for *example*, what enemies are you going to make? Eh? What enemies? You might get arrested, but you're not going to make any enemies. But Tim did. Somehow, somewhere, he did.

Tim was a pioneer of the British porno film. He directed nine films altogether, but who was directing him and what was their agenda, and where is Tim now?

I'll tell you where it started for me, give you the background and recount to you how it unfolded and then you'll know as much as I do. See what sense, if any, you can make of it.

Gibbous moon rising. A shy wind through the trees. Susurrus. November. Late in the year. Late in the day. A fat

Saturday meandering its way to an end and merging insensibly with a lazy Sunday.

I pulled the curtain across, turned over in the bed and lit a cigarette. The room was dark now aside from the television. I was watching a video of Mike Hodges' *Get Carter*. It's a *noir* masterpiece – the kind of movie that's produced about once every twenty years in the British film industry.

Michael Caine is Jack Carter, a gangster whose brother has been found dead in Newcastle, apparently from an accident – he'd been drinking and driving. Carter thinks it's fishy. There's more to it. Jack has a nose for villainy.

It's a film about nasty people in nasty situations. Jack Carter may be a crook but he's self-righteous and determined. He doesn't flinch at cruelty. He's smart and deliberate. And he's got self-respect.

The film opens on Carter standing behind French windows looking out. He's with some gangsters, the ones he works for in London and they're enjoying a slide showing of black-and-white porno stills projected on a screen.

Caine is looking pensive and mean. He's worried and concerned. He's got a different agenda and the other thugs sense this.

'*We* don't want you to go up north, Jack.'

But Jack is determined. He's already made up his mind.

Then Jack's on the train heading north from King's Cross. He's looking at the other passengers and out the window and reading Raymond Chandler's *Farewell, My Lovely*.

There are evening shots and then it's night as the train pulls into Newcastle-upon-Tyne station. Newcastle in the north of England.

Later, there's a superb cameo in the film of a provincial gangland boss, Kinnear, played by John Osborne, the playwright. Kinnear speaks with a semi-educated nasally voice that has a built-in resignation.

Jack is rescued from some hoods who are chasing him by

Kinnear's girlfriend in a white sports car. This is Glenda.

Glenda takes Jack back to her flat. They make love on her bed, reflected in the large mirror that serves as a headboard. Afterwards she goes to the bathroom and runs a bath. She lies in it smoking a cigarette, her heavy make-up still in place. She's smoking the cigarette like it's the last one she'll ever have and, indeed, it is.

Beside the bed is an 8mm projector. A roll of film is laced up and ready to turn over. It's a blue film. Local porno. Glenda has already said she appears in it. Jack switches the projector on. The projector turns over and throws a picture on to the small screen at the foot of the bed.

The film is a mute black-and-white production called *Teacher's Pet*. A schoolgirl gets out of a car. Inside a house she is shown into a room by a 'mistress' played by Glenda.

As Jack watches he realises that the young girl is his brother's daughter (though she may well be *his* daughter, the film is ambiguous). Tears silently roll down Jack's face as he stares at the screen. The drama unfolds. Set pieces. Jack knows what is coming next. A bit of this and then a bit of that. Anyone can write the script.

As I'm watching Michael Caine watch the film the sound is cut. I can see Carter call out something to Glenda in the bathroom. She mouths something but the sound has gone. And now the picture goes too. It's there and then it isn't and I'm left with a black screen with streaking white noise. From downstairs I hear the grandfather clock chime midnight.

Fuck!

I paid £15 for this bootleg tape. A prime copy of the full uncut version ... supposedly.

I run the tape fast forward. Nothing. Further fast forward. Still nothing. Just blackness.

As I light another cigarette the screen catches my eye. The black has given way to a solid grey, as though something is about to appear. I stare at the screen waiting for Michael Caine and the rest of *Get Carter*. I wait and the grey remains. Suddenly, in black and white, there's some film leader and the rapidly descending numbers of 10-9-8-7-6-5-4-3-2-1. They're over in as many seconds and the screen is now white. Then:

FUCKADUCK FILMS
presents

The words have been handwritten on white card with a thick black marker. The first line in caps and the second in lower case.

The card very nearly fills the screen. It's being held by someone whose fingers can be seen in the two top corners. Fingers with long false fingernails painted red. I assume it's red as the film is grainy black and white, and scratched.

And now a second card appears:

in association with
PRICK-A-DILLY PRODUCTIONS

rapidly followed by a third:

THE BOYFRIEND'S
SURPRISE VISIT

From the title alone I'd guess this is an authentic 1960s blue movie. A genuine slice of the underside of Swingin' London. A porno pic. A blue movie. A stag. A smoker. A loop. Call it what you will.

Is it here? Am I going to see it?

Yes.

The opening shot. Two of them. A blonde. A brunette. Two dolly birds in their late teens, early twenties. Both with the heavy eye make-up one associates with graduates of Dusty Springfield University. The brunette is wearing a floral patterned dress and white high-heeled shoes. Her hair is cut short. She has a pixie face with small eyes and large lips. The blonde has her hair straight and uncut. She's wearing a black skirt and a white blouse. She's the more attractive of the two but there's something hard about her angular features. She's stealing glances at the camera every so often and holding herself back. She would rather not be doing this but for some reason she is. The brunette is playing the role to the full.

The two girls are sitting on the floor of a room that looks like a bedsit (and indeed it is, or was). In front of them is a portable record player with an LP spinning. They are swooning over some photographs of Cliff Richard in a magazine, kissing him, holding him to their breasts, closing their eyes and thinking how wonderful it must be to be possessed by such a *fella*.

The room interests me more now than the girls. To their left is a small old threadbare two-seater sofa which has been put hard against the footboard of a high double bed, one of those old beds that stands about a metre off the ground. I remember as a kid being taken on holidays in the 1950s when every hotel room had just such a bed. They were ancient even then. Massive hardwood head- and foot-boards that looked like they would last a million years and, indeed, would have had not changing fashions ousted them. I can only see about a third of the bed and on it seems to be a quilted eiderdown, and not the more usual candlewick bedspread, usually a *sine qua non* of British sixties porno pix. The other obligatory prop of the genre is the Lloyd Loom chair but I can't see one in frame. Should the camera pan on the tripod, however, I would bet my pristine first edition copy of *The Crying of Lot 49* that one would sail into view (it didn't, so just as well). In the back-ground some heavy ceiling-to-floor curtains have been closed over the windows that occupy the centre of a wall with peeling arabesque wallpaper. To the right of the drapes – a tailor's dummy, a torso bereft of limbs on a stand. Is this going to feature in the action or is it just standing there in splendid surrealist isolation?

On the right wall was a sink in the corner with an odd-looking Ascot heater above it. The Ascot was the object that officially confirmed a room had changed its identity and was now a *bedsit*. This was objective, scientific proof that nobody could dispute. Landlords put them in for quick, cheap hot water so the renters wouldn't clutter the bathroom they shared with ten others (indeed, in some cases, it obviated the need for a bathroom altogether).

On this side of the sink was a table and above it, pinned to the wallpaper, were postcards and photographs. Then a big bulky armchair, a close relative to and contemporary of the sofa, followed by a largish bookcase that disappears from frame.

I wondered where this bedsitter was? Earls Court was the favourite locale, and if not there South Kensington or Swiss Cottage? No, Swiss Cottage did not seem right. How about Ladbroke Grove? More likely. A pound on Earls Court then, 50 pence on South Ken and 25 on the Grove. I would later find that my last bet was topographically the nearest: this little example of the secret cinema was shot in Bayswater, on Porchester Road, near the top of Queensway, a little over three-quarters of a mile to the east of Ladbroke Grove.

The camera is still statically staring down at the girls who continue cooing and oohing at Cliff. I'm wondering what will happen next? A dream sequence with a Cliff clone? And, God Almighty, there were enough of them about in the late fifties and early sixties! Hard to credit, eh?

The blonde looks to the camera and then quickly looks away. Whoever is behind the camera is giving her directions and telling her not to look into the lens. She stands up, kicks her shoes off, pulls up her dress, takes her panties down, steps out of them and throws them towards the sink. All of these actions are done with an expression of bored defiance – I don't have to do this! Pouty and spoilt. Very well, if I have to, *then*.

The brunette looks up from Cliff and says something to

the blonde. She says something in reply and then sits down on the floor peering over the brunette's shoulders at the photographs. The brunette turns and gently pushes the blonde back until she is flat on the carpet with her legs towards the camera. The blonde reaches over for the magazine and is reunited with Cliff as the brunette lifts her skirt, opens her legs, and begins gently massaging her almost hairless blonde pussy, all glistening and shiny (with baby oil?). The blonde begins moving her hips in a circular motion as the brunette's fingers explore more deeply. The camera zooms in until the action largely fills the frame. Now the brunette's head comes into view, led by her tongue which follows the course taken by her fingers over the labia and on to the clit. Her hair keeps falling forward and obscuring the action and, it seems, responding to instructions the brunette quickly pushes it back behind her ear (the punters have to see what is going on). She's licking with her eyes closed, giving herself up to the part.

The camera pulls back slowly to the full framing of the opening footage. The two girls stand up and begin undressing until they are both naked. They embrace and run their hands up and down each other's bodies. The blonde is still shooting glances at the camera.

They walk to the left and the camera, still on the tripod, pans and follows them without moving from its original position. The blonde sits on the edge of the bed, opens her legs, and the brunette goes down on her again. The blonde, to show how much she is really enjoying this, opens her mouth, rolls her head and stares at the ceiling.

I can now see more of the room. Behind the bed, against the wall to the left of the curtains is a mirrored dressing table piled high with books, mainly paperbacks. Above it is a painting in an ornate, carved if now worn frame. The glass appears to be cracked and the years of dirt, grime and, no doubt, cigarette smoke render it impossible to identify, at least on a video dupe of a twenty-five-year-old 8mm loop.

On this side of the bed at the head is a small, low bedside table with a Bakelite radio, an overflowing ashtray and some more paperbacks. By the foot of the bed is a squat television on an upturned packing carton angled for viewing from the bed.

Above the bed is a large poster of ... Charlie Parker! Bird is holding his alto and smiling. He's in a suit. One of those striped double-breasted creations the boppers favoured. He's staring out across the bedroom as the blonde and brunette gently rock to and fro in a sixty-nine position, the brunette uppermost. Bird's presence strikes me as incongruous, there's something too hip about him for a British blue movie. The ambient décor of home-grown stags has always been kitsch, terminal kitsch. If ever there's a painting on the wall it's the Oriental girl with green skin framed in white plastic that Boots the Chemists used to sell. That or a painting of a steam train or a Spitfire or the Italian kid with tears in his eyes. But *Bird*?

The couple uncouple and the brunette produces an unzipped banana from somewhere and gently inserts it into the blonde's vagina. The blonde starts staring at the ceiling again and impersonating ecstasy. The camera now moves: it and the tripod upon which it is fixed are lifted, carried nearer the bed, and set down. A slow zoom in to show the magical wedding of banana and labia in glistening, anatomical detail. The brunette's hand moves the fruit in, out, in and around. She's wearing false nails painted red, or certainly a dark colour. Were these the hands featured in the title card at the beginning?

After what seems an eternity of reciprocating motion the camera pulls back to the medium shot. The director should have told the blonde this because she is caught unawares. Instead of abandoning herself to the plateaux of pleasure she's scratching her nose and yawning. Somebody does say something to her because in a trice she's back to rolling her head and staring at the ceiling. And still the banana hasn't worn out. The brunette is diligently, if not mindlessly, pumping away with it.

Looking at the part of the room now visible and linking it with what was seen of the right-hand side I could see it was pretty spacious. The ceiling is high too. This is in a Victorian town house carved up into bedsits. The wall on the right was probably put in to divide the room.

The film so far has been one take. The first cut now occurs: same camera set-up with the two girls on the bed. The brunette is kneeling down with her buttocks towards the camera. The blonde is listlessly masturbating her with the neck of a bottle. The camera zooms in to show the penetration in greater detail but the available light at this angle is limited.

Another cut and the girls are fondling each other's breasts and kissing. The lens gently zooms in until lips and two extended touching tongues fill the screen. There's a slow pull back to a medium shot of the girls sitting on the edge of the bed. The brunette opens her legs and pulls back her lips as far as they will go. The blonde touches her with a hesitant middle finger and then moves it down and into her until it is lost within. The zoom lens brings the subject forward until it fills the whole screen. It holds for several beats and then pulls back as the blonde removes her finger and the brunette closes her legs.

The girls are now startled by something off-screen. A noise, perhaps? They duck under the bed's covers and wait. From camera right a figure walks into frame. He stands staring at the bed with his back to the camera. He's wearing tight-fitting cord trousers, Chelsea boots and a dark shirt. His hair is blond and longish (for the time), coming to just over his ears. He steps forward and pulls back the eiderdown to reveal the two naked girls underneath doing their best to act sheepish and embarrassed. He undresses quickly and pulls the girls from the bed. They kneel down in front of him, one on either side. The guy looks like he's in his early twenties. His features are sharp but not stern, almost like a young Paul Newman. He's smiling and enjoying himself.

The blonde takes his semi-flaccid circumcised member and begins rubbing it, deliberately and purposefully. She then sucks it with not much enthusiasm, barely taking more than its head in. The brunette comes over for a suck and does it with gusto, showing the blonde how it should be done.

The guy is now as hard as he's ever likely to be. He sits on the edge of the bed and pulls the blonde towards him. She climbs on him with her back to the camera and he's soon inside her. He supports her buttocks with his hands, parts them for the camera and gently moves her up and down. Her co-operation seems zero. The brunette kneels down in front of them to get a better look. Now the girls change position for another few feet of 8mm footage.

The brunette climbs off and kneels down on the bed. The guy stands up, turns, parts her buttocks and starts to fuck her from behind. The blonde manoeuvres herself round on the far side so she can caress the other girl's back. The detail isn't too clear from this distance and I wonder why the zoom lens isn't used for an anatomical close-up.

The guy withdraws and the blonde flops down with her legs open waiting for him. He seems to have some difficulty getting into her and then he's in and she's off staring at the ceiling again. The guy fucks her in what must be a difficult position, supporting himself on his right arm so that he's well above her, with his left leg at an awkward angle, so that the punters won't miss any of the action. Not that one can make out much from this distance. Again, why not a zoom? The brunette sits on the other side of the blonde caressing her breasts.

The guy withdraws quickly and the brunette reaches forward and rubs him as he ejaculates over the blonde's breasts. The blonde turns her head away to stop any come ending up on her face and then slowly gazes down at her breasts as if to say: what on earth is *that*?

The brunette leans forward and pulls the now detumescent penis to her mouth for a final quick suck. She then turns and scoops some come in a teaspoon that has appeared as if by magic and offers it to the blonde who opens her mouth and takes it in. She probably didn't swallow it, but whether she did or not we will never know as the film now cuts to a title card, again the black marker on white card:

That's all, Folks!
THE END
Copyright NGN MCMLXIII

Another card follows:

Watch out for our COMING attractions!

And then:

THE MIRACLE WANKER
FLORENCE OF ARABIA

and

SPLENDOUR IN THE ASS
Soon on a wall near you!!

Whoever made this had a rare sense of humour, certainly for the genre. The allusive coming attractions would seem to validate the joky copyright line of MCMLXIII (1963): the originals for these punning titles were all feature films released here in London in 1961 or 1962, years I can remember pretty well, cinematically speaking, as I had just left school and went to the pictures regularly, usually twice a week.

This was the first sixties porno film I had seen in nearly twenty years. I had forgotten how amateurish they were. Not only amateurish but almost simple and innocent, like a saucy Victorian pin-up. Artless and unaffected. I remembered that everyone in them looked like someone you could have gone to school with. They were the kids next door and the film could well have been made next door. Now the porno films from Germany, America and Scandinavia are shot professionally in good colour, with sync sound, incidental music and glam girls tarted up and expensively dressed like a page three bimbo opening a supermarket (well, in the opening scenes anyway – they soon strip off). But I guess it's what you're used to, what you grew up with. If I'm honest with myself I have to admit there's a nostalgia factor in the appeal of these loops. They're the first ones I saw, they are the ones I associate with my youth, with parties where I smoked my first dope, with the whole sixties whirligig.

The first blue movie I ever saw was at a party in a church in Chelsea, or rather a small chapel that had been converted into a house by a newspaper photographer who then lived there. I went with a girlfriend called Sarah Breakspear who I can still vividly recall after all these years. The only redhead I've ever gone out with. In the middle of the party someone switched on a little 8mm projector and we all enjoyed an hour's worth of sleaze. It was fun, there was a lot of laughter. Try doing that at your average party now.

I'm thinking about the film and the sixties generally when I get an epiphanic answer to the question as to why the zooms lens was used in the first half of the film but not the second. The reason was simple. The guy who appeared in the film was the director/cameraman. Of course! When he was in front of the lens there was no one to operate the camera. He was the *auteur* (if stags are allowed such a thing) and, further, it was his room the movie was shot in. After all, didn't he look the sort of guy who would have a picture of Bird on his wall?

The video had continued turning after the end of *The Boyfriend's Surprise Visit* ... showing nothing but solid black. But now there was movement and sound – the end credits of *Get Carter* were rolling, but I wasn't taking any

real notice. I was still thinking about the blue movie. Who
was the guy? What was his background? Did he make any
other loops? Where is he now? What's he doing? Who was
the blonde? Who was the brunette? Where are they now?
Did they travel by bus, underground, taxi or car to the
shoot? What did they do immediately afterwards? What
did they work at? Where *are* they now? If they're married,
do their husbands know about their work in the movies?
Why did they appear? How much were they paid?

The Boyfriend's Surprise Visit. Not a very original title but
then the whole genre is formula stuff right down to and
including the title. Boyfriend implies in this context a
sexual relationship, and if he's surprising his girlfriend
she's obviously doing something naughty. What you think
you're getting you usually get.

Years ago I had an inventory of British dirty films seized
by the police from a wealthy collector and dealer who lived
in St John's Wood. I remember going through the list and
thinking how dreary and unimaginative the titles were.
There were some 500 of them. Nearly half were of *The
Boyfriend's Surprise Visit* kind – titles like *Caught in the Act,
The Handy Man, The Casting Couch, Geisha Girl, Night Nurses,*
and so on. The next largest group were the explicitly direct,
Get Fucked, Arse Lovers, Dildo Delights, and similar. Out of
this long list only three were really memorable – two for
their humour and the third for its sheer bizarreness. The
humour award goes to *Los Effectos de La Marihuana* with
Incestral [sic] Home in second place. This is what passes for
urbane wit in this neck of the woods. The oddest title was
stolen from a British theatrical musical of the 1940s written
by Ivor Novello: *Perchance to Dream.* What a genteel title for a
fuck film even if it does feature a dream sequence.

As I lay in the darkness edging into sleep the film kept
running through my mind. Who were the girls? Who was
the guy?

The director's name I would later discover was Timothy

Purdom. Well, that was the name he sailed under in the early sixties. He was christened George Eric Purdom. His friends called him Tim or Timmy. Why? I don't know. And I never did find out.

George Purdom. George Eric Purdom. He wasn't an Eric. There was nothing about him that was Eric-ish, or George-ish. Given names that were misnomers, both of them. He was a Tim or a Timmy, the name suited him far better. A name he could live with. But where are you now, Timmy? Where indeed?

Timmy's a mystery all right. A real mystery. But, as I would discover, he was a mystery in an even bigger mystery. Forget about answers, we don't even know the questions.

This is a lost mystery of Lost London.

I step off the underground train, walk along the platform and up the stairs. There is no ticket collector so I drop the ticket into a waste-bin and continue bouncing along in my new Reeboks and out on to the street. Queensway. Back in the 1960s it was a bohemian sort of place whereas now it seems mainly populated by Arabs, the less well-off Arabs, the ones that can't afford Sloane Street and thereabouts.

It's a cold Sunday afternoon and big rain clouds are massing in the sky, yet the place is as bustling as Oxford Street on a Saturday morning.

To the south is the Bayswater Road and that part of Hyde Park that dissolves into Kensington Gardens, while to the north is Westbourne Grove where I now head. Up past the old Whitely's department store on the left, now revamped as some co-operative boutique collective with flags flying at high mast above it, and then across the Grove.

I continue, in an easterly direction, past the road that leads up to the Porchester Baths, past the old ABC Cinema.

I turn left on to Porchester Road and stop. I'm standing outside the Royal Oak pub, a place that looks like it must have been here for a hundred years or more. It's a pub with more local than passing trade I would guess, an unprepossessing place that probably hasn't changed since the war and one that won't until the day a developer gets planning permission to demolish and redevelop, then it'll become part of what it already seems – another part of Lost London.

And there's Timmy drinking at the bar, just in there, only a few yards away from me ... but nearly thirty years ago. He's part of Lost London too, the Valhalla of Memory. All the parameters are right except for that of Time. We could have met. Yes, indeed.

I turn my head slowly. I know what to expect from sly peripheral vision glances. What was there is no longer there. I'm dealing in the vanished. The stuff of memories. The London that is gone.

Here was Albert Terrace, built in the late 1850s or early 1860s. A tall terrace of mid-Victorian stock design – open basement, mezzanine, plus three storeys. Brick with stucco. Built originally for the middle levels of the middle classes who could not afford to live in the swankier area to the south along the Bayswater Road (which itself was for those who could not afford the airy elegance of Cubitt's Belgravia on the other side of Hyde Park). One family (and servants) in each house with their horses and carriages kept around the back in the mews. But a special configuration of late nineteenth-century topography and demography resulted in the terrace descending into cheap multi-occupancy ... and the plaster cracked and the wallpaper peeled and the carpets on the stairs got more and more threadbare while the rainwater pipes rusted and bracken and moss sprouted in the hopper-heads.

I raise my head slightly and then slowly open my eyes and see what used to be there. I picture it as it was. Then I see what is there now and I see how the whole corner of Porchester Road and Bishop's Bridge Road has been redeveloped in clean crisp brick. Gone is Albert Terrace and the

mews behind and the other buildings. The past has been
jettisoned like the rubble of Albert Terrace. Spacious expensive apartments rising high and protected above
Westbourne Grove and the Royal Oak. And here incorpo-
rated into the design at street level is a Pizza Express facing
the south, and a Budgen's supermarket fronting Porchester
Road. There is where Timmy's crowded and untidy room
would have been, just there I would say, behind an orna-
mental balcony that also no longer exists. Now a sheer wall
of brick.

This corner here is murmurous with time. Somewhere
the past is still the present. Somewhere ... there's music ...

How high the moon?

Tim is now loading a reel of 8mm black-and-white film into
the movie camera. A Charlie Parker or Thelonious Monk
record might be playing on his portable record player. It's
the early 1960s and then when you were young your
future, your life, had only one limitation and that was your
imagination. If you could think of it you could do it.
Anything was possible. It always is in the past.

'Hi. Come in.'
  'Sit down ... would you like a drink ... or something?'
  'No.'
  'You got any Pepsi?'
  'No, I haven't. I've got some lemonade ... I think.'
  'No.'
  'You're Elaine?'
  'Yes.'
  'You work with Brenda?'
  'No. We're just friends.'
  'Elaine and me went to school together.'
  'Uh-huh.'
  'Yeah. Elaine works in a shoe shop.'
  'In the West End?'
  'Marble Arch.'

'But I'm going after a better job.'
'Good.'
'It will be if I get it.'
'I hope you do.'
'I will.'
'This your place?'
'I live here. Yes.'
'Not very modern, is it?'
'Suits me.'
'Yeah.'

'Brenda says you're going to pay us £10 each.'
  'A tenner each … that's right.'
  'We get paid now?'
  'As soon as we've finished.'
  'Yeah. What's this going to be called then?'
  'I haven't decided.'
  'See, he doesn't know. I asked before … said he didn't know.'
  'Well, probably something like *Surprised by the Boyfriend*.'
  'You're the boyfriend?'
  'I'm the only fella here.'
  'What have I got to do?'
  'We can run through it … run through it in a minute when I've got the lights fixed … but it opens with you two alone here and you start getting fruity and playing with each other.'
  'Oh, yeah?'
  'Yeah. And then I discover … I surprise you when I walk in and we have a threesome.'
  'So you appear in it?'
  'Yes.'
  'Who looks after the camera when you are … doing it?'
  'Nobody. It's on a tripod. It looks after itself.'
  'I don't want to get pregnant.'
  'You won't. I'm not going to come inside you.'
  'I've got to catch my bus at nine o'clock.'

'I've never heard of any of these records ... where do you get them from? I haven't heard of ... any ... this lot.'

'Jazz shops.'

'Jazz ... I don't like *jazz*.'

'Where are the records from these Cliff Richard sleeves?'

'There aren't any. I just have the sleeves.'

'You just collect sleeves ... so it looks good?'

'No. They're props for this ... the film.'

'Props?'

'Just props ... in the film.'

'Don't you have anything worth playing?'

'There's a Beatles EP there somewhere. Put that on.'

'The who?'

'The Beatles ... you know ... from Liverpool.'

'I like Cliff.'

'He's all right.'

'You know Roy?'

'Who's he?'

'My boyfriend.'

'*That* Roy.'

'Yes. He's my new boyfriend. He works in a record shop. The Melody Bar ... in Charing Cross Road.'

'That sounds exciting. Can he get records cheap?'

'No. But Cliff Richard went in there last week and there were riots ... and the police were called. *Summer Holiday* got to number seven in the Hit Parade this week.'

'Did he meet Cliff?'

'Yes ... and he got his autograph for me!'

'Can he get me one?'

'If Cliff comes back in the shop, he can.'

'He's the tops.'

'Even my old gran likes him.'

'Everyone does.'

'Even the police.'

'And Elvis does too.'

'Does he?'

'Yeah. I heard this geezer say it on the radio.'

'When's he going to be ready?'

'Soon. He has to get all the lights and that right. They pay him a lot of money for this. That's how he can pay us a lot.'

'Only a tenner!'

'That's more than I earn a week at Maison Eve. And you don't earn that selling shoes!'

'I never said I did, did I?'

'It's good ... for an hour's work.'

'You see those photos in the paper today of Elizabeth Taylor wearing all that jewellery? Over £100,000 worth!'

'What I saw today was a really nice black dress in a boutique in Old Bond Street. It was six guineas and I'm going to get it.'

'That's nice. I'm going to save it. We're getting married soon and we need every penny.'

'To Roy?'

'I hope so.'

'Does he know you're doing this?'

'Course not, stupid!'

'Let's just run through it ... are you sure you two don't want a drink?'

'A drink?'

'Yes.'

'No.'

'This isn't going to be shown over here, is it?'

'No, it isn't. I told you. It's being exported to Thailand.'

'Thailand?'

'That's miles away, Brenda.'

'Thailand? Near India, The other side of India ... so don't take your holidays there!'

'Where?'

'Thailand. In Thailand.'

'Shouldn't think so. We only ever go to the coast some-place. Someplace … like Ilfracombe … or Cromer.'

'I've been to Cromer.'

'Lots of boys there.'

'But more in Ilfracombe.'

'We went in my dad's Dormobile.'

'Lucky thing!'

'Yes. He saved really hard for it.'

'I don't want to miss my last bus.'

'You won't.'

'I've got to get up early in the morning. I'm helping my sister-in-law.'

'I mustn't get my hair in a mess. I've only just had it done.'

'You won't.'

'I don't want what it cost me going down the drain. Seven- and-six it was.'

'That's steep. We don't charge that.'

'Let's do a dress rehearsal.'

'Can't you just film it?'

'We have to get it right.'

'I'm cold.'

'So am I.'

'I've put the electric fire on … full.'

'I'm all goose pimples now.'

'It won't show on the film.'

'Can I put the gas fire on?'

'If it worked you could.'

'Belongs in a museum.'

'Put that Beatles record on.'

'It's *Please, Please Me*.'

'Yeah.'

'This bedcover is filthy … don't you ever wash it?'
  'Are we ready?'
  'Where did I put the spoon?'
  'It's on the bed there … the other side.'
  'Here it is.'
  'Leave it there.'
  'Are you both ready?'
  'I am … yes.'
  'Yes.'
  'Sure you don't want to run through it again?'

'Ready? Ready … OK, then. I'm going to start the camera … and don't get in the way. The camera has to see everything. Everything. But don't look into the camera. I'll tell you … as we go along. OK? Running. Now. Action!'

A dowdy run-down pre-war council estate in Harpenden, Hertfordshire. A house more run-down than the others. A battered, rusted Ford Capri jacked up in the front garden and adjacent a redundant washing machine with weeds growing up around it.

The woman standing by the front door looks like Elaine's grandmother would have looked in 1963. But it's Elaine herself. She's wearing black slacks, a white blouse, a red bra. White high-heeled shoes. She's been married twice and divorced twice. She looks lived-in, as they say. She was fifty last week.

'It wasn't me and anyway I can't talk to you as I've got to pick my granddaughter up from the nursery.'

That evening when she was all alone she would look into the bathroom mirror, explore the intricate topography of her face, and say, 'I was young and silly then … but very attractive … *very* attractive.' She would stare into her eyes for some time and wonder: where have those thirty years gone?

A crematorium. Neat and ordered. Avenues of remembrance. Trained creepers and pruned roses. A tired fountain.

Here's a plaque set in the wall:

BRENDA JENNIFER BUTLER
7 July 1944 – 3 March 1965
'Now in Heaven'
Our Precious Daughter
Mum and Dad

She was crossing the road. Walking across the Edgware Road just south of Kilburn. Two black guys in a stolen car, stoned out of their minds. Hit and run.

I look at the plaque again ... one of the two memorials to her existence.

NICK ESDAILLE: Perhaps the sixties, the 1960s, started at midnight on 1 January 1960? Perhaps they started half an hour later? Perhaps they didn't get going until 1966 when *Time* magazine had that cover story about 'London – The Swinging City'? Was it 1966? I'm not sure. Yeah, it was 1966. Yeah, I always remember that because it was the same year as the Moors Murders trial. Perhaps ... perhaps the sixties, the 1960s ... .

This Yucatan is really *goooood*!

So ... so ... what I'm saying is ... that you ... is that you can ask a dozen different people and you'll get a dozen different starting dates. The sixties, I always think, didn't really get going until about 1964 and didn't end until about 1972 or 1973. The early 1960s were, in every way, the fag end of the fifties – post-war austerity, drab, predictable ... and not very imaginative or stylish.

You see the 1940s didn't end until about 1956. Then it was the 1950s until 1963 or '64 or so.

So Tim, you know, was a child of the 1940s who came of age in the 1950s and when he was out and about in London in the early 1960s it was still very fifty-ish. But I think he was, in his own way, one of those formative guys who sort of ... uh ... *pointed* the way. He was heading in the direction

a lot of other people would go, but a good few years earlier.
I suppose you could say he was one of the precursors of
Swingin' London, in his own way ... even if his was a life
on the margin.

Yeah ... paranoia ... paranoia ... there was a lot of paranoia about then. In fact it was a child of the sixties. No, it
wasn't all dope related. Dope paranoia is local, person-
alised stuff. Pretty small beer: me and my friends and
whether that guy in the bar is going to shop me to the local
drug squad. That kind of thing. Part of the drug culture.
What I'm really talking about is what you might call *political* paranoia. Political in the big sense of the term.
Conspiracies that affect the way we live and the way we
perceive things. Conspiracy theory, if you like, as opposed
to the 'accident' theorists like ... like, say Christopher
Andrew and his ilk. These guys see all sorts of conspiracies
with the left wing ... communist and socialist conspiracies
all over the place, the enemy within and all that, but as soon
as someone thinks they see a right-wing conspiracy or plot
these guys are on the platform shouting 'Conspiracy theo-
rist!' You know, as a put-down.

I date it from 1963, the paranoia. There were two events
then that got it rolling. First, the arrest and alleged suicide
of Stephen Ward, the osteopath at the centre of the Profumo
Affair. And then, a few months later, Lee Harvey Oswald
supposedly shooting John F. Kennedy. But *this* was a
double whammy: two days after Jack Kennedy got it
Oswald got it too! Shot in the police basement in Dallas by
a small-time Mafia hood, Jack Ruby!

Now, who really was Stephen Ward? Who was Oswald?
Who was Ruby? Thirty years later now, are we any the
wiser? Are we any the wiser in real terms? We know a bit
more, sure, but we don't have any definitive answers.
Plenty of surmises. Plenty of hunches. But no smoking
guns. No true confessions.

There was, I think, a mutually reinforcing feedback
between the drug paranoia and the political paranoia. A

dope smoker who is pretty sure that the local drug squad is up to no good – you know, licensing dealers, selling off seized quantities, fitting up people – is more likely to look at Lee Harvey Oswald and think, hold on a minute! What's really going on here? What's the real score? What's the sub-text?

I can't speak for other countries but for the generation that grew up here in the 1950s and 1960s dope got you looking at things in a different way. You found yourself questioning things your parents never did. That political sophistication may be the only valid legacy of the sixties. We'll see.

Nobody has the Big Picture. Even people on the inside don't have it, but, of course, their picture is a lot more comprehensive than the one you put together on the outside. I don't think Timmy ever thought he had it or, if he did, he never confided it to me. Nothing much at all was known at the time. The odd strange occurrence, the odd half-digested rumour, the odd suspicion. Nobody was sitting down and trying to put it all together. You couldn't catch it in a single focus. When you are working on a news-paper you hear things all the time. There's a kind of over-load. You prick your ears up when there is something that is of immediate use. But the rest? It goes to the back of your mind ... then out of your mind. Unlike American papers we don't have journalists working long-term on Big Stories. Your typical hack wants the big one placed on his desk – all trussed-up and oven-ready.

Sure, I was interested in these things and I made all sorts of inquiries and spent a long time with Tim but where could I have gone if I had nailed it? Do you think any sheet in Fleet Street would have touched it? Those were the days when every newspaper editor used to have a photograph of the Queen on his desk. These were the chaps who went to church every Sunday. God. The Queen. My Country. Truth was an unstable commodity that changed from day to day.

What was it that Carlyle said about history? History is present politics. Uh-huh. These guys would have told you truth is present politics. Nobody had to lean on them and say ignore this one, old boy. They didn't have to be told this. They knew what was expected of them. Now it's changed a bit, but not that much. There are other outlets now and television too and there you'll find some of the best shit-stirring investigative reporting around.

So, you hear this type of thing and you can't do much with it. And you can't do much with it because you haven't got the half of it. It's like being blindfolded and let loose in a library. You know it's all there but how are you going to find what you are looking for?

Tim didn't have the full story. Couldn't have. But he sensed that there was something going on and he sensed that he might have been manoeuvred but he didn't know why and, really, how. You can be used and not realise you are being used. You can also be used, realise you are being used, but misunderstand why and how you are being used. He got wind of something being afoot but that was it. You know something's there but you don't know what it is.

2

Sometimes I'm Happy

And diligently noting decaying rumours and dissolving memories.
– Caroline Severin *Out of Nowhere* (1967)

ROCHESTER. About 25 miles east-south-east of London. It was here that the Romans, like the Britons before them, forded the River Medway some nine or so miles upstream from where it empties into the Thames estuary.

Charles Dickens was here. Didn't he spend his early years in Chatham, a mile or so down the road? And here too is 'Cloisterham' of *The Mystery of Edwin Drood*, Dickens' uncompleted last novel. And nearby are the marshes where at the beginning of *Great Expectations* Pip encounters the escaped convict. This is where I will be going.

To start to know your subject, start to know the places he (or she) grew up in, lived in, died in. Place *is* very nearly person. Know something about the place and you'll know something about the person. The topography of Tim is drawing me in. But first I need a cup of coffee.

I drive out of Rochester, over the bridge and across the river to a place with the bewitching, adjectival-sounding name of Strood. Its name is its most attractive feature. Then off to the right and under the sweep of a railway viaduct and past the Steam Packet, a little Victorian pub built of stock bricks.

The road rises and threads its way through the Medway town environs and then it begins a gentle and deliberate descent and ahead I see the rolling chalkland and its open fields.

Now there are derelict railway lines and disused army earthworks, overgrown cattle paths and droves, pre-war bungalows 'modernised' to look like Texas ranch houses and electricity pylons taking seven-league steps to a monumental power station over by the estuary.

A little way past Lower Stoke the road crosses the here infilled Yantlet Creek, then a level crossing on a lonely railway track and you enter the Isle of Grain. There's a sign that says so, but now it is an isle in name only.

Isle of Grain. Parish of St James. And in that Saxon intermediate division between the parish and the county, the hundred, this is the Hundred of Hoo.

> He that rideth in the Hundred of Hoo
> Besides pilfering Seamen shall find dirt enow.
> – Ralph Holinshed *Chronicles of England* (1587)

Ahead, now, is the vast BP oil refinery. All pipes and towers and minarets glistening in the fading sunlight. At night it must look like a scene out of *Blade Runner*. And here a sign that says KENT TERMINAL but, more aptly, should read TERMINAL KENT.

> The Island of Graine lies very flat and low; the greatest part of it consists of pasture and marshes, the vast tracts of the latter in the neighbourhood of it, and the badness of the water, makes it a very unwholesome place; so that the inhabitants mostly consist of a few Lookers or Bailiffs, and of those who work at the salt-works, and such like, who have not wherewithal to seek a residence elsewhere.
> – Edward Hasted *The History and Topographical Survey of the County of Kent* (1782)

Here too are the saltings and the marshes and quays and wharves of the estuary waters where the coastal birds still bravely adjust to every fresh incursion into what has been their habitat since their ancestors first leapt from the trees. Here is the snipe, the sandpiper, the moorhen, the wild duck, the tern, and a hundred varieties of gull.

There's a gentle rise in the road and ahead is the village of St James's, more usually known simply as Grain. But village is the wrong word, it provokes images of some pastoral scene. Grain isn't like that now. It looks like a transit camp for refugees.

There are some old cottages on the left and then ahead the small Church of St James with its tiny squat tower that, at 31 feet, does not reach the height of the nave. This is a Norman church of masonry and mortar that replaced an Anglo-Saxon wooden structure that was old and decaying a thousand years ago.

The road continues past the church and by some ageing cottages and then the High Street becomes a mere trackway, its metalling chipped and disintegrating, past what remains of the cottages of Willow Place, and there a scruffy carpark strewn with dented beer cans and emptied ashtrays and dog shit. Here, beyond the sloping grassland and the geometrical concrete blocks designed to prevent the Germans invading, and beyond the weathered groins and piers and half-submerged abandoned barges on the mud flats, is Father Thames himself, emptying into the North Sea. Then a panorama of Essex coastland that shades gradually into the grey swells of the sea and the grey swirls of the sky.

Here is the end of the road. It goes no further. This is the end of the journey for us, but here was the beginning for Timmy. For here on the Feast of St Brocard, hermit, 2 September that is, 1937, a Thursday, just back there towards the church in a cottage now demolished, George Eric Purdom was born.

Now the watery light of the morning merges with that of the afternoon and memories are stirred.

MRS FLORENCE MIDDLEMOST: I've spent all my life on Grain. I was born here in 1918 just as the Great War ended. Mum and Dad had come down here from Gravesend. We lived in a clapboard cottage down near Home Farm. Dad used to put these poles up in the garden with a platform high above the ground and the herons used to come and nest. I think that's one of my earliest memories.

I never called him Tim or Timmy. I always called him Eric because that was his name.

Eric's mother was Joan and we were at school together at the National School by the church (the same school Eric went to). I had been there for a couple of years before she came. Her parents moved over from Borstal around 1930.

Joan lived with her parents just the other side of the church in Willow Place but that's not there any more, the cottage they lived in. Joan was a few months older than me, or I might have been a few months older than her. I can't remember now. We were very close friends and spent all our time together when we were young.

Joan had several boyfriends and then ... well, you know what happened and it's too late now to sweep it under the carpet. She was *expecting*. She wasn't the first unmarried girl in Grain to have a baby and she won't be the last. I think her mum and dad were very upset to begin with but they made the best of it.

A bonny, fat little baby was Eric. He was always called Eric by us here, but George was his first name. I don't know why that was so. And I certainly never called him Tim or Timmy. I don't know where that came from.

Joan never said who the father was and everybody used to whisper that it was him or him but nobody knew for sure. I think I know. I think it was one of those American engineers who worked down at the oil refinery where Port Victoria used to be.

I got married that same year Eric was born and didn't see much of Joan after that. When the war broke out she left Grain and took Eric to stay with her mother's family up in

Nottingham or Northampton until the war was over. I spent most of the beginning of the war with my little boy and girl in Oxford while George, my husband, was away in the Army. Then we came back to West Malling for the rest of the war and back to Grain in 1945. Joan and Eric came back soon after that and then Eric started school here by the church, where Joan and me had gone.

Eric was a lovely little boy, always full of energy and high spirits. A real handful. Also, very obliging. He used to carry my shopping back home for me, lend a hand in the garden and so on. A little gem.

Joan married some time in the early 1950s and went to live in Rochester. I don't know who she married. I think my friend Edna said he was a printer.

The last time I saw her and Eric was in 1953. She came back to visit. And I know it was 1953 because that was when we had these great floods and we couldn't get off the island. We were stuck here, we were! All of the Kent coast and the Essex coast too was under the sea.

I never saw Joan again after that visit though we still used to exchange Christmas cards. And then one year I didn't get one and I knew something had happened to her. She had died of cancer in St Bartholomew's in Rochester. A long illness, I heard. Very sad. She was a good woman ... and it will be nice to meet her again when I pass on.

Eric, I think, went to work in the dockyards. A welder, or it might have been in the machine-shop. I really don't know.

I didn't know he went to London ... what is he doing now? Is he married? Does he have a family?

VICTOR COULSON: Mrs Middlemost! I remember her very well. Is she still alive? She must be getting on for eighty! A real battle-axe in her day. She used to give us kids such a rucking if she ever caught us getting up to no good.

Apart from her and Tim's mum there was nobody else up there I would ever want to meet again ... and Tim. I wouldn't mind having a pint with him again.

I think his mother and Mrs Middlemost and the school were the only people who called Tim by his real name, Eric. Nobody else ever called him that. I don't know where it came from.

We lived in the coastguard cottages in those days. My old man was moved out there just after the war and that's where I grew up. I was about five then and I was twenty when we came back to Chatham.

Tim and I were at school together. We were best friends. We spent all our time together and used to get up to all sorts of tricks. We were always getting into trouble – even with the police! We once accidentally set fire to a hayrick!

We used to spend the summers beachcombing and playing pirates and digging up the mudflats looking for buried treasure.

Tim was always full of ideas, not just playing around ideas but ideas for making money and he used to involve me. Like this old rag-and-bone man who came up from Strood once a month. Tim chatted him up and we used to do the collecting for him, or some of the collecting anyway. We'd earn a few shillings each month doing that. Tim was about ten at the time. Then we used to go collecting empty bottles and taking them back to the pub and getting tuppence on them. We'd also catch eels.

In the summer we would cycle down to the beach at Lower Upnor and ogle the girls in their bathing costumes, and comb the beach for money and things people had lost. And as we were doing this you would see the old paddle steamers going up and down the river. They've all gone now.

Tim and I were just beginning to discover girls when he left the Isle and went to live down in the Medway towns. I bumped into him down at the public library in Rochester a few years later. I didn't recognise him. He came up to me and asked me what I was doing. Tim's mum was a lovely lady. I'd see her biking into Rochester on her bicycle, one of those things you don't see now that had a little engine mounted on the rear wheel. She was a legal secretary or something there, I believe. I don't think we ever thought about Tim not having a father. I suppose he considered his grandad as his father.

Tim was bright and intelligent and smart but he wasn't cut out for school work. I think school bored him. He never paid a lot of attention, but even so, he was brighter than most of the class. This was the little school out by the church. We had this teacher, Miss Chatteris: a real dragon with horn-rimmed glasses and an enormous bosom.

Tim was well off to leave Grain when he did. By the time you got to fifteen it was the most boring place on earth. An exciting evening was something like sitting around the radio at home, or wireless as we used to call it. Sitting around it listening to Hughie Green's *Opportunity Knocks* on 208, Radio Luxembourg that is, or listening to *PC49* on the Light. On really special days the old wind-up record player was dusted down and 78s of Reginald Foort or Ambrose were put on. There was one we had that I liked – the old Count Basie version of *Open the Door, Richard!* My favourite record as a kid.

'Tomorrow is ... tomorrow is ... what?'

'Saturday, Miss.'

'I know tomorrow is Saturday, but it is a special Saturday. Does anyone know why it is special?'

'It's May Day, Miss.'

'It is not May Day. May Day is at the beginning of May. Today is the 23rd of May and tomorrow is the 24th of May and tomorrow we celebrate something special. Goodsmith?'

'Because it's 1947?'

'Because it's 1947? Why should that be special?'

'I don't know, Miss.'

'You are a silly boy. Now, yes, Purdom, I know you know. But no one else does? Very well. Tomorrow ... every 24th of May is Empire Day. *Empire Day*. On Empire Day we celebrate the achievements and triumphs of the British Empire and give our thanks to God. *And* the King.'

'Miss, I heard it on the wireless this morning.'

'Well, you did not remember it until I reminded you. So, tomorrow is Empire Day and we celebrate it on the 24th of May because that was the birthday of Queen Victoria and it was under her that our colonies and possessions multiplied so greatly and over which she reigned so well and for so long. Now, because it is Empire Day we are going to have a special treat. Purdom is going to tell us a story … yes, come to the front of the class … there, yes. This is a story from *The Ingoldsby Legends*, one of Purdom's favourite books, and a story he has read many times. It is a local story, or certainly a near-local story. It takes place … if we were to walk over the embankment there what would we see? Kilmart?'

'Miss, we would see the sea.'

'Yes, we would, but what would we see beyond it?'

'Sheerness, Miss.'

'That is correct. Sheerness is on an island, as indeed we too once were. Sheerness is on the Isle of … the Isle of? Farmer?'

'Is it Sheppey, Miss?'

'Yes, it is, Eileen. The Isle of Sheppey … named so because of all the sheep there. The story we are going to hear is set on the Isle. It is a legend … and … Purdom, it is called?'

'*Grey Dolphin*, Miss.'

'Good. So Eric will now tell us *The Legend of Grey Dolphin*.'

'Sir Robert de Shurland lived in Shurland Castle which is not very far away from Sheerness.

'One day he was eating oysters and this sentry arrived. The sentry said that a sailor had been washed up on the beach who was dead and the friar wouldn't bury him. So Sir Robert went down there and he shouted at the fat friar and said you must bury this man and he wouldn't. So Sir Robert kicked him as hard as he could and the friar fell into the grave they had dug and was killed.

'When the Abbot in Canterbury heard the friar was dead he got all his men together and they got on their horses and went to the castle where Sir Robert was having dinner again, eating oysters. They attacked the castle but Sir Robert and his soldiers attacked them and they all went back to Canterbury. And then Sir Robert had some more oysters.

'The Abbot told the Pope what had happened and the Pope said Sir Robert must be killed.

'Sir Robert was going to tell the King about this and get a pardon because Sir Robert had fought with him on the Crusades.'

'And *who* was the King, Eric?'

'Uhm … he's called Longshanks in the book, Miss.'

'Yes, I know he is. But you don't think we had a King Longshanks on the throne, do you?'

'The book says so.'

'I know … but Longshanks was his *nickname*. Do you know what his real name was … ? Does anyone? Dyce?'

'Henry, Miss.'

'Henry?'

'King Henry, Miss.'

'You are a silly boy! None of you know? Very well, it was Edward I. He was known as Longshanks because he had long legs. And he was the son of Henry III. Purdom.'

'So Sir Robert was going to see the King and get a pardon. He heard the King was in a ship coming down the River Thames and he sent for his horse, Grey Dolphin, and rode him out into the sea and Grey Dolphin swam two miles out to where the King was in his boat and when the King saw him coming he thought he was a mermaid or a monster.

'The King recognised Sir Robert because they had been on the Crusades together and he was very pleased to see him. And he said I pardon you for killing the fat monk. And then Sir Robert got on to Grey Dolphin and Grey Dolphin swam back.

'When they got back to the beach Sir Robert got off Grey Dolphin and then an old lady who was a witch appeared suddenly. He said, what do you want, old woman? She said that Grey Dolphin had saved his life this time but Grey Dolphin would cause him to lose his life as well. And when she had said that she disappeared all of a sudden and Sir Robert didn't know where she went to.

'Sir Robert was ever so worried by what the witch had said and he looked at Grey Dolphin and he was very tired from swimming and he thought he was a very old horse and if he went into battle again on a crusade for the King he would need a young horse. Also, he didn't want Grey Dolphin killing him so he took out his great sword and cut Grey Dolphin's head off in one swipe. Now he had killed Grey Dolphin ... Grey Dolphin wouldn't be able to kill him and he went back to his castle and forgot all about it.

'A long time went by and Sir Robert had been fighting with the King in battles in Scotland and in other places. He had been away for a long time and now he had come home and he was marching along the beach with his men near the castle. He saw that old lady again on the beach sitting on a rock and he rode towards her and when he got there she disappeared in front of him. He looked down and saw that it wasn't a rock she was sitting on but the skull of Grey Dolphin. He was very angry and got off his new horse and kicked Grey Dolphin's skull into the sea. And as the skull of Grey Dolphin was flying through the air it laughed and everybody was afraid.

'There was a pain in Sir Robert's foot after he kicked it and when he took his boot off he found there was a tooth stuck in his big toe from Grey Dolphin's skull. It hurt him and he pulled it out and then went home to the castle.

'Sir Robert went to bed and the next morning his toe was really swollen and he couldn't walk and it got bigger and they sent for the doctor, who had to cut it off. They thought he was going to get better but the poison spread up from his toe into his leg and everywhere else and soon he died and as he did he was thinking of Grey Dolphin and the old witch.'

'Good. A good story, Purdom. We will now sing *I Vow to Thee my Country* ... .'

WILLIAM 'DIXIE' CHIVERS: I started in the Chatham dockyards in 1946 as soon as I was demobbed and I worked there right up until they closed in 1984. We got this bungalow here in Margate the following year and I haven't been back since.

It wasn't easy getting into the dockyards in those days. The main thing though, them days, was a two-day Civil Service examination. It was held once a year. And if you didn't pass that you didn't get in. Timmy must have passed it because he started work under me as an apprentice fitter. Then he went to work in the sheet metal shop ... on submarines, I think. We still had National Service in those days but if you were an apprentice you got it deferred. Tim was very happy about that, getting it deferred. I seem to remember that he never did do it in the end, though ... I can't remember why.

Timmy was a bright lad and worked hard. Thought a lot. But his heart was never truly in the job. He read a lot. Always had his nose in a book. Also good at photography.

He worked under me for about a year until he was transferred. Still used to see him about after that from time to time. Always cheery. Then he went to work for that photographer in Rochester who fell out of a train and got killed. What was his name? Hedgecock or something. Something like that.

I can't remember the last time I saw Timmy. Perhaps a year or two after he left the yards ... in Rochester.

Next time I see any of the lads I'll ask them. See what they can come up with. But as I told you, the bloke you need to speak to is George Treadwell. He was one of my apprentices. He owns all those car body-shops all over the Medway towns now. Very successful. Has a big car and everything. He was Timmy's best friend. He'll help you.

GEORGE TREADWELL: Dixie Chivers! Now there's a name! Haven't seen him for a few years!

I got to know Tim in the mid-1950s when we were both apprentice fitters in the dockyards.

He was my closest friend in those days and we used to do everything together. We had some right old times. I was a couple of years older than him and eventually I had to do my National Service. Two bloody wasted years that was, pissing about for a bunch of officer types who didn't know their arse from their elbow.

After being demobbed I went back to the yards but only stayed for about six months. It was a secure job but I didn't see any real future there for a working man. A working bloke could only go so far. I thought to myself, fuck this, and I went to work in the body-shop at Cooper's garage, just over the bridge in Strood. Tim and I were still best friends though.

So, Tim and I met in the docks when we were apprentices. I think it was 1956. Yeah, it must have been. There was petrol rationing. It was the Suez crisis! What a laugh that was. We worked all hours God gave us. Plenty of bubble – that means overtime. Some of the old guys there spent all their time getting nostalgic about the war. They used to say, 'Wars are good for the working man in the yard. He'll always have a full pay packet.' They all thought Nasser was a good thing because it meant more work.

Tim was living with his mother and this bloke she married over in Chatham and then he, the husband, died and Tim and his mum rented a small flat in Rochester. She got very ill and went into hospital and they soon realised that she wasn't going to come out again and that's when Tim moved into this funny place near the Banks. Well, it was just off the Banks. St Margaret's Banks. That's the raised bit of road on the High Street where the railway line crosses it. Sort of halfway between Rochester and Chatham. As you know, they say that no one knows where Rochester ends and Chatham begins. It was there he had this place. He had this big room and an adjoining bathroom. It was on the second or third floor and it was right next to the railway which is raised on a viaduct.

This flat was just around the corner from St Bartholomew's where his mum died. Only a few minutes' walk. You may even have been able to see the hospital from his window.

I used to spend all my time at Tim's flat. I was still living at home then and of course I'd be a bit restricted turning up there with Tim and a couple of girls! And Tim was very good at pulling the birds back then. Always had a good-looking one on his arm.

When we were at the docks you used to get all sorts of ships coming and going from around the world. Tim would always get matey with the sailors to see if they had any interesting stuff. All sailors stash something away that they might be able to trade or sell. There was a pretty hot Customs and Excise department in the docks but they only went after obvious stuff – you know, expensive watches, gold, drink. A sailor could come in with a couple of kilos of Mary Jane, marijuana that is, or grass and the Customs officers would just think it was some exotic local tobacco. They didn't know about getting loaded and that. Neither did the police.

The first reefer I ever smoked was walking along Rochester High Street on a Saturday morning with Tim who gave it to me. We walked along getting totally loaded and passing it back and forth and falling about all over the place and laughing. Nobody had ever heard of dope in those days.

There was an old record Tim used to play. A song that went:

> Have you seen that funny little reefer man?
> He's got a notion
> To walk the ocean,
> That funny little reefer man.

That really used to make us laugh!

Tim left the yards and went to work for this local photographer who did portraits and weddings. He really liked that and he was very good at it. Had a natural flair for taking pictures. We still spent all our spare time together. I was working at Cooper's then and I could always borrow a car at weekends, not that old man Cooper knew. So we'd go off driving with a couple of girls on Sundays. No insurance or anything! We used to go down to Margate and Ramsgate and have a good time.

We used to listen to a lot of music. In the beginning he had this old wind-up 78 r.p.m. record player and then about 1958 or whenever it was he got a record player for LPs and that. It was there I first heard Thelonious Monk and Chet Baker and Gerry Mulligan. I used to think we were the only two guys in the whole of England who listened to jazz like that. We were really cool. We also listened to Parker and Gillespie and all the others. Nobody else could bear it, especially the girls. All they wanted to hear was Pat Boone and Tommy Steele.

Tim was always reading. He'd get books out of the library on people and things you'd never heard of. He also read a lot of Henry Miller. And I did too. His books were banned then, but we certainly enjoyed them.

After his mother died Tim got very restless and decided there had to be some changes in his life. I turned up at his flat just after she died. It was the summer of '59. The most glorious summer of the century, they said. The weather was fabulous – day after day of it! The door was open and Tim was sitting on the bed smoking a joint and just staring ahead. We passed the reefer back and forth. It was dark outside and the window was open and whenever a train went by it drowned the music. We just sat there for ages and then he looked up and said to me, 'We're already history.' I thought that was a funny thing to say and it's stayed with me all these years. 'We're already history.'

'What's that mean?'

'It means this is already the past.'

'I thought now was *now*?'

'It's gone before you can ... .'

'Your turn.'

'Yeah. Thanks.'

'It's ... it's ... I cannot believe my mother is dead. She's history now. She's in the past. You try and prepare yourself for it, but you can't really.'

'She's not suffering now.'

'She's not anything any more.'

'I can't imagine my mum dying.'

'I can't either.'

'You now.'

'Uh-huh.'

'Mind if I close the window?'

'It's a nice night out there.'

'But the trains ... .'

'If you want.'

'OK.'

'There's nothing to hold me here now. I'm going to go somewhere else. Move on. Hit the road.'

'Where are you thinking of going? Chatham?'

'Chatham? No! Move away altogether. London probably.'

'What do you want to go there for? This is where you belong.'

'I don't belong here now. You might, I don't.'

'You're my best mate, Tim. Rochester wouldn't be the same without you.'

'You'll survive all right.'

'When are you going?'

'Soon. Sort out a few things. Settle some things. This and that.'

'This is good stuff.'

'I'll do another three-paper one and we can go down the road and see what's happening.'

'Good idea.'

'Come and visit me when I'm in London.'

'I will. You got any sweets? Anything at all?'

'There's a Crunchie bar over there if you want one.'

'Yeah. Good. Where you gonna get the dope when you're in London?'

'West Indians have always got it.'

'I was reading that they're brought up on it.'

'Something like that, George.'

'You're really going, aren't you?'

'Yeah.'

'Why?'

'I told you. Lots of reasons. I need a change from all this. I don't see much opportunity in Rochester. I don't want to spend all my life here.'

'Yeah, but you said the other day you don't know what you want to do.'

'I know I said that. If you don't know what you want to do then you don't stay somewhere where there's little opportunity to do *anything*. You go somewhere where there's lots of opportunity to do different things. Like London.'

'Like London?'

'Yeah, like London.'

'Hey! I didn't know you had Earl Bostic's *Flamingo*!'

'Yeah. You can have it when I take the train out of here. Now, this little three-paper beauty is ready, so let's light up and get our feets to do some walking!'

'I'm with you, brother.'

'Into the night life ... .'

GEORGE TREADWELL: We're already history! He was right. That was over thirty years ago. It's like we suddenly jumped from then to now. All those years! Yet if I close my eyes I can still see myself sitting in the room in that armchair. Listening to the music. Hearing the trains going by. Smelling the soot. Inhaling the joint and getting high.

A few weeks later Tim was gone. He got the train to London and started a new life up there. Goodbye Rochester. I looked after some of his things and he came back and got them a few months later. I went to see him a couple of times ... that would have been late 1959, early 1960. And then we sort of lost touch. My business started to take off and I got married and we started a family. I often thought of Tim. Still do.

How old would Tim be now? Well, I'm fifty-six this year and he was a couple of years younger than me so that would make him about fifty-four. I can't imagine him in his fifties. There was something Peter Pan-ish about him. He's always stayed in my mind at the age he was when I first met him.

Something very odd happened a little while ago concerning Tim but I'll tell you about that after we've had dinner.

Part Two

1

All the Things You Are

You do your best with what goes on at the time.
– Max Roach, quoted in Ira Gitler's *Swing to Bop* (1985)

I DIDN'T WANT to be stuck in Rochester for the rest of my life and if I hadn't made a move then I would never have done, so, on Friday 19 June in the Year of Our Lord one thousand nine hundred and fifty-nine, at the beginning of the seventh regnal year of *your* Gracious Majesty Queen Elizabeth II, in the midst of what would prove to be one of the finest summers of the century, at a little before 3 p.m., after having had a farewell drink with the local lads, I picked up my tattered cardboard suitcase which contained 50 per cent of my worldly collateral, amongst which a toothbrush, a comb, Jack Kerouac's *On the Road*, and a 12-inch long-playing microgroove record of Thelonious Monk small group recordings from the late 1940s and early 1950s, I walked along the Banks and down the High Street to the station where I caught what I thought was the first available train to London which, as it turned out, did not go to London, resulting thus in numerous changes and delays too boring to recount here that ended up with me not arriving at Charing Cross until 8.30 p.m. on this aforementioned Friday.

On the journey up I found a copy of *Queen* magazine someone had abandoned. I read about the Aston DB3 that could do 120 m.p.h. and only cost £3,358 with purchase tax, about debs in pearls and twin-sets who have coming-out parties that cost £500, about the actress Valerie Hobson who is now married to a Tory millionaire called Profumo (odd name) buying at an auction a fur coat that used to belong to Lady Docker for £80, and I take out my wallet and count my life savings and I have exactly £23 12s.6d. to show for nearly twenty-two years of existence, *and* I consider myself ahead of the game.

It was too late to do much when I got to Charing Cross so I caught the Circle Line underground to Bayswater and started looking for a cheap bed-and-breakfast hotel in which to stay. I'd been to this area before and I knew there were quite a few places over here. Most of them were full of tourists (it was June, after all) or too expensive but I eventually found a place that was almost empty. It looked more like a common lodging-house than a bed-and-breakfast hotel and it was situated at the Hyde Park end of Inverness Terrace. The outside of the building was crumbling and peeling and water dripped out of the rainwater pipes on to arc-shaped patches of moss. The sign over the entrance porch hung at an angle and said 'The Ararat Continental Hotel' and it looked like it was evacuated during the war and no one had ever come back. It was £1 4s. a night and for that I got a box room out the back with a hard bed and for breakfast a kipper, a cup of coffee and three pieces of toast.

The next day, a Saturday, I spruced myself up and went down to Soho. I thought if I'm in London I might as well work in the centre. So that's what I did. I went down to Soho and just worked my way up and down the streets going into every place that was open and asking if they had a job. I didn't mind what I did until I got on my feet. Now Saturday was not perhaps the smartest day to look for a job but after a good few hours' non-stop tramping about I got a job that was not bad to begin with and has now become pretty good ... of its type. I got it on the Saturday and I started on the Monday.

I've been in this job for six months now. I average working about 72 hours a week over six days. I get £10 12s. a week clear, which is not bad – about the same as a beginner policeman only he has got to pay tax and that. But I do a lot more hours. I started on £6 for a 40-hour week but my hours and responsibility increased – Mr Calabrese, who is the sole proprietor of the Modern Snax Bar at the Shaftesbury Avenue end of Wardour Street, is getting old and wants more time to himself.

At the Snax I work as washer-upper, coffee maker, sandwich maker, sweeper-upper, and errand runner for Mr Calabrese, Mr Emilio Calabrese, who is as old as the century and who arrived on these shores in 1920 from, where else? but Calabria down in the boot of Italy. He was interned during the war for being an enemy alien but harbours no grudge against the British.

We've got a 1940 Wurlitzer jukebox in one corner but it doesn't always work. Mr Calabrese usually prefers *Housewives' Choice* and *Workers' Playtime* on the radio and all that Light Programme stuff but I don't want to hear Godfrey Winn (known in Fleet Street as 'Winifred God') introducing records and Patti Page singing *Mockin' Bird Hill*. When he's here we have the radio on and when I'm in charge it's the jukebox, not that there are many records on it I care for. It's just that it's a bit better than the BBC.

We get a pretty varied clientele here. We get freelance strippers and girls from the Windmill. Actors and actresses from the theatres on Shaftesbury Avenue. Taxi drivers. Musicians around the corner from Archer Street, usually when they've been turned down for work (we're cheap, they go elsewhere when they get a booking). Maltese ponces. Retired spivs. Trainee thugs and crazy self-styled hoodlums in suits that are two sizes too big. Prostitutes, black and white and mixed, but mainly white and mainly old enough to be grandmothers and none of them with a heart of gold, least not the ones I serve espresso to. They go on like the old guys in the dockyards about the last war and how good it was for business and how well they did with all the servicemen and Yanks about. Business was never better. The best news you could ever give them would be to tell them that World War III has just begun. They'd love you for that.

After I got fixed up with the job I had to get somewhere to live and that proved a little more difficult. There were plenty of places about but the suitable ones, the ones not too far out (because I didn't want to spend too much time travelling to and from work) and in an OK sort of area were too expensive, while the places I could afford had frontages on Skid Row and were in out-of-the-way places, and you'd always be plagued with the thought as to whether you were going to wake up in the morning or not.

The place I eventually found was just around the corner from the Ararat Continental, funnily enough. In fact, not around the corner, but straight up the road, on the continuation northwards of Inverness Terrace the other side of Westbourne Grove – Porchester Road, no less, as scummy a thoroughfare as ever graced the capital. Everything changes once you cross Westbourne Grove – it comes down a peg or two. But this suited me. A largish room on the second floor of a terrace for £3 12s. a week. Perhaps expensive for the area but all right in its own way. Albert Terrace, Porchester Road, London W2.

The terraces here are all pretty run down, all let out into rooms. Nobody has done work on them for years. There's a few local people here, but there aren't many of them now I'm told. They die off and are replaced by people like me. People from outside London. Transients. Transients with great expectations who've arrived in London to seek their fortunes. Folks on the move. Folks on the run. In from the provinces (and even other countries), here to do, like me, what they couldn't do back home. They're in London to find something or to forget something; perhaps both even. After a while most of them have their hands so full just surviving they forget what originally brought them here. They slide from being ambitious to being merely on the make. Their eyes glaze over and they develop a stare fixed on infinity. Frank in the room opposite me is just like that.

He's from up north somewhere. Durham maybe. Works as a barman in a rough old pub near Paddington station. He's a compulsive gambler, running up big bills with what in this area passes for the Mafia. They may not be organised but they're nasty. He's had a few beatings. He also borrows off them: 'five for six'. Like the serfs in the Bible – the interest grows faster than he can ever pay it off. He's trying to outpace the treadmill, but he's spent so much time on it he doesn't know any different. He wants it that way. He likes it that way. It's a drug he couldn't survive without. Debt is his destiny. If he was free of debt he wouldn't have a purpose in life.

That's Frank.

Then there's Brizio downstairs, the Italian.

He says he's a tailor but I don't think that's true. He does something pretty lowly in the garment trade. He's been here since just after the war, yet he still lives in a dosshouse like this. He's addicted to buying new suits and seems to have a new one every week. If you saw him walking down the street you'd think he was some nabob from the Italian embassy. He buys new suits to impress little secretary girls and typists.

He wants an English wife. English women like well-dressed men, he thinks. Therefore he's got to dress well and that's all he ever does. He'll exist on a loaf of bread for a month. Cash can't be diverted from clothes.

South of Westbourne Grove there are plenty of nice houses in between the hotels. Big smart cars, quite a bit of money. But it's going downhill, it'll soon be like our area: crumbling tenements, absentee landlords, the rootless and the restless. It isn't as bad over here as it is to the west in

Notting Hill – there the houses are crammed with West Indians newly arrived.

Westbourne Grove. Westbourne means the place to the west of the bourne or stream, according to a book on place names I borrowed from the library which I have yet to return. It is impossible to believe there was anything like a stream here. Hasn't around here been built over since Creation? Could there ever have been green fields, wood-land, meadows, and a bright flowing stream dancing over glistening pebbles here? But there was ... and somewhere it still flows.

I often vary the way I travel back home from the Modern Snax Bar, just for the sake of it, but I always travel into work the same way. I take a lazy stroll down Queensway and catch a bus on the Bayswater Road opposite Kensington Gardens. It takes me about ten minutes at this clip and it's about the only exercise I get. Queensway has an air of raff-ishness and bohemian dissolution about it which I like. There are quicker ways of getting to work but this suits me. It isn't so good when it is smoggy – it's bad to breathe it in and you have to wear a scarf around your face.

I always buy a newspaper from the newspaper man who stands outside Bayswater station. He's a frail old man with snow-white hair and a tatty, wispy beard who looks like the wind could blow him away. No matter what the weather he is always wearing the same heavy full-length army coat. A coat that looks like it could match him year for year. One day I asked him what the silver badge was he wore on his lapel. He said he was an ex-serviceman and had been wounded on the first day of the Somme during the First World War.

I catch a bus outside Queensway station. There's an old accordion player who stands on the corner here playing a never-ending medley of pre-war popular tunes. He doesn't open his eyes and may be, for all I know, blind. I don't know what time he begins in the morning but he's always

there when I arrive just after 7 a.m. There are very few
people about and I wonder who he's playing for? Perhaps
himself?

The bus takes me past Kensington Gardens and Hyde
Park, which is why I sit upstairs on the right-hand side: there
are good views across the parkland. I am back in the country
then, day-dreaming of Arcady. I get off at a stop nearly
opposite the top of Wardour Street and then it's only a few
minutes' walk down to the Snax Bar. There's an old shoe-
shine geezer here and every Friday he shines my shoes
(with Kiwi polish – nothing less would do!). I give him a
shilling and he says, 'God bless you, guv.' He really does.

Wardour Street is where all the film companies have
their offices, and Wardour Street is in Soho. And Soho is the
Sin, Sex, Scandal and Crime Capital of the World. The
reason I know this is easy – the *News of the World* tells me it
is every Sunday … and why would they make it up?

Soho is also, according to the same newspaper, the following: the Racket Capital of the World (why not of the
Universe?), The Shame of a Nation, The World's Worst Red
Light District, The Evil Web at the Heart of a Nation, The
Sink of Sinfulness ('sinfulness' doesn't really pack a punch
and, besides, the phrase is The Sink of Iniquity, but it lacks
alliteration, and how many readers would know what iniquity was?), The Den of Degeneration, The Vortex of Vice
(what else begins with a V?), The Pervert's Playground (the
apostrophe was wrongly positioned, it was about several of
them), and for those readers who take a shine to a biblical
allusion, Britain's Brazen Babylon, Lucifer's Lot and
Satan's Square Mile (it's a lot less than a square mile. A
square mile would take in Mayfair and Fitzrovia), and so
on. The papers say this when they're exposing the odd
petty criminal here because with this accident of topography that petty criminal can then be painted as Public
Enemy Number One, a Master Mind, a Notorious Mister
Big. This is Soho. Anywhere else he'd just be a little
hoodlum, a delinquent. Here he's Important. Reality and

reportage aren't stored in the same jar, least not in these parts.

There's a tarnished trinity at work here: the cops, the criminals and the newspaper hacks. It's a three-sided conspiracy with each side playing an equal part. The small-time criminals want to be portrayed bigger than they are, it increases their standing, makes them feel better. This, naturally, makes the police look better when they collar them. The public can see that they're not just arresting no-hope amateurs, they are arresting Major Figures. Now, of course, the bigger the arrest the bigger the story and this is where the journalist plays his part. This is the Sinful Symbiosis operating daily in the cheap papers. What a merry-go-round, and no one to shout boo!

I can think of a personified example to illustrate the trinity of cops, crooks and Fleet Street hacks.

There's a journalist who comes into the Snax Bar about twice a week named Desmond. Desmond Raeburn. He must be in his late forties, perhaps older. A big guy with shifty eyes and a clammy handshake. He has this air of intrigue and conspiracy about him, like a corrupt detective: *I know something you don't know*. He can ask if we have any bacon sandwiches and you feel like you've got to be careful in your reply. Charlie who works with me says he'd sell his mother down the river for a tip-off and I think he's right.

He looks a lot older than his years. You can smell the drink on him across the room. White, white skin. Eyes that have almost disappeared. Dirty greasy glasses. A half-smoked cigarette permanently in the corner of his mouth. Traces of his last meal always in the corners of his mouth too. A manner that is simultaneously ingratiating and intimidating. He's the chief crime correspondent of one of the Sundays, 'Scotland Yard's Most Trusted Correspondent', 'The Reporter with the Ear of the Metropolitan Police' and, in his own words, 'The Crown Prince of Crime Reporters'.

Desmond would not know how to investigate a story to

save his life. He writes what the police tell him to write.
He's a publicity agent for the coppers pure and simple. His
office should be in Scotland Yard not Fleet Street. They call
him in, give him the bare details and he jazzes it up and
makes them look like the Lone Ranger. All detectives are
'gang-busters', 'crime-fighters', or 'knights in the war
against crime' who 'wage war' on the underworld with
'scarcely a thought for personal safety' and are content to
know 'the job is done' and 'the citizens of London can
sleep peacefully in their beds'. This sort of drivel is trotted
out every weekend. The close relationship doesn't end
when the copper retires. Then we get the obligatory
*Murder on My Manor: The Memoirs of Detective-Chief Inspec-
tor Backhander* ('As told to Desmond Raeburn'). Plugs for
the book follow in his column over the next few weeks and
this saves work as Desmond can then recycle what's
written in the book (which is just recycled from his column
anyway). He gets paid for the same stuff three times. Nice
work if you can get it.

Desmond is always saying that if I hear anything I
should tell him, as he pays well for a good story. I told him
about the Duke of Edinburgh regularly visiting these two
black prostitutes in Dolphin Square, and how I overheard
one of the coloured girls talking about it to her friend, in
hushed tones, in the Snax Bar. But that's not all. The Duke
was being blackmailed by an international syndicate of
guys in expensive suits with Italian names who had
secretly taken photographs. A great story. A really great
story. I know it was because I made it all up.

The first thing Desmond does with a good story is
phone his pals up at the Yard. He's shopped more petty
criminals than the rest of London. And I wouldn't be
surprised if he also collected an informer's fee. 'Money is
what it's all about, son,' he says, and I guess it is. That is
certainly what motivates the bent coppers who take
weekly 'contributions' from all of the bigger villains in
London. It's known as 'licence money'.

One Saturday morning Desmond staggered into the
Snax Bar and said he had a problem and that I had to help
him. He led me to a corner table, sat me down, looked
hither and thither as though we were in a den of spies (or,
worse, other journalists), pulled his chair up, sat down
himself with a sly glance to the door, leant forward, looked
around once more, and said in a barely audible whisper,
'The ... blue ... film ... racket.' Nothing more. That was it.
The statement hung there in the air. I didn't know what to
say. The blue film racket *what*? He didn't say anything
further, he was looking about again. What was I supposed
to say, Yes, please!? The blue film racket? I began to think I
was being thick. There was something I should say in
response but I didn't know what it was. He's just staring at
me. Is my name going to be put in the frame as a Mr Big to
protect someone else or what? I was waiting for him to start
talking like one of his detective friends: 'It's all right, son.
We've got you bang to rights. You can tell me everything.
Be helpful to me and I'll play fair with you.' All detectives
talk like this because that's how they talk in Desmond's
books, and I've read two of them, *Robbery on My Patch* and
Villainy on My Doorstep. But hold on, Desmond is about to
say something.

'It's worth a fiver.'

'A fiver? What's worth a fiver?'

'The story. The whole story. The whole inside story ... the
fearless truth.'

Fearless truth!!?? This guy thinks like he writes, no less.

'Desmond, I haven't got any fearless truth. I don't know
what you're talking about.'

A long silence. The face of the Crown Prince of Crime
Reporting drops like a schoolboy who's just had a bar of
chocolate confiscated.

'You don't know about the blue film rackets then?'

'I don't know anything about them.'

'I just thought you might. Nobody else about today. I've
got a problem.'

'Why?'

'A very quiet week. We need a feature for page two. The editor says we have to do a major exposé of the blue film racket about every six months and tomorrow is as good a Sunday as ever, and it's been a lean week … and I'm a bit burnt out, old boy, to tell you the truth.'

Desmond's problems are also his listener's problems. It is a childlike egocentric world he inhabits. He's irritating me no end now.

'You've written these stories before, you know what to write.'

'I need something fresh. I'm stymied.'

'OK then. How's this? For the first time ever blue films are being organised, promoted, in a big way in this country. It's a slick operation. They are all professionals. And, what's more, they are regularly making films over here now and not relying on old foreign films made in the 1920s.'

'Yes. A slick operation!'

'High profits. A wave sweeping the country.'

'A wave sweeping the country!'

'The police know who the Mr Big is but he's surrounded himself with expensive lawyers. The police are patiently waiting for him to make a slip.'

'Patient crime-busters. A slip. I want lots more plausible detail, Tim.'

Well, I gave it to him and the following appeared, featured over two pages under his byline, the next day. A fitting counterpoint to the greasy bacon and burnt toast on the nation's breakfast tables.

I GET THE PASSWORD TO
THE SECRET WORLD OF BLUE FILM FILTH

From the murky back alleys of Soho to a more fashionable and smart area of central London I have followed the trail of the 'blue' film traffic. There are no shady advertisements, no ex-directory telephone numbers. The only 'passport' is a personal introduction.

Even in the basement clubs of Soho the subject is taboo.

This 'blue' film traffic is a subject for concern.

This is what Lord Kilmuir, the Lord Chancellor, said about it in the House of Lords during the second reading of the Obscene Publications Bill:

'We must face it that grossly obscene films in houses or the rooms of clubs are one of the evils of life. There have always been places which try to attract people to shows of this kind. I think they ought to be struck at.'

Lord Denning said films exhibiting obscenity could be smuggled in from another country and bought at a cost of some £50. These would be displayed in private at £2 to £3 per seat.

I have news for his Lordship. This filth is no longer imported from abroad. It is made here in Britain. There is a 'blue' wave sweeping the country.

I set out on a voyage of discovery.

Though the 'blue' film business is one of the underworld's most closely guarded secrets, the frontier can be crossed.

Especially with a well-filled wallet. The wallet is important. Very important.

So too is perseverance.

This is how I did it.

First I browsed for hours in Soho bookshops specialising in pin-ups, books of nudes and nude 'stills' at 10 shillings for five.

In these shops totally obscene photographs were displayed.

If the bookshop manager thought you looked like a 'good punter' he would invite you to see 'something stronger' at the back of the shop. Here in a half-light you could buy photographs of the most depraved activities for £1 to 25s. for a set of five. These 'specials' showed sexual activities that would make a hardened crime-buster reach for the banister.

As Detective-Inspector Greenslade of Scotland Yard once said to me, 'The depths of depravity to which the common pornographer sinks knows no bounds.'

It was in one of these Soho bookshops that I was granted my 'passport' to the underworld of filth.

I was approached by the dark-haired, black-eyed, Levantine-complexioned [Levantine – Fleet Street codeword for Jew. Desmond can boast anti-Semitism amongst his many talents.] manager of one of these shops who offered me expensive, coloured photographs. I said I was more interested in films.

He looked at me quizzically and then hurriedly scribbled a telephone number on a scrap of paper. He said the number was written in reverse so it would remain secret. He said, 'Mention me and you will have a good time, honourable sir.'

I rang the number. A well-spoken woman answered and we arranged to meet outside Baker Street underground station.

I waited five minutes at the underground station. A smartly dressed woman appeared from the shadows of a building.

I mentioned the name of the bookshop manager. The woman asked me to follow her.

'It's not far,' she said. 'We cannot be too careful. The police are keen and I don't like toughs. I don't like trouble either. It's not good for business.'

'This will cost you ten [£10]. I know that's a bit steep but there's no nonsense. Any further services are extra.'

We walked about 300 yards to a block of luxury flats. I followed the woman up to the first floor and into an expensively decorated flat. We went into a well-furnished sitting room.

A large radiogram played softly in the corner. On the wall above it was a silver screen measuring 5ft. 6ins. by 4ft. 9ins.

In the middle of the room on an elegant coffee table was a projector. It was angled at the screen.

'Sit down and make yourself comfortable,' said the woman. 'I'll be back in a jiff.'

She left the room.

There was a divan in the corner of the room, a large settee and two easy chairs. Behind me was a very expensive writing-desk.

The woman returned with three small reels of films.

'I think you will like these,' she said. 'They are all new and made in England. We do not import old films from abroad. We make them ourselves.'

The first film like the other two was revolting.

It was called 'Up Skirts and Down Slacks' and the cast

numbered two, a young man and a young woman. It was filmed in a flat that looked very much like the flat I was now sitting in.

When it was over I was offered a drink – 'At no extra charge.' I declined.

The first film was very carefully re-wound and then the second one was shown.

It featured a blonde girl with two coloured girls and was named 'Two Blacks Make a White'. It was the most disgusting thing I had ever seen in my life.

The third, 'Gymkhana Sluts', featured a blonde and a brunette with a man. It was made in a riding school.

Each film lasted about fifteen minutes and was made in black and white. There was no soundtrack. The films were run to music from the radiogram.

'I've had a busy day,' said the woman. Her name was Stella. 'I have to pay £10 per film per day to the distributors. There are lots of girls organised like me. We get our films from the man who makes them. He is very rich and successful. But I have to be careful. I have nosy neighbours so I never have more than twenty-five men a day here. Would you like any additional services?'

I made an excuse and left, after I handed over £10.

Stella is one of many girls caught up in the new 'blue' film web run by the Mr Big of 'Blue' Films. A man who has sworn to turn England into the 'blue' film capital of the world and to make the racket a million pounds a year business.

You can rest assured that the crime fighters at Scotland Yard are working on his case and that it is only a matter of time before they have him where he belongs – in prison.

This was virtually all invention. My invention. I particularly liked the fake film titles! The Lords Kilmuir and Denning quotes I dare say, were dug out by some sub on the paper, yet the lad himself takes the money and the glory for doing fuck all.

I didn't know it at the time but my fictional venture into blue films presaged a bizarre invitation some weeks later courtesy of French Joe, another Modern Snax regular who'll soon be appearing on the horizon.

I've only ever seen one blue film and that was down in the docks at Chatham. I suppose there are blue films in Soho but I haven't noticed them. What we have mainly are small cinemas showing subtitled French 'X' films and such. You won't see much more than the odd naked tit. That's about it. *The Nudist Story* opened a little while back. Just about the biggest thing that ever hit these flea-pits. They're packed out. Nudist films have become big business now.

Charlie says these pits are really just full of dirty old men giving themselves one off the wrist or paying a street-walker to do the same. That's why, he says, the seats are wet and sticky and why there's tissue paper all over the floor. Fellows go there to play pocket billiards, to have a hand shandy.

If I continue conjugating the depravity hereabouts we next come to the striptease joints (with the emphasis on the tease) and then the medical-goods shops and the book-shops.

The medical shops sell condoms, contraceptive creams, pessaries, and all kinds of preparations (good word that!) that add to the pleasure of the act of sexual union. They also sell pills and trusses and special underpants for the incontinent. You only ever see old men going in and out of them and the window displays are full of faded products covered in dust and look like they haven't been changed since 1933.

A typical window announces:

DAMAROIDS – THE GREAT BRITISH REJUVENATOR
HYGEOLENE – THE PERFECT CONTRACEPTIVE
DUREX – THE NAME YOU CAN TRUST

And how about this from the Charing Cross Road?

OTHER RUBBER GOODS
* * *

Please ask the MANAGEMENT for Further Details
of Your REQUISITES if not on Display.

Also in the windows you will find several types of book.
The marriage stuff with titles like:

IDEAL MARRIAGE
IMPOTENCY – ITS CAUSES AND CURE
MODERN SEXUAL RELATIONS
PRACTICAL EUGENICS [*Huh*!?]
WEDDING NIGHT ETIQUETTE

... and then on the other side the 'art study' titles:

BEAUTY'S DAUGHTERS
CURVES AND CONTRASTS
OF THE HUMAN FIGURE
THE FEMALE FORM IN LIGHT AND SHADE

... wherein too there are always some titles on nudism, or
'naturism' as the devotees thereof call it:

EXERCISING AS NATURE INTENDED
BEAUTY FROM GERMANY
SUN WITHOUT SHAME

... and so on. German naturist books are always popular
and they have titles like *Körperkultur und Erziehung* (I'm
quoting from memory) and are full of buxom heavy blonde
Bavarian maidens called Lotte who look like they were
enthusiastic breeding units for producing Hitler Youth.

Charlie describes these books as strokers' manuals,
wankers' digests and '*hand*books for geezers who want the
solution in their fists.' He also says they are for blokes who
like dating handkerchiefs and practising five-finger exercises. He's a fund of sexual slang and colloquialism.

There's something fascinating about these farther shores
of 'vice'. It brings out the voyeur in me.

If the medical shops cater for the needs of the practical man, the man of action, the dirty bookshops, perhaps a dozen in number, cater for the man of imagination. They supply the stuff that gets him soaring in his reveries and showing blue films all night long on the back of his eyelids.

The windows are always crammed full of American 'girlie' magazines. They're tame enough, glamour stuff like those dreary pin-ups put out by Harrison Marks. You go inside the shop and you're starting to see nipples now and air-brushed crotches. Hang about here for a while and look serious enough and the manager will ask you if you would like to 'come out back and see something stronger?' He lifts one side of the counter and you walk through to the back-room where the real action is. Here rows of photographs are kept wrapped in cellophane in packets of five in long wooden trays. The trays are labelled so you can go straight to your partiality.

JUVE is old streetwalkers dressed as Girl Guides or in schoolgirl uniforms being rogered by Sir. LES or LEZ is lesbian stuff. FLAGE is flagellation and sado-masochistic material. PERV is girls dressed in rubber and tied up, or a white girl being screwed by a black guy, while STRAIGHT is a white couple doing it missionary style or side by side (but certainly not doggy style). That's it. Sometimes you may see some BEST[-iality] which demonstrates that a girl and her dog are not to be parted, but you'll never see any HOMO. You'll have to go to Paris or Port Said for that. This London stuff is produced *by* straights *for* straights.

The quality of these photographs is awful. The exposure is nearly always right but the lighting is harsh and flatly uniform, rather as if the shots were taken under strip lighting. The poses and composition are as unappealing as the old scrubbers and the fellows who appear in them. They all look as though they were shot in a basement in Paddington in 1945, and, indeed, they could well have been.

Some of these shops are reputed to have a turnover of

£200 or more a week. Of course, the police don't close them, because most of the police are on the take from them, certainly the Obscene Publications Squad at West End Central who are supposed to deal with them. One of these days this whole story might come out, but I doubt it.

A few of the shops, like the 'long shop' in Old Compton Street, next door to the bomb site, always have a shelf or two of 'readers' out in the back. 'Readers' are books. As magazines are invariably called 'books' by the semi-illiterates who manage and frequent these shops another term had to be conjured up for actual *books*. Thus 'readers', as opposed to the rest of the stock that might be termed 'lookers'. Readers might be sexological textbooks such as Krafft-Ebing, Magnus Hirschfeld, Stekel and their modern imitators who have MD or PhD after their (pseudonymous) name and choose to publish their studies of female auto-erotic practices (or whatever) through cheap American paperback houses operating out of unlikely addresses, like Cleveland, Ohio. They might be what antiquarian book-sellers call curiosa or *oeuvres galantes*, such as a history of corporal punishment or an anthropological study of female circumcision (with plates, yet) or even some reprinted drollery. They could also be what is known as 'Soho type-scripts'. These are short stories a few thousand words or so in length churned out on Gestetner duplicating machines and printed on blotting paper. They are written by local hacks for £1 a thousand words. The hacks are semi-literate too and the stories are bereft of wit or saving graces. They are even bereft of imagination. One typescript I had was called *Nurses Like It Always* (there was some confusion in the 'story' as to whether it should have been All Ways). Here's the opening sentence verbatim:

Pretty Staff Nurse Susan of Saint Hildas' hadn't had a good hard cock up her for at least 24hrs so when Syd the decorator walked up to her in the Laundry cupeboard her juices start flowing right away and she says "Get them offand show me your a Man" and he did and she took his big cock and gave it a real sucking while she rubbed herself and brought herself off and then he said lay down there Im going to stick it right up you and he did and while they were doing this Harry's mate came in [who's Harry?] and saw the real horny action for himself and got his big dick out and decided she'd have it at the same time up her arse.

The other hot titles to be found on the reader shelves are the Olympia Press 'Traveller's Companion Series', paperbacks smuggled over from Paris. These are often called greenback readers, from the colour of the covers. The Olympia Press has published dozens of obscene novels with titles like *Roman Orgy*, *With Open Mouth*, *Rape*, *Tender Was My Flesh*, and so on, but it's also published serious stuff like Vladimir Nabokov. Indeed, I saw a copy of *Lolita* on one of the shelves a few weeks back. What would the average punter make of that when he got it home?

If, as we now know from the Sunday broadsheets, Soho is the current centre of the pornographic trade in England, where was it before? Where, one hundred years ago, would you have gone to purchase a hot reader? Where would you have gone to buy an obscene engraving, an erotic chromolithograph, a dirty photograph? The answer is Holywell Street. But that's disappeared now. That's where one hundred years ago and, indeed, two hundred years ago, all the dubious action was.

There you could buy anything almost, and certainly sheepskin condoms and other devices. But you'll search for it in vain now – it was all pulled down in 1901 and Bush House and Aldwych were built upon its site. If London is haunted by any pornographer's ghosts then the southern end of Kingsway is where you'll find them.

Something that really pisses me off about England (and I suppose this is true of other countries as well) is this: fucking and so on is legal to do but illegal to show in any way, whereas murder is the exact opposite. I can walk down the Charing Cross Road and go into Foyle's or any of the other big bookshops and see walls and walls of shelves full of murder books: detective mysteries, amateur sleuths, non-fiction studies and so on. Acres of them! There's even a publisher who has a series called the Murder Club. I can go up to some virginal spinsterish shop assistant and say 'I want your top dozen murder books.' But try asking for the top dozen fucking books.

2

Intermission Riff

If you couldn't change the room, then the room changed you.
– Charleen Page (1969)

AN ANECDOTED INVENTORY OF MY ROOM AT NO.
16 ALBERT TERRACE, PORCHESTER ROAD, LONDON
W.2., AT 4.30 P.M. ON SUNDAY, 20 DECEMBER 1959

The 'furnished' (*sic*) room measures approximately 30 feet
by 16 feet by about 9 feet high. It is on the second floor,
above the mezzanine. The room is directly over the front
door. When I look out of the window I am facing west-
south-west.

Ignoring just a few degrees of direction I will refer to the
four walls of the room as the north, the south, the east and
the west. The single door in (and out) of the room is situated at the end of the east wall where it joins that of the
north. I will begin the inventory here and work my way
around in a clockwise direction. But first, a word or two on
the floor, walls and ceiling.

The floor is covered in a brown linoleum that was badly
in need of replacement during the Abdication Crisis. A
large square carpet of indeterminable age and pattern (so
grubby is it now) floats on the centre of the linoleum but
falls short of reaching the walls in every direction except on
the north side.

The wallpaper, hither and thither peeling, ceased being
wallpaper some time during the last war when it became

wall-*covering*. It must originally date from the early 1920s.

The ceiling is a darkish brown colour but, many years ago, must have been white. There are pleasing decorative plaster-work cornices and edges about the room, and in the centre an ornate wreath-like design from which descends a length of flex terminating in a light-bulb socket that has never worked.

There is music in the room right now and I should say something about that. On the carpet, just to the south of the north wall, is a Dansette Major portable record player. New, these are about £17 but I acquired this one for a fiver from Charlie who said that his Uncle Archie was selling it so cheap as he was about to emigrate to Australia.

All however-many-cubic-feet of my room are full right now with the Thelonious Monk Trio playing *April in Paris*.

We enter the room and turn left down the east wall:

A CLOTHES RACK at a jaunty angle for maximum inconvenience and spanning the carpet and the brown linoleum.

FOUR CARTONS stacked against the wall. These may or may not contain lost items of clothing, old newspapers and magazines. They certainly do contain *imponderabilia*.

A MASSIVE WARDROBE over 6 feet high with twin mirrored doors. It must be as old as the century, perhaps a bit older. It is beautifully and solidly constructed from some rare, dark hardwood. It would make a good air-raid shelter.

On a panel on the front, between the two doors, the following has been carved in irregular letters about an inch high and a good eighth of an inch deep:

KEN AND PEGGY! 1949
M.O.A.T.

What does M.O.A.T. mean? I've been told that it is obviously like S.W.A.L.K. (Sealed With A Loving Kiss) and other things sweethearts used to put on letters during the last war. An acronym, no less. But MOAT? Nobody's ever heard of it.

A FRAMED ENGRAVING OF Rochester Castle dated 1796 and measuring, in the frame, nearly 2 feet by 1 foot. I bought this for 17s.6d. in a junk shop on the King's Road in Chelsea a couple of weeks ago.

GAS FIRE set in wall. This has never worked since I moved in. I believe the mains has been cut off elsewhere. Certainly no gas flows when you turn the tap. To the fore here:

ALADDIN CONVECTOR HEATER. This burns paraffin, smells awful and makes the whole room damp.

A BEDSIDE TABLE about 2 feet high made of carved oak. It has no shelves or drawers and supports itself somewhat precariously on four cross-braced spindly legs. Upon it is a cream plastic Bush mains radio that barely works, and upon this is a small bedside lamp with a 60-watt pearl bulb *sans* shade. Next to it is a chipped enamel ashtray. It is white with a red and black six-pointed star in the centre. Around the edge is written: USHER'S AMBER ALE, again in red and black but the colours are now faded, and fading.

A packet of Player's Navy Cut cigarettes is adjacent.

Also on the table are several paperback books, mostly American.

A HIGH DOUBLE BED contemporary, I think, with the wardrobe. The head- and tailboards are solid hardwood and rise about 2 feet above the top of the mattress which itself is nearly 3 feet off the ground.

CHARLIE PARKER POSTER above the bed showing Bird in a thickly striped suit with a shirt and tie holding an alto and smiling into the lens like butter wouldn't melt in his mouth.

A FRAMED PRINT of Henry Bowler's *The Doubt – Can These Dry Bones Live?* published in 1865. The painting shows a woman in a graveyard leaning against a gravestone and having religious doubts. May date back to the original occupants.

A DRESSING TABLE runs from the far corner of the south wall along the west wall. It has three mirrors and four drawers and is finished in veneer. It dates from the late 1940s.

On it are two untidy piles of papers and magazines.

There's a photograph of my mother here in a free-standing frame. It is a studio portrait taken by Frank's of Rochester some time in the early 1930s. It is the only photograph of her that I have. She has on a light-coloured print dress that I can remember her still wearing in the early 1950s. There is a half-smile on her lips and expectation in her eyes.

78 R.P.M. RECORDS are stacked on the brown lino next to the dressing table in two piles. There are about forty of them altogether, mainly Monk, Bird, Dizzy Gillespie, Chet Baker.

WINDOWS now, some 6 feet wide altogether with chipped and flaking paintwork. If you can jemmy open one of them there is a small decorative balcony outside which you can lie down upon providing you don't mind sticking your feet over the edge.

AN ELECTRIC BAR HEATER with a circular concave reflector for maximum heat. This type is only really any good for warming your toes, but that's academic because it has never worked.

A TAILOR'S DUMMY stands at the other end of the windows. It was here when I arrived in the summer and I have not had the energy to remove it.

A DEFUNCT GAS REFRIGERATOR is next against the wall here in the corner. Probably dates from the 1930s. It shows no sign of having worked within living memory, but it's insulated and useful for keeping the milk from going off on hot days.

A PORCELAIN SINK, deep and white (originally), begins the run of the north wall in the corner. Above this is a splashboard, a mirror, and an old wall-mounted gas-fed Ascot heater for hot water.

A KITCHEN TABLE. It is some 4 feet long by 2 feet wide and is abutted against the sink. The top has been covered in self-adhesive Fablon, in a pattern known as 'Vino' which against a black background has gaily coloured freehand drawings of wine bottles, carafes, glasses and so on, and which was not my choice and cost some 12s.6d. (as to who was responsible, see below).

A SMALL PINBOARD is affixed to the wall above the table and pinned to it are postcards people have sent me (Scarborough is the furthest any friend of mine seems to have travelled).

A SOLID BULBOUS ARMCHAIR covered in a maroon velvety cloth. It is faded, torn, grubby and comfortable. It must be fifty years old or more and matches the sofa at the foot of the bed.

A STANDARD LAMP stands to the fore of the armchair. It is about 6 feet high and made of turned, decorated wood.

A CAMPAIGN FOR NUCLEUR DISARMAMENT poster is on the wall above the armchair and shows the devastation at Hiroshima after the big bomb went off.

A BOOKCASE stands against the north wall next to the armchair. It measures about 3 feet by 3 feet and has three shelves (excluding the top). It was here when I arrived and is almost full of books, mainly authors like Vicki Baum, Hugh Walpole, Stanley Weyman, Jeffery Farnol and Rafael Sabatini, those popular authors of a previous age who have largely died with it.

THE LAUGHING CAVALIER occupies a frame immediately above the bookcase. I like the man.

I have now completed the circuit of my room, the perlustration of my kingdom. It only remains for me to inventory the following:

AN OLD SOFA that is placed against the foot of the bed. It is almost exactly the width of the bed and as I have already noted is the mother and father of my reading chair.

THE DANSETTE MAJOR record player, detailed above, is on the floor to the fore of the sofa. The sleeve for the Monk LP now playing is on the floor beside it together with copies of today's *Observer* (Est. 1791; No. 8790. Price 5d.) and (crumpled) the *News of the World* (No. 6056. Price 4d.).

A WOODEN TEA CHEST is this side of the bed and near the foot. Upon which is my 12-inch Murphy TELEVISION SET which I bought in the Portobello Road second-hand for £3 12s.

I have everything I need except a Goblin Teasmaid (or is it a Teas*made*?), but there is one 'item' I have not yet listed on the inventory. To wit:

GIRLFRIEND, BRUNETTE, on her side on the bed in a see-through baby-doll nightie and nothing else reading last month's issue of *Ideal Home* magazine, biting her nails and smoking a cigarette. This is Veronica. She prefers to be known as Ronnie. I won't shorten Veronica so we often argue about it. I usually call her Princess Fablon.

She's got a short pageboy haircut and dresses sharply. Beautiful big dark eyes. She almost looks like Bardot from across the street, but a close-up would reveal a sharper more angular face with thinner lips, and more generous breasts. She's waif-like in appearance but not in manner or temperament. Her temper can be fearsome indeed. She wears a trench coat the whole time and a black sweater.

That's her 'uniform'. Though sometimes at weekends she wears a horizontally striped sweater (she has dozens of these) and black stretch pants. Veronica chews gum the whole time, even when we're kissing. She's chewing gum now while she's flicking through the magazine and biting her fingers and smoking.

I have never known her not to smell of Pagan perfume. I'm so used to it I don't notice it except when I come back to the room after she has been here. Pagan is, I suppose, a mid-priced perfume. It is advertised with the line 'Don't wear it if you're only bluffing'. Veronica doesn't bluff.

Veronica's full name is Veronica Hilda Emily Stainer. Her two middle names which she hates people to know come from, respectively, her mother and her granny. Her name does not do her justice. She was born on 10 October 1940 in the house she still lives in with her parents in Kensal Rise. She was nineteen last birthday. She works as a stylist in a hairdressing salon on Westbourne Grove called Yvette of Mayfair. I met her one evening through Charlie's sister in the pub opposite here on the corner, the Royal Oak, the weekend I moved in.

Veronica lets out a big sigh, throws the magazine on the floor and stretches back on the bed. She sees that I am looking at her. I am standing in front of the door with a pencil in one hand and a shorthand notebook in the other. Ronnie is daring me to say something, but gets impatient.

'Well? Why don't you tidy up this place? And give that awful music a rest, please.' There's an expectant pause. Then: 'There's an article here about this new Morris Mini-Minor … it's only £537 … including purchase tax. You'll never be able to afford one … will *you*?'

Probably not, I think to myself, but who knows?

Veronica and I in our relationship have each notched up personal bests in incongruity and mismatchedness. We are so ill-suited every meeting is a Roman candle of surprises, every phone call an adventure. We thrive on differences that would have reduced other couples to patients in the

locked wards of Colney Hatch asylum. We should enter
competitions and appear on television shows. We're so far
apart we've backed into each other, because human space
is, like Einstein's space, curved.

'Well, then? Are you just going to stand there *gormless*?'
Veronica is a tough little thing who will probably end up
marrying some flash car dealer and living in a detached
new house in Watford or some such place. She's fond of me
and thoughtful and kind but she's just treading water for
the time being. I think I amuse her but she sees no future
with me. In fact, she sees no future *for* me. In ten years'
time, she avers, I will still be living in this 'poky' little room
listening to 'funny' music and pissing away my life in the
Modern Snax Bar. She may be right. She may be wrong.
And she knows I don't like being made to think about Big
Personal Issues, a fact that goads her further.

'I'm going down the Pyramid.'

Veronica will not say, Shall we go down to the coffee bar?
or Would you like to go down to the coffee bar? She just
makes flat pronouncements: *I am* going down to the
Pyramid, and that's that. Now you can, if you want, tag
along. Or you can stay here. It doesn't seem to make much
difference to her. In reality it does but she will not tack on
Why don't you come too? But I'm not complaining. She's
feisty and spirited.

Her parents, Hilda and Reg ('Mr and Mrs Stainer, *if* you
don't mind') tolerate but don't approve of me. They won't
be happy until she brings home the flashy car dealer:
working-class girls should always better themselves by
marrying well. They see me as a layabout and n'er-do-well
'who thinks he's someone special because he's always got
his nose in a book'. And books, as we know, are for the
upper classes only. Her parents seem quite well off. Her
dad does something down in the docks, in the warehouses.
He was quite impressed when I told him I had an appren-
ticeship down in Chatham but he's gone off me since then.
They've got a brand new 14-inch Bush television set and a

Bendix Dialomatic washing machine no less, *and* a Ferguson radiogram. Not to mention a Ford Popular. I know dockers are pretty highly paid but I suspect our Reg also does a bit of dealing in bent goods.

Veronica is now looking at me through her big doleful eyes. She's kittenish and frolicsome all of a sudden.

'If you were to buy me a box of Meltis Savoys tonight we could have a ... little *romp* ... now. Just a little one.'

She laughs and slides under the eiderdown. A long sustained note at the end of Monk's *Ruby, My Dear* slowly spreads over the entire room engulfing me and Veronica, who is now in my arms.

3

Red Top

> Vice drew me, but I could also trace the ruinous course of its effects,
> and note the political and economic forces that sustained it, and
> know who profited from it.
> – Luc Sante *Low Life* (1991)

COFFEE BARS AND MILK BARS have sprung up all over
the place in London in the last year or two and have, as
they say, become very very much the *thing*. If the mums
and dads have their pubs and stuffy corner-house restau-
rants, then the kids have got these places, places they can
regard as their own where they can linger over espresso or
milkshakes and listen to their own music. This is why Mr
Calabrese tarted up his little family café and gave it the
name it now has: Modern Snax Bar (it used to be called
Emilio's). Anyway, nearly all his regular customers had
died or moved away, and Soho had changed too fast and
too much in the 1950s for him. He says it used to be a
village and now it isn't. Mr C. will make what money he
can before his lease finally runs out and then he will go and
join the rest of his family down on the south coast.

Just around the corner from us in Old Compton Street is
the 2i's Coffee Bar. This is a pretty famous place and we're
always getting kids and journalists coming in and asking
us where it is. I tell them I'll have to ask somebody out back
and would they like a coffee while they're waiting? So at
least we pick up some incidental trade from it.

Mr Calabrese took Charlie on to help out part-time. Charlie
is about twenty and lives up Holloway Road. He's a sharp

dresser who buys all his stuff on Shaftesbury Avenue, but if it's cold he puts on a big old duffel coat that jars a bit with the sharp stuff underneath. Charlie tells me he is just 'passing through' here, he's 'developing interests', and that he's a 'well-known face' in certain quarters. He's always on the make and I'm quite sure that over his bed he has a photograph of Sgt. Bilko. But he's likeable and has a lot of Italian generosity.

His grandfather came over in the 1890s as a plasterer doing work on stately homes in Bedfordshire and I think there is some distant connection between his family and the Calabreses. Old Man Calabrese certainly always calls him Carlo, and this drives Charlie batty.

Charlie has an encyclopaedic command of slang and colloquialisms and I've often told him to write it all down and produce a handbook or little dictionary. It would make a good paperback if you could find a publisher brave enough to publish it, but being as most of the slang is sexual and pretty explicit no publisher over here is going to put his neck on the chopping block and get done for obscenity.

Charlie is growing bird-seed in a window box out in Holloway because he read somewhere that it contains marijuana seeds. He's going to harvest a crop and sell it off and make a good few bob. It'll complement his small-time drug dealing, or rather pill dealing. He carries black bombers and purple hearts around in those small circular tins that Gibbs Dentifrice comes in and sells them to kids in the amusement arcades where he spends a lot of his time.

Amongst the many angles Charlie occupies himself with is the odd bit of merchandise that has fallen off the back of a lorry, been lost in transit, gone for a walk, developed legs, become ownerless, lost its collar, appeared on his doorstep, was found adrift in the canal, or was given to him to mind by a geezer who never came back. All euphemisms for stolen or, as he prefers to call it, Little Red Ridings (rhyming slang: stolen goods = Little Red Riding Hoods,

and don't ask me where the finial 's' came from). These are
bent goods and it seems he's friendly with some fence in
Camden Town and works on a freelance commission basis.

Charlie has a different girl on his arm every time I see
him. All good-lookers, all seemingly besotted with him. I
think he regards women like his shirts. This one might be
OK for tonight but it certainly wouldn't do for tomorrow
night. He regards me as semi-married because I've only got
one girlfriend and see her regularly, so, in his eyes, I am
old-fashioned and well past it (whatever 'it' is).

My other good friend is a black guy from Barbados called
Sonny. We got talking one night at Mrs Bill's stall by St
Anne's church. It must have been about two o'clock in the
morning. Here's how we met. I was standing there
drinking some coffee and having a cigarette with a Sonny
Rollins Esquire LP under my arm that I had bought earlier
that day from Dobell's in Charing Cross Road.

Sonny came over and said he'd renamed himself after
Rollins. It turned out his name was originally Michael de
Salle which came from some French plantation owner or
something a hundred or so years ago. He said he didn't
want to be named after a French count so he called himself
Sonny after Rollins instead. He told me that he played a bit
of trumpet, and that Dizzy Gillespie and Fats Navarro were
his idols but adopting their names would have seemed too
affected. So he settled for Sonny instead.

Sonny works most evenings in the Be Bop Club behind
the bar. He also plays on some nights. The Be Bop is not
much bop but plenty of dope and, inevitably I suppose, he
does some dealing. Most of the West Indians when they
were back home used to smoke some *ganja* so they do so
over here too. Sonny deals in most things including some
hard stuff which is mainly used by white society people (I
believe him). He used to sell occasionally to Brenda Dean
Paul who was found dead in her flat in Kensington back in
July. She was society.

Sonny lives just off Ladbroke Grove in a basement flat that is dark and dank. The rest of the house seems to be full of ponces and prostitutes, all black. Sonny 'runs' girls from time to time for a few extra bucks. He has lived in this room since 1955. His parents, his mother and stepfather that is, brought him over from Barbados when he was fifteen. He lived with them for a couple of months in the East End somewhere, had a row, walked out and has never seen them since. He has been self-sufficient since then. He's had to seize whatever opportunities he could. This is a life without an awful lot of choice.

He's never been interested in black girls (except, that is, for business). It's only white pussy that gets him going. It doesn't matter about the size or quality, just as long as it's white. Up until recently he had been living with a tarty Welsh girl called Mary but she ran off with some (white) bank robber to Greece. He still keeps a picture of her tacked to the wall above his bed and, perhaps, still loves her.

The 1950s finally came to an end and we are now three months into the 1960s. I haven't noticed any changes yet but there's a feeling in the air. I can't quite put my finger on it, but there's something: a feeling of expectancy about, things are going to happen but no one knows what yet. It'll take a couple of years for this decade to discover its own identity. Everybody seems to feel that Macmillan's 'wind of change' isn't going to be limited to whistling through South Africa, it'll blow wider. I'm still living over in Bayswater (OK, *near* Bayswater) and still working at the Modern Snax Bar. I'm still seeing Veronica and she's still telling me I'll never be anything. This year so far I've bought myself an expensive suede jacket (via Charlie, it fell off the back of an airliner and only cost me £5 10s.) and discovered Claude Thornhill's band.

Apart from that, what else?

The police are having a big crackdown on pep pills and Charlie and Sonny are being very cautious, and the

Queen's sister says she's going to marry some snapshot artiste ... I was going to say, as *if* anyone cared, but the trouble is the whole fucking country cares. The whole fucking country thinks this is news and that the Queen's sister is more important than what's going on in Algeria and what's going on with the black students down in Alabama! What hope for a country as parochial and insular as this?

It's a quiet Wednesday at Modern Snax today and not much trade aside from the regulars. A warm day and I feel bored. Mr Calabrese is in for a couple of hours so we've got the radio instead of the jukebox. He turns on the radio and what starts blaring out? Yes, *Theme from A Summer Place*. You can't escape the bloody tune. Everywhere you go they are playing it. I wouldn't mind a shilling for every time I've heard it. And if it's not that it's bloody Adam Faith singing *Poor Me*. What about *poor us* having to put up with *him*? Christ!

We've had a couple of the real regulars in today, the 'faces' as Charlie calls them. Harold the Knife Grinder was in first thing this morning, telling me (yet again) that Queen Boadicea of the ancient Britons is buried underneath a platform at King's Cross station and that there is some occult connection between this and the widespread reports of flying saucers in the neighbourhood – reports, incidentally, that are kept out of the newspapers, or so he says. And, further, this is all tied in with Merlin's Cave nearby and St Chad's Well too. They all fit in somewhere, but Harold hasn't quite figured it out yet.

I used to be a bit condescending towards Harold when I started here. But as Mr Calabrese says, all this stuff is Harold's truth, *mia verita* in Italian (if that's how you spell it). Even if Harold's quest will always defeat him he is living in a world of magic and enchantment and hope. Anything is possible. Hope burns brightly in his universe.

Harold's speech is often slurred and indistinct but if you listen carefully you'll hear the vestiges of a fine, upper-class accent. Nobody seems to know who he really is or where he came from, though it is rumoured that his family had a large house somewhere in the country. He's always been around Soho. The story is that during the First World War he was sent back to a hospital here in England suffering from wounds and shell-shock. He never recovered. He drifted to Soho and has stayed here ever since. His left hand is badly shattered and his left temple displays a dreadful scar so there may be some truth in this. It's no use asking Harold about his past. He has none. He has his knife-grinding and his quest. He lives in an all-consuming perpetual present.

Mr Calabrese gives him a free cup of tea every day and if we're doing well Harold might also get a free sandwich or a cake.

His eyes are the bluest I've ever seen in my life and when I look into them I see a child's innocence.

The other face we had in today is a character bereft of honesty, integrity, vision and truth. In other words, a human being at the opposite end of the spectrum to Harold. This is French Joe, though he isn't French and Joe isn't his real name. Nobody knows what his real name is, though there is a rumour that it is Cyril, but this seems unlikely. A real name is too honest for Joe; a nickname is enough. He lived in Soho for ages but his landlord finally threw him out because he hadn't paid the rent on his room for years and years. He lives in Somers Town now, somewhere up behind Euston station, a neighbourhood on the wane. He must be around fifty but looks seventy-five. He is stained and decrepit and smells of drink, cabbage, photographic chemicals, old cigarettes, failure and opportunism in roughly that order.

Charlie said if you gave him some Omo washing powder he'd put a spoonful in his tea, he wouldn't think to use it to wash anything. He lives in a polarised world where things are either 'bleedin' awful' or 'handsome'. He's been on the run ever since he deserted from the Army in 1940 and he now lives a hand-to-mouth existence ducking and diving and turning his hand to whatever comes along. He is bereft also of principles and is a well-known tea-leaf (rhyming slang for thief) who would steal from anyone, including his friends. We keep a close eye on him whenever he comes in.

French Joe has had regular jobs in the past but always got the sack for nicking stuff. At one time he worked in various capacities in different night-clubs, like Kate Meyrick's 43 Club in Gerrard Street and the Shim Sham Club in Dean Street where Benny Carter once played, or so he says.

French Joe says he was born in Soho, in D'Arblay Street, and this is apparently true. His mother was reputed to be a French whore (as, indeed, were most of the girls on the game fifty years ago – French, that is) and this might be how his moniker arose. He says he remembers Zeppelins dropping bombs on Soho when he was a small kid during the First World War and during the 1939-45 fisticuffs he was standing just down from St Anne's church when it was bombed. The bombs during the last war drove him out to Tottenham for a while where he raised pigs in the back garden for sale on the black market.

Even if Joe was living out in north London during the war he was down in Soho every day. He says the war years in Soho were the best years ever in its history for making money. The place was full of servicemen out for a good time and you couldn't help but coin it in.

When Joe was in today he asked me if I was free on Sunday evening to give him a hand doing a little job? The job was so bizarre and out of my ken that I said yes.

Sunday night came and so did 7.30 p.m. but Joe didn't. I was stretched out on the bed reading *Moby Dick* and listening to some string quintet playing *El Relicario* on the radio when Joe finally turned up at about nine o'clock and honked his horn. I walked down and out and joined him in his little battered Austin A35 van. This is the unlicensed vehicle with DOBSONS OF PLAISTOW – HIGH CLASS GROCERIES signwritten down the side.

'What kept you? I been giving this horn stick for ten minutes!' spluttered Joe.

'How do you close this door?'

'You don't. You hold it shut by that strap. See? Or, if you want, you can lock it shut and climb through the window. OK?'

'I thought you said 7.30?'

'I did. But I had to pick up something in Notting Hill.'

And with that we jumped and jerked forward and spluttered around the corner into Bishop's Bridge Road, and then down the Harrow Road, and across the Edgware Road, stalling and starting all the way.

We went down the Marylebone Road into the Euston Road and then turned left up the other side of King's Cross station where we turned right into a side turning and came to a halt. All done without so much as one word passing between us.

The cobbled street is narrow and dingy, with run-down Victorian warehouses and shops on either side. This is a little backwater in the lee of the station. A backwater that time has passed by.

'We're here then.'

Joe said this and then turned in his seat and started shaking something in the back of the van.

'Wake up, Sambo. We're fucking here. Come on! Stop dossing. You're on next. You're not here for forty winks!'

I turned and could just make out in the dark a black bloke rubbing his eyes and yawning. This was the *something* that Joe had to pick up in Notting Hill.

We get out the van and I follow Joe through an open door and up a flight of stairs with the black guy trailing behind us (his name, I later learnt, was Clarence, but Joe never called him anything other than Sambo). We stopped on the landing and Joe knocked on a door that had EVE stencilled on it.

'Vera! You in there, Vera?'

I could hear a radio blaring some Paul Anka record inside. A tinny small radio turned much too loud, the speaker distorting the sound. I looked around the landing. The paint and wallpaper were old and grimy. There were three other doors but none of them looked like they were ever opened. The floor was bare boards except for a half-moon-shaped rug, badly worn, in front of the EVE door. Clarence still looked sleepy and hungover. He had a perpetual half-grin on his face and was standing with his hand in his pocket, bent slightly forward. I kept on expecting him to straighten himself but he didn't. It was as though he was frozen.

'Come on, Vera! I ain't got all night!'

'Coming,' said a raspy female voice from inside.

Then the door opened and there was Vera standing in a pink dressing gown with a cigarette in a holder about a foot long. She was late thirties, early forties, had long bleached hair and was heavily made up. Her lips were as red as red apples and full and sensuous. She wasn't particularly beautiful but she had the vestiges of beauty. A tired, used beauty, all spent. Her lips parted into something that could equally well have been a sneer or a half-smile.

'Come in. I don't want all the heat escaping,' she said.

We trooped in and she shut the door behind us. There was another woman sitting on the bed painting her toenails. She gave us a glance as though the three of us had been dragged in by the dog. She was a few years younger than Vera and was in a similar dressing gown. She had short black hair, small eyes and very thin lips. This, I would later learn, was Olive. She looks a bit like Janette Scott the actress, but older.

'I must finish doing me toes.'

Nobody objected.

I looked around the room. It was about half the size of mine. The window overlooked King's Cross. Or, to be more accurate, underlooked King's Cross. The other side of the street was a brick wall that went up as far as the eye could see. The room was dominated by the large double bed Olive was sitting on. A pink candlewick bedspread was stretched over it. There were some kidney-shaped cushions thrown about at the head.

On one side of the bed was a dressing table with mirrors and on the other a wardrobe, also with mirrors. Two Lloyd Loom chairs were at the foot of the bed where we were standing. It was a cramped room and our presence made it more so.

In the corner was a hand-basin with a couple of grubby white towels thrown over it. There was also some soap and a bottle of medical disinfectant.

The bedside table is littered with half-eaten packs of biscuits, ashtrays, packets of Durex and other types of contraceptives, and a Pifco vibrator with all manner of attachments. There are also a couple of tins of Vaseline and a large container of talcum powder. *And* a leather thong with metal studs fixed to the business end. The top drawer of the table is about a quarter opened and inside I can see a large pink plastic something-or-other – a strap-on dildo, no less.

The room is damp and clammy. There's a convector heater by the washbasin. A smell of unguents and emollients, rubber and cigarettes.

Vera is now sipping a Cherry B and going on to Olive about how she paid £19 for a beaver-lamb fur coat that had a ripped lining and how she took it back. She finishes the conversation we had interrupted and then turns to us.

'Who have we got here then?'

'This is Tim who's helping me and this is Sambo who's going to do a turn.'

'He looks clean enough … but tell him to go and wash *it* and tell him I don't want his gravy going all over the bed-spread.'

'You hear that, Sambo? Wash yourself properly over there and don't shoot it over the furnishings or you'll be for the high jump. Tim, you go and get the equipment ... and don't lose the keys.'

When I got back with the Photax floodlamps and Joe's carrier bag Clarence was standing naked in the corner washing himself and Joe was counting out £1 notes to Vera and Olive, who were holding them up to the light to see if they were genuine.

'I want the lamps looking down here.'

I plugged them in and set them up.

'OK, girls. Positions.'

Joe takes an old battered twin lens reflex Rolleicord from the carrier bag. It probably dates from about 1938. It was probably thieved. He then cleans the 75mm lens with a dirty handkerchief after breathing on it (the lens, that is). The lens is scratched and still covered in grease. The camera's casing is dented and covered in mildew. Joe must keep it in the van.

'A lovely camera this, Timmy. Had it years. Never lets me down.'

He reaches into the bag again and produces some rolls of HP3 black-and-white 120 film (and only 12 exposures a roll).

Vera and Olive take their dressing gowns off. Olive is completely naked while Vera is wearing a cream-coloured suspender belt and stockings. They sit down on the bed and wait, Vera still sipping her Cherry B and Olive now smoking. Vera has biggish firm breasts with very large erect nipples. Olive's breasts are small and point up at the end. They've both got passable figures. It's their faces that look worn and used.

Clarence is now standing next to Joe waiting for instructions. He's still got a half-smile on his face and looks like he isn't quite with us yet.

'Over there then, Sambo.'

Joe accidentally drops the camera and curses. He picks it up and shakes it to make sure it is still working. A Rolleicord! I suppose I would not have been more surprised if he had turned up with a Speed Graphic. With Joe, the f-stops here, you could say.

Clarence sits on the edge of the bed next to the girls. He's a big guy all right and the girls have noticed.

Vera turns to Clarence and tells him that there is not to be any kissing. They don't do that. Plenty of sucking, yes, but no kissing. Clarence continues smiling. He'll do as he's told.

Joe then produces an old Avo light meter! An Avo! Not even a Weston! An Avo. I haven't seen one of these in years. They stopped making them in the late 1930s. It belongs in a museum. Little cream-coloured thing in Bakelite with a flat light receptor – not even a dome. Joe holds it in the direction of the girls, taps it, takes a reading and then twists the calculator disc for the exposure. I'm not even sure the thing is working and neither is Joe. Then he guesses the exposure just to be sure and throws (yes, throws) the Avo back in the bag. He sets the Rolleicord and shakily holds it at waist level telling the three of them not to move. I don't think it would have made much difference if they had, Joe's hands are so trembly the camera is vibrating anyway. That and the grease on the lens diffusing the image is going to make for a thin blurry neg. But will the punters notice? I wouldn't have thought so.

'Yeah, this seems all right.'

He looks up from the camera and gives the lens another polish.

'Right. Vera, Olive – it doesn't matter what you do to our West Indian friend here. You can do whatever you like as much as you like, he'll never lose his horn.'

'He won't?'

'He won't. He's got a medical condition. Ain't that right, Sambo?'

Clarence shakes his head gleefully. But the shaking continues for a moment too long. I wonder if he isn't doped up on something. Vera wants to know if this medical condition is infectious.

'No, it's a nervous medical condition. A condition every bloke wishes he had. It gives him a permanent hard-on!'

Vera and Olive are a bit sceptical.

'Right. Now let's get on with it. First shot. You lie on your back there in the middle, Sambo. Vera, give him a suck ... and pull your hair back so we can see what's going on. And you, Olive, give him a tit to suck. Yeah, that's about right ... lean back a bit. Hold it. Watch the birdie! Now change positions and hold it. Yeah. That's right. Take it right in. Watch the birdie! OK. Now you stay where you are and you lie by the side, Vera, with your legs open and your lips pulled back. Yeah, that's good. But a bit more. Watch the birdie! Stay where you are and I'll get it from over here. Don't move. Yup. Hold it. Watch the birdie!'

And so it will go on for four rolls of HP3. Clarence sticks it wherever Joe tells him to and the girls roll their eyes and lick their lips and sigh and groan and give out little cries of pleasure that would do St Teresa proud and which would be great if only Joe's camera had a sound stripe. But it doesn't. This is the iconography and sound-ography of purchased sex and this is what the girls' punters expect and get, in spades. The girls are so used to putting on the sighing and aaaahing they even do it for the camera. While Joe reloads the camera the girls return to their normal mien, bored, impatient, stand-offish.

Clarence eventually comes over Vera's tits and later over Olive's face and he is very careful that it doesn't go else-where. The girls don't mind having semen over their lips but woe betide Clarence if he gets it on the bloody candlewick. He pumps away and they groan and push and Joe snaps away.

By the second roll I'm really bored. What I see going on over there on the bed has nothing to do with what I asso-ciate with sex. Dirty photos are sometimes exciting but this is too real. Photos allow you room for your imagination. This doesn't. I say that, yet would I feel any different if the two girls over there were a couple of real crackers, like

some of Charlie's girlfriends, and not the two old scrubbers
I now see? I wonder.

Joe gets paid £10 for a session like this from Mr
Messalino who runs a few dirty bookshops here and there
but mainly in Soho. Now I know who takes those dirty pix
you see floating around Soho. French Joe, the plain man's
photographic genius, the happy snapper. French Joe – a
Weegee without talent or technique – producing those
washed-out photographs of lifeless fornication with over-
ripe scrubbers. Washed out but uniformly hard lit, no sense
of lighting. Next to stuff like this Harrison Marks starts to
take on the mantle of Man Ray or Bill Brandt.

Before the session is finished I wander down to the car. I
didn't want to be a spectator any longer (and I certainly
don't want to be a participant). I stand in the street and
smoke a cigarette and watch the people and traffic coming
and going from King's Cross and looking up at the too
brightly lit window and think this evening would make a
fine chapter in a book of Henry Miller-style memoirs
should I ever write one.

I wondered why Joe had asked me along. To take part in
the activities? He never said anything or indicated that he
wanted me to join the girls. He was anything but subtle. If
he had wanted me to take part he would have come out
with it. He didn't. I wasn't asked along for any second
photographic opinions. Joe is quite confident in his own
expertise and doesn't need some kid to tell him how to do
it. Did he think he was doing me a favour letting me come
along and watch? Joe has no idea of what friendship is and
has never been known to do anyone a favour in his life.

This puzzled me.

I also learnt later that Clarence wasn't doped up. He was
mentally defective and Joe had collected him from some
halfway house hostel in Blenheim Crescent. So an evening
that began as being merely grotesque ended up as being
totally gruesome ... and all on the Sabbath too.

The net result of this night out was a week of diminished libido. I just didn't fancy doing it at all. I wasn't impotent or anything, just uninterested. Veronica said the evening sounded awful but didn't want me to spare her any of the details and I duly obliged. Sonny said he would be happy to take over whenever they wanted a black guy to give it to the white mamas and I told him he should get in touch with Joe as I certainly wasn't going to be involved in that scene. Charlie thought it was funny and wanted to know why I hadn't taken part. I told him. He didn't understand.

French Joe came by the bar a couple of times during the week sporting a smirky smile and acting like I owed him a big favour. He didn't mention the Sunday at all but I could tell it was on his mind. He asked if I would lend him 10 shillings and somehow thought I should and when I didn't he stormed out in a huff. A couple of days later he came back in, sullen and wounded. It still puzzled me why he had asked me along and I tackled him on it. He seemed to get nervous. He shuffled about and avoided looking me in the eye.

'I just thought you might like to come along.'

'What, as a favour?'

'Yeah. That's right.'

'You've never done a favour for anyone in your life.'

'I'm always doing favours ... for friends.'

'You are not ... because you don't have any.'

'That's not a very fucking nice thing to say, is it? You saying that ... you're talking like a real cunt, you are.'

'Perhaps I am a cunt.'

'Perhaps you are, Timmy. Perhaps you are. I didn't think you was but perhaps you are ... a real prize cunt.'

'Thanks.'

'Yeah. You got ten bob I could borrow to the weekend?'

'No.'

'What do you mean, *no*?'

'I mean I haven't got ten bob to lend you.'

'I'll remember that if you ever want to borrow a few bob

off me. Don't ever come to me on the earhole when you're skint.'

Joe's policy of asking everyone all the time for money probably results in a few shillings here and there but as he never pays any of it back he could never put the arm on someone a second time, except, of course, if they were real mugs.

Joe's explanation for inviting me along was untrue. I could not figure it out. The probable reason came out in a conversation with Desmond the journalist: Joe was very nervous about black guys and thought at any moment they could 'go jungle', revert to type, that is, and start acting like cannibals. He always wanted another white guy about to act as his minder. Joe is certainly a coward and a blinkered, ignorant one at that so I suppose I could buy this explanation, but how come he was alone when he picked up Clarence in Notting Hill Gate?

Joe came in the following day and the business of the ten bob was not mentioned. It was early evening and quiet so I took my coffee over to Joe's table and he told me the following:

'First job I had when I left school was with Cox & Harris over on Long Acre. Commercial and industrial photographers. Worked there for a few years up until about 1926. Got a grounding in photography there. Worked for some other photographers too later on. Never came to much. In the 1930s I used to do the odd bit of glamour photography as they now call it. Only then it was hot stuff and sold only in certain places. You never saw anything more than bare tits and arses.

'There was this French geezer up in Camden Town, on Delancey Street, who used to publish little pocket-size magazines with titles like *Spicy Ladies*, *Parisian Nights*. I used to make a few bob doing photos for him.

'The only dirty photos you saw in those days was brought in from abroad. You know, sailors and people who

went abroad brought them back. They came from France ...
or Egypt, I think. I mean there might have been somebody
doing this stuff over here but I never saw it.

'Then it all started to change during the war. Troops were
coming and going through London like nobody's business
and they were bringing these dirty photos over from the
countries they had been stationed in. So there was a big
demand for the stuff. They didn't just want to see foreign
women and niggers and that, they wanted girls who
looked like Vera Lynn. You know, English girls.

'There was this fella over on Greek Street called Wally
Gulliver who was originally a Highbury lad but he bought
this shop there near the Pillars and was a photographic
sundries man, a bit of this and a bit of that. He asked me to
do some photographs and he sold them under the counter
in his shop. We did a roaring trade! First off, all we sold was
photos of single girls with their legs open but then the
punters wanted to know why we didn't have any lezzy
stuff and fucking stuff. So we obliged.

'The girls never asked for masks or anything. Sometimes
one or two might have worn a wig but you could still see
who they were.

'So that's how I got going during the war. After the war,
in the late 1940s, things started getting back to normal but I
stopped doing pictures. Then about 1948 ... yeah, it was
1948 because it was the year Freddie Mills became the
world light-heavyweight champion, this Maltese geezer,
Franco Messalino, comes up to me and says would I like to
do some business for him? He's opened this shop selling
Yank mags and pin-up mags and he wants some pictures
for "out back". Stronger stuff for the punters. So I say
what's in it for me and we work it out. I been taking
pictures for him ever since.

'There are a couple of other geezers doing the photos too
but most of the stuff you'll see about was done by me. And
I've shot it all on my old Rolleicord. The box has never let
me down.

'When I began the stuff I shot was always the same. Just a boy and a girl. Just simple fuck and suck stuff. You never saw the bloke coming or anything like that. That came much later. Then it moved on to group stuff with two men and a woman, or two women and a bloke, and even two couples. Later on you got the jigaboos, the niggers in the pictures. There was a black girl I used a lot in the 1950s from Shepherd's Bush called Nancy. She did a lot of photographs with white blokes, usually two at a time. She used to love it.

'About six or seven years ago the stuff started getting pervy. The punters wanted pictures of girls getting it up the arse and stuff like that. Also, the flage stuff. I used to draw whip-marks on their arses with lipstick. Leather and rubber gear. That came along too.

'I don't do as many pictures as I used to now. Just two or three sessions a year. All my old stuff gets reprinted but I don't get paid for it. Sometime Mr Messalino might bung me a drink for old times' sake but there's no money there, not for me.'

There's never much trade on Saturday mornings so I left Charlie in charge of the bar and wandered over to the Fox for a quick drink. The place was almost empty. I got a pint of light ale and sat down and started reading the *Telegraph*. About ten minutes later Veronica appeared. She gave me a light kiss on the cheek and told me she'd like a gin and tonic which I instantly and dutifully got for her. She knocked half of it back in one gulp.

'Shopping always makes me thirsty.'
'You're always thirsty.'
'I'm always shopping.'
'I thought you were coming by this evening?'
'I was. But we can go to the pictures another evening. My friend Babs is having a party tonight so we can go there instead. I'll be around at your place about eight.'
And with that she finished the drink and was up and

away. I returned to the paper and the light ale.

Half of the *Telegraph* later as the pub was getting crowded I heard my name being called and looked up to see French Joe striding across the floor towards me.

'What you going to buy an old soldier, son?'

'Hello, Joe.'

'What you going to get me then? A gold watch? Huh?'

'You can have what I'm having.'

'What, the light stuff? That's for nancy boys and women!'

'And you can even sit here, but let me get on with the paper, eh?'

'Sure. You keep your nose in the paper. I'll sit here quiet.'

I got Joe a pint instead of a Scotch and returned to the paper.

'Amazes me what you find to read in that paper.'

Joe could not sit still and quiet for five minutes to save his life. He's looking around the room, drumming his fingers on the table, sighing and murmuring to himself, rubbing his nose, blowing his nose, picking his nose, inspecting the wax he has extracted from his ear with his little finger and then wiping it on the lapels of his jacket, belching, farting, clearing his throat and slurping his drink. I persevered with an article on Monday's Budget which, amongst other things, had put twopence on a packet of cigarettes. I didn't smoke that many, perhaps a dozen a day, but the twopences would add up. The cost of living was rising. Inflation had averaged out at about 5 per cent over the last three years if I understood the diagram correctly. People hadn't noticed this because weekly earnings had gone up about 14 per cent in the same period while salaries over the same stretch were now up around 17 per cent. The pound had held strong against the dollar throughout the 1950s at $2.80. But this is the sixties now and I wonder how we'll be at the end of it. As the article says, more and more foreign competition is challenging our traditional overseas markets ... . Still, I can't ever imagine our heavy and light industries going under. Who else could build a ship, a motorbike, or a television set so well?

'Joe. How are you?'

A quiet well-spoken voice with the trace of a foreign accent. Who was it? I looked up and saw this man standing by our table. He was only about 5ft. 4in. and was sharply dressed in an expensive grey suit and a silk shirt that must have cost him a good few guineas. He had a silk tie too. Short grey hair greased and plastered back and a thin taz. He wore glasses and was carrying a walking stick thing more like a cane. His skin was olivey in colour and he didn't look English. His smile showed a couple of gold teeth. He looked like Adolphe Menjou.

Joe immediately stands up out of deference and respect.

'I'm all right, Mr Messalino. And how are you and the family?'

'We're good, Joe. Everything is good.'

'Oh, I'm very pleased to hear that. Very pleased indeed, Mr Messalino.'

'I see you already have a drink, Joe.'

Joe has social graces like the Sahara has lakes. He must always angle for something and he does:

'Yeah, that's true. But it'll be gone in a minute.'

Joe says this in a joky fashion and when there is no response from his sometime patron his face contorts in embarrassment and he fidgets and shuffles. So even poor old Joe has some vestigial sense of the niceties of behaviour. Mr Messalino turns to me and smiles. Joe jumps into the breach.

'Yeah, Mr Messalino. This is my friend Timmy. He runs Modern Snax across the road.'

'Ah, you work for Emilio?'

'Yes, I do.'

'I have known Emilio well for many years. He is a good man … as were his brothers.'

'Yes, he is.'

'You will please give him my best wishes.'

'I will.'

'Joe ... Mr Timmy.'

And with that Mr Messalino bowed towards us and went off to join some cronies on the other side of the pub.

'Important man, Mr Messalino. Very important.'

'Seems pleasant enough.'

'I know all the important people. Know 'em all.'

That night Veronica didn't show up until nine o'clock. It was too late to go to the party so we stayed at Porchester Road. She was wearing a pair of knee-length leather fashion boots she had bought in Oxford Street that day. I'd never known a girl with boots like that before. I told her I thought it was only Russian princesses who wore them. Later we made love and I told her she had to keep them on. She says I am 'kinky'. Afterwards I walked her down to the bus stop. On Saturdays she can stay out till 11.30 p.m. She said she'd had enough of her parents' domination and wanted to get out. In fact she was going to move out this week and in with me.

'After all, it's only a couple of minutes' walk from your place to the salon.'

She said this so I didn't get any wrong ideas about why she was moving in. I told her it would be good to have someone to share the housework with and she said she'd clear up the mess she makes but not the mess I make. I told her she had a deal and gave her a big kiss as the bus drew up.

I walked back to the flat feeling dead chuffed. I put my *Chet Baker Sings* LP on and sat back on the bed with a full tumbler of cheap red wine. I lit a cigarette and thought that perhaps the 1960s were going to be good to me yet.

I was walking up Charing Cross Road the following Wednesday afternoon with Charlie when we bump into Joe dragging a sack along the ground out of Manette Street, by Foyle's. He's hot and sweaty and out of breath.

'You two, 'ere! I need a hand.'

'Not from me you old Richard!' shouts Charlie.

'You're a fucking tosser, Charlie. Just like every other soddin' Eyetie.'

A Richard is a turd, a word that rhymes with Richard the Third. No wonder Joe felt socially humiliated. Hence his witty rejoinder.

Charlie whispers to me: 'What's he got in that sack then?'

'No idea. His dirty washing?'

'Looks heavy enough to be a stiff.'

'But not big enough.'

'You sort him out. I'm going to Brighton [Brighton Pier = disappear] down the arcade. See you. I'm gone.'

I walked over to Joe who was now sitting on the kerb mopping his face with a black handkerchief.

'Gimme a hand getting this lot in a taxi.'

'What is it?'

'Old glazed tiles. Picture ones. I nicked them from the demolition site back there. These will be worth a fortune down in Chelsea. I'll get a cab down there and flog 'em.'

I went across the pavement and soon got Joe a cab. The cabby didn't mind having the sack in the luggage space up front so I dragged it across. It occurred to me that Joe probably didn't have the money to pay the fare at the other end so I gave the cabby a few bob to cover it.

Just as the cab is about to pull off Joe winds the window down and hands me a grubby bit of paper.

'Phone her. She wants to speak to you. Important. Vera. You met her the other night.'

The cab pulls away and I wave Joe off in relief. I look down at the scrap and written on it in pencil is:

Vera EUSton 2385

It looked as though it was written by a child. The characters were different sizes and at odd angles. Presumably the fair hand of Joe.

There was a telephone kiosk just down Manette Street behind the Pillars of Hercules. I looked in my pocket and found I had four pennies so I shuffled down. The kiosk, like all kiosks in the West End, stank of urine. I lifted the receiver, put the four pennies in and let it ring. It was answered and I pushed Button A.

'Hello? Vera?'

'This is Vera. Can I help you?'

'It's Tim. Timmy Purdom.'

There was a silence.

'I thought you would have phoned me sooner, dear.'

'I only ...'

'I can't talk now because I've got a gentleman visitor who has a train to catch. Phone me this evening ... about nine-ish.'

And she hung up.

What did she want to speak to me about?

I didn't get to phone her that evening because Veronica had decided to move in earlier than planned and this involved borrowing a bubble car off Charlie's cousin and going over to her parents' place while they were out and grabbing all her stuff.

It was good having her there when I arrived home in the evening and even better going to sleep with her and knowing she would still be next to me when I awoke in the morning. We'd watch telly together, listen to my music, listen to her music, get drunk and argue. It wasn't a relationship that was going to be long term and lasting but then I don't suppose either of us were prepared to commit ourselves like that anyhow. It was a relationship of the present, pro tem, and none the worse for that.

I finally got around to phoning Vera from the stairway phone at Porchester Road a few days later.

'I thought you were going to phone me back the other day?'

'I've been busy. I'm sorry.'

'I need someone reliable.'

'Hold on a minute ... *you* need someone reliable?'

'Didn't Joe explain?'

'Joe didn't explain anything. He just gave me your number. Nothing else. Said I should call you.'

'Oh, I'm sorry dear. I thought he explained.'

'No.'

'Well, let me explain. There's a gentleman I know in the West End who often has a party ... '

A party? A birthday party? An end of term party or what?

'You know, dear. A *party*.'

'Oh, yes. A party.'

'That's right. And at the party he's usually too busy entertaining the guests and the young ladies to ... to ... to undertake the duties and responsibilities of being a cinema projectionist ... *if* you get my drift?'

'I don't know anything about cinema projection.'

'The cinema projection that I am referring to is, it should be said, that of the home variety such as you might find on the table top of numerous smart West End addresses.'

She means 8mm stuff. I'm now warming to her genteelisms.

'May I be so bold as to inquire into the exact nature of the cinematographic footage I will be projecting?'

'People enjoying themselves, dear, and doing no harm to anyone else. That's all.'

'But I don't have any films.'

'No, but I do. And I also have the projector.'

'Why don't you go around and show them?'

'If I'm entertaining the guests I can't be working the projector as well. I've only got one pair of hands. That's if I'm there.'

'Why doesn't he do it himself?'

'Well, dear, you are either interested or you are not. You may pick up as much as one pound in tips.'

'What do I do if I'm interested?'

'Do you have a fountain pen?'

'Not with me.'

'Any writing instrument?'

'There's a pencil here.'

'Good. His name is Stephen and his telephone number is Welbeck 9378.'

'Thanks.'

'Good-night.'

'Yes, good-night.'

I went back upstairs and told Veronica.

'I'd like to come.'

'It might be an orgy. It might be full of awful people.'

'So, I don't have to take part.'

'I haven't decided whether I'm doing it yet.'

'You will.'

She was right.

I phoned this Stephen a few days later.

'Is that Stephen?'

'This is Stephen.'

'I'm Timmy Purdom. Vera said I should call you.'

'Oh, Timmy. Thank you so much for phoning. I had been expecting you. I'm *so* glad you rang.'

It was a soft, beautifully educated voice with deep and rich intonations and … yes … almost a feminine lilt to it. Was he a fairy? What was I letting myself in for?

'Vera mentioned a party.'

'Yes, we're having a little get-together next Friday if you would like to make a note. It starts about 9 p.m. and it's in a very good friend of mine's house in Culross Street.'

'Where's that?'

'You don't know Culross Street?'

'No. I'm fresh up from Rochester.'

'What an intriguing coincidence!'

'Why?'

'My father was a dean at the Cathedral there.'

'I don't think I ever met him.'

This was silly, smart-arse remark but somehow the context demanded it.

'Culross Street is a very charming mews right behind that bright new American embassy.'

'In Grosvenor Square.' I knew that at least.

'Exactly.'

'What number?'

'You know I can never remember. But you'll see a Bristol parked outside in British racing green. That one.'

'Right.'

'Good. You'll tie up with Vera and bring the things over, Timmy?'

'Yes.'

'Good. I do so look forward to meeting you, and do bring a girlfriend if you wish.'

'Thanks.'

'Until then.'

I told Veronica about the conversation but I didn't mention what he said at the end. She graciously allowed me to go on the understanding that (1) I didn't screw any girls, and (2) if it wasn't too awful she could come along to the next one, if there was one. I agreed. But what I didn't tell her was I didn't intend going to any second one ... in fact, why was I going to the first one?

The following Friday at about 7 p.m. I left Charlie in charge of Modern Snax and went upstairs to the maisonette and had a bath and washed my hair and changed into my suede jacket and good clothes that I had brought in with me in a bag. Then I caught a cab over to Vera's at King's Cross. She gave me the projector in a folding case, but no screen ('Just point it at the wall, dear'), and a carrier bag that contained three rolls of 8mm film and an empty spool for take-up. I then walked down to the underground and got a train over to Marble Arch after changing at Holborn.

Culross Street I found right away, right behind the US embassy. A small narrow mews street with houses dating from the 1700s, all immaculately kept, all with big cars parked outside. I soon found the Bristol. I knocked on the door of the house.

The door was eventually opened by a man of medium build and height wearing glasses and holding a cigarette in the air just to the right of his head (a position he would not deviate from throughout the evening). He looked like he was in his early forties. He was wearing a darkish suit, a white shirt and some sort of regimental tie and his hair was receding slightly at the temples. His eyes were wide open and he had a bounciness about him as though he had just won a prize. This I felt must be Stephen. I was right.

'It's Timmy, isn't it? Do come in, *dear* boy. Do come in.'

He waved me in and pointed down a corridor that seemed to go on for ever. At the end a door opened on to a large room at a slightly lower level, down a few steps. The remarkable thing about the room was that it seemed much bigger than the frontage of the house would allow.

Stephen waved me in and announced to the guests: 'The movie man's here, boys and girls!'

'Oh, good.'

'Yes, please.'

'The film chappie!'

'Good show!'

'Let's hope so!'

There were five or six blokes standing and sitting around in day and evening suits. All talking with frightfully good accents. Their ages were from the late forties upwards. One geezer with grey hair looked like he was about seventy. There were about seven girls there. Well made-up in expensive suits and dresses with hairdos and pricey handbags. A couple of them were younger than me but the rest looked mid- to late twenties. They were standing around talking and drinking. The girls were doing all the laughing.

'Timmy, put your things there and let me get you a drink. What would you like? Gin and tonic perhaps? Something else?'

'You haven't got a brandy and soda?'

'I'm sure we have. Let me go and see and while I'm doing that you can put your projector thingy over here and set it up.'

Which I did while Stephen Brightoned. All of the guests carried on talking and I was left alone at the end of the room getting sorted. There were some really attractive girls there but I felt that I was a bit out of my depth. I wouldn't be the kind of bloke who figured on their shopping lists. This lot was after bigger things that could not be provided by even Mr Calabrese's star employee. A bottle of champagne popped and there was more laughter and giggling. I watched the 8mm film through as the projector autothreaded.

Stephen suddenly popped up at my side and silently offered me the brandy and soda. I nodded and took a sip.

'How have you been keeping, Timmy?'

He said this like we were old friends who hadn't seen each other for a while. A puzzling remark. He was standing just a couple of inches closer to me than people normally do and I felt awkward and, strange as it may seem, threatened. I leant back against the table and he inched forward. I moved to the side. He remained where he was.

'You're a friend of Vera's, I believe?'

'No. I know *Vera* ... sort of.'

'Yes, I remember now. *Vera*. Dear Vera. Have you ever done it with Vera?'

I thought to myself, What a bloody cheek! It's no business of yours, but I answered him anyway: 'No, I haven't ... actually.'

'She's very good. She has a vagina that can clasp you with the firmness of ... of a sailor's fist.'

His eyes were looking me up and down as he said this. As if he was sizing me up for something. The femininity of his voice that was so apparent on the telephone wasn't so noticeable in the flesh but his mannerisms made up for it. One thing I've always noticed about homosexuals, particularly closet queers, is this eye movement thing. Their eyes are always wandering over you. There was a bank manager down in Rochester who often used to come by the photographer's for film. He was just like that. He got discovered in a public convenience with a lorry driver and got a prison sentence. He was just like that. Always stood just a bit too close. Always had the eyes going all over you. Perhaps I've got Stephen all wrong, but I think at the very least he must be bisexual. Vera says he's always got pretty girls around him but that doesn't mean anything. Not a brass farthing.

I guess he knows all about sailors' fists …

A fat balding guy in an evening suit waddles over to us and saves me from this situation.

'You're the film chap.'

'Yes. Timmy Purdom.'

'Purdom. Don't come from Crowhurst way, do you?'

'No. I've never been there in my life.'

'Oh.'

'Timmy, this is Dudley Fleming. Our host tonight.'

'Pleased to meet you.'

We shake hands.

'Pleased to meet you, Timmy.'

Dudley wanders back to the chesterfield and some blonde with big tits who is all over him.

A tall girl with long black hair in a white evening dress walks by and Stephen takes her arm.

'This is Carol. Carol is flying out to see Brasilia for herself tomorrow. Aren't you, Carol?'

She nods in an aloofish sort of way.

'One of her many admirers is paying for the trip, isn't he, Carol?'

There's a frosty smile. She doesn't want to meet me, the hired help.

'Carol is a lovely girl, Timmy. From a very good background. But I'm really afraid her penchant for the black boys is going to get her into serious trouble. I'm very worried about her.'

Stephen goes across the room and raises his hands. The talk and laughter dwindles to silence. He says, 'I think it is time, ladies and gentlemen, for a spot of movie magic. Peter, if you will take care of the lights and ... Mr Projectionist, *if* you please.'

The room went dark and a white beam from the projector shot across to the far wall. What would we see first?

There were four films and I'll describe them individually in the sequence they were shown. All were scratched and damaged with odd frames missing and, in one instance, a scene or scenes missing. These prints had been about a long time and the sprocket holes were ripped in odd places and sometimes missing altogether. All were black-and-white and mute.

FIFI ET SES DEUX AMIS

Three minutes of three people: a good-looking buxom blonde and two blokes with moustaches. It looks like it was made in the 1920s, probably in France. The film opens with Bloke One being given a blow job by the girl. Then they start fucking in different positions. The door opens and Bloke Two walks in unaware. Bloke One remonstrates with him and Bloke Two exits. Bloke One re-joins the girl and she whispers something in his ear. He gets off the bed and shouts out the door to Bloke Two, who then comes back in and gets on the bed. The girl has both men at the same time.

The production values are not bad for the time. There's plenty of inter-cutting of close-ups and whoever directed it gave some thought to the action. The girl is a vigorous performer and quite obviously enjoyed it. The two blokes were a bit wooden and stiff (no pun here).

SMART ALECK

This looks like it was made in the States in the early 1950s.

If the previous film had been made by a gifted amateur this one was made by an un-gifted professional. It has all the surface slickness of a professional film but it is lazy in direction and detail.

A salesman at a hotel (or is it called a motel?) invites a young girl up to his room for a drink. She gets a bit tipsy and they start to have sex. Later, she won't suck him so she calls in another girl, who does. Then the three of them carry on together.

THE NYLON MAN
This is older than *Smart Aleck* and dates from some time in the early 1940s. American (again).

A salesman (again!) sells a girl a pair of inferior stockings and he calls by later just as a large hole appears in them. The girl is furious. The salesman offers to fix them with his magic salve and this together with his smooth talking soon leads to them making love. At the end she realises she has been hoodwinked again and throws him out.

RIN-TIN-TIN MEXICANO
A very bad print with whole scenes missing. Mexican. Shot some time in the 1930s.

A woman takes a shower, has sex with a dog who mounts her from behind after licking her, then has another shower (or is it the same shower?), then makes love to an older man on the floor while the dog is asleep.

Stephen had thoughtfully placed a small lamp on the table next to the projector so I could switch it on and see what I was doing while changing films. The laughter and giggles subsided in the intermissions and gave way to rustlings and murmurings. I wasn't sure what they were doing but they were certainly doing something. When the lights came on at the end I could see a few shirts and blouses unbuttoned but that was all.

The guests began drifting upstairs in twos and threes as I started to rewind the films on the projector. Some old guy had a blonde on each arm. Then I was alone in the room. Then Stephen appeared through the door waving a fiver in the air, which he gave to me.

'*Splendid*, Timmy. You must come again. I hope you enjoyed yourself?'

'Yes, it was fun.'

'Perhaps you'd like a drink with me in the upstairs drawing room before you go? You could tell me all about yourself. I'd so like to hear *everything*.'

'I'd love to, Stephen ... but I've got to be going.'

'What a pity ... a great pity indeed.'

I packed up the projector and the reels and Stephen showed me out. He asked me to call him next week. I said I would. I returned the stuff to Vera and was home and in bed with Veronica by just before midnight. She wanted to know all about the evening and I gave her a quick once-over of what happened and said I'd tell her the rest in the morning. After seeing the women at the party and the films I should have felt really horny but didn't. I just wanted to get to sleep as I would be getting up at six in the morning.

The following day I was out the back of the bar making some cheese and tomato sandwiches ('And, remember, Timmy, just *a suggestion* of salad cream and salt') when Charlie came out and said some old geezer out front wanted to see me. Charlie didn't know who it was because the geezer didn't say and because he, Charlie, was too uninterested to ask. I wondered who it could be. I took my apron off, wiped my hands and walked through.

Charlie pointed to the number 2 table over by the door, next to the jukebox. Sitting there, stirring his cup, was Mr Messalino. I recognised him right away. What did he want? I walked over. He smiled and indicated to me to sit down.

'I'm pleased to see you again, Mr Timmy.'

'Thanks. Timmy is, actually, my first name.'

'I'm so sorry. I thought it was your father's name.'

'No. That's Purdom.'

'Purdom. A name I have never heard before ... is it English?'

'Sort of. It's Old French. It means honest man.'

'I'm sure you are.'

'I try to be.'

Messalino then took a small manila envelope from the leather attaché case he had on his lap. The envelope measured about 6 by 5 inches. He placed it on the table in front of me and waited for me to pick it up. I did. There was something in it.

'Please,' indicated Messalino.

I took out five black-and-white photos. They were pictures taken the other Sunday at the photo session by French Joe. Each shot was overexposed and blurred. You could just about make out what was going on.

'This is very sad.'

'Pretty bad, aren't they? I was there when he did them.'

Poor old Joe had finally fucked up in a major key. I doubted if Messalino could even have given these photos away in his shops.

'Joe is too old to do any more. It is sad but true.'

'Why are you showing them to me?'

'Are you not a photographer?'

'Of sorts. How do you know?'

'I had a drink the other evening at the club with Emilio. He said you were trained as a photographer. He says you are very dependable.'

'I had some training.'

'Good.'

'I don't think I'm the person you're looking for, Mr Messalino.'

'Why is that?'

'I've seen enough of Vera and Olive in that situation to last me a lifetime. I don't want to get involved in that.'

'Olive and Vera, yes. I remember them when they were fresh young girls. That was a *few* years ago.'

'Yes.'

'Timmy, Joe is old and dirty. I tell him many times that we need fresh young girls in our photographs. Fresh and young like Olive and Vera were once. But what fresh young girl is going to be enticed by Joe? We need a young person to take photographs of the young girls. Joe only knows old women.'

'Why ask me?'

'You are young. You know about cameras. Emilio speaks highly of you. You are reliable. It is that simple.'

'Well … I would like to help you, Mr Messalino, but I don't really think this is me. I'm sorry.'

'I would pay you £2 10s. for each negative I accept. Please think over the proposal.'

'That's a lot of money.'

'If it is of the right kind with good-looking models I would consider that a fair price.'

'Right. Thanks. I'll think about it.'

And back to the cheese and tomato sandwiches I went, leaving Mr M. to finish his tea.

That night as I lay on the bed staring at the ceiling I told Veronica about Messalino's offer. She was sitting on the sofa at the foot of the bed mending a blouse and trying to block out the Monk LP I was listening to.

'He'll pay you £2 10s. a negative?'

'Uh-huh.'

'How much is a roll of film?'

'What film?'

'The film you'd shoot this on.'

'Thirty-five millimetre black-and-white, 400ASA, 36 exposures. It's about 7s. 6d. a roll.'

'How much to develop it?'

'Three bob or so.'

'And the prints?'

'What prints?'

'The prints he'd buy from. He's not dumb enough to buy from the negatives, is he?'

'I don't know.'

'How much are they, then?'

'Postcard size … about tenpence each.'

'You said Joe pays the girls £3 each and doesn't ever pay the fellas?'

'Uh-huh.'

She went quiet and I drifted off to sleep listening to that glorious seven-minute version of *Blue Monk* that Thelonious recorded in September 1954 … .

I don't know how much later it was when Veronica started shaking me and telling me to wake up. The record had finished and the room was quiet apart from her voice. She was sitting on the side of the bed with a pencil and one of my notebooks.

'I've done the sums on this and you'd be a fool not to do it.'

'Not to do what?'

'Take these photographs for that bloke.'

'Why?'

'Listen to this. Say you had two girls and two fellas. That would only cost you £6 for the evening. So what you'd have to do is make sure you took as many pictures as you could. Two rolls of film with the developing and printing would come to another £6. So your total costs are £12 and you've got 72 negatives you could sell at £2 10s. each. If you sold every one of them you would get £180 back. Take away your costs and that is a clear profit of £168!'

'Oh, yeah. And what if he only bought ten of them? Tell me that!'

'If he only brought ten of them you'd make … only £13, which is more than you earn in a week anyhow, *thick-head*!'

'You'd really like me to do this, wouldn't you?'

'When are you going to wake up?'

'Don't you have any shame?'

Shame? Shame! The word just came out. It must have been the first time in my life I'd ever used the word. Shame!

'I wouldn't appear in them, but what's the harm? You're not robbing anyone or making them do something they don't want to do, are you?'

I turned over in a huff and pulled the eiderdown up over me.

'I'm going to sleep … I'm not doing it … and, besides, I don't know any girls.'

'I think *I* do.'

4

Epistrophy

There is a great deal of vice which really is sheer inadvertence.
— Benjamin Disraeli (1879)

IT WAS COMING UP TO eight o'clock in the evening when I arrived at Gledhow Gardens, a street off the Brompton Road about ten minutes' walk down from South Kensington underground station. Eight o'clock on Sunday, 1 May 1960.

I rang the bell for the top flat. Sally opened the door and said Sonny had arrived already, but Charlie hadn't. Janet was upstairs talking to Sonny. Would we cancel it now or what? No, we'll give him half an hour or so, see what happens.

Sally and Janet shared a couple of poky rooms at the top of the house. Two single beds, an old sofa, some armchairs, a rickety kitchen table shoved over near the gas ring. The communal bathroom was on the next floor down. There were pictures and calendars they had put up on the walls themselves, but these served to accentuate the anonymity of the place rather than reduce it. There was an Ella Fitzgerald record playing in the background.

Sally was nineteen and worked as a secretary in an import-export company over in Victoria Street run by an 'Indian gentleman in a cashmere coat who drives a Jag'. This was the fourth job she had done since arriving in London from Coventry some eighteen months ago.

Janet was a year older and worked in Whitely's store in

Queensway, in the linen department. She was from Cambridge and had held the job down for two years. Veronica is Janet's favourite hairdresser, hence the connection.

It doesn't look as if Charlie is going to arrive. Sonny is smoking some dope and the two girls are both getting a bit tiddly on red wine. Perhaps we should get going now?

Janet comes over with her glass and sits next to me on the bed.

'Are you a photographer, then?'

'I was ... I *am*.'

'What sort of photographs do you take?'

'All different types. A lot of portraits ... well, I used to.'

'Have you ever taken any of these pictures before?'

'No, I haven't.'

'How do you know what to do, then?'

'That's not too difficult ... is it?'

'Suppose not ... I didn't know he was going to be black.'

'What, Sonny?'

'Yes.'

'He's always been black. Does it make any difference?'

'No, not really. But I've never done it with a black man before. I suppose they're the same as us?'

'Uh-huh ... but bigger!'

'Are they?'

'I'm joking. I don't know.'

'They say they are.'

'We'll both find out, won't we?'

'Heads it's you, Sally. Tails – Janet. Looks like you win ... or lose, Sally. If you lie on the bed like that ... but undo your blouse ... yes ... take them off ... so we can see ... open your legs, yes ... close your eyes ... put your tongue slightly out ... you are enjoying it ... caress yourself ... like that ... open them wider and start rubbing yourself ... just carry on ... higher ... wider ... I'll just take shots ... more ... hold the end and put it in ... right in ... push it in and out and pretend you are enjoying it ... more ... like that ... stay still ... yes ... I'll get different angles like that.'

'Same thing, Janet ... take your stretch pants off though and just pull the sweater up ... like Sally ... yes ... more ... use that ... right in ... yes ... now turn on your side with your leg like that ... keep doing it ... you're really enjoying it ... yes ... *more.*'

'Sally ... just hold him ... Sonny put your arms around Sally and hold her breasts ... yes ... now start licking him only ... move back a bit because I can't quite see ... take him right in your mouth ... now hold your breasts against him ... squeeze him like that ... Sonny, if you get on top and let her suck you like that ... OK, now a sixty-nine position ... and just carry on and I'll get different angles ... good ... just a few more ... If you kneel by the side of the bed you can lick Sally from there ... lie on your side now and Sonny will enter you from behind ... Sonny, hold her leg up ... keep going ... now get on top of Sally ... good ... don't stop ... can you get on top of Sally now, Sonny? Right ... more ... support yourself so I can get some shots from here ... stay still ... just a few more ... OK, then ... take it out and come over her tummy ... don't move ... good ... stay still ... lick your lips ... hold it ... rub him ... yes, just a few more shots ... good.'

'Sally, you lie on the bed and Janet, kneel just there ... play with her breasts ... yeah, suck them ... and rub her at the same time. Yes, good ... like that ... good ... keep going ... now swing round ... and lick her like that ... well, pretend to ... push your tongue out then and stay like that ... and pull her lips back ... yes, don't move ... close your eyes so people think you are enjoying it ... good ... now push that in ... and hold it ... now lie on top of Sally ... on your back on top of Sally ... like that ... OK, just a few more ... Sally, you pretend to lick Janet now ... that's good ... keep like that ... pull her lips right back ... now push it right in ... close your eyes and bite your tongue, Janet, like you are really enjoying it ... good ... now just a few shots in a sixty-nine position ... keep your tongues out ... right out. That's all.'

'You stand there, Sonny ... and Janet, kneel in front of him ... yes, take him right in ... move your hands ... can we do it with you sitting in the armchair now, Sonny ... good, Janet ... now get on top of him ... move up a bit and I can get shots from back here ... stay still like that ... good ... now kneel down and Sonny can enter you from behind ... look back over your shoulder so we can see you ... move around a bit Sonny ... yeah, so I can see what's going on ... some more ... good ... Janet, can you hold Sonny while he's in Sally ... yeah, like that ... look interested ... excited ... and ... hold it. Right. When he comes this time hold it in your mouth ... then let it out so it runs back down him ... and keep your head there. Uh-huh. Good ... good...now, yes. Rub it over your lips ... put your tongue out. Yes ... lick it off her.'

And so it went on until nearly eleven o'clock. And had I been apprehensive before the evening began that I would write myself into the action, I needn't have worried. A more asexual evening I have never had. The whole evening to me was something more akin to gross anatomy than eroticism. I felt a flicker of arousal when the comely Janet sat next to me but the moment she and Sally stripped off my interest evaporated. I didn't get a hard-on all evening. I was merely a photographer and this was merely a job. I could have been shooting printing presses at Mackay's of Chatham for all the arousal it gave me. And the other funny thing was that there seemed to be no connection between what was happening on the bed here and making love to Veronica. Nothing at all. Sonny certainly enjoyed himself. He was like the proverbial dog with two cocks.

Altogether I shot four rolls of 36 exposures, a total of 144
pictures, on my little Ilford Sportsman. They may not be as
well composed as the stuff that appears in *Amateur
Photographer*, but the lighting and exposure will be spot on,
certainly head and shoulders above anything Joe ever shot.
How many Mr Messalino will want to purchase from me is,
of course, another question. We shall see.

Afterwards the girls made Sonny and me a cup of instant
coffee and we chatted about where we would all like to go
for our holidays and it was as though we'd all only just met
up in a pub. Nobody mentioned what had been going on.
That was the past now, ancient history, all forgotten about.
Over with.

Soon, Sonny and I were walking up to South Kensington
station.
    'We going to come round here again and take some more
pictures with these young ladies, Timmy?'
    'I don't know. Perhaps. Ask them.'
    'You set it up.'
    'I partly set it up.'
    'Uh-huh. You gave them £3 each.'
    'That's the rate.'
    'How come I don't get no three quid?'
    'Guys don't.'
    'Why's that?'
    'Because guys get the action instead, that's why. I
explained this to you.'
    'You didn't explain the girls get paid.'
    'Would that have made any difference?'
    'Sure. You expect me to work for ... uh ... like *love*? Do
you?'
    'You weren't working for love. You were thinking and
working with your dick. You know?'
    'I think you should give me something.'
    'You do? When I told you you were going to be giving it

to two young white girls you couldn't get your dick around here quick enough. *You* would have paid me. Now you've got your rocks off and your tubes cleared...*you* want some money?'

'I do. That's only right.'

'Sonny, you're such a small-time hustler!'

'I'm a big-time hustler if I'm a hustler!'

'Nickels and dimes.'

'You can fuck yourself, man!'

'See you around.'

'Fuck you, white boy!'

'And you, brother!'

I walked the rest of the distance to the station by myself. I left Sonny storming down the road waving for cabs. Dope gets to him sometimes. He doesn't always think straight. I now need to get down to Rochester and get Arthur to process and print the shots for me and do a set of dupe negs just for safety's sake. Perhaps I can do that next Saturday, take the day off? Better clear it with Mr Calabrese first. Shouldn't be a problem.

How long have I been up in London now? Eleven months only. And already I'm a pornographer with all the qualifications for being splashed over the front page of the *News of the World*. I guess I'm now an active part of Britain's moral decline. Part of the scum in this great nation of ours. One of Her Majesty's subjects actively engaged in dirty pix. A potential white slaver and drug fiend! Just another guy on the make, that's all. Another guy on the make.

'You've got a postcard from that friend of yours ... Stephen,' said Veronica as I walked into the room after a real pig of a day in Wardour Street.

'Have I? Where is it?'

'On the table there ... somewhere.'

It wasn't.

'Well, it was earlier.'

'But it's gone.'

'So?'

'So you've been the only person here.'

'So?'

I couldn't find it anywhere.

'What did it say?'

'Nothing much. Just phone him. About a party. Saturday or something.'

'I'll call him.'

'Don't forget you've got to get down to Rochester and get the pictures developed.'

'I know. What's that got to do with it?'

'Nothing. But you've got to do that.'

'I know I have.'

'If I don't push you you'll keep on putting it off.'

'I haven't kept on putting it off and I won't, all right?'

'Good.'

I got through to Stephen later that evening on the third attempt.

'You are a dear boy for phoning.'

'I got your card. But it's lost.'

'Good. Did you like it?'

'Uh … I haven't seen it. Veronica lost it.'

'What a shame … a beautiful portrait of the Duke of Edinburgh. Just the sort of thing to pin above the mantel-piece.'

'I don't collect pictures of the royal family.'

'Well, you should … especially of Philip. A very good-looking man. Very good-looking. I used to see him about in the late 1940s, early 1950s.'

'You get about a bit, don't you?'

'That's what we're here for, Timmy. Getting about and getting to know each other.'

'I'll remember that next time I'm full of existential despair.'

'I don't know if you've got your little appointment book

with you but on Saturday week, that's a week this Saturday, we're having a little party at Dudley's again in Culross Street. Perhaps you'd like to come?'

'What, with the projector?'

'No, no projector this time. We may have a magic lantern show instead. Teddy will do it himself.'

'I think I can make it. Do you mind if I bring someone?'

'Who?'

'Veronica – the girl I live with.'

'Not at all … as long as she has a full set of lips and cheeks and knows how to use them!'

'You'll have to ask her yourself.'

'I will.'

'Until Saturday, then.'

'Until Saturday.'

I turned up at Stephen's party in a new sheepskin coat I'd got from Charlie for £6. It looked very smart. Veronica was wearing a tight-fitting black dress and had her hair piled up high. I guess we both looked smart for our type but I'm not sure how well we fitted in with the crowd who were there. It was the same lot as last time plus a few more – middle-aged and elderly geezers and tarty-classy young ladies. Stephen was all over me and all over Veronica when we arrived and then he spirited her off to meet some friends of his who were at the other end of the room. I just stood there with a brandy and soda until I heard a woman's voice call my name. I turned. It was Vera: 'Hello, dear.'

'Hello, Vera.'

'We are going to have a little film show after all, and I hope you don't mind taking care of the projector.'

'I don't mind.'

'Good. The equipment is out in the hall. Perhaps you'll go and get it in a jiff?'

'Yes.' Vera was rubbing her forefinger around the edge of the glass and staring at me. I sensed she wanted to talk. 'Have you been to many of Stephen's parties?' I asked.

'I've known Stephen since just after the war. I've been to hundreds of his parties.'

'Are they all much the same?'

'They are attended by people who like to get the most out of life. Uninhibited types. Girls who want to get on. People like that.'

'Just out for a good time?'

'Exactly ... and doing no harm to anyone else.'

'Where do you come in?'

'I'm a very old friend of Stephen's and I help out. We all do what we can, don't we?'

'What's Stephen's particular type of sexuality? What is it he enjoys doing?'

'I think you'd better ask him that yourself, dear.'

'I'm asking you, aren't I? What do you do for him?'

'A bit of this, a bit of that, but I haven't done either for a long time.'

'You are being very coy.'

'Not coy, just discreet.'

'Tell me ... for old times' sake.'

'We don't have any old times.'

'I know.'

'He needs the vibrator now ... it takes a lot of work. He likes watching, mainly. I don't think he's a very sexual person himself. He has sex through other people.'

'What else?'

'A little bit of domination.'

'What about other men?'

'I think I've said quite enough already.'

'You haven't started.'

'I've started and finished, dear.'

'What do you mean by, "He has sex through other people"?'

'He likes hearing about what other people do. He likes watching them. He takes up and adopts these young girls, introduces them to his friends ... they go to bed. Favours are owed.'

'That's all?'
'That's enough, isn't it?'
'I guess it is.'
'He has very influential friends.'
'He does?'
'Yes, he does.'
'Very influential.'

Stephen's voice cut through the general hubbub. 'So, it's all the talk of the town! One of my dear friend Baron's assistants is going to marry the Queen's sister. Tony Armstrong-Jones is going to marry Princess Margaret. When they told Tony it was May the sixth he didn't know whether that was the wedding date or his new title!'

There were two films that evening:

LA VIBORA
A very poor print. Made in Mexico, Cuba or somewhere like that. Looks old, could have been made in the 1930s. A man goes to see a girl and they soon start making love. Then another man arrives and the first one hides in a cupboard. Later he comes out and all three of them go at it.

ESPRIT DE FAMILLE
A French film from the late 1940s (?), reassembled by some cutter who apparently didn't have a full print to work with. A man and two girls. The shots are out of sequence – in one shot one of the girls is undressed, in the next she is walking into the room fully clothed. Just a couple of dozen takes of sexual activity thrown together in no particular order.

After the showing couples wandered upstairs again and we hung around for a little while eating and drinking. We left about 11 p.m.

I walked up Wardour Street and down the alley that led across to Dean Street. About half-way down on the right-hand side was a large, freshly painted front door. Freshly painted in black. There was nothing on the door aside from a polished knocker, a dolphin, and a small bronze plate that had engraved upon it: MIDEX LTD. I knocked and waited, then knocked again. A small grille that I hadn't noticed on the upper part of the door slid back and a voice, with an Italian accent, said, 'Who are you?'

'Timmy Purdom. I've come to see Mr Messalino.'

The door opened and I was waved in by a young Italian kid in an expensive blue suit. He waved me on further, up the stairs. Mr Messalino appeared on the landing at the top and showed me into his office.

'Please sit down.'

Messalino walked around the desk and sat down too. He smiled and rubbed his hands together.

'You have been busy?'

'Pretty busy, yes.'

'You have something for me?'

I handed him the large manila envelope I had been carrying. Of the 144 pictures I took on May Day I judged that 110 of them were OK for his consideration, the other 34, though better than Joe's, I didn't really consider good enough.

Messalino thanks me for the envelope and takes from it the pile of photographs. He removes the rubber band that secures them and then takes a pair of glasses from his breast pocket.

'You have been *very* busy.'

'I hope they are what you are looking for.'

'I hope so too.'

Messalino carefully scrutinises each picture in silence. Some are put in a pile on the left, some on the right. He works his way through them, carefully and deliberately.

'Two very attractive models, Timmy.'

'They are.'

'I wonder if they would be available for other work?'

'I have no idea.'

This little room must be the hub of Messalino's empire. An antique desk, two chairs, a drinks cabinet, a filing cabinet, and dozens of family photographs all elaborately and ornately framed on the walls. The one window is draped with bright red velvet curtains and nets and over-looks the back yards of some buildings on Old Compton Street.

Messalino considers each photograph individually. He squints at it like a diamond dealer, carefully assaying its quality. Some will pass, others will not.

'Very well. I have made a selection. Perhaps we can now do some business?' He hands me the larger of the two piles.

'These I would like. Would you count them?'

There are sixty-five photographs. Sixty-five sold out of a total of 144 taken. That's very nearly 50 per cent. Not bad going, eh?

'That's sixty-five, Mr Messalino.'

'Good. You have the negatives with you?'

'Yes. I've numbered them. Call out the numbers on the back of each print and I'll sort the negs.'

I didn't want to just hand over the rolls of film so I cut all the negs and separately bagged and numbered them. Messalino would only get what he paid for. Nothing more. Nothing less. We spent twenty minutes sorting them and then Messalino went over to the wall-safe that was behind a family photograph on hinges (just like in the films). He took out a metal cash box and walked back to his desk.

'Sixty-five photographs, Timmy. And we agreed £2 10s. per negative?'

'Yes, we did.'

'That is a total of £162 10s then?'

'Right.'

'That is one hundred in ones ... sixty in fives ... two further ones ... and a ten-shilling note.'

'Thanks.'

'I am very pleased with these ... but my customers will

be the final judge. Let us see how well they react. I will be in touch with you presently.'

'I've never held so much money in my whole life. I hope you'll be able to make your money back.'

'I'm sure I will. These are very good pictures.'

I said goodbye to Mr Messalino and walked out on to the Soho streets like a tit in a trance. One hundred and sixty-two pounds and ten shillings! Can you believe it? Can you honestly believe it? All that money for doing what? Doing fuck all! Just a few lousy photographs. Big simple money this! And what did it cost me? A few hours on the Sunday, a Saturday afternoon in Rochester, and a total of about £25! One hundred and thirty-seven pounds and ten shillings clear profit! Staggering. Still, I've got to split this with Veronica, but that still leaves nearly seventy quid to myself. Seventy quid, no less! I can even afford to bung a few pounds to that mean black bastard, Sonny.

It was late on a Thursday afternoon and we had been very quiet for an hour or two when I heard my name being called across the place. I looked up from the cheese sand-wich I was making and saw Stephen sitting at a window table with a slim brunette who somehow looked both nervous and full of herself at the same time. I guess she was about nineteen, late teens certainly.

'Tim, dear boy, do we merit table service?'

I wiped my hands and walked over. Stephen was rabbiting on to the girl about those 'influential' friends he had. She looked suitably impressed – impressed enough to take time off from inspecting her manicured long red fingernails.

'Tim, I want you to meet my very dear friend, Linda. Linda, this is Tim.'

Linda and I nodded at each other. She smiled, but it was a thin and forced smile, a smile that had its origin in the social etiquette pages of a woman's magazine. She was wearing a classy black dress and a wide-brimmed hat.

Around her neck was a string of pearls.

'Linda is one of the newest models in London ... and *very* successful.'

Stephen said this in a measured, considered way as it if was very important. Almost in the way Richard Dimbleby would announce some royal event on the television.

'Linda is particularly successful in ... photographic modelling.'

The emphasis was on the word *photographic*. Photographic. There was something curious about this statement because though it was aimed at me Stephen was looking at Linda as he said it and he continued looking at her, with a leery smile. She stared at him and giggled. They were talking about something I was not privy to. Something else was going on here.

'Linda cannot stop. She has to be somewhere ... don't you, love?'

Linda got up at the end of this sentence, smiled at me, waved at Stephen and left, without even saying a word. I watched her as she crossed Wardour Street and headed down towards Shaftesbury Avenue.

I fetched Stephen a cup of coffee and sat down with him. He had been boozing and his speech was slightly slurred.

'I didn't know you knew I worked here ... did I tell you?'

'You must have done. Or someone did.'

I could tell from Stephen's eyes that things were racing through his mind. There was a stifled smile on his lips as though he was thinking, I know something you don't know. Just like Desmond, but in his unique way.

'Have you known Linda long?'

'Gorgeous girl, isn't she?'

'Yes.'

'She's very well liked ... has a lot of admirers.'

'Have you just been somewhere?'

'Yes ... we have. And have you?'

'Just here and home.'

'Nowhere else?'

'No.'

'I've heard you've been quite active.'

'Active?'

'Yes, photographically speaking ... if you get my drift, Tim.'

Stephen's smile ceased to be stifled, it spread across his face. His eyes opened up. His expression said, you can trust me! This was his little secret. This was what he had wanted to say to me.

'How did you know?'

'Tim ... I know lots and lots of people ... I really do.'

'Word travels fast around here.'

'It does. All I wanted to say was that I could be of great help to you ... you have only to ask.'

'Help? How?'

'I know some very good girls, photographic models ... .'

'Like Linda?'

'Exactly.'

Somehow I could not picture Linda getting her giggling gear around Sonny's stiff black cock ... but who knows?

'I think it is so important for friends to help each other. Don't you, Tim?'

'I suppose it is.'

'But just do me a little favour in return.'

'What's that?'

'You know I'm a bit of a dirty old man ... let me have some copies of the pictures. I can put them in my ... *family* album. I do so like photographs of the dear girls I've helped ... given a helping hand to ... see them as I best remember them.'

'Uh-huh,' I said.

'Would you like some tickets for *Psycho*, the new Hitchcock film? It opens here at the end of the month.'

'Would you like another coffee?'

'I don't think I quite have time.'

And that was that.

I was walking down Wardour Street with Charlie early one evening when some geezer in a big black Mercedes starts honking his horn. I didn't take any notice. Then Charlie says to me some bloke in the car is waving to me. I looked around and it was Mr Messalino.

'Good evening, Mr Messalino.'

'Good evening. How are you?'

'OK.'

'Business is good. Business is very good. I need more photographs from you. I need new photographs. You come and see me on Saturday morning. We discuss it then.'

'Yes. Right.'

The Mercedes pulled forward and headed down towards Old Compton Street.

'He a friend of yours, Tim?'

'That's Mr Messalino.'

'Some car, huh?'

'Yeah. I think I've just made myself a few more bob, old mate.'

'Good. It's National Pakamac Fortnight now. You'll be able to get yourself a different one for each day of the week.'

'And you too.'

'Don't bother.'

When I first met Mr Messalino he had three shops in Soho. Now he has seven, I'm told. Dirty pix and adult mags have really taken off in a big way. He must be making hundreds of pounds a week. And easy money at that.

I didn't get around to setting up the second photo session of my career until the beginning of September. The 2nd of September, funnily enough. My birthday: 2 September 1960. My twenty-third birthday. And as good a way of celebrating the event as any.

The session was shot in Charlie's rooms up on the Holloway Road near the Nag's Head. The two blokes were Charlie and Sonny and the two girls were two secretary types that Stephen had sent over called Angela and Beverly. They were both brunettes in their early twenties. Angela was slim and had no tits but made up for it with enthusiasm while Beverly was big (about 36D) and a bit frigid: she just acted like a robot. Which just goes to show you can't get everything right.

We started at 7.30 p.m. and finished just after 10 p.m. I shot a total of four reels again. It was just the usual couples and foursome stuff (the girls didn't want to do any heavy lesbian things) but I got some good shots of Angela with two cocks in her mouth at the same time. I also discovered that condensed milk looks just like semen so I cheated a good number of ejaculation shots.

The girls were friends who had met Stephen at a pub down in Chelsea. They had been around to the mews house he has somewhere near Portland Place for another party but didn't really know much about him. They both wanted to be models and he said he could introduce them to the right people (not me, surely?). There was an air of evasiveness about them both and a reluctance to discuss personal specifics. I let it go at that. Stephen had told them the photographs would only be sold in Scandinavia and I didn't tell them otherwise.

I took the negs down to Rochester and got them processed together with two sets of prints.

Of the 144 pictures I took I ended up with 70 that I felt were good enough to show Mr Messalino. He bought 40 of them and gave me £100 which is nice work ... if you can get it. When I was with him I couldn't help thinking of Laurence Olivier as Archie Rice in the film *The Entertainer* which I had seen the day before. Messalino is just like a Latin equivalent of Rice, but a bit meaner perhaps.

Veronica is lying on the bed in our room watching TV. Stephen is sitting on the sofa at the foot of the bed going through a set of photographs of Sonny and Charlie and Angela and Beverly that I've just handed to him. I'm

standing in front of the sink with a bottle of beer playing
Monk's original 1947 recording of *Round Midnight* in my
head. I'm also thinking about the lovely money Veronica
and I made from this session (OK, she didn't do anything
this time, but she is my partner).

Stephen is drooling over the pictures and breathing excit-
edly.

'Tim, you are a very naughty boy ... making the girls
work like this. Very naughty ... isn't he, Veronica?'

'He's disgusting – really disgusting.'

'Tim, Tim, Timmy. Such an imagination!'

I'm thinking that I would like to buy a really good stereo
record player. A real hi-fi job. Listen to Monk on something
decent instead of this tinny little speaker on the pathetic
Dansette. A couple of big speakers. A good stylus. Fill the
whole room with blue notes from his piano.

'You realise, Tim, that you have become precisely the
sort of person the Sunday papers like to put on their front
pages and expose?'

I guess he's right. I guess I am the sort of person they like
doing over. I am a living, breathing part of the decline of the
British Empire. I should wear a badge.

'The *News of the World* might get to *you* first,' says
Veronica to Stephen with a chuckle.

Stephen is a bit put out by the remark, unduly so. He
says in a snappish, high-pitched voice, 'I don't think *that*
will happen, dear.'

Veronica responds in character: 'How can we be so sure,
dear?'

'Because, dear, I have very influential friends.'

'Pride before a fall, Stephen. The bigger your friends the
quicker they'll drop you if something goes wrong!'

'Tim, I don't know how you can live with this *woman*.'

I don't either, but it works somehow.

Stephen continues looking through the pictures and then
he has a bright idea. 'Couldn't you go professional,
producing pictures like this?'

If some guys have girlfriends and wives who finish their sentences for them, I've got a partner who not only does that but also starts the sentences as well. Without taking her eye off the TV Veronica says, 'The money is in distributing and selling them, not in producing them ... and Tim's not got a very good business brain.'

Stephen sighs and looks at me. I smile and say, 'I see it really as a sort of hobby that produces the odd bit of revenue. It certainly isn't enough to live on.'

Veronica looks across at Stephen: 'See, what did I tell you?'

The third photo session took place on Friday, 18 November 1960, around at Sonny's place in Ladbroke Grove. It was two days after Clark Gable died. The day after he died someone in Wardour Street told me the joke about this bloke going to a bar in New York and picking up this great-looking girl. Anyway, they end up back at his place and one thing leads to another and the girl goes down on the guy. Then she suddenly stops sucking him, leans back and says, 'Clarke Gable died today.' The guy says, 'Yeah, I know. But carry on, he would have liked it that way.'

Sonny had got two black girls for the session, Shirley and Lorna. They were both on the game. I started off getting a roll of lesbian stuff and then Sonny joined in and I did some threesome shots and then more stuff of Sonny with each of the girls separately. I ended up with nearly a hundred shots of which about half were good enough for presentation to Mr Messalino, the Archie Rice of the dirty book trade, as I now think of him.

Mr Messalino ended up buying twenty only, which netted me a mere £50. Not one of my most lucrative evenings.

'It's nice stuff, but white people don't want to see niggers doing it to each other. Niggers might want to but not enough of them come into my shops to make it worth while. White people don't mind seeing photos of jigga-

booes but there's got to be whites there too. I'll take a few,
these twenty. They've got a novelty value. If I ever open a
shop in Africa I'll let you know.'

On the way home I bought a copy of *Lady Chatterley's
Lover* which is now on sale everywhere since the jury at the
Old Bailey decided it wasn't obscene.

It might not be obscene but it is boring. I passed it on to
Veronica. The opening pages didn't even fire me enough to
search out the dirty bits.

The first session of 1961 took place in late January, four
days after John F. Kennedy became the 35th President of
the United States of America. The cast was Sonny, Sonny's
prostitute friend, Shirley, a friend of Stephen's called Nancy,
an American girl, and Harry, a mate of Charlie's from the
Nag's Head in Holloway: in other words, a black guy, a
black girl, a white guy and a white girl, which gave me
quite a few varied combinations. I ended up shooting some
six rolls of film, a total of 216 pictures, in about four hours.
On the earlier sessions I had always spent some time
arranging the lighting so that I had highlights and
shadows, pictures with some depth and atmosphere. Now
I just bang in the lights like French Joe and shoot. Subtleties
of lighting are lost on the people who buy these pictures.
They just want pictures that are sharply lit and in focus.
Give them what they want. They are close-up detail devotees. They want the sort of pictures that appear in medical
textbooks. Anatomical high definition. Vulvas and dicks
glistening with baby oil.

There's a limit to what two, three or four people can do
together, sexually speaking, so I vary the setting and the
props. I had some shots of Nancy sucking Sonny's dick
while Shirley was sitting beside her looking at an Adam
Faith LP. Then I had some shots of the two of them doing it
doggy style while watching television. I suppose this is all
lost on the punters, the humour of it (such as it is). But then
it's just my little joke. The thing is that there is a decided

tediousness now to these sessions. But then I'm only here for the money. This session was shot in a hotel room on the Bayswater Road. Veronica arranged it through the receptionist from the place who goes into her salon to have her hair done. I had to bung her £5 and the assistant manager another fiver, but it was worth it to get out of bedsits and grotty rooms. The room wasn't grand, just a couple of armchairs, a double bed, bedside tables and a TV, but it looked like a hotel room, which was the main thing. I've been thinking about other locations lately, like in a train, on Hampstead Heath, on top of a bus, and others. This could add a bit of spice to the pictures.

After the session was over I walked with Nancy down the Bayswater Road. She needed a cab to get back to Hampstead. I asked her how long she had been in London.

'Six months.'

'Have you got a job?'

'I'm a secretary-researcher in the House of Commons.'

'Really?'

'Uh-huh. Just temporary. An exchange scheme arranged through my old university.'

'What for MPs and that?'

'Yes … but don't tell Stephen I told you that.'

'Why ever not?'

'He might not like it. He's funny about who knows what … odd.'

'I won't mention it. Do you know him well?'

'A little … not well.'

'Have you had an affair with him?'

'No. They say he's only interested in watching. I think he prefers other men, really.'

'Is that a guess or a fact?'

'A guess.'

'Why did you agree to appear in the photos?'

'Something different to do.'

'Something different? Just for a laugh?'

'Yeah.'

'Just a whim?'

'You could say that.'

'That's all?'

'Yes, that's all. That's the picture, Tim. You ask too many questions. You might get into trouble one day carrying on like this.'

'Perhaps I'm in trouble already?'

'I wouldn't know.'

'Is there something going on I don't know about?'

'I don't know what you know and what you don't know.'

'I'll tell you something I don't know.'

'Tell me.'

'Your other name and your phone number.'

Nancy thought this was funny. She laughed. She didn't reply.

'What is your other name?'

'I don't think it would be a good thing for us to see each other again, Tim.'

'Why not?'

'It wouldn't.'

'Is Nancy actually your real name?'

'There's a cab over there. I've got to get home.'

Of the 216 pictures I shot I took 120 around to Mr Messalino and he bought 50 negs from me so I ended up with £125 which, minus expenses of around £75 (I'm now paying the actors £10 a session), left me with some £50. He liked the stuff but said I should now shoot some 'flage' material as the punters were always asking for it and the pictures he had were very old.

'Tie the girl's hands behind her back and put some lipstick lines on her arse and have that nigger standing over her with a whip ... that kind of thing. But get girls who can act like it is hurting them.'

It's a coldish afternoon as I walk up Marylebone High

Street to the coffee bar Stephen has asked me to meet him in. I find it up at the top, the Mocambo: espresso and pastries and prints of Italian seaside resorts on the wall. This is the carriage-trade end of the coffee bar world. Expensively dressed secretaries. Professional types in suits. Dean Martin records in the background.

Stephen is sitting at the very back in a cubicle. He waves me over and orders some coffee for us both. He's in one of his subdued manic moods again, his eyes flitting about, his hands dancing with each other.

'So good to see you again, Tim. So good. Have you got some little snapshots for me?'

I hand him the manila envelope that contains a hundred or so prints from the last session. He opens it under the table and hurriedly begins riffling through the postcard size prints.

'Excellent, Tim. Very good. Who is this marvellous black lady?'

'She's from Notting Hill, or rather, Ladbroke Grove. She's on the game.'

'Does she do any governess work?'

'Governess? What, teaching?'

'I suppose one could say that. I rather had in mind a little of the old spanking.'

'I don't know. You'd have to ask her.'

'I imagine she would. These negresses are often very good at administering corporal punishment to naughty white boys. Very good. And quite merciless.'

'They are?'

'Indeed, they are. You might like to try it one day … if you haven't tried it already.'

'Perhaps I could ask Nancy to give me a couple of strokes?'

'Nancy? Who's Nancy?'

'That American girl there you sent along.'

'You mean Julia?'

'Do I?'

'Yes. She was obviously a little shy at telling you her real name. Girls are so difficult to predict. Some of them change their names as often as they change their knickers.'

'Is there anything about her I shouldn't know, Stephen?'

'Search me, old boy.'

'Like she works in the House of Commons?'

'Does she? How interesting ... I say, this black girl looks so fetching with the dildo strapped to her ... so proud ... I wouldn't like her to surprise me from behind on a dark night, would you? *That* could be very, very painful!'

Sitting here listening to Stephen and listening to Dean Martin I had an epiphany as to what it is about Stephen I don't like. I always knew there was something about him that irritated me. Now I know what it is. The bloke is so fucking plausible ... even when you know he is lying. Just so fucking *plausible*.

'Tim, I've had a rather splendid idea.'

Stephen is now piloting the conversation even further away from the subject of Nancy (alias Julia).

'You have?'

'Yes. Now that you are such a whiz at taking these photographs, how about taking some of chaps? You know, fellows frolicking together and doing things ... like they do?'

'Queer stuff? Homosexual stuff?'

'I know a very rich viscount who would pay you royally indeed for some sets.'

'I'm not the bloke for that. You'll have to get someone else.'

I finished my coffee and left. Stephen was still gazing at the pictures and smirking.

It was a quiet, hot July Monday afternoon. Trade was slow and limited to bottles of Pepsi-Cola and strawberry milk-shakes (we'd run out of chocolate and banana syrup). I'd sold three corned beef and three cheese and tomato sand-wiches since lunchtime. I was leaning against the counter

having a quick fag while Charlie was sitting down at a table
with his feet up reading a car magazine.

'See this new E-type Jag, Tim?'

'No.'

'Cruises at 100 miles an hour. Tops at 150!'

'How much?'

'Two grand … 2,000 oncers, Tim. I bet you'd like a car
like this, wouldn't you?'

'Yes, I guess I would.'

'Well, you'll never be able to afford one, son!'

'Thanks.'

'Imagine bombing up that new motorway in this little
beauty. You'd be in Birmingham in half an hour. You'd
really pull the birds driving it! They'd be eating out of your
trouser zip for a ride in this … slobbering all over you!'

'Did you hear about Ernest Hemingway yesterday?'

'Who's he?'

'Just some American writer … he blew his brains out
with a 12-bore shotgun.'

'That must have been a surprise for his charlady. How
about you and me, Tim, half-inching one of these Jags for a
joy-ride? We could be in Scotland before they noticed it was
missing! Up the old A1, the wind in our hair … vroooom!'

I was gazing down at my suede shoes and puffing on the
cigarette when the door opened. I looked up and saw
French Joe shuffle in and shuffle over to one of the window
tables where he sat down. I had only seen him once or
twice over the past couple of months. Each time he had
looked the worse for wear and each time I had given him a
tenner out of guilt. I know Mr Messalino would have
elbowed him doing the photographs without me appearing
on the scene, but I felt my presence had hastened his
demise. Somebody said Joe was living in some hostel in
Camden Town and earning pennies working as a pot-man
in a pub on Chalk Farm Road.

I took Joe over a cup of coffee and a corned beef sandwich and some custard cream biscuits.

'Here you are, old fellow, on the house.'

French Joe just stared ahead. His eyes were red. He was crying.

'What's up?'

He took out a dirty handkerchief and wiped his nose and his eyes (in that order) and then turned to me and managed a half-smile. He took a bite from the sandwich and swallowed it without chewing it.

'You hear the news?'

'What news?'

'You hear all those police cars and sirens this morning?'

'Yeah, you always do here. I don't notice them any more.'

'You should have done.'

'Why? What happened?'

'Some tearaways went out with their shotguns … they blasted Mr Messalino out his window.'

'He's dead?'

'Course he's dead. He never knew what hit him.'

'Christ Almighty. I don't believe it! I saw him only last week!'

'What's that got to do with it? An audience with you ain't going to give him immortality, is it?'

'Who did it? Why?'

'Everybody knows who did it except the Old Bill. Bernie Narrizano's the bloke. He's the boss now. He'll take over the shops and the clubs. He's a vicious bastard … not a gentleman like Mr Messalino. A real fucker … strong-arm stuff. Things are changing around here. This is the 1960s now. I'm still living in the 1940s. I don't recognise it. It's all different. The game has lost me.'

And I've lost Mr Messalino and a nice little earner … .

It was a stiflingly hot August Saturday night about a month later when there was a loud thump on the door of our room. Veronica and I were half undressed on the bed watching that old Dane Clark film, *Moonrise*, on the TV.

Veronica wasn't expecting anyone and nor was I. I opened
the door and these two blokes who were built like brick
shit-houses just walked into the room. They had evening
suits on and were either on the way to some function or
had just left one. They looked like bouncers, which is sort
of what they are. They were marinated in cheap after-shave
or cologne.

The slimmer of the two (but still pretty big) said: 'You
Timmy Purdom?'

'Yes, I am.'

'And who's this?' He nodded towards Veronica.

'My girlfriend.'

'Right then. Bernie asked us to come round and see you.'

'Bernie?'

'Mr Bernie Narrizano.'

'Oh, right.'

'Now you did some ... uh ... work for Mr Messalino,
right?'

'Yes.'

'You had a good run for your money with him?'

'I guess so.'

'That's what Bernie heard. Bernie also heard you were a
dab hand with the camera. You know how to take pictures
that look like they were taken by a bloke with a head on his
shoulders.'

'I can use a light meter.'

'Well, Bernie says that he don't need you to take any
snapshots as his own lads can do that. But what he does
need is someone who can use an 8mm cine camera. He
wants some 10-minute films ... all the usual ingredients ...
plenty of humping and that.'

'I've never shot a movie before.'

'Shouldn't be too difficult for a man of your achievements, should it, son?'

'I wouldn't know where to get the footage processed.'

'That's ain't a problem. We've got a lab up on the Seven
Sisters Road that can do it at night.'

'What would the deal be?'

'Bernie is generous ... very generous. But the market and Bernie's programme of expansion and diversification have put a little bit of a brake on his good heart. But he'll look after you. Anyway, I'm Ronnie Swindon ... and this is my card. I run the day-to-day operations for Bernie ... it has been a real treat meeting you and your lovely wife, Timmy, and we shall talk shortly I'm sure. Good-night.'

And they sailed out the door and thumped all the way down the stairs and slammed the front door so hard the whole house rocked.

Veronica was laughing.

'What's so funny?'

'Your new friends.'

'I wouldn't say they are friends. More business acquaintances.'

'They won't let you get away with anything, Tim.'

'I'm sure they wouldn't.'

I got back on the bed and tried to watch *Moonrise* but I couldn't concentrate. Eight-millimetre films, eh? They wouldn't be very difficult to shoot but they would require a more extrovert performer than the stills, someone who would listen and do exactly as they were told. Still, I couldn't make worse films than those old pictures I showed at Stephen's parties if I tried, could I? The punters don't expect great acting anyway; the fact that it is moving is enough for them. I could do for dirty films what Harrison Marks has done for glamour films. But I need a distinctive name to sign the pictures with ... how about lopping off the 's' of Marks and swapping the names around? Mark Harrison presents ... that sounds right. Sleazy and yet with a bit of polish. Mark Harrison presents ... A Moonrise Film ... *Au Pair Girls in a Chelsea Sandwich*!

But what would the deal be? And is Bernie's idea of generosity my idea of generosity? And who am I and what am I doing here anyway?

First 8mm:
DOLCE VITA FOR FOUR
125 feet (10 minutes), black and white, mute.

The Ronnie/Bernie Deal, as Veronica called it, was simple. I would submit an expenses budget and 'story' outline and if they approved it they would reimburse me the costs once the film was made and pay me £75. I paid the performers, bought the stock and organised the camera and lights. They would pay the development costs at the lab. So while it wasn't the good money I had been making with Mr Messalino it wasn't to be balked at: £75 clear for just a couple of evenings' work – an evening to shoot it and an evening later on to edit it.

My contact man up at Finsbury Park was a bloke called Ernie Trundle who worked nights in a small 8mm lab. He was the night-shift supervisor and could do what he wanted. He was an elderly guy and apparently was an old friend of Ronnie Swindon's dad, Harry, a once well known bank robber who now, funnily enough, runs a caravan site down on the Isle of Sheppey just across the Medway from Grain. ('You ever want a caravan for the weekend, Timmy, just give me a shout and I'll fix it with my old man.') We were limited to 8mm black-and-white because no independent lab yet had colour processing facilities. When you bought a reel of 8mm Kodacolor or Gevacolor the processing costs were included in the purchase price and only those companies have the means to process colour. So, until such time as a safe contact is found in one of these big labs or colour processing becomes easier and simpler the punters are stuck with black-and-white.

I wasn't too familiar with 8mm cine cameras so I bought some copies of *Amateur Cine World*, studied the ads and spent a day going around the West End shops checking the gear out. The camera I decided on was the new Eumig C5 that was only just out from Johnsons up in Hendon. A beautiful bit of Austrian engineering and just what I needed because, unlike all the other 8mm machines, it has reflex viewing and a built-in zoom lens, an f/1.8 10-40mm, no less. So there would be no messing about with lens turrets and no framing cock-ups arising from a parallax viewfinder. Further, it runs off five pen-light batteries so you are not constantly rewinding a clockwork motor. The thing costs £117 8s. 3d. new and while I had some savings I didn't want to blow that amount on something I didn't need myself. Luckily I found a dodgy photographic dealer down in Streatham who was prepared to hire the camera to me overnight for 25 shillings.

I shot *Dolce Vita for Four* on Friday, 18 August 1961, in a bedsit in Courtfield Gardens that a friend of Veronica's had. I had two guys from a pub on Westbourne Grove I knew, Audrey who had come via Veronica, and a friend of Stephen's called Tina who was half English and half Chinese. She said she was an old friend of Stephen's but didn't seem to know much at all about him. But she was a real wildcat on camera and was the only performer who didn't keep looking into the lens.

The storyline of the film was minimal. Audrey and Tina are alone in the bedsit drooling over a Cliff Richard magazine. Audrey gets very excited by Cliff and then Tina produces a dildo. In the middle of the lesbian high-jinks the two boyfriends walk in unexpectedly and join in. There was a slight problem with one of the blokes, Terry, who couldn't keep it up, so I had to be careful how I shot him. The problem with Bill was that he got too excited while I was reloading the camera and came in Tina's hand when she gave him a playful squeeze. Luckily I had some condensed milk for come shots, but I don't see how one can fake an ejaculation itself. The zoom lens came in handy for big close-ups. You can zoom right in for close-ups that fill the screen. Give the punters what they want!

I stole the title from the Fellini film that I had seen the week before at the Berkeley Cinema. As a title it seemed apt and contemporary. The phrase appears all over the place now, even in the *News of the World*, and it is important to reflect the times. I didn't actually think a lot of Fellini's film, it had some nice moments but it went on too long. Perhaps I wasn't in the right mood to see it, having just had an enormous row with Veronica who had originally agreed to come but at the last moment stormed off to see *Exodus* at the Astoria instead. ('I don't want to see a bunch of Italians – I want to see Sal Mineo. He's really dreamy!') The night after Ernie processed it I went up to the lab and 'edited' the film together. Joining would be a better term. There was nothing much really to edit, aside from cutting in the opening titles I had shot in my room:

Card One:

Mark Harrison
presents
A Moonrise Production of

Card Two:

DOLCE VITA FOR FOUR

This was really *film d'art* as they used to call it, filmed theatre. Next time I'll think in terms of cutaways and editing and see if I can't come up with something a little more cinematic. But Ronnie liked it and gave me £75 in fivers. Good on you, guv. It ain't the old Messalino money but it supplements the few bob a week I make at Modern Snax.

Second 8mm:
HOT STUFF
125 feet (10 minutes), black and white, mute.
This was shot in my room on the afternoon of Sunday 19 November 1961. It featured a young guy named Brian Westgate who is a projectionist in a Soho cinema, Shirley the black girl, and a girl Veronica found named Janet Hutchins, a small dark-haired beauty with the finest set of big firm breasts I've ever seen. I shot it in less than an hour

and it came out pretty good. Brian was a good performer and could get it up at a flick of a wrist (providing the wrist was someone else's). He came twice in the hour, once in Shirley's mouth and once between Janet's tits. I eschewed a storyline in this. It is just a straight fuck-and-suck film.

I got some good three-way screwing shots and the girls had some fun with each other and with the brand new green nylon umbrella I had bought on Friday at Hector Powe's. I introduced some forced humour at the end. Janet turns to Brian and says by way of a title card:

'Does it burn after sex?'

... and he replies:

'I don't know. I've never tried lighting it.'

That's an old schoolboy joke. One we all heard years ago.

After the session we all went down to Au Père de Nico in Lincoln Street, just off the King's Road near Sloane Square. Very Chelsea-ish. We sat in the courtyard out the back and had some really good crêpes and wine. The whole bill only came to £4 12s. 6d., which wasn't bad at all. I spent a bit of time editing this film together. I had shot cutaway close-ups of the faces of each of the performers as they rolled their eyes, licked their lips and sighed. I could inter-cut these as reaction shots away from the main action. I had also realised after shooting the first film that one shot of a girl sucking a guy, or whatever of some sexual activity, is much the same as another and that it was not necessary to shoot it from another angle again. Just dupe your original shot, which is what I did. Dupe it or flip it. I shot 100 feet of film and ended up with 125 feet. The cuts and inter-cuts certainly gave it a more cinematic feel. After Ernie had done his neg cutting and produced a new print I took it along to Ronnie, who pronounced it a 'gem'.

I was walking down Charing Cross Road one evening on

the way to meet Stephen in a pub over in Covent Garden when I saw French Joe on the other side of the road leaning against a lamp-post and smoking a cigarette. I walked across. He was shaking and tears were running down his face.

'How you doing, Joe?'

'I'm doing all right … but poor Jimmy ain't.'

'Who?'

'They hanged him this morning … at the prison. He's dead. He was a really good mate … he was. Really good.'

'Who hanged him?'

'The fucking prison hanged him … the rozzers. Who do you fucking think hanged him? The taxman?'

I then connected what Joe was saying with the news I had heard on the radio earlier. James Hanratty had been hanged for murdering some bloke called Michael Gregsten who was married but having an affair. Hanratty had discovered them together in the car, surprised them, and then with a gun got them to drive for miles up to Bedfordshire somewhere and there he had shot Gregsten, raped the girl and then shot her, believing she was dead. She wasn't. She recovered and eventually identified him. Why was French Joe upset by this?

'Was Hanratty a friend of yours?'

'Yes he was. And you knew him too!'

'I did?'

'Yeah, I came into your place enough times with him. He was a good mate.'

I remembered when Joe said that. Hanratty was a slight guy, a young guy who often used to hang about with Joe. A harmless sort of guy, did a bit of thieving but that was about it. We had even given him some casual work in Modern Snax. Very polite. Gentle. Harmless. This was the guy who was supposed to be Public Enemy Number One? The Worst Murderer of Our Times? The thing hit me like a lead cosh. I staggered.

'Did he do it, Joe?'

'No, he didn't. He was set up. The rozzers know he was set up. There's this bloke up on the ********* *****. He's the ******* of the murdered ******* ****. He took a dim view of Gregsten carrying on with another woman so he decided to take the law into his own hands and have the frighteners put on Gregsten. He got this loony Peter Alphon to go in there with a gun and frighten him. You know, just frighten him. But Alphon is a real loony and he ends up shooting the guy and raping the girl. The shit hits the fan then but this geezer's got friends in the police so it all gets hushed up and they can't do Alphon because he'll lead them back to the geezer who set it up so they get poor Jimmy instead.'

'How the fuck do you know this?'

'I know it … Alphon told me, that's how I know.'

'Haven't you told anyone?'

'I've told the pigeons and I've told you … should I write a letter to her fucking Royal Highness, the Queen? Dear Ma'am, There's been a bit of wrong business going on in your kingdom? Do me a favour!'

'What about Desmond the journalist?'

'He couldn't hang Jimmy quick enough.'

'There are other journalists.'

'There's something else going on here. I heard that this geezer up on **** **** ***. *********** *** ****** ******* *** **** ******* *** **** **** ** ****** ** ***** *** ** *** *** ** ********* * *** *** **** * *** ** ** *** *** ** *** ** *** **** **** ****** *** * ********* *** *** *** ******* ** *** ******* ** ***** ***** *** *** *** *** '

1962 is getting even more bizarre than 1961 … .

Needless to say, I never ended up seeing Stephen that evening. I slouched up Charing Cross Road and caught the underground down to Queensway and I had a quick drink in every pub between there and home. I got in and fell asleep on the sofa.

I caught up with Stephen about a week later in his little coffee bar in Marylebone. He had been pestering me to get

a print of *Dolce Vita for Four* for him. I put it on the table and
told him that he owed me £15.

'That's an awful lot of money, old boy.'

'That's what it cost me. Times are changing.'

'I think you are forgetting I sent you cute little Tina.'

'I paid her the rate, £10. Why should I now fork out £15
for you? I can't get them free. I have to pay what the
punters pay if I want a print. These blokes run everything
as a business.'

'They do?'

'Yes, they do. If you can't afford £15 I'll flog it to
someone who can. All right?'

'Calm down, Timmy. I need that print.'

'And I need £15 or I'm off. Got it?'

'It'll have to be a cheque. You'll take a cheque?'

'If I have to … yes.'

'A post-dated cheque?'

What a mean fucker this guy is when it comes to money.
The cheque will probably bounce but what choice do I
have?

'Start writing,' I said.

Third 8mm:

ALADDIN'S LAMP, OR, RUB VERY HARD!

125 feet (10 minutes), black and white, mute.

This was shot one Friday evening in April 1962 in the room
in Porchester Road. I didn't really have my heart in it. It
was shot and cut professionally enough and Ronnie liked it
so I guess that is all that matters.

The actors were Frank from next door and a girl Stephen
had sent over called Trish who works in travel agent's
somewhere in the city, or so she said. Frank didn't mind
appearing because he could wear a disguise.

The story was pretty basic. Trish is reading the new
Sunday Times 'Colour Section' ('A Sharp Glance at the
Mood of Britain'). It was the first issue and had come out a
couple of weeks or so before. She gets bored reading this so

she starts sorting through the wardrobe. She's ready for bed in her baby-doll nightie. She finds an old brass lamp. She rubs it and a fairy princess appears (played by Veronica in a hat and curtains). The princess says she will grant Trish one wish. Trish's wish is for a big stud so, who should walk into the room, but Frank in a mask and loin-cloth! He gives her a jolly rogering and she is left exhausted. She falls asleep and when she wakes up in the morning she looks perplexedly into the camera: was it a dream or did it really happen?

Frank performed pretty well but had difficulty keeping it up after a while so we had to cheat some of it. He managed a good come shot over the girl's tummy. Trish seemed a bit of a raver and was eager to appear in another film. When I gave her a tenner she nearly had another orgasm. Frank told me afterwards that he is moving out next week. He's found somewhere cheaper to live. And smaller. A broom cupboard or something over a laun-dromat on the Harrow Road just to the north. My feeling is that he's doing this to avoid his creditors.

It was about 10.30 p.m. on a Tuesday and I had just walked up Queensway. It had been a real pig of day at Modern Snax that was crowned by a £5 discrepancy in the till. I just wanted to get into bed and get unconscious. As I turned into Porchester Road a car that was parked in front of the house flashed its lights. I took no notice and was walking by when I heard my name being called. It was Stephen. He was sitting in a white Jaguar. 'Jump in,' he said, indicating the back.

I climbed in and pulled the door shut. 'Are we going for a ride or what?'

He turned in the driving seat and just stared at me. His face was intermittently illuminated by the headlamps of passing cars. He seemed agitated. Nervous.

'Why don't you come upstairs? We can have a drink,' I said. 'You look like you could do with one.'

'I haven't got time tonight.' This was said in a clipped unemotive manner. Something was on his mind.

'What are you doing Friday night, Timmy?'

'Not much I shouldn't think. Why?'

'I need you to take some photographs.'

'Some photographs?'

'Yes, photographs.'

'Of what?'

'Of a woman I know. She wants to be photographed with a couple of black guys … big *black* guys. Not light-skinned chaps … really black ones. Her husband wants to see them too … the photographs, that is, not the … uh … *chaps*.'

'She does?'

'Yes. Can you supply them?'

'I'll get Sonny and a mate of his … it might cost her.'

'That is not a problem.'

'Right.'

'Bring a camera.'

'A movie camera or a stills camera?'

'A stills camera is just fine.'

'Where do we show up?'

'At my place at eight o'clock.'

'I don't know where your place is … do I?'

Stephen pulled out his wallet, took a card from it and gave it to me.

'Eight p.m., then?'

'I'll see you then, Stephen.'

'Off you go, Timmy. I'm late.'

I got out of the car and slammed the door. He accelerated forward at a fair old lick and disappeared in the traffic. I glanced up and saw our light was off. Veronica was out again.

In the hallway I looked at the card Stephen had given me. It was a stiff white card and measured about 3 inches by 2. Printed in a cursive, embossed script typeface was the following:

Dr. Stephen Ward
Osteopath

4, Wimpole Mews,
Harley Street,
London, W.1.   WELbeck 9378

A doctor, huh? But not a GP.

I turned up on Stephen's doorstep at the agreed time with
Anton and Nelson, two friends of Sonny's, as the lad
himself was playing trumpet at some benefit in Shepherd's
Bush. Anton and Nelson were big and mean looking and
thought it might be a bit of a laugh. They were each 6-foot
plus.

I rang the bell and heard a ringing somewhere upstairs.
A light went on and footsteps came down the stairs.
Stephen opened the door with a sports jacket over his arm.
He smiled at me and then looked at the two fellows.

'*My* … and what do we have here then? Clasp your eyes
on these two! What big boys they are!'

The two blacks shuffled about and didn't know how to
react. They'd never met anyone like Stephen before and
were unsure how to respond to him.

'Milady is certainly going to be in for a good time
tonight, isn't she? In the hands of these two brutes indeed!
How lucky!'

Stephen pulled the door shut and, jangling his car keys
about like Carmen Miranda, led us over to his white Jag.
Anton and Nelson ducked into the back and I sat in the
front with Stephen.

We got to Portland Place and drove south into Regent
Street and then along Piccadilly. It was dark and drizzly
and town seemed empty. Stephen was talking non-stop to

the spades about all the white women he knows who like black dick, about his experiences with black girls, going to West Indian clubs and smoking charge and so on. On the mention of reefers Anton said that he just happened to have some on him and would Stephen mind if he and Nelson smoked? Not at all, says Stephen, but forgive me if I don't – I'm driving.

The car was soon full of the sweet-sour smoke. I opened the window. The spades were now giggling like schoolgirls and talking in this Caribbean patois that whitey can't understand.   We drove round Hyde Park Corner and headed down Grosvenor Place towards Victoria. I was fidgeting with the camera on my lap and feeling edgy for no discernible reason.

'Who am I going to be photographing?'

'A dear friend of mine, Tim. A very dear friend.'

'Yeah, I know that, but who?'

'Anonymity is the best policy I've always found. I think she would prefer to keep her identity a secret.'

'What does her husband do?'

'He's well off ... has various interests ... the usual.'

'Why am I taking the photographs and not you? And not *him*?'

'Timmy, we can take snaps but you're a professional. You can take *photographs*.'

Stephen is a real snake when he's being evasive. He wasn't going to say anything more. We'll wait and see what happens.

The drizzle had turned into rain as we drove past Victoria station and into the warren of backstreets that lead down to the Thames and go under the name of Pimlico. Pimlico. A strange name for a strange area. Nobody knows where it begins and where it ends. I've got lost down here. The stuccoed Victorian streets all look the same. People keep to themselves here in a way they don't in other neigh-bourhoods. A lot of secrecy about, not like Bayswater where there's life on the streets. This is an area that people retreat to. Here they know they won't get disturbed or bothered. There aren't even many pubs down here and if you do find one you'll see that it is full of solitary individuals drinking in silence. This is a part of London I don't think I could ever get to know. Foreign territory. Pimlico. Nobody even knows the origin of the name.

Stephen parks the car behind a derelict Dormobile on Lupus Street and says we'll walk the last bit: 'Just around the corner.' The Dormobile is dented and rusty and has no rear wheels, it is jacked up on bricks. This is a drab and decaying neighbourhood. Lupus Street. Where does that name come from? I thought lupus was some sort of disfiguring disease.

These terrace houses are now divided up into bedsits and small flats. The windows are crammed with plants and junk and threadbare curtains in conflicting colours that let the light in and out and serve as silhouette screens when the occupants walk in front of the naked 60-watt bulbs. The open basements are full of rusting dustbins.

There's a chill smell of rain and rotting vegetables, not that Nelson and Anton would notice it as they pass another reefer back and forth. Stephen is leading us along like a schoolteacher who has had one gin and tonic too many – a nervous concern, a sort of forced hilarity and a lot of gesticulation. We must look an odd foursome.

'I hope those reefers aren't going to get in the way of you boys performing tonight!'

'I only gotta sniff some white cooch, governor, and I'm there,' says Nelson, and then he laughs and pats Stephen on the back.

'Yeah, that's right,' says Anton, coughing as he exhales the charge.

We turn a corner. A sign on the railings says St George's Square. Here are two rows of Victorian terraces facing each other across a narrow oblong of grass and trees. This isn't one of the great squares of London. Down there on the other side is Dolphin Square, that vast development of flats

put up in the 1930s, and beyond, the Thames. The same
Thames that flows on and laps against the Isle of Grain ... .

Stephen turns abruptly when we are halfway along the
square and walks down the stone steps of a basement. He
knocks on the door and turns and smiles at me. One of his 'I
know something you don't know' smiles. Stephen might be
able to keep secrets but what he cannot withhold is the fact
that he has a secret. He won't tell you what it is but he'll let
you know that he has it. Stephen would have been a good
actor, I've always thought. He has the vanity, the self-
centredness of a Shaftesbury Avenue chorus boy.

I look at the door. Peeling paint illuminated by the street
lamp above. The letterbox is missing, just a rectangular
hole in the door. A large brass knocker shaped like a boot.
On the right of the door someone has recently nailed a
square of hardboard as if to hide something. There are
marks to one side of it that seem to have been made by
someone forcing the door with a crowbar or something.

We are still waiting. Stephen knocks hard again. Twice in
rapid succession. The door opens and there is a guy in his
late twenties in an Italian-style suit and striped Cecil Gee
shirt sporting a Perry Como haircut. The guy doesn't say
anything. He stares at Stephen and then at me and then at
the spades. His face is expressionless. Stephen mumbles
something to him. I can't make out what it is. The guy's
eyes look up and back to me and then back to Stephen.
Everything seems to be in order. This bloke has seen too
many B-films. Petty hoods behave in real life in the way
petty hoods do in cheap films. They need to. They need a
reference for their manner. By themselves they wouldn't
know what to do. I stare at the guy's face. Motionless still.
It fascinates me. There's something borderline about him.
Borderline psychotic, that is. There's a slight movement in
his head which Stephen recognises as an indication that we
can go in. We follow Stephen, who seems to know where
he is going because he walks straight down a long bare
corridor, through a door and across an open yard and into

the back of another building that faces on to a parallel street. Another bare corridor.

I'm wondering where we are going. The two spades are just passing a joint back and forth.

'What's this all about, then?' whispers Anton, the *ganja* fresh on his breath.

'Ask Stephen,' I whisper. 'You know what I've told you and that's all I know.'

But Stephen is a man on a mission. He has a purpose. Ahead, he stops, opens a door and waves us in. This is a decrepit old bedroom that looks like it hasn't been cleaned since the Armistice. There's a smell of cheap musky perfume and mustiness and cigarette smoke. The curtains are faded with some Edwardian flower pattern on them. There's a massive old wardrobe with a door hanging off. A dressing table with a cracked mirror. The remains of a coal fire in the grate.

The focal point of the room is a double bed with monumental wooden head- and footboards that looks like something out of a cemetery.

On the bed is a woman in, I'd guess, her mid-thirties. She's dressed in an expensively tailored black suit with a white silk blouse. Her long blonde straight hair stretches out on the pillows. She has pearl earrings and a pearl necklace. On her fingers are several rings, diamond I would think, including a wedding one. Her skirt is halfway up her thighs and reveals part of her stocking tops. Stephen points at her and says, 'Let me introduce you, boys. This is Elizabeth.'

Nelson and Anton are smiling the biggest smiles of their lives. They've only ever seen class white pussy like this on the cinema screen. They can't believe their luck. This is what they've been dreaming about since they were kids.

'Elizabeth', for that cannot be her real name, continues to stare ahead. She doesn't say anything. She doesn't react. I then realise why. She's neither conscious nor unconscious. She's hovering between the two not knowing where she is.

She's been drugged. She tries to say something but the words die in her throat. As I approach the bed I can smell the perfume she is wearing, a more subtle fragrance than the one that pervades the room. She isn't here out of choice. It's one thing photographing, say, some randy deb who likes the West Indian brothers; it's another thing altogether photographing somebody who is coerced into it, who isn't aware of what's happening. I don't want any part of this. I turn to Stephen.

'What's all this about? She doesn't know what's happening to her.'

'Of course she does. She takes a few pills so she can relax. She likes to be used. She's a masochist.'

'And her husband?'

'He gets his kicks looking at pictures of her getting her kicks.'

Am I being told the truth? She could be some sort of masochist I suppose, but …. Good old *plausible* Stephen.

There's a young tart in slacks sitting in a worn red armchair on the other side of the bed. I hadn't noticed her. Mid-twenties. Beehive hairdo. Chewing gum. Slim. Hard lips. She goes to say something to Stephen who smiles at her and lays a forefinger over his lips. Her words freeze in her throat. She remains silent. I want to know who the woman on the bed is. I'm not going to let Stephen off the hook so easily.

'Before we go any further, Stephen, I want to know who this is. Do you understand that?'

Stephen looks at me and his lips part briefly in a forced smile. He says nothing. I repeat the question.

'I really don't think you should trouble yourself about that.'

'I'm not troubling myself. I just want to know, OK?'

'If I were just to say that she was a friend of a friend … could we leave it at that?'

That old disarming plausibility. There's a strained atmosphere here now, even the tart senses it. The spades

don't. They are still having difficulty believing their luck.
They are rarin' to go.

'My,' says Stephen, looking at his watch and feigning
agitated concern, 'look at the time. We really must get a
move on!'

Curious phrasing. The statement hangs in the air. Anton
and Nelson look at each other – they know what to do but
they need someone to say Ready, Steady, *Go!*

'We must undress her,' says Stephen to Nelson and
Anton. They don't need telling a second time. They're on
the bed and undoing buttons and belts with a delicate
dexterity you would scarcely think possible. 'But do leave
her stockings and suspender belt on.'

'Sure, governor,' says one of them.

I watch the spades as they sit the woman up and remove
her jacket and blouse. I watch Stephen watching them, his
lower lip quivering. This excites him. This is his sexuality.
The sexuality of a voyeur. He's really going to enjoy this
evening. I'm not. And if I were to hang around I'd wake up
in the morning hating myself. I don't want any part of this.
This is Stephen's sick scene. He can keep it.

'I'm off, Stephen. This isn't for me.'

Stephen stares at me and nods. He understands. He isn't
going to argue. Very well, then.

'Rosie, could you show Mr Purdom out?'

'Yes, Dr Ward,' says the tart as she languidly pushes
herself up from the chair.

'Well then, Tim, I'll just have to take some amateur snaps
with my own little camera … won't I?'

'Yeah, happy snapping.'

'Don't be long, Rosie. We'll need you to lend a hand.'

I followed Rosie out and down the corridor and across
the yard. Standing in the shadows was the guy in the Cecil
Gee shirt smoking a cigarette. He said nothing. He just
stared at us as we walked across. Who was he? Was he
Rosie's boyfriend? No, Rosie doesn't have boyfriends.
Rosie only has gentlemen friends.

'Was that your boyfriend?'
'Was who my boyfriend?'
'The bloke in the yard in the suit.'
'What bloke?'

It was raining again as I walked up St George's Square and into Lupus Street. I held my camera under my jacket and legged it down to Belgrave Road for a cab. I stood in a doorway of a shop and waited. There were no cabs or buses about. In fact there was hardly any traffic at all. The rain was falling harder now and there was distant thunder.

I thought back to the bedroom and what was going on there now. Who was the guy in the suit? What did he do when he wasn't keeping an eye on a photographic session like this? Who was the tart? Why was she there? How did Stephen know her? Who was the woman on the bed? Was the story Stephen told me true? It could have been ... knowing the sort of people he knows ... then, again, there was an equal possibility that it wasn't ... in which case ... in which case what? What could I do? What *should* I do? Go to the police and tell them that some woman is being photographed with a couple of West Indians against her will? Yes, sir, and how do you know this? I'd be digging my own grave.

And why had Stephen been so understanding, so very understanding, when I said I was going? Why so obliging? Why couldn't he take the photos in the first place? He was just too obliging ... but perhaps by then he could afford to be. I'd delivered the spades, hadn't I? I guess that was what it was all about. I don't know.

5

Dizzy Atmosphere

So why's everyone suddenly interested in me, huh?
– Al Capone, attributed (1930)

Fourth 8mm:
BLACK BUGGERY
150 feet (12 minutes), black and white, mute.
This was shot at the beginning of June 1962 in Sonny's basement and features him and a couple of girls from around the corner who I think are both on the game part-time. One of them certainly is. I shot it after seeing Jeanne Moreau in *Les Liaisons Dangereuses* at the Columbia earlier in the day, which I'd watched just to remind myself what cinema was really all about.

Ronnie had said he wanted a fuck film: 'Some black guy giving it up the arse to a couple of white mysteries ... would be very popular ... particularly with the German tourists. They're always asking for stuff like that.'

I wanted to call it *Zulu Frolics* but that was overruled. Ronnie said nobody would understand what it was all about with a title like that. Anyway, he came up with *Black Buggery*. He thought it a gem, and original.

One of the girls – her name was Treena Ellis – was doped up on pills and had needle marks all over her arms. Sonny paid her in pills and told me that he would have to give her ten quid for her daddy (whoever he was). I didn't argue. Treena was attractive but disintegrating fast.

Mary, the other girl, was from Northern Ireland and

worked as a receptionist in some no-luggage hotel in
Leinster Square. She said if I ever wanted to shoot in one of
the rooms there she could arrange it. I said I'd bear it in
mind. While I was setting up the camera she asked me if
she had time to do some knitting before we began? Sonny
had been passing a joint around and I just found her question so funny, I cracked up. I decided to incorporate this in
the action. *Black Buggery* must be the only blue film
showing a girl being buggered while she knits.

When I was talking to Sonny about Eichmann's hanging
a couple of days before, Mary said it was only because he
murdered Jews and that if he had killed anyone else they
wouldn't have bothered. She said that next to Catholics the
Jews are the most godless and evil race. They should be
wiped off the face of the earth. I guess this is the authentic
voice of the Ulster Protestant.

Veronica thought the film was shot without any thought
or feeling. And she was right. Ronnie thought it was my
best yet. He said he's even going to make some stills from
the frames. I asked him if this means I would get a few quid
more.

'No, but I owe you a drink.'

How about increasing my rate anyway?

'Not the money about right now, son.'

Fifth 8mm:
SCHOOLGIRL FROLICS
125 feet (10 minutes), black and white, mute.
This was shot in Frank's new room over on Harrow Road
on a Saturday night in the middle of August.

I got there early and found Frank cutting out pictures of
Marilyn Monroe and sticking them on the wall. He was
always a big fan of Marilyn's and still couldn't believe she
had just committed suicide. Frank always liked them big,
busty and glamorous.

He was pretty sloshed and had been drinking most of
the day. He said he had to rush off and meet someone down

in Paddington and could I pay him for the use of the room now? Sure. I gave him the fiver and he buzzed off, but not before saying to me, 'I don't want your slags messing up the bathroom or the bed and I don't want come stains all over the mirror.' I told him this was an all-girl film and I think he wished he could have stayed.

About twenty minutes later the bell went and it was a girl Stephen had sent along, Maureen. She was tall, about 5ft. 6in., and slim without any noticeable tits. She was about nineteen or twenty years of age. Her black hair was long and straight, almost down to her waist. She was wearing a white dress with white stiletto shoes and carrying a white handbag. I was smoking some charge which she didn't want so I made her a gin and tonic (not Frank's, I had brought a bottle along myself).

I asked her what she did.

'I'm a secretary but I want to be a model. Stephen said he is going to help me. He knows all the people in modelling. He can get me on a modelling course.'

She had emptied the glass in about two gulps and she held it out to me for another one. I filled her up and asked her how long she had known Stephen, knowing what the answer would be. 'Just a couple of weeks. I met him at a friend's. Then I met him again at a party.'

'How come you're here?'

'Here? This was the address he gave me.'

'I don't mean *here* … I mean doing this. I mean why are you going to do … appear … in this?'

'Something to do … a bit of a laugh.'

'Really?'

'Yes. That's all.'

'Have you ever been in any other blue films?'

'No.'

'Have you ever been in any photographs?'

'Photographs?'

'Yes, blue photographs?'

Maureen was silent. She stared at her drink like it wasn't

there and then she quickly raised the glass and took a long, slow mouthful. Her eloquent silence hung heavily in the room.

'Were these with Stephen?'

After a pause: 'Stephen was there.'

Stephen was there. Not with Stephen, but Stephen was *there*. What was Stephen doing, a spot of dusting in the background? Making the cheese sandwiches in the kitchen while the boys and girls enjoyed themselves? I wanted to ask her and yet I didn't want to know. I changed tack.

'What did Stephen say to you about tonight?'

'Nothing much really.'

'He must have said something.'

'Just would I like to appear in a film.'

'And you said yes?'

'I did.'

'So Stephen just sidles up to you at a party, asks you how you are, and then says would you like to appear in a film? You instinctively know what sort of film and, Bob's your uncle, you're here?'

'Yes.'

'OK. Now what did he say?'

'He asked me if I'd like to appear in a film.'

'How did he describe the film?'

'He said it was with some other girls ... that's all.'

'Stephen thought it would be a good idea for you to appear in it?'

'Yes. He thought it might be good ... good experience.'

There was something Maureen wasn't telling me and wouldn't tell me. This cyclical cross-examination was spiralling away from what I wanted to know. But I didn't know what I wanted to know. And was Maureen aware of it anyway? Did she know something that she knew I shouldn't know?

'Stand up, Maureen.'

'Why?'

'Please, just stand up.'

Maureen put her glass down on the carpet and stood up in front of me. She placed her hands just below her breasts and brushed the folds out of her dress. She stood motionless, her lower lip pouting slightly. I stared into her eyes and then looked her up and down.

'Turn round.'

Maureen did as she was told.

I stood up. I parted her hair and kissed her on the nape of the neck. She neither moved nor said anything. I then began unbuttoning the back of her dress.

'What are you doing?'

'Undoing your dress.'

'If you want to make love we better be quick ... before the others arrive.'

And exactly then the bell went. The others had arrived. Damn and fuck! Maureen turned and held my face in her hands and kissed me lightly on the lips.

'I'm sorry,' she said.

'Me too ... and I want you to go now.'

'Why? You haven't done the film yet.'

'I know. I don't want you in the film and I don't want you to see Stephen again ... ever.'

'He'll be very angry with me.'

'Fuck him. So what? He can't do anything to you, can he?'

The bell rang again several times.

'Don't see him. He'll never help you. It's all talk with him. Nothing more. He'll just get you involved in all sorts of crazy scenes.'

Maureen followed me down the stairs and disappeared into the Saturday night crowds as Valerie and Christine, two contacts of Veronica's from the salon, tumbled in.

'Not disturbing anything, are we?'

'We're only doing this if we can wear masks.'

I'm quite sure that Maureen ignored my advice. I'll never know, but I'd bet a pound to a pinch of shit it went in one ear and out the other.

As for the masks, Ronnie thought they added a bit of mystery to the movie. 'A bit of tantalising intrigue, son.'

When I got back to the room that evening Veronica was propped up in bed reading some glossy magazine.

'How did it go?'

'Not bad.'

'Uh-huh. I want a cuddle.'

'I'll give you a cuddle and that's all. You know I never feel like it after a session. It puts me off a bit. It really does.'

'Oh, yeah. Stephen phoned. Important. Can you call him.'

'What, *now*?'

'Whenever you got in,' he said.

I sorted out some pennies and walked down the stairs to the hall. I put the pennies in the box, dialled his number and waited. I only had to wait about ten seconds until it was answered. I pushed the button.

'Stephen?'

'A real raver, isn't she?'

'Who are you talking about?'

'Maureen. The girl I sent round. A real raver.'

'Maureen, yeah.'

'Well, isn't she?'

'She wasn't suitable.'

'What do you mean she wasn't suitable? All the girls I send you are suitable.'

'This one wasn't.'

'What on earth do you mean by that?'

'Just what I say. She wasn't suitable.'

'You didn't use her?'

'Right. I didn't use her. She wasn't suitable.'

'I went to great trouble ...'

'Don't tell me you went to great trouble. That ain't my problem. I have who I want in my films. Got that?'

'It was important that ... .'

Stephen never finished the sentence. What was important? What did he start to say that he didn't complete? I was now too tired to worry. Another day perhaps, but not now.

'Don't you ever do this again to me, Timmy.'

'Get lost!'

'I wanted her in that film!'

'You'll have to be satisfied with the photos you've already got ... OK?'

Stephen went silent. I kicked myself for letting him know that I knew about them. I kicked myself again for betraying Maureen's confidence. I shouldn't have said it. Damn. Stephen was still silent. I was too angry with myself to say anything.

'Did Maureen say anything ... else?'

'Nothing else.'

'Perhaps we had both better get some sleep.'

'Yes.'

I hung up and punched the coinbox. Can't I keep a secret? OK then, so I let that slip. What's the worst that's going to happen to Maureen? Stephen doesn't invite her around any more? Isn't that what I wanted anyway?

Sixth 8mm:
THE RANDY FRENCH MAID
150 feet (12 minutes), black and white, mute.
October 1962. Three days into the countdown for the start of World War III wasn't the best time to shoot a blue film. In fact, it wasn't the best time to do anything, I thought. My actor and actresses in this little epic didn't read newspapers, watch TV or listen to the radio and were deliriously ignorant about what was going on in Castro's principality. President Kennedy had said there were Russian nuclear missile sites in Cuba and that he was imposing an arms blockade on the country. Russian ships were sailing out there and God knows what would happen when they came upon the patrolling US vessels. This time next week we could be atomised, a billion zillion fragmented bits of

matter in deep space. Nothing at all surviving. Not even a memory. Armageddon in spades. The Twilight of the Gods.

I sometimes felt I was the only person out on the street who took this Cuba crisis seriously. People's perceptions of nuclear weapons are so uninformed. Veronica said that if push came to shove and a couple of nuclear bombs went off it would only mean a few large craters here and there. Nothing to worry about. Pamela, the girl in the film, the randy French maid herself, said fallout wasn't at all dangerous, the wind just blew it away in any case (!). I sometimes feel I am surrounded by idiots, and wilful idiots at that.

The Randy French Maid was shot in the Hotel Exquisite on the north side of Leinster Square just down the road from me in Bayswater. This is the hotel Mary, the Ulster Protestant, works in and she had fixed me up with one of their bigger rooms for the evening. I gave her a fiver for the favour in addition to the tenner she got for performing.

Trevor, a minicab bloke I know from Notting Hill, plays a businessman. He checks into a hotel at night and tries to get some sleep. He can't, he's too restless. Then the French maid walks in to do the room. She's played by a buxom girl Stephen sent round named Pamela Page, another erstwhile model who currently works for a dress manufacturer down in Margaret Street. She turned up with her own French maid costume in a carrier bag.

The maid is all tits and thighs and soon she and Trevor are at it and then Mary walks in, surprises them, and joins in for a Chelsea sandwich. The story is shit and I didn't even attempt to explain Mary's presence.

Ronnie thought the film was pretty good and paid me on the spot. He said he had never seen a girl suck with the enthusiasm that Mary showed. Where could he contact her? I told him to phone the Hotel Exquisite.

There was an eeriness about in London as the Cuba crisis progressed. I think the facts had finally got through even to the idiots. If this was going to be the end it was going to be the End for all time. And even if there were any survivors they would soon be, in that grim phrase of Herman Kahn's, envying the dead.

Veronica and I went down to the Chelsea Potter pub on the Saturday evening to escape the gloom. At least the clientele there never pays any attention to what is going on in the outside world and that night we were glad of it. We met a couple of guys I knew from Modern Snax who work in an advertising agency in Dean Street and ended up going with them to a party in Sydney Street held by some rich antique dealer and his wife. There was plenty to drink and eat and some black cat was rolling joints and handing them out pell-mell (all courtesy of the host and hostess). I took a few hits and wandered out to the front steps to get some fresh air. Some fresh, chill air. It was a damp night and there had been showers earlier, but it was clear and every star was bright and in sharp focus. The street was empty and silent. The only noise came from the house behind me. I was steadying myself against the railings, flying really high, giggling to myself, when I heard footsteps. Hollow echoey footsteps on the pavement, but I couldn't tell from which direction they came. I staggered forward down the couple of steps, still clinging to the railings. Two figures were walking towards me. A man and a woman. They were walking hurriedly as though they were late for something. The man was wearing a long heavy coat. The woman was wearing a cloak. It looked like a cloak, but perhaps it was just a coat with a hood which she had over her head.

As they walked by me it was like a slow-motion sequence from a film. The woman was nearest to me. As she passed she turned and looked at me. It was Maureen, the girl Stephen had sent. The man was pulling her along. She silently mouthed something to me. It could have been 'No, not now.' I fancied it was, but it could have been anything. Her head turned further as she continued down along the street. The man stopped and said something to her. They both looked back at me, and then turned and increased their pace towards King's Road, disappearing into the shadows.

I felt there was something sinister about the bloke but why I felt this I don't know. Just an intuitive feeling. He reminded me of ******* ******. It could have well been him. In fact the more I think about it the more I'm sure it was him. He'd been on television that week going on about public spending, declining standards of morality, and so on – the usual Tory diagnostic litany of what's wrong with this country.

But what was a Conservative MP doing with a girl like this? A girl with a present that's fast becoming a past? It is said that he ****** ***** ****** *** ** *** *** ******. Who knows?

And whither little Maureen?

What, indeed, would become of us all? And will we be here next week anyway? I looked back at the house and heard the laughter and the music … I guess all that one can do when Rome burns is fiddle. Enjoy yourself while you can.

I woke up about midday on Sunday, lit a cigarette or two, made some percolated coffee, woke Veronica up, and then went across the road to get the papers – which I wish I hadn't. The Sundays were full of nothing but Cuba in the news sections. I threw them over to Veronica and started flicking through the *Sunday Times* 'Colour Section'.

Then I put a Monk record on. The Riverside *Monk's Music* which is a Thelonious septet featuring Coleman Hawkins and John Coltrane on tenors. I put side one on which opens with a version of that nineteenth century hymn, *Abide with Me*, scored by Monk for the horns only. I've always felt really moved by it and this time I feel tears gathering in my eyes as I listen to it. I also start thinking of Grain, of my mother, of her time at the hospital. She always liked this tune ... but I don't suppose she ever heard this version. Grain. Rochester. My mother. Gone now. I will never ever see her again ... and when did I last even visit her grave? Oh, God almighty. I start quietly sobbing into my handkerchief and later, but not much later, I slip off to sleep.

When my eyes open the record has ended but is still turning on the deck, the arm at the centre. Veronica is sitting up in bed reading the papers. I make some more coffee, roll a joint and get back into bed with her. We smoke the reefer together and begin to slowly doze off. Veronica turns the radio up. It's the one o'clock news. I brace myself to hear that nuclear missiles have been launched and this is going to be the last ten minutes of my life. Is ten minutes long enough for me in this state to get an erection and make love to Veronica? Perhaps our orgasms could coincide with a 20-megaton bomb going off over London? Sweet thought. I snuggle up to Veronica and listen ... but the news is totally unexpected. The Soviet freighters have turned back from Cuba! Khrushchev has backed down. The missile bases on the island are going to be dismantled! I really could not believe it. I was convinced this was the end. I give Veronica a big hug and we both start laughing with a near-hysterical relief. The end of the world has been postponed. We made love and then I dozed off again.

I'm awoken by a bell. Our bell. There's someone at the door. Veronica won't go down so I get up and descend the steps as nobody else in the house seems to be bothering with it either. Who's at the front door? Stephen, no less. He's beaming one of those manic grins of his.

'You've heard the news, Timmy?'

'Right. Fantastic.'

'I would have let you know about it sooner, old boy, but it was all a bit hush-hush. You know what these things are like.'

'Sooner? I heard it on the news about an hour ago.'

'I knew about it last night. Couldn't tell though.'

'It was only just announced.'

'Yes, but some of us are privy to higher levels of intelligence.'

'Jack Kennedy phoned you?'

'No, but I knew him when he was a young senator.'

'You are full of shit … you really are.'

'Aren't you going to invite me in?'

'Come in.'

Stephen follows me up the stairs.

'These are very exciting times, Timmy. Aren't they?'

Very exciting, Stephen. But I don't answer him.

I give him a cup of coffee and get back into bed with Veronica. Stephen wanders about the room like he's inspecting it on behalf of someone who is going to rent it.

'Looking for something, Stephen?'

'I was, actually.'

'What?'

'The *French Maid* film.'

'It is in the can over by the sink there … and that'll be £15. £15 *now*.'

'I've only got a fiver on me.'

'Leave that and a cheque.'

'It'll have to be postdated.'

'It always is.'

'What did you think of my girl, Pamela?'

'Not bad.'

'No, she isn't bad at all. She'll go far with the right direction. I've told her to start under a wealthy man … and work her way up.'

'Sage advice there, Stephen.'

'It always is … from me.'

'Isn't it just?'

'When will you be making your next little film?'

'Why?'

'Why? Well, I have a doctor friend who has the most marvellous mirrored bathroom in Harley Street. Very luxurious. You could use it as a location. You wouldn't have to

pay him anything … just let him hang about.'
    'And watch?'
    'And watch.'

Seventh 8mm:
SEX AND SUDS
150 feet (12 minutes), black and white, mute.
Which is how the idea for this film came about … It was
shot on a bitterly cold Saturday at the back end of
November.

Ward's friend turned out to be a doddering old libertine
called Dr Quantick. He must have been in his late seventies.
He shook a lot and I thought perhaps he had Parkinson's
disease, but I guess he was just excited. He didn't leave the
bathroom once. He just stood there the whole time, but
fortunately it was a big bathroom, as big as my room
almost.

I used three actors. A layabout from Greek Street called
Leon White who is an electrician in the West End theatres.
One of Stephen's dopey girls, Susan O'Reilly (though I
doubt that was her real name), and a divorcee acquaintance
of Veronica's from Fulham called Eileen McElroy. Both
Susan and Eileen were buxomish with big tits so the film
opened with them in the bath together soaping each other's
boobs. Then they start playing around with the loofah and
a bar of soap. Susan straddles the bidet and I did a shot of
her pissing into it. While she is sitting there Eileen uses a
dildo on her. The bathroom door opens and there's Leon in
his electrician's overalls. He strips down and the three of
them get in the bath together. There are the usual threesome scenes and the final shot is Leon coming into Susan's
mouth as Eileen masturbates him.

If Eileen hadn't been a friend of Veronica's I think I
would have told Susan that I wanted a further shot of
someone fucking her and done it myself. I quite fancied her
for some reason. Strange because shooting these dirty films
puts me off it more than anything. After the session I asked

Susan if we could perhaps meet for a drink? She didn't
want to know.

I thanked Dr Quantick as we were leaving. He said I
could use his bathroom any time I liked 'as long as you
bring some young ladies'.

Stephen had asked me to phone him right after the
session and I called him from Oxford Circus underground.

'Did it all go OK, Tim?'

'Yes. Why, shouldn't it have?'

'Quantick wasn't a nuisance?'

'No. Not at all.'

'Good. I must have a copy of this film as soon as
possible.'

'Why the hurry?'

'I want to see my little beauty, Susan ... that's all.'

'As soon as I've edited it together and it's printed you
can have one, OK? About a fortnight. I've got a lot on right
now.'

'You will phone me?'

'Yes.'

I then rushed back home to see the very first edition of
this new satirical show on BBC, *That Was the Week That Was*.
Some of the *Private Eye* people were involved in it and it
promised to be good.

I saw Stephen about two weeks later when he called by
Modern Snax for a copy of *Sex and Suds*. He didn't stop a
minute. Just gave me £20 (the films had gone up in price)
and zoomed off. I wouldn't see or speak to him again for
some four months. Something was about to explode in his
face and he would never be the same again. In fact, it ended
him.

It was late on a Friday when I got back home. I'd shut
Modern Snax early but I'd gone for a drink in the French
with Charlie and this had led to a bit of a pub crawl
through Soho: after all, Christmas was only a couple of
weeks away and the festive spirit always arrives early in

Soho. I was sober, but a little the worse for wear.

Veronica was writing a letter when I got in (probably to her sister who had emigrated to Australia). She didn't look up but said, 'Your friend has been on the radio.'

What friend on the radio? Perhaps Sonny has been giving a talk about West Indian culture on the Third Programme? Or has French Joe been reminiscing about all the writers and painters he's known in Soho?

'Which friend?'

'Stephen.'

'What was he talking about?'

'He wasn't *talking*. He *was* the news.'

'Doing what?'

'Doing nothing. They just mentioned him. There were two models staying in his house and this black man turned up and started firing shots at them ... with a gun. That's all.'

With a gun? That's all!? Christ almighty!

'Was anyone shot, hurt?'

'I don't think so. I don't know.'

Who were the two models? Were they girls I had photographed or what? I ran down the stairs two at a time and phoned Stephen. I could not get through to him. The phone had been left off the hook ...

The shots in Wimpole Mews that Friday night would, over the coming months, ring around the world like those at Sarajevo had nearly fifty years earlier. These shots heralded the unfolding of what became known as the Profumo Affair, the name coming from Jack Profumo, Harold Macmillan's 'Minister of War', who had been shagging one of the models who had been fired at, a Christine Keeler (how apt that Profumo means perfume in Italian). I didn't know her, thank God, and I didn't know her mate either, some blonde with the preposterous name of Mandy Rice-Davies, soon to be known throughout Albion as Randy Mice-Davies. News of the ministerial shagging came out after Profumo had denied it and then he had to resign (I think that was the sequence anyway). Each week the papers were full of new stuff about Stephen and his friends. Keeler sold her memoirs to the *News of the World* and there were rumours about all sorts of goings on. A Russian diplomat called Ivanov was mentioned as being a friend of Stephen's and then it turned out he was reputedly having it off with Keeler while she was also doing it with Profumo. The affair now became a matter of national security.

The newspapers teased the story out daily from Ward's tangled past. Whenever you picked up a newspaper there were pictures of some new girl who had once drifted into Ward's orbit, some new story of sex and drugs, some new tale about Lord this or that. Russian spies were all over the place. Macmillan put a brave face on it all but his government was crumbling.

For the first few weeks I was convinced that my little arrangement with Stephen was going to come tumbling out. Somebody was going to say something and then hordes of journalists would be turning up at Porchester Road or at Modern Snax. But they didn't. Neither did I recognise any of the 'Ward girls' who were being paraded almost daily in the papers.

Stephen wouldn't say anything about our cosy arrangement because, of course, that would only get him further in the shit. Veronica wasn't going to go around incriminating herself either, for the same reason, so who did that leave? It left Sonny and Charlie. Charlie knew I knew a geezer called Stephen who occasionally pushed girls in my direction, but he had no reason to link my Stephen with Dr Ward. So that left Sonny ... and Nelson and Anton. Sonny knows exactly who Stephen is, but can he be trusted? He's a bit unpredictable but I can't see him calling attention to himself with all the skulduggery he's got going on. The last thing he wants is the Old Bill snooping about, which is precisely what would happen if his name appeared in the papers. Nelson and Anton? They'd be a real danger if some journalist with a chequebook started waving money under their noses, but how would a journalist know about them? They'd have to be found. They're too out of it and too wrapped up in big fat mamas and *ganja* to flog themselves down Fleet Street.

Who else is there? The girls of course. The girls Stephen sent along. They are the real wild cards in the pack ... but again, would they incriminate themselves? Would they have to? Couldn't they just blow the whistle on me ... and Stephen?

This worried me all over Christmas and down through January of 1963. The coldest winter for years and I've got the worry of this! Any moment now I was going to be tumbled. Any moment now there was going to be a knock on the door and I was going to be Public Pornographer Number One with my face plastered all over the papers. I lay low. Just went to work each day. Didn't contact Stephen or Ronnie or anyone. I'd battened the hatches down. I was waiting for things to blow over...or up.

Then I woke up one morning in the middle of February (the 14th actually, the day Harold Wilson became the new Labour leader) and realised that I was now worrying unnecessarily. If I was going to be exposed it would have happened by now. The papers were just interested in Ward and Keeler and Rice-Davies and the satellites that orbited about them, Profumo, Lord Astor, Douglas Fairbanks, and Keeler's two West Indian lovers, Lucky Gordon and Johnny Edgecombe. This was where the action was. The rest was peripheral. Thank fucking Christ neither Christine nor Mandy had ever turned up at a session! I'd be on the public grill by now.

Eighth 8mm:
BEATNIK SLUTS
125 feet (10 minutes), black and white, mute.
This featured two girls I'd got talking to in Modern Snax, June and Paula. Both fresh down from Leeds and very cute.

It was shot in a flat in Sandringham Mansions on Charing Cross Road opposite Dobell's jazz shop (where earlier that Saturday I had picked up George Russell's *Ezz-Thetics*, a Riverside LP, with the most amazing version of Monk's *Round Midnight*, featuring Eric Dolphy on bass clarinet and alto).

The flat belonged to a geezer, Eric Klein, who frequently came into Snax and had something to do with horse betting. I'd lent him a tenner when he was down on his luck and he'd never got around to paying me back. I cornered him earlier in the week and told him that I wanted to use his flat for the afternoon. I wanted to take a girlfriend there. We had nowhere else to go. He agreed. I told him I wanted the place spotless and I didn't want him turning up. He kept his side of the bargain.

The girls eventually arrived and changed into what passes as beatnik gear: black tight-fitting pants, floppy sweaters, hair tied back, sandals, dark lipstick. I suppose they'd pass as beatniks to the punters who go to watch this rubbish.

Johnny and Nello, two Soho no-hopers, arrived about an hour late. So I had an hour of listening to the Beatles! The girls were gaga about them and had just bought *Please, Please Me*. I'm not sure I wouldn't have preferred listening to Adam Faith and Craig Douglas – at least there is no mistaking their lack of talent and originality.

Johnny and Nello had both been drinking. Nello came the moment Paula touched his cock and shot it all over June's neatly folded Gor Ray skirt that was over a chair. As he couldn't get it up again he had to mime the rest of the time.

The film was badly shot, badly thought out and badly acted. I gave the guys a fiver each for old times' sake and they buggered off. I paid June and Paula a tenner each. I gave each of them two of those crisp new fivers that have Britannia on them without a helmet on. They'd only just been issued. The girls had never seen them before.

Paula walked up to me as I was loading the Eumig in its case and just put her hand on my crotch.

'Don't you fancy some?,' she said, very matter-of-factly.

'I guess I do,' I replied.

While still rubbing my trousers she turned to June and said, 'Hang on a jiff. I'm going to do it with Tim before we go.'

'Go ahead,' was the reply. 'I'll watch if you don't mind.'

So, while June hand-jived in the armchair to the Beatles, we did it on the couch. And I enjoyed it.

'That didn't take you long, Tim,' said June, 'you need to discipline yourself.'

'Paula isn't complaining,' I said, rather foolishly.

'She wouldn't. She's a lady,' replied June with a laugh.

I asked for that.

'Not very good at all, my son,' said Ronnie in his third-floor Soho office. 'If I were to buy this I wouldn't be doing right by Mr Narrizano. He'd think I was on the take from you … and we wouldn't want him to think that, would we? We don't want to do anything that would upset the goose that lays the golden egg, right?'

'Right. So you're not buying it?'

'It is a piss-poor piece of work … and no mistake.'

'You're right. What do I do with it?'

'Take it home and keep it and when you're an old man without any friends in the world you can get it out and . remind yourself of all the good times you've had.'

I guess it had to happen in the end. A refusal. I was forty-odd quid out of pocket.

I cheered myself up by buying the Thelonious Monk with John Coltrane LP at Dobell's. It set me back 39s. 8d. Veronica was out when I got home that night so I got smashed on gin while listening to Monk and Trane.

Ninth (and last) 8mm:
THE BOYFRIEND'S SURPRISE VISIT
125 feet (10 minutes), black and white, mute.
This was shot a couple of weeks after *Beatnik Sluts* on Friday, 8 March, in Porchester Road. Brenda Butler and Elaine

Cutter were two contacts through Veronica. Brenda worked in a hairdresser's in the Edgware Road and Elaine in a shoe shop at Marble Arch. They were both better looking than their names implied. Charlie was supposed to turn up for this session but when I got home there was a message pinned to the telephone saying he couldn't make it. I'd laid the money out on the Eumig and the stock and the girls were expecting to be paid. Sod it, I thought, I'll do this one myself and I did. Fittingly, perhaps, it was the last film that I made.

The film opens with the two girls chatting and listening to records. They get fruity over Cliff Richard and start amusing themselves. When they've stripped down and got on the bed I walk in and surprise them and then join in the fun. It wasn't too difficult using the camera on the tripod but it wasn't easy giving the girls directions while I was on camera. Still, the film didn't turn out too bad.

Brenda was wearing a Maidenform bra. This gave me the idea for a better title than *The Boyfriend's Surprise Visit*. How about *I Dreamt I was Buggered in my Maidenform Bra*? A good title but for two things: (1) Ronnie doesn't have a sense of humour, and (2) there was no buggery in the film. But a good title nonetheless.

'Very nice, my son! I never knew you had it in you. Very nice indeed. I thought you snap artists just liked watching and not doing anything.'

'Is it good enough then, Ronnie?'

'Is it good enough?'

That was my question.

'Well, Tim, old son, it is like this: things have moved on a bit lately.'

'What's moved on?'

'The old blue film lark.'

'Moved on? What's moved on?'

'There are some lads in town now who can shoot a film in colour.'

In colour? I couldn't believe it.

'Where do they get it processed, then?'

'I don't ask them a question like that, Tim. That's their professional secret. They might do it abroad for all I know. The black-and-white market is shrinking a bit. The other thing is that over in Sweden and in Germany they're making good films. I can buy them by the hundred over there, ship them back, put a hefty mark-up on them. The price comes out dandy. They're all colour. Some of them even have sound. No hassles this way. Know what I mean?'

'What about Customs?'

'What about them? You cost it that one shipment in five is going to be seized. Simple.'

'So you don't want the film then?'

'I'd love to have it, Tim. But I've got all this other stuff. Take a tenner, son.'

'Have the film anyway ... I've got no use for it.'

'I'll take it. I'll give you a call if we ever order up any prints.'

'I'll see you, Ronnie.'

'Yeah, see you around.'

And as all good things come to an end, my career as a director of blue films was over there and then. I was ill-inclined to pursue it further.

The Profumo Affair creaked on and the eponymous 'Minister of War' resigned from Macmillan's government after he admitted lying to the House of Commons about his relationship with this 'model', Christine Keeler (a photographic model? It seems so, according to informed gossip down in Fleet Street). He had originally said there had been no impropriety. Then when it was proven that there had been, away he went. The government was getting shakier by the day. The Labour Party had a field day and latched on to the scandal like a dog to a bone.

I frequently thought about Stephen but I didn't try and contact him. I figured he preferred it that way. He knew where I was if he needed anything. And then, in the middle of April, late on a Sunday night the bell went and who was it on the doorstep?

'How are you, Tim? *So* good to see you,' declared Stephen.

'I'm fine. What about you?'

'I'm fine. Can I come in?'

'Of course.'

'But let me ask you something first.'

'Yeah, what?'

'The police haven't been round to see you, have they?'

'No. What about? They haven't been here.'

'About me? About anything?'

'No police have been here at all.'

'That's the truth?'

'That's the honest truth, Stephen.'

'OK, then.'

I ushered Stephen in and followed him up the stairs. He was carrying a medium-sized suitcase. He didn't say anything and neither did I.

We got into the room and I made him a gin and tonic while he chatted to Veronica.

'I want you to do me a favour, Tim.'

'What?'

'I'm about to be arrested.'

'Arrested!? What for? What are they arresting you for?'

'All sorts of nonsense … but they are going to do it.'

'The police?'

'Who else?'

'Christ.'

'I want you to look after this suitcase for me until the whole business blows over.'

'Sure, yeah. What's in it?'

'Personal things. I need to leave it somewhere safe.'

'Leave it here.'

'Good. Now over the next few weeks, months, you might read some strange things about me in the papers.

Don't believe all you read. Just trust me. There've been reasons for different things. When it's all over I'll ... put you in the picture. But now, just trust me.'

'I will, yeah.'

'I'll see you both ... eventually.'

He finished his drink, smiled at us both and was gone.

I looked down at the suitcase in the middle of the room. It was heavy ... and locked.

Veronica asked me what I was going to do with it.

'We can't keep it in here ... just in case. I'll put it in the landlord's store room for now ... and then drop it round at Frank's.'

'Why don't we open it and see what's inside?'

'Why don't we respect Stephen?'

'I want to know what's in it.'

'I don't. Anyway, it's locked.'

I stashed the case away under a mattress in the loft and then Veronica and I went across to the Royal Oak and got pretty smashed.

Stephen was arrested on 8 June and the papers were full of it. He was charged with procuring, living on the proceeds of prostitution and, I think, arranging an abortion. That was the Saturday.

On the Monday following I closed Modern Snax at about 7.30 p.m. Sonny appeared and asked me if I wanted to go round to Ronnie Scott's with him for a while. I asked him who was playing and he said Tubby Hayes, so I went. Sonny had plenty of money on him and he wouldn't let me get a round in. He said he had done a rather spectacular bit of dealing that day. I didn't ask for further and better particulars. I left Sonny about ten o'clock at the club and got back to Porchester Road half an hour later. Veronica usually went to see her mum and dad on Monday nights so I didn't expect to find her in. I could see the light wasn't on as I turned into Porchester Road.

I let myself in the front door and jumped the stairs two

at a time to our floor: the light on the stairs only stayed on for about twenty seconds once you pressed it and I always liked beating it up to our landing.

I got out the Yale key and as I pushed it into the lock the door just swung open. And as it swung open the landing light popped off. I was in darkness. I called out Veronica's name, quietly, tentatively. There was no reply. She wasn't there. There was a menacing silence engulfing the room. A heavy silence. Something wasn't right and I didn't know what it was. The curtains had been pulled some time during the day. Had Veronica been back or what? I was staring into the darkness hoping to see something. I stood there frozen.

Then I put the light on.

The whole room had been turned inside out. Every drawer had been emptied. Every box emptied. All the furniture had been moved. Nothing had been left alone. Someone had gone through the room item by item looking for something ... but what? I stumbled through the mess. Over by the sink I found the Old Holborn tobacco tin I kept some £50 in. All in fivers. They'd found that and opened it. But they hadn't taken the money. The fivers were all over the floor. Whoever did this wasn't a thief. They were looking for something.

I raced upstairs and fiddled the padlock off the land-lord's attic store-room. I crawled past the tea chests and furniture and through the cobwebs to the far eaves: Stephen's suitcase was still there under the old stained mattress.

I lay on my back on the rafters breathing heavily. Who knew I had Stephen's case? That must have been what they were after – they weren't regular burglars. Nobody knew ... but then how come they came looking for it here? Someone must have known. I haven't told anyone. Veronica wouldn't have told anyone. And Stephen would hardly jeopardise himself by rabbiting on to somebody ... but whoever it was, they knew. They really knew. Should I tell Stephen about this?

If I did, what could he do? It would just be one further
thing for him to worry about. I suppose he knew someone
would be after the case, would want what's in it. That's
why he gave it to me ... and what is in it? Should I break it
open and see?

I stumbled back to the room, poured myself a gin and
tonic, straightened the television set and sat down in front
of it. I was in a state of shock and I just sat there watching
A.J.P. Taylor giving a lecture about Lord Palmerston until
Veronica arrived and screamed: 'What the fucking hell has
been going on!!??'

I wish I knew. I really do.

'There's a black car over there with two men in it,' said
Veronica.

She was standing at the window looking down on
Porchester Road. I was going through the papers. Since
Stephen's arrest I've been buying every daily newspaper
and reading everything I can about the case. Acres of it.
Acres and acres of coverage but not an awful lot of infor-
mation. The same stuff printed in each paper five different
ways. It seems these two coppers from Scotland Yard,
Herbert and Burroughs, have taken London apart while
investigating Stephen. They've interviewed nearly two
hundred people by most accounts. They've tracked down
people who said hello to Stephen once in 1945 and have
never seen him again since. They haven't left a stone
unturned ... but they haven't been here ... yet.

The more I've thought about the break-in the more I've
become convinced it was someone other than the police
who did it. The Old Bill could have turned up here any
time, said they were looking for drugs, and then turned the
place over. It was someone else who did it. But who?

Who indeed? The security services?

If I knew the answer to that I would know the answer to
a lot of other things as well. I then might also know if
Stephen is and has been on the level with me ... which is a

pretty intriguing question.

'It's been there all day, Tim. It was there yesterday too.'

I went over to the window and peered through the side of the curtains.

'Where?'

'The black Humber just up from the Royal Oak ... see?'

There was a black Humber there but I couldn't see anyone in it as the light was being reflected from the windscreen.

'There were two blokes sitting in it all day yesterday and they're there now. I saw them just now when I came in.'

'I wonder what they're doing?'

'They're doing something ... aren't they?'

'Waiting, I guess.'

'For what?'

'For me?'

It was a possibility, but one I could not face directly, not at the moment anyway.

The following morning the first thing I did when I got up was peek out through the curtains. The Humber was still there.

I left for work at the usual time. I walked directly across the street to the newsagent's and glanced to my left. There were two men sitting in the car. Just sitting there and staring ahead. I bought a paper and took a right as I left the shop so that I could walk down and abreast of the 'watchers' (as I had come to think of them).

The Humber was four or five years old and in good nick. There were no aerials on it, no distinguishing features. It was plainclothes all right. The two blokes sitting in it were in their thirties, in suits and collars and ties. They could have been anyone. Nothing remarkable at all ... except they were here ... waiting and watching. I nonchalantly strolled by and continued down to the Royal Oak and then turned into Westbourne Grove. The moment I was round the corner and out of sight from the car I broke into a sprint and raced down past the ABC Cinema and into the turning that was the continuation of Queensway north of the Grove. There was a furniture removal van parked a little way up so I ran behind it to get my breath. I'm not in good shape and even this little burst taxed me. I moved around to the far side of the vehicle where I could get a clear view across the Grove and down Queensway without being seen. It was early. There was hardly any traffic about: a taxi or two heading down to Paddington, a milk float, a couple of buses. I could see half a dozen people only, a couple of workmen, a newspaper boy, two women cleaners (if that is what they were) nattering to each other on the corner, some beatnik type with an armful of LPs standing at the bus stop smoking, a delivery van at the baker's.

I waited.

If those two blokes were sent to tail me I would expect to see one of them appear soon on foot or for the car to drive by ... wouldn't I? I continued waiting. Nothing. Not a dicky bird.

Now, if I were under surveillance it would be important for them to know exactly what I was doing and where I was going the whole time. They couldn't make any assumptions. They couldn't assume that I was now going to work and, say, pick me up again in Wardour Street. I might break the journey. I might lead them somewhere. A tail would have to be on me the whole time.

I stood behind the pantechnicon for ten minutes. Neither one of the blokes nor the car appeared. Nothing. Nothing remotely suspicious.

What do I do now?

Is the car parked around the corner still? Are the blokes still sitting in it? I decided to find out by going back to the newsagent's and getting some cigarettes.

As I turned by the Royal Oak on the corner of Porchester Road I could see the Humber ahead of me. The two of them were there still, just sitting. Doing nothing. Saying nothing. Just waiting

Does someone else take over from them when I go off?

Over the next few days I walked around with one eye over
my shoulder the whole time. I didn't know if I was under
surveillance or not but it seemed prudent to assume that I
was. I kept my routine straight and simple. I got up, went
to work, had a drink in Soho, went home. I did not do
anything different. I'd walk down Queensway every
morning and catch the bus to the top of Wardour Street and
amble down from there. I did our shopping on Westbourne
Grove. Went home. And all the time glancing back, regis-
tering faces, filing them away. Waiting for somebody to
give themselves away.

And still the two guys sat in the Humber. I had now
figured out there were six of them altogether working two
at a time in eight hour shifts. They just sat there. They had
become a fixture in Porchester Road. And still, under an old
mattress in the eaves above, was Stephen's suitcase.

Was there any connection?

'They make me very nervous just sitting out there, Tim,'
said Veronica.

She worried about them more than I did now. She was
convinced they were after me, after us. This was a war of
nerves guaranteed to chip away at our equilibrium.
Veronica said they would continue like this and if that got
nowhere – they'd raise the ante. She didn't want to be
about when that happened.

'Why don't you just give them that bloody suitcase?'

'We don't know if it's that they want, do we?'

'Of course it is!'

'We don't know.'

'It's the suitcase! What else could it be?'

'I don't know. I just don't know.'

Give them the suitcase? This remark of Veronica's
alarmed me. She wouldn't do anything silly like telling
them about it, would she? I'm sure she wouldn't … but she
is getting worn down by this. She could get over-wrought,
have a drink or two, and then do something stupid. It is not

a good idea keeping the thing here. But what do I do? My life seems nothing but an endless series of questions lately … and uncertain answers.

That night I checked out the back exit to the house. I went down to the basement and along the corridor to the glass-panelled back door. This opened on to a yard about 30 feet long that was surrounded by a high wall. Beyond the wall at the far end I could see the mews houses which, at one time, were linked with the main houses here. But that was before the dividing wall was built. No escape here. There was only one way in and out of this fucking decrepit house and that was through the front door that opened on to Porchester Road *and* the black Humber. I'm back to square one.

The anxieties about Veronica and the suitcase were dissolved the following day, at a price. Veronica told me she could no longer stay here while '*you* are under surveil-lance'. Not *us*, but *me* … under surveillance. She was going to stay with her friend, Audrey, who lived down on Blenheim Crescent. She'd stay there until all this blew over. She was very sorry and she knew she should stand by me and give me support but it was all too much for her and if I were anything of a man I'd understand anyway.

I did.

I was now alone with the men in black and the suitcase.

The waiting game. But waiting for what? And when? And was it just the suitcase?

I pulled the edge of the curtain back and looked down to the Humber parked where it always was: heavy, black and silent. It then struck me how obvious this all was. They wanted me to know they were there. This was all part of the game.

I met Nick Esdaille in the Swiss on Old Compton Street on Wednesday after work. He's a good friend and used to be a regular at Modern Snax. Works down in Fleet Street on a newspaper. I can trust him. We had a drink or two and then went to Jimmy's for a meal. A noisy place but you can talk with privacy. Also, the Greek food is good and cheap and the portions are large. The front part of the basement had a few people scattered about but the back was empty. We took a corner table and both ordered the mousaka. I got a cheap bottle of retsina too, it was 4s.6d.

'Did you see the papers today?' Nick asked.

I hadn't. I still bought the *Telegraph* most days but I hadn't today.

'No,' I said. 'More about Stephen?'

'No, something else.' Nick held up the front page of the *Daily Mirror*: 'NEW THIRD MAN SENSATION: FOREIGN OFFICE FOUND PHILBY A JOB.'

'You didn't see this about Philby?'

'The Russian spy? No.'

'Interesting. The FO got him a job on the *Observer*. They said there was never any reason to doubt his loyalty. They recommended him to the *Observer*. The paper sent him out to the Middle East and then in January this year he disappeared from Lebanon ... .'

'And surfaced in Moscow.'

'Yeah. Surfaced in Moscow. You know who was Foreign Secretary back in 1955? You know who cleared Philby then when it was first rumoured he was the Third Man in the Russian Spy Ring?'

'No? Who?'

'Harold Macmillan.'

'Jesus. I didn't realise that.'

'Uh-huh. On Monday Philby was officially named as the Third Man in the House of Commons. Doesn't look good for old Harold, does it? And it's getting worse for him over all this Profumo business. Profumo says he never fucked Keeler and Macmillan says he'll stand by him, won't accept his resignation. Then it turns out he was screwing her while she was seeing the Russian naval attaché, so Profumo does resign and Macmillan is left with a lot of egg on his face. The government is looking decidedly dodgy ... very iffy.'

'And Stephen's trial is coming up … God knows what birds that is going to scare from the trees.'

'Exactly.'

The waiter put the bottle down in front of me together with two glass tumblers. I poured us a glass each. I took a sip. I've always been a sucker for the resinous taste of retsina. It haunts your palate like mouthwash.

'Yeah, your friend Stephen is up to his eyes in it.'

'He is, now that Profumo is out of the game.'

'A fast lifestyle, surrounded by leggy tarts who don't mind putting it about. Orgies. Sexual favours. Whispers of espionage. It's the sort of story Fleet Street editors have wet dreams about. They'll bleed it dry. They'll bleed him dry.'

'What's going to happen to him?'

'No idea. What do you think's going to happen to him?'

'I've got no idea either … but I know what he thinks.'

'What's that, Tim?'

'He thinks it's going to blow over. He thinks this is a little charade he has to go through. And then at the trial the cavalry arrives and saves him. That's what he thinks.'

'Who's telling him this?'

'I don't know, but someone is. I thought you might have some idea?'

'No idea. No idea at all. Perhaps he got it from a ouija board? Or how about the husband of the drugged blonde you were supposed to photograph? You tell me. Could be anyone, right?'

'Yeah, that narrows it down a bit.'

'Anything is possible. Listen, there's a rumour going around that the whole Profumo thing was orchestrated, brought into the open, to camouflage something else to do with Ward. Have you heard that?'

Nick said it like he thought there was something to it.

'No. I've heard a lot of other rumours though.'

'There are dozens of them each day. They spring up overnight. But some of them might have some truth in them … you never know.'

'You never know.'

'Tell me about the girls again.'

'There isn't much to tell beyond what I've already told you. When he heard I was doing the photographs and then the films he said he could supply girls. These girls turned up and that was it.'

'You never saw them again?'

'No. Well, I saw one of them late one night walking down a street in Chelsea. We didn't talk or anything.'

'They never appeared in your pictures a second time is what I meant.'

'No.'

'And Stephen always wanted copies of whatever they were in?'

'Uh-huh.'

'Did you ever wonder why?'

'Not really. He was supposed to be a bit of a voyeur. He just liked watching his girls getting it ... I suppose. I didn't think anything more of it at the time. It's only since then that I've started thinking about it.'

'Did the girls have anything in common?'

'I've thought about that a lot. The only thing they had in common was Stephen. I can't think of what else they had in common ... beyond the willingness to do ... what they did.'

'Yeah, but why were they willing?'

'Stephen said it was a good idea ... they wanted to get on ... I remember they all more or less said the same thing ... like parrots. They wanted to be models ... the usual.'

'Perhaps they had been rehearsed, Tim?'

'Why?'

'Search me.'

'I keep thinking that there's something here if only I could recognise it. Some clue. A key. But I don't know what it is.'

'Why don't we go round and have it out with him?'

'What with Stephen? I want to keep as far away from him as possible. I don't want the Old Bill turning up on my doorstep. And that's the other thing – you've got these coppers going through Stephen's life with a magnifying glass and they've turned up hundreds of people and yet I've never had a visit. How do you explain that?'

'They can't know everything … be everywhere. Just think yourself lucky, mate.'

'Suppose so, Nick. But then who was it who turned my place over and who are the geezers in the Black Humber?'

'They're not coppers.'

'I know that … but who are they?'

'They're people who know a lot more about Stephen than the flat-footed coppers do, that's who they are. Kim Philby could probably tell you all about them. Security. That's who they are.'

'That's chilling.'

'It is.'

My appetite disappeared there and then as the mousaka arrived.

6

Algo Bueno

It's an accident I got anything to do with history, you know?
– Benny Harris (1965)

SATURDAY. I was up early and like I do every morning now I peek out from behind the curtains to see if the Humber is still there. Today it was gone. It had driven away. All that remained was the mute testimony of a large patch of leaked oil.

This news put me in a good frame of mind for the rest of the day and as custom was pretty slow at Modern Snax after lunch I closed the place at 3 p.m. Fuck it, I thought, I'll go down one of the clubs and have a drink and thus I found myself climbing the narrow steps of the Colony Club, or Muriel's as it is better known, in Dean Street. Muriel herself was sitting on a stall at the near end of the bar. She looked at me like I was a dollop of dog shit.

'Here's Sir Tim!' she said to the bloke behind the bar. 'He's finally got tired of staying at home and playing with himself!'

'Hello, Muriel.'

'I'll have the same again, if that's all right with you?'

I told the barman to fill Muriel's glass up and give me a gin and tonic.

Muriel swivelled around on her perch and eyed me up and down again.

'You look like you've been eating out of Christine Keeler's lap. Do you want something to take the taste away?'

'I think I do.'

'Good, dearie. And you shall have it. Now toddle down to the end there and be a good little cunt. If I want to talk to you again I'll send Ian down with a message.'

I had two or three gin and tonics in rapid succession. The place was beginning to fill up but not with any faces I knew. Muriel's piercing laughter echoed about the place. I ordered another drink and an arm bearing a crisp new fiver appeared in front of me and I heard the words, 'Make it two and *I'll* pay for them.'

I turned. It was Sonny. Sonny in an expensive three-piece suit looking like a Super Pimp from Harlem (or, failing that, King Shit, the mythical reefer dealer all the young black hoods aspire to be).

'Sonny, how good to see you!' I said this impersonating Stephen's plausible insincerity. It was lost on Sonny.

'Good to see you too.'

'I didn't know you were a member.'

Sonny pulled his waistcoat down and said, real cool like and unruffled, 'I didn't know *you* were a member.'

'Yeah. You look really prosperous.'

'I've wisened up to a lot of things. I've got all sorts of things on the go now.'

'You must have.'

'Yeah, I do. What about you?'

'Not a lot. I'm still down at Modern Snax. Not much else.'

'Still making films?'

'Not lately … the train pulled away without me.'

'Uh-huh. It's the sixties now, man. The *sixties*. Things are different all the way down the line. You got to remember that. The *sixties* now.'

There was something about the way he kept on saying the sixties that irritated me. Fuck, I know it is the sixties all right. What's he telling me that for? But there was something else about him. We used to be good mates together. Two guys on the make. Now it was as though there was a

pane of glass between us. Sonny was in the money and I
wasn't. Perhaps he didn't want to be reminded about the
way it was?

'How come you're here this afternoon, Sonny?'

'I like it here. I often come by. Today I thought I'd celebrate Cassius Clay beating the living shit out of Henry-
fucking-Cooper.'

'Did you see the fight?'

'I had *tickets*. I was *there* at Wembley.'

'You didn't listen to it on the radio then?'

'Two good seats I had. The best five rounds I've ever
seen in my life.'

We had a couple more drinks and talked aimlessly. It
wasn't so much a conversation as two interweaving mono-
logues winding in and out and above and below each other
and drifting nowhere. I sensed Sonny was tense. There
were other things on his mind.   Our chat eventually
petered out after about twenty minutes. There was just
silence punctuated by Muriel's guffaws and the hum of the
other dedicated drinkers.

'Do you want to come to a party, Tim?'

'Is it going to be a good party?'

'Sure is. Upper class. Plenty of drink. Good-looking
women.'

'Tonight?'

'Yeah.'

'Where?'

'Hitchin.'

'Hitchin? Where's Hitchin?'

'North up the A1. Off the A1. An hour's drive.'

'Out in the country?'

'Where the fields are.'

'How do we get there, Sonny?'

'In my car.'

'I didn't know you had one.'

'I got two.'

Sonny's two-year-old Ford Consul was parked on Dean Street a few minutes from the Colony. All bright and polished with shiny chrome. He opened the nearside passenger door first and waved me in.

'You're going for a ride in black-man's car.'

'Indeed I am.'

Sonny got in and the car started up right away. He pushed the gearstick into first and we moved off down to Old Compton Street, took a left, and then up into Charing Cross Road. Sonny was a better driver than I would have given him credit for. He slipped from one gear to another effortlessly and was mindful of the other traffic. Who'd have credited it? Sonny said he got the car second-hand about three months ago. He'd spent a few bob on it to get it in tip-top shape. His other car was an MG Sports that was currently having a new engine fitted.

Whence the spondulicks that paid for all this?

'A bit of this and a bit of that. Some hefty drug deals to begin with. Charge at first. Then I moved to stronger stuff. Cocaine is where the money is. Cocaine people ain't like the street riff-raff. They got money and class. They're discreet. They ain't going to cheat you none. So I did really well out of that and made a bit. The I started to diversify, man. This is the sixties and that's what you gotta do. I got an interest in a dress boutique on Portobello Road and I'm the manager of some rock groups. You heard of the Beatles? Well, the Maybellines are gonna be bigger than the Beatles ever could be. They're some real cool black kids from Tottenham and they are gonna make me a millionaire. This is the *sixties*. You gotta diversify and swing with the mood. That's what I'm doing.'

We drove through Camden Town and past Swiss Cottage on to the Finchley Road. A mile or so up we took a left after the Blue Star garage and headed down the Hendon Way and then on to the A1 that would, if we just kept going, take us all the way to Edinburgh.

We've left grimy crowded London behind us now and

the semi-detached suburban villas soon give way to fields and woods.

How long has it been since I last saw a hedgerow?

Sonny is getting twitchy and says he could do with another drink. I want to take a slash. So we pull in at the first pub we come to – a 1930s road-house of a pile called the King's Arms that's situated by a roundabout somewhere just inside the border of Hertfordshire. Before Sonny gets out of the car he reaches under the steering wheel and produces a brown carrier bag which he carries into the pub. The place has only just opened and is virtually empty. Sonny gets the drinks while I go for a slash. When I come out of the Gents Sonny is nowhere to be seen. The drinks and a packet of crisps are on a table by the entrance, but no Sonny. I sit down, sip my gin and light a cigarette and wait. I wait about ten minutes and then a door opens on the far side of the bar and Sonny walks through clutching the carrier bag. No, he strides through it and strides over to me. He sits down and picks up his glass and empties half the contents in one gulp. He's hot and sweating and very anxious about something.

Sonny says, 'Good drink, man ... and a nice evening, huh?'

He is manifestly agitated but he's not saying anything. He can't be as dumb as to think I haven't noticed, can he? Or can he?

'Where did you get to?' he asks.

'Where did I get to?'

People always throw back a question to you when they want to buy some time to think up a plausible alternative to the truth. Where did he get to? Where could he have got to?

'I thought I'd lost you.'

'No. No. Had to make some phone calls.'

'Just looking after business?'

'Yeah. Business.'

'And how is business?'

'Good and bad.'

Sonny wouldn't look at me. His eyes were darting every-where except at me sitting on the opposite side of the table. Sonny starts swinging his arms in time with some music that's being played over the pub's loudspeakers. The carrier bag sits on his lap.

We finished our drinks and the crisps and left. On the way out I noticed that there was a public telephone just inside the main doors. But Sonny hadn't been there. He'd come through a door on the other side of the pub. Is this phone out of order and is there another one behind the bar? I wondered about that. I also wondered whether I wasn't getting a little 'paranoid' as they now call it.

Sonny carefully places the carrier bag somewhere under the steering wheel.

I tease him: 'A little bit of business in there?'

'A big bit of business,' he replies.

So what's Sonny doing now? Supplying cocaine to the leisured country classes?

'Why don't you drive now?' says Sonny. 'I'm a bit tired, man.'

'OK.'

We get out and swap places. I haven't driven for a few weeks, in fact, about six weeks. I drove over to Bromley in Mr Calabrese's van to get some spares for the Gaggia coffee machine. That was the last time I was behind the wheel.

I pull out of the pub's carpark and get back on to the A1 going north. It's a fine summer evening with a warm breeze and there's not much traffic about. I drive leisurely and keep at around 50 m.p.h. The fields on either side stretch to the horizon, rich dark greens and golden browns. There's another 1930s road-house here that looks like an enormous thatched barn, and then the road is lined with poplars on either side like you see in France.

More fields, more ribbon-development bungalows, a road-house or two and now we're going through Hatfield and past a pub called the Comet (complete with a model

Comet aeroplane on a plinth).

After an old coaching pub (that's what it looks like) called the Red Lion the road starts a sinewy descent down a wooded hill and soon we're driving through some country village that has a White Hart and a Green King but no people and then we're out in the country again and the road meanders through the fields.

Sonny isn't saying much and he doesn't strike me as someone who much wants to go to a party. But perhaps he's not going there for pleasure but for business: the business in the paper bag. He's lying back in the seat nodding off. This businessman has got a lot of worries.

We drive through a straggly village and then we're out in the country again with vast open fields on either side and no hedgerow or fence to separate them from the road. The road twists and turns and seems to be unsure of its course. High yew hedges spring up from nowhere and enclose the road and to the right I catch a flash of something that looks like the entrance gate to a vast medieval castle, but the trees envelop it and then it's gone.

The ground gently rises on either side here and is well wooded. The breeze has increased to a wind and has become chill. There are dark clouds above, rain clouds. I wind the window up. Signposts with odd names point down sunken lanes that are not much wider than a cart-track. Little sheltered communities here unaware of the Big City and its vices (unless, of course, Sonny is on callout).

'We've passed it,' says Sonny. His first words for a good few miles. 'We've passed the pub.'

'What pub?'

'The turning was back there.'

'How do you know?'

'It was the turning on the left before the Royal Oak we wanted. There's the pub ... so we've passed it.'

This Royal Oak didn't look like my Royal Oak in Porchester Road. This was a rambling farmhouse of a place, a sort of coaching inn, miles from anywhere. You could almost smell the straw and the horse shit.

I pull up, reverse the car into a field entrance and take off back in the direction whence we had come.

Sonny points to a narrow country lane on our right that is signposted to some village called St Paul's-something-or-other.

I head down it. The trees and hedges on either side grow up high and almost meet above the road. It's dark now with the rain clouds, time to switch the headlamps on.

I can see Sonny out of the corner of my eye shifting about on his seat. He can't settle down tonight. He's nervous. There's something on his mind.

'Pull over here, man. I gotta take a piss.'

'Can't you wait?'

'I'm bursting.'

The road is descending here down the middle of a valley. There's dense woodland on either side and nowhere to stop. Then ahead on the right I see a muddy lay-by to the fore of a three-rail gate that leads into the woods. I pull over.

Sonny jumps out and says he won't be a minute. He climbs the fence and disappears into the undergrowth.

I light a cigarette and gaze ahead. It is quiet here. Very quiet. Quiet and still. Just the wind in the tree tops, a gentle rustling murmur. No other traffic. Not even any birds. I look down the valley ahead of me with the towering mature hardwoods on either side and think the view must have been unchanged for centuries. You could bring back some sixteenth-century farmer, show him this, and he'd know where he was.

I look down and see that the carrier bag Sonny has been clutching is partially pushed under the front seat. I'm curious what's in it? Dope? Can't be anything else. Should I risk a peek? No, forget it. I don't want to know.

I laughed to myself at the thought of the police suddenly appearing here and searching the car. I'd have a tough time explaining the shit away: 'I wonder if you could hold on for a few minutes, officer. My black dealer friend is in the woods there taking a piss. He's the chap you need to speak to.'

'Certainly, sir. You are obviously completely innocent. We'll wait over there until the black gentleman reappears. We're sorry to have troubled you.'

'Not at all, officer. Any time.'

A tough time indeed!

I flick the end remains of the cigarette out the window and lazily yell to Sonny to get a move on. There's no reply. What's he doing? Has he got a stricture or something?

I get out of the car and stretch. I've got a slight ache in my lower back so I lean forward and touch my toes a dozen times. That always gets rid of it. I light another cigarette and go over to the wooden gate.

'SONNY! SONNY!' No reply.

I can see some distance into the wood in most directions. There's no sign of Sonny anywhere. How far does he have to go before he feels it's safe to take a leak? Half a mile? What a dumb black fucker!

I climb the gate and sit on the top rail facing the car and the road. I puff on the cigarette and wait. I look up the road in the direction we just came. Still and silent. I look down the road. Still and silent. Everything's still and silent. I'm the only thing here ... I'm the only thing here. I'm the centre of the universe. It's just me ... and the car ... and the dope.

But what about Sonny?

Sonny wasn't coming back. This thought swept through me with such certainty I shuddered. Sonny had gone. I was here alone. A sitting duck. A patient sitting duck.

There was a sound coming from back up the hill. An urgent sound. I could hear it but I couldn't identify it. An urgent sound getting louder ... getting nearer. Racing. It was a speeding car. It was two speeding cars. It was three.

I threw my cigarette away, swung my legs over the gate, jumped down and began running through the undergrowth and through the bracken. The only sounds I could hear were my heavy breathing and the crash of my feet. I stumbled and fell several times but I was on my feet again before I hit the deck. Onward. The ground begins to rise steeply and more of an effort is needed to maintain my pace. I crash and career through the bushes. Don't stop. Don't look back. Just keep going.

Then I'm out of the wood and fall on my face. I'm in the middle of a narrow lane, my face hard against the road surfacing. Tar fumes filling my head. I can hear my heart beating like a kettledrum. I can also hear a car far off. Several cars. I can hear shouts. Dogs barking.

I'm up and on my feet again. I'm running again. I'm running through a gap in a hawthorn hedge and then I'm racing through a field that skirts another wood.

Any moment I expect a hand on my shoulder and some copper saying, 'That's far enough, son.' Any moment now it is going to happen. It really is.

I steady myself against a massive pollarded oak tree. I take some deep breaths. The sweat is pouring off me. I don't know what to do except keep moving.

I can hear muffled shouts and muted dog barks coming from far below in the valley, borne up on the evening wind. And then I hear a sound nearer. Much nearer. A car comes to a violent halt in the lane behind me. I hear more men and dogs. There are shouts. The vehicle's doors are slammed. I listen. Who's there? What are they doing? What's going on?

I listen intently. I listen for every sound. They don't seem to be coming this way. No, not this way. They're going off into the woods back down the way I came. They're going away from me.

Now I'm running again. I've got to keep moving. I cannot stop. I must keep going. Must keep moving. I'm running for my life. Running. Don't stop. Don't ever stop. Run and run and run and you'll get away. But don't stop. Just don't stop.

My feet now leave the ground. I arc through the air. I don't have to run any more. I'm propelling myself through the air. I'm airborne. Sailing. Speeding through the ether on sails made of gossamer. Borne by the winds. I'm flying away. Up and away. Just like a dream, only this isn't a dream. This is for real. I'm a soaring kestrel. I'm Icarus.

And like Icarus I now crash to earth, against something hard and unforgiving. Masonry. My face hits part of it first and then my shoulder crashes into another part. I lie there on my back taking deep breaths as my consciousness reassembles itself. I'm staring at the dark clouds and waiting. Something cold and wet runs down my face, then down my neck and under my shirt collar. There's a crescent moon up there looking like a child's painted cutout. There's silence here. Pure silence. Not even a murmur of wind now. And an enveloping blackness. A pit of unknowing.

Later my eyes slowly opened and focused on rare and strange shapes towering high above, vaulting into the night sky. Ahead of me in the darkness I see a wall silhouetted. Several walls thrusting up. Ghostly arches. Walls and arches enshrouded by ivy or clinging vines. What is this? I look to the left and then to the right. Isolated walls detached from any structure. A sepulchral silence. An abandoned overgrown shell.

I open my mouth and my face seems to crack down my left cheek. I bring my hand up and feel some dried sediment that streaks down to my neck: blood. My fingers trace its path up past my temple to a dried gash just within my hairline. There is a sharp pain here and a dull pain in my shoulder, I'm motionless and I wait for something to change, but nothing does.

Why am I here? What has happened?

Slowly fragments of memory float up from some abyss of mind and dance into order. Sonny. What became of Sonny? Why was he gone for so long? Where is he now? Did something happen to him in the woods?

Quiet. Still. I listen with every cell in my body but I hear now only the light wind caressing the trees. No footfalls. No voices. Nothing. Whoever was in pursuit is in pursuit no longer. They have lost me. Lost me.

I push myself up and lean against a wall. I take deep breaths and hope I have the energy to do something. A cloud passes from the moon and a cold light illuminates this tableau: a deserted, ancient church overgrown with centuries of neglect.

I take shaky, tentative steps ahead, one at a time. I must not rush. I will get there. Each and every step is carefully considered and worked out. This is important.

The wood gives way to a field and I am upon a footpath that is straight and undeviating. The path dissolves into the darkness but is obviously aligned on the twinkling lights far ahead.

My steps become more steady and certain as I continue. I see other lights and car headlamps sweeping in great arcs through the night.

I've got to get back to London.

The path brings me to the side of the Royal Oak pub, the same Royal Oak our directions were based on. I walk quickly past the people drinking outside and continue along the road. Several cars pass me and I realise I am teasing Fate by appearing as a roadside attraction. Whoever was after me back there must now be out looking for me, searching the roads and lanes. I climb over a gate and follow the road from behind the hedgerows.

I do not know where I am going but this looks an important road and it will lead somewhere, eventually. Houses appear and I am forced to resume walking along the road itself. I walk so as not to attract attention. I walk at not too fast a pace with my back straight which is now no easy task with the increasing pain in my shoulder.

Ahead to the right I see across the fields a small bridge. I walk diagonally across the field and discover a small stream where I clean away the blood from my face and neck. The water is warm and tastes sweet.

A signpost points to somewhere called St Ippollitts and, straight ahead, to Hitchin: 2 miles. I have no alternative but to continue. Detached country houses appear on either side of the road and I continue. I am now in the environs of Hitchin and soon I will be in the town itself.

I now go down a sunken curving lane with tall trees towering above. There are some eighteenth-century houses on the right and, some distance later, a vast church over to the left beyond what appears to be a market-place or a car park. The church looks almost like some ancient cathedral, big, but not quite big enough.

I merge with the Saturday night revellers. I feel safer here: better to be lost amongst people than lost in the country. I stop two girls and ask them if there is somewhere I can get a cup of coffee? They point to beyond the church and I head along an alley that brings me to a modest little café full of teenagers. Not so much a coffee bar as a tarted up transport caff. But the coffee is hot and nobody looks at me, they must see enough victims of Saturday night pub brawls not to give them a second look. That dreadful *Telstar* pop record is blasting out of a jukebox, exacerbating my headache. Every time the door opens I look up to see who is coming in. I don't know who to expect but there are people out there looking for me … and I don't know who they are.

I buy a second cup of coffee and a pork pie and a Kit-Kat. I stare into the cup and try to make sense of what has happened. What became of Sonny in the woods? How did the police know where to find us – if, indeed, they were the police? Who but the police have dogs anyway? Were we followed from London? Did they know Sonny's destination? Did some grass tip them off? Each question spawned further questions. Each question fragmented into a further dozen unanswered puzzles. But the dominant question, the one I kept returning to was: why was Sonny so long in the woods? Was he setting me up? If so, why? Was he some 'licensed' drug dealer delivering up bodies to his corrupt police contact or what?

I was wasting time sitting here and trying to reduce the unknowable to the known. It was time to get moving. I'll finish the coffee and go as soon as Stan Getz stops playing *Desafinado*.

A young bloke at an adjoining table said there was a railway station about ten minutes' walk away. I could get a train to London from there.

I went down a wide street called Bancroft with graceful houses on either side. This leads to the suburbs of Hitchin and then, further on, past a looming granary (or malt-house?) was a turning with a sign saying STATION APPROACH. The Approach is more like a broad drive leading to a country house. Stacks of chestnut trees in an avenue to the right where the ground rises steeply. Sylvan, all right. Ahead a solid brick Victorian Gothicky building with BOOKING HALL above the entrance. Looks friendly enough.

Some taxis waiting patiently in the forecourt. Some kids in leather jackets strutting around a couple of motorbikes. A couple of railway workers rolling cigarettes.

I was cautious about just walking in and buying a ticket. There might be somebody waiting for me. I could see no police cars, nobody suspicious. I had to chance it.

The ticket clerk told me I had a 20-minute wait for the next King's Cross train. I bought a single ticket and went down the steps and along the passage underneath the tracks to the far platform.

I got a bar of chocolate from a slot machine and sat down on a bench which afforded me a good view of anyone who might come through from the ticket office. It wasn't unreasonable to think that whoever had the resources to mount tonight's little operation also had the resources to travel over here.

If the police were to appear I could head down the track and into the darkness. It would take them a few minutes to get across to where I was, enough time for me to vanish ... I hoped.

I finished the chocolate and lit a cigarette. An elderly couple appeared on the far platform followed by a few of the leather jackets. The couple sat down while the kids hotfooted it to a waiting room. An express train thundered by without stopping and temporarily blocked my view across.

When the train had gone and the smoke and steam had lifted nothing appeared to have changed on the far platform, but I felt a rising unease. *Something* had changed. But what? I couldn't put my finger on it. The elderly couple were now staring in my direction. They were still, silent and staring.

There was a noise from somewhere in the darkness down the track in the London direction. A noise like a muted cry or shout. I could see nothing. I looked across to the couple and they were walking back into the booking hall. A noise again, like muffled footsteps. There was something or someone down the tracks. I stood up. Some movement. Two men in suits were walking down the track towards me. The station lights now illuminated them more, I could see the shine on their shoes. These were not railway workers.

I turned and walked quickly down the platform away from them. I'd head down the steps, along the passage under the track and make good my escape. But as I approached the steps two other men were coming up them. They were looking at me and smiling. They were both in their forties, expensively dressed in suits and light raincoats.

'Hello, Tim,' said the taller of the two.

'Who are you?'

'We've got some friends of yours across there. Please follow us.'

The two figures who had appeared down the railway track were now standing a couple of yards behind me. Just standing there staring at me. I looked down at the men on the stairs and then I looked along the platform in the 'up' direction. A further two figures stood motionless at the far end of the platform.

My question was ignored. I rephrased it: 'What's this all about?'

'I've asked you to follow us.'

And so I followed them down the steps and along and up to the booking hall in silence.

The taller figure now said, 'Inspectors Cox and Weatherburn of the Metropolitan Police are waiting to take you back to London.'

'Who are you, then?'

Cox and Weatherburn were leaning against a black police saloon smoking. They looked precisely what they were: two fat unprincipled and probably corrupt Met detectives forever on the make. Two greasy bastards with short hair, tiny moustaches and crumpled suits from Burton's ... and so unlike these other guys, whoever they were.

'This is Inspector Cox.'

Cox threw his cigarette away and strode over to me.

'You've given us a fucking song and dance tonight, haven't you?'

Weatherburn was quick to get his tuppence in: 'A right little cunt you are. I should have been home with my wife hours ago.'

I was looking at Weatherburn when I saw a blur of movement in my peripheral vision. Cox was doing something. I couldn't quite decide what exactly ... and then something hit the side of my face with force. I fell. My face was in a puddle and I could taste dirt on my lips.

'That should give you something to think about, cunt.'

And then I was kicked in the ribs. It did not hurt at first and then waves of pain spread over my body and I was hardly aware of my wrists and ankles being tied with cord that cut into my skin like a blunt razor. Pain upon pain. It was as though it was happening to someone else.

I have blurred memories of being pushed into the back of

a car. Then the smell of leather as my face scuffed the upholstery. A long ride into the night. The pain of my shoulder and head. The pain in my wrists and ankles, incessant. My head spinning off into unconsciousness.

First my left eye opens. I saw the naked sun high above. Then slowly my right eye opens. The blinding sun, the blaze of noon. I am on my back staring into the sun. Perhaps I am sunbathing? Am I? Could this be what I am doing? It isn't.

I am on my back on a mattress on the floor of a small room. A cell. I am imprisoned by four walls, a floor and a ceiling. I and my mattress are the only objects in this box aside from a recessed light-bulb directly above me. There are no windows.

I am not moving and I do not know whether I can move. I decide to see what I can move. I must think what I can move and then decide to move it.

My hand. I will raise my hand that is situated at the end of my arm. So, my arm needs to be moved in order to bring my hand into view. Once that is done I can then attempt to move my hand.

My arm rises as I command it. It is naked as is my hand, but around my wrist are thick bandages through which blood has seeped. The blood is now dried. My hand moves but it takes all my reserves of energy.

I am tiring quickly and soon lapse back into the unknown. My consciousness drifts in and ebbs away again many times. I have no knowledge of time. Minutes, hours, days, years mean nothing to me. I am now living beyond temporal restraint. I have transcended it. I am free and I am unknowing.

I am sitting upright on the mattress. I do not how long I have been here. I do not know where 'here' is. It could be in Aberdeen for all I know, but I suspect it is in London. The two Met coppers were hardly likely to take me anywhere else.

The cell is very well insulated. Sounds may travel out of the cell but they do not travel into it. Sometimes there are far-off and distant rumblings but I cannot make out what they are. There is a metallic clank. It comes from the door. I look up and through the spy-hole see an eye looking at me. A key is inserted in the lock and the door opens. A young uniformed police officer in shirtsleeves walks in carrying a tray. Upon the tray is a cup of tea, a white bread sandwich, and some biscuits. The officer smiles at me.

'How long have I been here?'

'Nearly twenty-four hours … I'll put this down here.'

'Why am I here … do you know?'

'No, I don't. Inspector Cox brought you in. He's not back until tomorrow. Dare say he'll be in to see you then.'

I looked at the tray and wondered if I could eat anything. The officer saw my quizzical look and volunteered an apology: 'Yeah, sorry about this. Sunday, you know.'

Sunday … the 7th of July, in the Year of Our Lord one thousand nine hundred and sixty-three. A Sunday like any other Sunday?

'Where am I?'

'You mean where's this?'

'Yes.'

'West End Central … I'll turn the light down a bit so that you can get some sleep.'

'Was anyone else brought in with me?'

'I wasn't on duty … and I wouldn't be at liberty to say even if I had been.'

'I see … yeah. Have I been charged?'

Charging somebody while they're unconscious is a regular practice in London. I've known a couple of people it's happened to.

The copper didn't reply. I don't know whether he heard me or not. I asked the question again. He looked at me for a beat and there was something funny about his eyes as if he wanted to tell me something but couldn't.

'There's nothing in the paperwork.'

He said this slowly and deliberately, weighing each word. There's nothing in the paperwork. This was like an uncompleted sentence with a built-in inference. There's nothing in the paperwork ... but there *should* be.

And now he was gone. The door thudded shut and the lock was turned.

I sipped the sweet tea.

What was I doing at West End Central police station? Why here? Was Sonny here? Where was he? What was happening to him? More importantly, what was happening to me?

No answers would be forthcoming tonight, but tomorrow is another day. I will sleep now.

'Up you get and down to the bog. You've got five minutes and five minutes only.'

A big burly sergeant. Grey hair and a red face. Perpetually wearing a look of manic outrage. Them and us. Civvies versus the police. Don't ever show them you're human. School of Trenchard. Monday morning at West End Central.

I'm led down a long corridor. Brickwork painted green to waist height and then an institutional cream-brown up to the ceiling. Chipped paintwork. The smell of vomit and disinfectant.

'There you go, lad. Five minutes.'

I'm shunted into a small square room that contains a lavatory and a washbasin. I take a leak and look over my shoulder and see the sergeant peering through the spy-hole in the door. His eye doesn't move. He may consider watching prisoners piss a police perk.

There's one tap above the sink. The water gushes out, icy cold. I wash my face and hands as best I can with the sliver of ivory-coloured soap. I dry myself with the paper towels and place them neatly on the ledge of the sink as there is nowhere else to leave them.

The sergeant follows me back to the cell at the end of the

corridor. He doesn't say anything. His heavy breathing and wheezing and puffing echoes off the peeling paint and richochets about in the silence.

'Do you know what's going on?' I say.

A pointless question but asked nonetheless. The sergeant ignores it. Civilians should only speak when spoken to. Any speech initiated by a civilian, and particularly a question, is at the very least an impertinence. The NCO mentality. Freedom through discipline and respect. The *weltanschauung* of the sergeant-major. Where else could a bloke like this go after the Army but into the police?

Now get in there and let's not be having any more lip from you or you'll be in real trouble, Sonny Jim. This is what he thinks but leaves unuttered.

The cell door bangs shut. The lock is turned. Precise military footsteps fade into the silence.

I look around the cell but there is nothing to look at except the four walls, the door and the bed. A little self-contained universe that is all mine. My own ready-made reality for, I guess, as long as I like … as long as someone likes.

I ease myself down on to the bed and stare into infinity. The pain ebbs back into my body and I begin sweating. I imagine a big clock someplace with a second hand like a hammer on an anvil. One second after another. Consecutive seconds. Millions of them stretching ahead to the end of time. I'm going to be fully conscious of every last one of them until something happens. Billions and billions of fat seconds, each one longer than the last, because this is what it is all about. Waiting. Waiting and waiting. Letting you stew. Letting you fall prey to your very own anxieties and insecurities. Suspending you in a time warp where your defences are peeled away a layer at a time until you are raw and naked.

A couple of years ago I read Kropotkin's autobiography. He was locked up in the Peter and Paul Fortress in Moscow in a cell. He says how he was determined to keep his mind and body together while imprisoned and he drew up this rigorous schedule of activities. He would do all sorts of mental and physical exercises each day. He'd walk 35 miles a day, backwards and forwards and around the cell. You have to keep occupied, keep active, keep busy.

I pushed myself up off the bed, moved it out into the centre of the room so I could walk around the walls, and paced the distance off. The room is square and each side is four paces exactly. My paces are about a yard, so one full circumnavigation is a distance of 16 yards. There's 1,760 yards in a mile. Sixteen into 1,760 is one, carry one, one, nought. One, one, nought. One hundred and ten: 110 circuits equal a mile. Add another 40 for clipping the corners, say. That's 150 laps to the mile. Begin now. Keep count. One lap. Two laps. Three laps. Four laps. I'm feeling better already. Five laps. Keep going. Six laps. Seven laps.

At 50 laps the door swings open and a young copper brings in a tray with a bowl of cold porridge and a mug of tea.

'You a fitness fanatic?'
'Only when I'm banged away in here.'
'I'll put this down here on the bed.'
'Thanks.'
'What you here for?'
'You're the copper. Shouldn't I be asking you?'
'There's nothing on your sheet.'
'That's because I've done nothing.'
'Oh, yeah?'
'Oh, yeah.'
Fifty-one laps. Fifty-two. Fifty-three … .

I completed two miles straight off. The exercise made me feel good. The achievement made me feel good. I was keeping busy. Now some mental exercises. I lay on the bed. I'd work my way through the alphabet thinking of something for each of the twenty-six letters. Countries? Colours? Famous people? Book titles? Yeah, book titles.

A for *Ape and Essence*.

B for *Billy Budd*.

C for ... C for ... C for ... *Crime and Punishment*.

D for ... *Dombey and Son*.

E for –

'Right, lad! Come with me.'

The words are out before the door is open. It is the fat sergeant bristling with *purpose*.

He comes into the cell, looks me up and down, looks around the place to see if I've nicked anything, and says I'm to follow him. 'They've got a few questions for you.'

'Well, as long as it is only a few. I'm a busy man.'

'You're too clever by half, son. Too clever by half.'

Here's the interview room. A square room about the size of my cell. A table and three chairs. Two of the chairs are occupied. The two CID blokes who 'nicked' me last night. One of them is, presumably, Inspector Cox. They both stare at me like I'm a radioactive dog turd.

'Here you are, sir,' says the fat sergeant.

There's no reply. They're just staring.

'Sit down there,' the sergeant orders.

I sit down and face the two detectives across the table. They are both smoking. They are both still wearing those cheap Burton suits. They both look like a couple of villains which, I guess, is what they are.

'We'll call you later, sergeant.'

'Sir.'

The door bangs shut.

'I'm Inspector Cox and this is Inspector Weatherburn.'

The statement hangs in the air like a bad smell. Am I supposed to be impressed? Am I supposed to say 'Oh, in that case, I'm bang to rights on this one, guv'? Or should I say 'I'm very pleased to make your acquaintance'? I say nothing. These are a couple of self-proclaimed 'crime busters' – bent coppers who get good publicity in the cheap Sunday papers. Always on the make.

'You're in dead trouble.'

'I am?'

'You are. You were in possession of a stolen car in which was found a quantity of dangerous and illegal drugs.'

'And?'

'And you'll go down for it. Get a spell inside. You are obviously an individual who deals in these substances.'

Substances. What a strange word! Sub-stance. Substances.

'When are you going to charge me, then?'

'This is serious.'

'I'd like to see a lawyer.'

'He'd like to see a lawyer,' says the silent one. They chuckle. They're preening themselves on knowing something I don't.

'A lawyer isn't going to be much use to you.'

'None at all.'

'In that case … let me see one for laughs.'

'He's a joker.'

'Ain't he?'

'What's this all about?' I ask.

'It's all about you being in dead serious trouble.'

'So you keep saying.'

'Dead serious trouble.'

'Where's Sonny?'

'Sonny? Who's he?'

'The black guy I was with in the car.'

'We don't know any Sonny. You're the only one we know. You are quite enough for us … but if you want to give us some names it would look good for you in court. They might even knock a few years off when we say you've helped us.'

There's some cat-and-mouse game going on here. They're putting on the frighteners, softening me up. They're after something else, but what I don't know.

'Drugs are a very serious offence and you're going to have the book thrown at you, lad, unless … .'

Unless what? Spit it out.

'Unless you are prepared to give us a little help.'

Help. Such a little word! Help. Four letters only but what treachery can hide behind it. Help.

'A little help.'

'Yeah, a little help.'

'What sort of help do you have in mind?'

They look at each other and swap knowing smirks.

'There's a friend of yours we're interested in. A smart chap. Got himself into a bit of bother lately. Very dodgy case. A lot of unwholesomeness.'

'Unwholesomeness?' A bizarre word in this context.

'You know, drugs, perversion, pornography … little innocent white girls being forced to suck big black men's cocks and getting a mouthful of sperm. Stuff like *that*.'

'Yeah, we've seen the photographs. Black men's jism all over their pretty, innocent faces.'

'And in their hair.'

'Putting on little spectacles like this for his friends. You know the sort of thing. Fair enough. But then hidden cameras. A bit of blackmail. Very nasty.'

'Who are you two talking about?' I had a pretty good idea who they were talking about but I wasn't going to say the name.

'You know who we are talking about.'

'Tell me.'

'You tell him, Donald.'

'Ward. Dr Stephen Ward.'

'I've been reading about him in the papers,' I said, like I was unconsciously distancing myself from him.

'Now it seems that nice Dr Ward gave you something to look after a little while back. Something very important.'

'He did?'

'He did. And you can save yourself a lot of bother by telling us where it is.'

'Where what is?'

'You know. Now, where is it?'

'I don't know what you're talking about.'

'You are going to be sent down for so fucking long they're going to throw away the key, lad. You've fucking had it all right. Sergeant!'

Ninety laps. Ninety-one laps. Ninety-two laps. I'm concentrating on doing a mile. There's too much going on here to confront it head on. I can only look at it obliquely. Ninety-three laps. Ninety-four laps. But how did they know about Stephen giving me something? How? Stephen must have told somebody who told them. But who? Ninety-five laps. Ninety-six laps. Why would he tell someone? And who? It's useless thinking about this. I don't know who Stephen's friends are, do I? Is there some police or security spy in his camp or what? Ninety-seven laps. Who did I tell? I didn't. I didn't tell anyone ... but Veronica. Veronica knows. Would she tell anyone? No, she wouldn't. But I don't know what pressure could have been put on her. I guess they know what's in the suitcase. I don't. If ever I get out of here I'll take a peek all right.

Where was I? Ninety-something. Ninety-five. Ninety-six. Ninety-seven. Ninety-eight. Ninety-nine. One hundred. Made it. Only another fifty to go and I've done a mile.

If anxiety served any positive purpose I'd immerse myself in it. I'm prone to it if I don't keep a grip on myself. I have to block it out. I've got to keep aware of the source of it, but only through my peripheral vision. What is going to be is going to be.

Today, straight after breakfast, I did two miles non-stop. Pretty good going. Now I'm doing an A to Z of places in England and I'm stuck on Q. P was for Preston. But what's Q for? U always follows Q so it would be a place spelt Qu-something. Qu-? Quentin? Is there a place called Quentin? No, I don't think so.

Fuck it.

Sonny.

Sonny?

Where's Sonny? The cops didn't seem to know anything about him. Perhaps he's still hiding in the woods, living the life of a wild man? Living on berries and rabbits?

Now the big question here is, how did the police get on to us? Us? Sonny and/or me? They could have been on to him *or* me. Me seems more likely now in the light of the Stephen business. Me. I've been half-thinking of this always as some drugs operation that has Sonny in its sights. But no. Perhaps not. It was about *me*, not him. Sonny was just delivering me up.

Had they been following us out of London? If so, why didn't they apprehend us earlier? Why wait until we've stopped? Easier, I guess. Why didn't they make sure they had Sonny? Perhaps they just fucked up? Just one big fuck-up. Cox and his mate seem a couple of prize wankers. And who were those other blokes at the railway station?

I hear the key going into the lock and the bolts being thrown. I look up. The door swings open and there's a young copper there in shirtsleeves. Blond. Smiling. Looks a regular sort.

'Purdom?'

'Uh-huh.'

'On your bike. You're free to go.'

'Free to go? Walk out of here?'

'That's right.'

'This some trick or something?'

'No. I've just been told to release you.'

'Why?'

'They don't tell me more than I need to know.'

'Does this mean I'm not being charged?'

'Must do. Come on. I got to clear the room out before the next guest arrives.'

'Right.'

I followed the copper down a couple of corridors and up some flights of steps and through a couple of doors and before I knew where I was I was out on the street, standing on Savile Row looking up at the West End Central building.

'Nice day,' I said to the copper.

'A beauty.'

'Aren't you supposed to tell me not to get into trouble again or something?'

'Not me. I'm an acting gaoler not a sermoniser.'

'See you around.'

'Who knows?'

A bright sunny day with a cool breeze. Cars and traffic and black cabs. Women in summer dresses and tourists by the cartload. A bright sunny day, all right. But what day? What day of the week?

I asked some civil servant type what day it was. He looked at me like I was a loony, said Wednesday and then hurried off. Wednesday, 10 July 1963. I've been in there for four days. Since Sunday. Jesus fucking Christ!

I walked across to Regent Street and then down to Brewer Street and along to the Snax Bar. Charlie was there with a couple of the part-timers.

'Where you been?' he said. 'The old man's been looking for you.'

'When's he back?'

'Tonight some time.'

'Tell him I'll be here tomorrow.'

'Will do.'

'You seen Sonny at all?'

'Not for about a week. Why?'

I gave Charlie an abbreviated version of events since last Saturday. I told him everything except the Stephen stuff. He looked at me incredulously. I told him not to pass it on to Mr Calabrese, he might get worried, might think I'm not a fit person to look after the shop. Charlie's cool.

I sat down with a coffee and two rounds of corned beef sandwiches. White bread never tasted better.

'OK, Tim. What do you do now?'

'Keep my head down and hope nobody notices me.'

'If you ever learn that trick tell me how.'

'I will. Can you lend me a fiver? I've got no cash on me.'

'Sure.'

I walked down Wardour Street and along Old Compton Street looking for a cab. None about. I finally picked one up near the top of Charing Cross Road. I told the driver Bayswater, Porchester Road. But I changed my mind and decided to go to Sonny's place instead. Ladbroke Grove, just up past the station. See what that black dude has got to say for himself. Quiz him about a few things. See if he knows something I don't.

As the cab sped down Oxford Street I kept thinking about last Saturday night, about us stopping and about Sonny going for a leak. He'd seemed a bit nervous that evening. He says he wants to take a leak. He disappears into the woods and he's gone a long time. Where is he now? Perhaps I'll soon find out. Perhaps he'll tell me he had no choice but to set me up?

The cab dropped me on the corner, a few doors down from Sonny's place. I gave the cabby a two-bob tip. A couple of little black kids were playing on the pavement and when they saw me coming they stopped and stared at me, suspicious like. I went down the steps to the basement. The door was ajar. I pushed it open and called Sonny's name.

A slim black woman in her twenties appeared in the corridor. She was dressed in a cutaway housecoat that showed the upper reaches of her tits. Her lips were bright red. Her eyes were made up in thick layers. Great big eyes. Shining saucers. She was sexy all right.

She looked me up and down, very disdainfully. She exaggerated the disdain in her face. She wanted whitey to know she was most disdainful. Mightily disdainful.

'We not open now. You come back tonight.'

So, Sonny was now using his place as a knocking shop. The lad's lust for money stops at nothing.

'I don't want any business. I want to see Sonny.'

'Sonny not here.'

'When is he due back?'

'We don't know.'

'Have you seen him today?'

'No Sonny today.'

'When did you last see him?'

'Who are you?'

'Tim. Timmy. I'm an old friend of Sonny's.'

'A real friend?'

'A real friend, yes. I've been around here stacks of times. Smoked a lot of dope with him. Lent him money.' I could have added that I'd shot dirty pictures and a porno movie here too, but an inner voice told me to keep my big mouth shut.

'You know where he is?'

'Do I know where he is? I'm asking you where he is.'

'You come in.'

She led me through the flat to the room at the back that opens on to the garden. She took a lighted cigarette from the ashtray that she had left. On the table there a copy of the *Gleaner*, she'd been reading about the homeland where the sun shone every day and where you could smoke as much *ganja* as you liked and nobody said nothing.

She sat down at the table. I loafed down on the old threadbare sofa.

'Where Sonny then?' she asked. She puffed away at her cigarette and stared at me quizzically. In the position she was sitting I could see more of her breasts now. Big full breasts.

'You tell me when you last saw him.'

'He here Saturday morning. He say he going out for a few hours. Back at night. He don't come back.'

'So, you haven't seen him since then?'

'No Sonny since then.'

'Has anybody else seen him since then that you know about?'

'Nobody see him. You know where he is now?'

'No, I don't. I saw him on Saturday too … last.'

'Where you go?'

'Just in Soho. We had a drink together.' I didn't think it was a good idea to say anything more to her. Loose talk loses lives, as I think they used to say.

'He said he was going to a party. Did he say anything about that to you?'

'Party? Don't know about party.'

'Yeah. A party in Hitchin … near Hitchin. Have you ever heard of the place?'

'I only know London.'

So old Sonny hasn't been home since Saturday. Unusual. So, where is he, then? He could still be in the wood, in which case he's probably dead (but how?). He could be in police custody, but what for? Drugs? If they've got him for that they would have turned this tip over to see what else they could find.

'Have any police been here since Saturday? Any at all?'

'No police here.'

It doesn't seem the police have got him then … unless, of course, Sonny is sitting there in silence refusing to co-operate. Is that likely? Is that possible? No. Sonny loves talking. He can't stop talking. He'd be trying to talk himself up a deal. Anything the police wanted to know would come tumbling out.

So what does that leave? Sonny lying low? Keeping out of the way until it all blows over? (Until what blows over? Me?) But why? I believe her, whatever her name is.

'What is your name?'

'Shamay.'

She's telling the truth is Shamay. She hasn't seen him since Saturday.

Sonny is a homebody. If he hasn't been home for four or five days something's up. Something's not quite kosher. But what? Am I going to come up with any answers? Do I want to? Do I really care about this, about the Stephen business? About what happened to me? About what's going on? Yeah, I suppose I do, but for no noble reason. Just idle curiosity, I guess. Intellectual inquisitiveness. That's all. There's yesterday's truth, today's truth, tomorrow's truth. Some things you never find out about.

'You live here with Sonny?'

'Yes. Me and Susanna. We live here. Work for Sonny.'

'Business good?'

'We're busy. You want some business?'

'Another time, perhaps,' I said.

'You want cup of tea?'

'No. No thanks. I better be going.'

'You come and see me again some time?'

'Yeah.'

'You let me know about Sonny?'

'If I find out I will.'

Sonny, that dumb fucker.

'Has anyone else been around asking about Sonny?' This question just came out, popped out straight from my unconscious. The first thing I knew about it was when it was on my lips. Why did I ask it? Indeed, why didn't I ask it earlier?

'Few days ago gentleman come here and ask about Sonny. Nice gentleman.'

'Who was he?'

'Just a gentleman.'

'A copper?'

'Not policeman.'

'What was his name?'

'Didn't ask name. He not say. He same age as your father be. He say Sonny not show up. Sonny supposed to.'

'Show up where?'

'Don't know.'

'When was this?'

'Beginning of week he call here. Monday.'

'You'd never seen him before?'

'No.'

Who was this? Could have been anyone. Sonny knows all

sorts of people. Some upper-class dope fiend? Anybody.

'If Sonny turns up here will you tell him I called?'

'Yes. What your name?'

'Tim.'

'Yes, Tim.'

'See you about.'

I walked out and then south down Ladbroke Grove. I'll head for home, see what's been going on there. Catch up with a few things. I turned into Elgin Crescent and then across Portobello Road and along Colville whatever-it-is-called to Westbourne Grove. I got some bread and cheese and sausages in the grocer's shop just past Hereford Road and a *Telegraph* from the newsagent's next door. I was walking along with my brown carrier bag when my eye caught Veronica's salon across the road. She had been so out of mind I'd forgotten she was here. I crossed and peered in the window. Veronica was giving some old dear a cut. I went in and caught Veronica's eye. She nodded for me to go out back to the staff room. I waited there, idly flicking through an old *Vogue*.

'I can't stop. I'm in the middle of a client. Where have you been? I came around a couple of times. Nobody had seen you.'

'It's a long story. I'll tell you next time you come around. But listen, have you been visited at all by the police or by anyone making inquiries about me?'

'When?'

'When? This week … any time, I mean.'

'No. Why?'

'No one at all?'

'No. I'd tell you if I had.'

'Good.'

'Are the police going to come around and see me then? What about? Why?'

'It's something to do with Stephen, but they won't be coming to see you. It's all blown over.'

'I better get back. I'll come around on Friday.'

'Good idea. Yeah.'

I followed Veronica out and waved goodbye. I started walking quickly back to the flat. I was getting apprehensive about what I'd find. I didn't have good feelings. Something was amiss.

Just by the Royal Oak I turned into Porchester Road and stopped. I looked up at my window. It was there still and it wasn't broken. The house looked the same. So did the terrace. And the road, for that matter. What had I expected to find? A police cordon? Press and TV crews?

I let myself in the front door and closed it. I leant against it and listened. Silence. Then an old Scottish lady who has a room at the back on the ground floor shuffled across the hall. She saw me and said hello. I smiled back at her. She always knows what's going on here. If anything had happened she would have known about it and said something to me. I begin to relax. I take some deep breaths and start up the stairs, counting them as I go, some interesting anxiety-induced bit of obsessive behaviour.

I stop as the door of my room comes into view. It's there still. There are no axe marks on it. The hinges are intact. I approach it and take out the key. I put it in the lock and slowly turn it. The door swings open. I look around. Exactly as I left it. Nothing moved or changed. But there's an icy feeling I get. Someone *has* been here. Someone has carefully gone through everything. There's a vestige of a presence here. In the stillness there's a suggestion of somebody. They've done the job very carefully. I wouldn't ever know, would I?

I put the carrier bag on the side by the sink and hunt about for the old Ever Ready torch. I find it on the floor on the other side of the sofa. I switch it on. There's a faint light. The batteries are going but the dim, yellowy glow is enough.

I walk out of the room and up the flight of stairs that leads to the roof. I fiddle with the lock on the landlord's store room and ease it off the hasp. I shine the torch into the darkness. All the crap and clutter is still there much as I remember it. I get on my knees and crawl along the duck-board that leads to the eaves and – when I get there – it's *gone*.

Gone.

The case has *gone*.

Stephen's case has been taken. *They've* got it.

Once they had it, of course, there was no need to keep me in the nick. They found it and I was released. Free to go.

But just what was in it? What was I looking after?

What about Stephen?

Do I tell him it's gone? His trial begins at the Old Bailey on Monday. He's got enough to worry about. Perhaps I'll give *that* a miss.

Is there anyone I should tell? Is there anyone I can tell? I better keep my mouth shut. That's always good advice in any situation. Keep it shut. Good advice.

But do I tell Stephen? Do I? Does this missing case have any bearing on what's going to happen at the Old Bailey? A dumb question. How would I know the answer to that? So why don't I tell Stephen? Am I afraid to? Do I feel I've let him down … even if it was through no fault of my own?

I was really stupid not to find out what was in the case. I should have asked Stephen when he gave it to me. No, not just asked what was in it, but asked to *see* what was in it.

What are they charging Stephen with at the trial? Living off Christine Keeler's and Mandy Rice-Davies's immoral earnings (huh!) and then something about procuring a young girl or two. Pretty small beer you'd think for the Old Bailey, eh? Pretty fucking small beer. The whole thing is a fix, but who's fixing for whom?

7

Misterioso

Mystery is merely knowledge displaced.
– Robert Porpentine *Arrene: A Romance* (1926)

LIFE HAS TO CONTINUE, and continue it does.

As Stephen stood in the dock at the Old Bailey this morning at the beginning of his trial having the charges against him read out I was serving the umpteenth cup of espresso at Modern Snax and doing my best to block out the events of the last week. I'd spent most of the weekend trying to understand what had happened and got absolutely nowhere. I was trying to make sense of things without having a full hand of cards. I could only guess, and one guess is much the same as another in a situation like this. It was a waste of time. Different people know different parts. It's like the blind men and the elephant: they're all saying contradictory things and they're all speaking the truth.

I was reading an old Penguin Special a few weeks ago. I found it on a barrow in the Portobello Road. *Germany Puts the Clock Back* by Edgar Mowrer. Published about 1938. In the Introduction Mowrer says things have changed this century – it's fundamentally different from other centuries – the state's means of control and suppression are so vast it has meant the death of that old liberal belief that The Truth Will Out. Not true any more, says Mowrer. And he's right.

Mr Calabrese was very understanding about my few days off. I said I had to go down to Rochester on urgent family business. I didn't like telling a lie to him but in the circumstances (that is, self-interest) this appeared the best thing to do. He said that if I needed to borrow some money he'd help me. I said it wasn't necessary. I felt a real heel in the face of his kindness. I think what I should have said to him is that I had to go away for a few days and left it at that. No colour. No detail.

I'm on the bed smoking a joint with Veronica. She couldn't make it the other evening so she came around tonight instead. I made her a paella. We split a bottle of claret. I told her about last week. She was incredulous. Then we made love … but perhaps *screwed* is a better word. It was good. It always is with her. I like staring into her fiery little eyes while I'm thrusting into her. Fucking her. Fucking her hard. The only time she really ever opens up to me is when I'm inside her. Then she has a look of vulnerability. Then there's an expression on her face that says Don't Hurt Me, Be Kind to Me and it lasts until she comes and then it evaporates instantly.

'Why don't you move back in, Veronica?'

'What, me?'

'Who else do you think I'm talking to?'

'Let me have that joint.'

She thinks it's a silly suggestion. One not even worthy of a reply. I watch her taking some hits on the joint. A glassy look in her eyes. She coughs and hands it back to me.

'You're still at the Snax Bar, aren't you?'

An accusation posed as a question.

'Yes, I am,' I say guiltily.

'Isn't it time you did something. I mean go out and *do* something with your life? Huh?'

What a loaded question. If I answer *Yes* it means I'm not doing anything and should do something. If I answer *No* it means I'm not doing anything and don't want to either.

'You got anything in mind for me?' I ask.

'Haven't you got *anything* in mind for yourself? Don't you want to do anything? You want to be serving teas and coffees all your life? Waiting on tables? Pissing about like some cretin?'

Pissing about like some cretin!? Boy, you really get it from your friends.

How long have I been in London now? I came up in June 1959. How long's that? 59, 60, 61, 62, 63. Four years and … and a bit.

It's gone quickly. So quickly. So fucking quickly. You think of how long four years is when you are a kid. An eternity. A passage of time stretching to infinity. But now, a twinkling. It just zips by. Four years ago I was living and working in Rochester. I thought that little cathedral town on the Medway was the last word in civilisation, that it had just about everything to offer any city could have.

Four years in London and what have I got to show for it? What have I done? I've held a job down in a café. Kept myself together. Taken some photos. Made some blue films. Put a little money away in the bank. Loved Veronica. And what else? I know where I've come from but where am I going? What's going to happen in the next four years? What am I going to be doing in 1967? And four years after that, in 1971?

The seventies – another decade!

'Do you really think I'm pissing about like some cretin?'

'Yes, I do. You've got some talent … you should use it.'

'Yeah. I always put off answering big questions … making big decisions. There always seem to be other things occupying me.'

'I know. I've seen it in you.'

'I'll get my head screwed on first thing in the morning.'

Veronica takes the joint from me, has a couple of last drags and stubs it out in the ashtray.

'You got any films planned?'

'No. Why do you ask?'

'Just curious.'

'Things have changed. New faces on the scene. All this stuff is coming in from Scandinavia now. Beautifully made. Nobody's making the stuff over here now. It's cheaper to import films from abroad, and they're better.'

'You're going to feel the economic pinch.'

'Perhaps I'll supplement my wages with a bit of dealing.'

'You'll get banged up. Spend some time inside. I'll visit you once a month. A good ending to a not-so-promising career, huh?'

'We'll get married while I'm inside.'

'Everything is one big fucking joke to you, isn't it?'

'You want me to be heavy and serious like all those fuck-ups we see out there every day?'

'You know what I mean.'

'I don't.'

'Well, Timmy, it's too late in the day for me to explain.'

'Tell me in the morning.'

'I'm not staying over. I've got to go. Jesus! It's eleven o'clock already. I've got to be running.'

'Stay.'

'Can't.'

I lay there and watched her dress.

I've always liked seeing her dress, seeing her nakedness disappear a bit at a time as she puts on her clothes. It's like a formalised ritual. Women seem oblivious to you when they are dressing, they're so preoccupied.

'You going to see me down?'

'I always do.'

'Come on then.'

I pulled my cord trousers on while still on the bed and then hunted around for my lumberjack shirt. It was over by the sink.

'Come on.'

'I'm with you.'

I followed Veronica down the stairs with my hand up her miniskirt. She felt warm and damp. On the last landing I pulled her towards me and kissed her. She struggled so I held her tighter. She started pushing her hips into me. I got a hard-on. She noticed this and pushed me away and laughed.

'You'll have to take care of that yourself!'

We walked down the last flight of stairs and across the hall holding hands. I opened the door for her. She turned and gave me a quick kiss on the lips while rubbing the palm of her hand against my now semi-stiff dick.

'See you later.'

'Come around for dinner again later this week.'

'Yeah. How about Friday?' she shouted from the pavement.

'Fine. Good. Yes.'

I watched her cross the road and disappear from sight past the Royal Oak. She has an elegant walk. More a glide. She moves just from the hips downwards. A slide almost.

It was a cool, clear night. The sky was a rich, dark blue littered with diamonds of light, all glistening. Somebody or other further up the terrace had their window open and I could hear a version of Duke Ellington's *Mood Indigo* drifting down the street above the noise of the few cars and taxis. I took out my cigarettes and matches from my shirt pocket and lit up. It was a gorgeous evening and I felt especially good having seen Ronnie … I mean Veronica. It's as exciting fucking her now as it was when we first met. More so, actually. I get a thrill just thinking about her. But we're so different in other ways. Poles apart.

What's going to happen to us?

I'll tell you. We'll carry on like this until she meets some guy who has a few shekels and he'll cart her off. Wooed in the city. Married in the suburbs. I'll become a non-person. Get the big kiss-off.

When she says I'm a cretin pissing about it really gets through to me because I know she's telling the truth. But I'm going to have to start getting myself organised and back on the tracks. I just hope that this side of my 26th birthday ain't too late to start doing it. I'll get a decent 35mm camera. Start doing some serious photography … .

I flick the cigarette end into next door's garden and wander back into the house. As I shut the front door I see a white envelope in the letter cage that's fixed to the back of the door. I take it out, glance at it and go to put it on the shelf where the mail sits. I didn't think it was for me but I glance at it again.

My name is handwritten on the envelope in black ink in a beautiful italic. Not Tim Purdom or Timmy Purdom, but Eric Purdom. Who other than my mother and a couple of other people ever called me Eric? My given name, yes, but not one anybody else has ever used. Curious. I look over the envelope. The envelope is square, about 6 by 6 inches. Odd shape. Expensive laid paper. The sort of thing you buy at Harrods. Nothing else is on the envelope. Just my name. No address. No stamp. It must have been delivered by hand. I open the envelope and take out a folded sheet of paper. It feels expensive all right. It's got crinkly edges. The letter says:

> *Eric*
> *Please phone me when you have a moment.*
> *AMBassador 6532.*
>
> >   *Vicky Stafford.*

It's written in the same italic hand as the envelope ... which figures.

Who's Vicky Stafford, and why is she calling me Eric? She doesn't know me ... or does she?
I tried this Vicky Stafford number several times the next day from the bar but there was never any answer (as, indeed, there wasn't on Monday night). The phone just rang and rang. Wednesday it didn't answer either and by Thursday I was convinced the whole thing was some fool's errand or a case of mistaken identity.

Friday night I was at home alone watching the news on the TV (and waiting for an overdue Veronica). There was a news report from some BBC journalist outside the Old Bailey talking about Stephen's trial – it's been hard to get away from it. The papers are full of nothing else. Then one of the guys who lives on the ground floor knocked on the door and said there was someone on the phone for me, that it was important

I nearly said I never have important phone calls but I thought better of it. I thanked him and followed him down the stairs. Who was this going to be? Veronica saying she couldn't make it? Charlie saying he needed to sleep over again for the night? Mr Calabrese saying the burglar alarm had gone off again and could I go over and take care of things?

I took the big black phone in my hand and sat down on the stairs.

'Hello?'

There was silence, just static.

'Hello?'

'Oh, hello.'

A woman's voice. Educated. Youngish.

'Yes?'

'Oh, is that Eric Purdom?'

'Tim Purdom, you mean. Nobody has called me Eric for years.'

'Tim then. I'm so glad I've got hold of you ... Tim.'

First-name terms already. She sounds OK. Affectionate. There's an eagerness about her voice. Charlie would say that she sounds like she's been about.

'Who are you?'

'I'm Vicky Stafford.'

'The note.'

'Yes, the note.'

'I phoned you a good few times. I never got any reply.'

'I am sorry, Tim. I had to go down to the country after I had the note delivered. I've only just got back.'

'Right.'

'Look, we need to meet ... *soon*.'

Do we? Why? I've never heard of her. Why do we need to meet?

'Sure,' I say, 'but why?'

'I'd prefer not to say on the telephone, Tim. If I say we

met some time ago through Stephen perhaps you'll understand?'

'We did?'

'Yes. You may not remember it, but we did.'

'I'm sorry … I don't.'

'It doesn't matter.'

'Where do we meet then?'

'I've got a studio in the East End. It might be safer there
than at the flat here.'

'When?'

'Next Wednesday is the earliest I can do.'

'I think that's OK with me. What time?'

'Say about nine?'

'In the morning?'

'No, Tim. The evening.'

'That's a bit late, isn't it?'

'It's easier for me at that time.'

'Uh-huh. Where do I come to then?'

'Caroline House, Caroline Street.'

'Where's that?'

'Get an underground to Shadwell. About twenty
minutes' walk.'

'Shadwell? I've never heard of it.'

'In the East End, between Whitechapel and Stepney.'

'Uh-huh.'

'A railway goes across Caroline Street. Caroline House is
right there … next to the railway.'

'I see.'

'Until Wednesday, then?'

'Yes.'

'Good-night.'

'Good-night.'

I hung up. I can't remember meeting her. The name
doesn't ring a bell. Did Stephen give her my number? My
address? But Stephen doesn't know I was christened Eric
… does he? I suppose I could ring him and ask about this
Vicky. He's probably sitting at home right now having a

relaxing evening watching the TV after a long day at the
Old Bailey just waiting for me to call: Tim, dear boy. So *very*
glad you've called. I wanted to ask you about my suitcase.
You know the one. The one you're guarding for me.

Slack Tuesday, all right. And I'm sitting here in the room
smoking a fat joint. I'm holding it about a foot or so in front
of me. Just gazing at it. Fascinated. If I close my left eye it is
on the left of the TV, and if I close my right eye it is on the
right. It flicks backwards and forth as fast as I can open and
close my eyes … just like that scene with the kid and the
knife in *Knife in the Water.* Exactly the same.
    As I take another hit on the joint my eyes focus on the
television screen. There's a news reporter talking straight
into camera. He's standing outside some building. There
are crowds of people. Then there's a photograph of
Stephen wearing a suit and an open-necked white shirt.
He's got a cigarette in his hand and a smile on his face like
he's won the football pools. Then there's a not very flat-
tering photograph of Christine Keeler and then we're back
to Lunchtime O'Booze outside the court, the Old Bailey. I
wonder what he's saying. I can't hear. The volume is
turned down. All I can hear is Sonny Stitt on the record
player.
    I take another hit and stare back at the TV screen. I'm
looking at one thing and listening to something else. The
reporter is still rabbiting on about Stephen's trial. I think
the *Standard* said this evening that the judge begins his
summing up tomorrow, though fuck knows what he's got
to sum up – the percolated 'evidence' of a whole stream of
dubious, dodgy and suspect prosecution witnesses leant
on by the police, all with something to lose and gain.
Justice always triumphs, said H. L. Mencken … seven
times out of ten. I flick the remains of the joint into the sink
and then I go over to the bed and lie down. The record has
finished but the arm hasn't lifted. There's a continual click
as the LP turns endlessly. I'll have to fix that some time but

not right now. Not right now … I've slipped my moorings
and I'm drifting out into the ocean of sleep.

A peal of bells. No. A siren? No. A fire bell? No.
Something. What is it? And again. There it is again. A bell.
The bell. The one outside the room door. Why is it ringing?
What's happening? Yes. There must be someone down-
stairs.

I push myself to the side of the bed and swing my legs
over on to the floor. I push myself up with the palms of my
hands and topple across the room.

Now I'm going down the stairs real careful. One at a
time. Negotiating my way with all due diligence. Down
and down. Up above me I hear the bell again, ringing with
muted immediacy. Down still further and then across the
hall.

I open the front door.

'Hello, admiral. Mind if I kip down for the night?'

It's Charlie. He's got a new suede jacket on and a hat
with a band round it and he's smoking a cigar and looking
like a male model in *Town* magazine.

'Timmy. What have you been up to, son? You look like
you've been going in for some mental self-abuse with the
substances.'

'Yeah. Something like that. Come in.'

'Any left? I ain't got any.'

'All gone up in smoke.'

'Anything to drink then?'

'Just that half-bottle of sherry from Christmas.'

'Fancy going out and scoring something?'

'Not tonight.'

'OK, then.'

Charlie followed me up the stairs whistling and
humming *Big Girls Don't Cry* and I tell him to keep it quiet
as he'll wake the residents. He ignores me and I realise he's
more loaded than I am. But pills, not dope. Those little
purple hearts and black bombers are his taste. He likes
pharmaceuticals.

'What's there to eat?'

'Nothing I don't think. Some stale bread ... some cream crackers. Look over there.'

Charlie rummages about amongst the used plates and dirty milk bottles.

'Nothing here, squire. We'll find Sonny before we find anything worth eating here.'

Sonny. I'd almost forgotten about Sonny in the last few days.

'You heard anything about him lately?' I ask casually so as not to let on about anything.

'He's vanished. He's one stupid nigger who's got himself totally lost all right. One of his girls has reported him missing ... to the police.'

'You fancy a drive up to Hitchin at the weekend?'

'Hitchin, Tim? What's up there?'

'I want to have a look round a wood.'

'Sounds a rave. I'm starving. I'm going down the Grove to grab something. Gimme me your key and I'll let myself back in.'

'It's on the hook on the back of the door.'

'Great.'

And Charlie slams the door shut with such force the walls seem to wobble. The sound echoes down the stairwell. The remains of the joint in the sink are sodden. I carefully flush it away. I then gather up three or four ashtrays and go through the ash and fag-ends looking for the remains of any other joints. I find a couple and flush those away too.

There's a thump on the door and somebody calls my name. It's Charlie. There's another thump. The door opens.

'Some geezer downstairs on the phone for you.'

I nod to Charlie and follow him out.

'You want me to bring you back anything to eat?'

'No. No thanks.'

He takes the steps two at a time and disappears ahead of me. I take the steps a little more cautiously and wonder who's calling me at ... if my watch is right ... 11.30 p.m.

Veronica, probably. Or Mr Calabrese about the burglar alarm?

I see the phone ahead of me at the bottom of the stairs. The receiver is dangling just above the floor.

'Yeah?'

'Timmy, *dear* boy.'

A soft, warm resonant voice. Stephen's. I'm a bit taken aback. Why's he phoning me? Not that it isn't good to hear from him, but I'm surprised he's calling me. Timmy, dear boy – said in a bouncy manic-depressive on the upswing way.

'Stephen. Fancy hearing from you!'

'I thought I'd give you a quick call. See how you are.'

'I'm fine, but what about you?'

'Fine, Timmy. Just fine.'

'What about the trial?'

'Oh, that. Well, I don't think that's anything to worry about. Just a little sideshow, really. All blow over, you know.'

All blow over? I'm reading in the papers that he could be sent to the slammer for a few years and he says it'll all blow over? I seem to be more worried about it than he is.

'Is it all going to blow over?'

'It will all blow over … yes.'

'I'm glad you think so.'

'Uh-huh. I just wanted to make sure everything is … uh, *safe.*'

'Safe?'

I stupidly repeat the word in order to give myself time to think. Safe? He means the case. Is the case safe? What do I tell him?

I then get a paranoid shiver, a feeling that I'm being suckered into something. Whatever answer I give is letting me in for something.

Stephen puts his hand over the receiver. He's talking to someone else. There's another person with him. Who? I can hear some strangled whispering.

'Safe, Stephen? Everything is always safe.'

There's a silence at the other end of the phone. An uncharacteristic silence.

Stephen bounces in with 'I see, Timmy. Good.'

'Let me ask you something.'

'What?'

'Does the name Vicky Stafford mean anything to you?'

'Vicky Stafford? Vaguely rings a bell. One meets so many people. Why?'

There's a weariness about the way he says 'Why?'

He's got more important things to think about. A weariness over the question that contrasts with the studied way he says 'One meets so many people.' That alerts me to something, though I don't know what.

'Somebody I met … Stephen.'

'I must be toodling off now. I'll be in touch.'

'Yeah, take care, Stephen.'

'I certainly will … and you too. And we must get together soon. We really must.'

'Bye.'

'Bye.'

I slump down on the stairs and try to figure out what that call was all about.

First and most importantly, I guess, it was about the case being safe. But why?

What a fucking idiot I was never to see what was inside it! A dumb fucking idiot. Then again, perhaps it was better that I didn't know.

But why was I entrusted with it?

Why's Stephen so bouncy and bright?

Does he know something I don't about the trial? He must do.

And Vicky Stafford?

He didn't say yes and he didn't say no.

'One meets so many people.' A nice neat noncommittal answer.

The way he said it, though. Does he or doesn't he know her?

I think maybe he does. But why wasn't he saying?

Charlie was fast asleep on the sofa when I got up the following morning. I reheated last night's percolated coffee, had a couple of cigarettes and did some tidying up. I went across the landing and had a quick bath (the Ascot only produces tepid water now. I'll have to tell the landlord) and then got dressed. Charlie was still snoring. I tried to wake him but he was really gone. He can wake up in his own time. I'll see him later.

I left the house, walked down Queensway at a fair old clip, picked up a *Telegraph* and caught the bus down to work. There was a lengthy report in the paper about Stephen's trial, mainly detailing the prosecution summing up of Mervyn Griffith-Jones, the bloke who prosecuted in the *Lady Chatterley* trial and who asked the jury then if it was the sort of book they would leave around for their servants to find?

Stephen had been painted pretty black at the trial. But what did it all amount to? It amounted to this. He had some pretty girls around him who introduced him to other pretty girls and a few of his friends got laid. A couple of prostitutes talked nonsense, and what if money had changed hands? Big fucking deal! Who really cares?

I hoped Stephen's optimism was based on something sound. It sure didn't look good to me.

I got into the Snax Bar about ten minutes early and opened up. Charlie eventually wandered in just after 9 a.m. muttering apologies and blaming me for not waking him.

Business as usual here.

About 9.30 I was out the back making some corned beef sandwiches when the music on the radio was interrupted by a newsflash. I didn't pay much attention until I heard Stephen's name. Apparently he had been rushed to a hospital in Fulham – St Stephen's, funnily enough. He was unconscious. Why? They didn't say, or if they did I hadn't heard. Something was going on. If this had only just happened I'd have to keep my ears glued to the radio. But, the newsreader announced, the trial has continued without him. The judge is doing his summing up.

I wondered about this. Doesn't the defendant have to be there for a trial? Perhaps he only has to be there for the prosecution and defence cases, not the summing up.

About midday on the radio in the main news it was announced that Stephen had taken an overdose of barbiturates. An empty bottle of pills was found at his side by the guy whose flat he was staying in. Down in Chelsea somewhere. They reckoned it was a suicide attempt. The doctors weren't too sure whether he would pull through but they'd given him a stomach pump and moved him to a ward. He was under close observation.

I kept thinking that when I spoke to him last night he sounded bright and optimistic. The trial didn't seem to worry him. It would all blow over. Nothing to worry about, he said.

What had happened to change him?

Had he, indeed, attempted suicide?

I needed to talk to Nick Esdaille, find out what he knew and what was really going on. Hear what the gossip was down in Fleet Street, but Nick wasn't in the office and they didn't know where he was. He wasn't at home either. I tried him all afternoon.

I thought I could trawl around the bars in the evening looking for him but then I remembered I was supposed to go way down east and see this Vicky Stafford and see what she wanted. Fuck it. I tried the number I had for her half a dozen times but there was never any answer. Damn it.

EMBANKMENT. TEMPLE. BLACKFRIARS. MANSION HOUSE. CANNON STREET. MONUMENT FOR BANK. TOWER HILL. ALDGATE EAST. WHITECHAPEL.

The names fascinated me. This was *terra incognita* to me. I'd never been further east than Fleet Street before and here were all these station names on an underground line I'd never travelled before. I wondered where their names came from and what these places looked like. They were names I'd only ever seen in street atlases and books on the history of London and on the underground and tube maps. This was part of the metropolis I knew nothing about.

At Whitechapel I had to change trains. Goodbye District Line and hello Metropolitan. Shadwell was the first stop out of Whitechapel. Just a few minutes down the tunnel.

I supposed I should start wondering about Vicky Stafford and why I'm here. I couldn't muster up the enthusiasm, however. I just kept thinking of Stephen and this 'suicide' attempt and contrasting it with how he was on the phone last night.

None of it quite added up. But then a lot of things lately haven't. It shouldn't come as any surprise.

Shadwell. There's a big black ticket collector sitting on a high stool reading the *Mirror*. I'm the only person who gets off the train. He looks at me and indicates with his eyes that I'm to leave the ticket in a wooden box in front of him, and then he returns to his paper.

Outside the station I look at my watch. Twenty to nine. I've got twenty minutes. Should be there right on time.

It's been raining. There's that musty smell of cold rain on the hot pavements. Big rain clouds up in the heavens. Dark. Night time. Blocks of flats built in the 1930s. High brick walls. Narrow shops in a Victorian terrace. A dingy corner shop with ageing, chipped signs strewn all over the side wall. Enamel signs that must have been put up at the time of the First World War, certainly not much later:

ICED DRINKS by the glass

And here something adrift with the grammar and sense:

SEND A
GREETINGS CARD
FOR ALL OCCASIONS

Next door is a tailor's. A sign swings in the wind above the pavement:

S. GRONOFSKY
Suits Made to Measure
Misfits a Speciality

What, making misfits is a speciality, or correcting them?

There's no traffic here, no people. Just some dirty-faced kids on the other side of the road kicking a football over the cobbles. This is the famous Cable Street, no less. This is where the people of the East End turned out on a Sunday in 1936 and saw off the hordes of Oswald Mosley's Blackshirts who wanted to march through the East End. The Battle of Cable Street.

That's thirty years ago and, perhaps, on a quiet night you can still hear the clamour borne on the breeze. Perhaps.

There's a different feeling to this part of London. I try and figure out what it is. It's not just that it's new to me. No. There's a different and distinct tenor in the air. I think it's maybe that people live here. This is their *home*. People don't live where I live. They're just passing through. This, however, is home. This is the patch where you're born and where you stay.

I walk eastwards down the street, a solitary figure, my footsteps echoing.

If I remember the *A-Z* map correctly Caroline Street is about half a mile down on the left. Just keep going, past the derelict bombed sites, the dock warehouses and the Victorian 'improved dwellings for the labouring classes'.

There's a hundred year old street sign set into a brick wall: CAROLINE PLACE. And in front of it, some milk crates and an old plastic-covered sofa somebody has dumped.

I see the railway sweeping high across the street supported by brick piers and RSJs and I wonder whence it comes and to where it goes? No matter where you are in London you come across railway lines. Everybody knows about the major lines but these subsidiary tracks and branch lines, nobody ever knows their origin or destination. They criss-cross London with a secret logic of their own, stealing through the night.

Caroline House isn't this side of the railway. It must be the other. I walk under the bridge and stop and listen to the water dripping from high above and hitting the cobbles of the road. Each splash resonating in the brickwork cavern.

On the left here is a vast building towering up *sans* windows. It looks like the back of a cinema and doesn't look like Caroline House, but who knows? This other place on the right seems more the ticket.

There, stretching up to the height of the railway, is a three-storey Victorian commercial building done in some Italianate style with cornicing and stuck-on monumental decorations. Italianate, but Gothicky too. Squat and solid. Looking like it was built in the last century as the headquarters of a patent medicine company.

A solid wooden front door about seven feet high at the top of a short flight of steps. Big heavy brass fittings. A brass rectangle upon which are engraved the words CAROLINE HOUSE in serifed caps. Just that. Its name and nothing else. No clue as to what goes on here. This is Caroline House. 'Nuff said.

There are no lights on that I can see on the top floor, or the next one down, or on the ground floor. Is anybody in?

There's a bell-pull set in the jamb at the side of the door. A heavy pull of enamel in a brass surround. I pull it out and let it go. It shoots back in accompanied by a grinding sound and then a bell rings deep inside the building. I can just make it out.

I wait.

Nothing.

I step back and look up the building. No lights. No sign of anybody.

I look up and down the street. It's deserted. The north end of the street hits a busy road. There's plenty of traffic and noise, but here in this little inlet all is still and silent.

I pull the bell again.

And wait.

Nothing.

I look down the street again and see a cat scurrying through the shadows.

Well, this has certainly been a waste of fucking time all right! Why didn't I say to her, 'Listen, lady, if you want to see me tell me what it's about.' Why didn't I? Huh? I must be dumb. Totally dumb. Why didn't I tell her to come and see me?

I only got a single ticket on the underground so I'm free to go back whatever way I want. I'll walk up there to the main road, perhaps take a leisurely bus ride back.

At the top of the road on the left there's a quaint little pub that must be as old as Caroline Street itself. It's a Victorian local called the Brewery Tap. It doesn't look much bigger than my room. The windows are engraved glass. It looks friendly enough.

Inside it seems smaller than my room. It's crowded with locals. All blokes. Nobody seems to be under the age of about sixty-five. This must be some old age pensioners' pub. They're all wearing old suits with turn-ups, many of them have waistcoats and white handkerchiefs tied around their neck. Most of them are wearing cloth caps. This is how you picture the East End.

All these old geezers are too busy nattering away to notice me. I negotiate my way across to the bar where the only two women in the place keep an alert and proprietorial eye on the proceedings. The two old dears look like sisters. Both in their late fifties with lots of lines on their face filled up with powder.

'What would you like to drink, ducks?'

'A large gold watch, please.'

She turns and takes a glass and gives two hits to the optic. I hand her a pound note and while she's getting the change I pour some water into the glass from a blue jug

that says on it in white brush script lettering: A PRESENT
FROM SUNNY CLACTON. She hands me the change and I
light a cigarette. I take a large sip of the whisky. The
barmaid is looking at me and she is about to say something,
there's a pause … and then she does: 'Haven't seen you in
here before?'

'No. I'm not local. I live over in Bayswater.'

'Bayswater, eh?'

'Yes, Bayswater.'

'I went there once.'

This was said with some pride, as if going to Bayswater
meant travelling through dangerous countries to the other
side of the world. Should I congratulate her?

'Did you like it?'

'Didn't think much at all of it … not like home.'

Home, of course, being hereabouts.

I then thought I might ask her about Caroline House.

'I was supposed to meet someone here, down the road …
tonight.'

She nodded at me, a nod that meant she approved of
what I had said so far and that it was permissible for me to
continue.

'At Caroline House.'

'Caroline House, dear?'

'Yes. Do you know what goes on there?'

'It always used to be Snaith Bros and Drax.'

'Who were they?'

'They made dental powder. They were there when I was
a little girl. Been there for years. Business closed down just
after the Coronation.'

'What happens there now?'

'Don't know. It's changed hands a good few times. We
often see a young girl in a sports car going in and out there.
Very fancily dressed. Long blonde hair. Not from around
here. I don't know who's spoken to her. I haven't. She had
the decorators in last summer. They were there for ages.'

Well, all that tells me absolutely zero about Vicky Stafford.

I look at my watch: 9.30. I should be moving. I'm not
going to get home until 11 p.m. I down the remainder of
the Scotch, thank the landlady and make my way across to
the door.

I look at all the wizened faces and guess quite a few of
them were there in Cable Street all those years ago.

It's raining a bit now and I look back down the street
before I head back. There's a light on down near the railway
bridge that wasn't on before: streaming out of the main
door of Caroline House and illuminating a little sports car
now parked outside.

A beckoning light.

So Vicky Stafford's at home for visitors.

I walk diagonally across the cobbled street and then up
the steps to the door which is wide open. It leads on to a
carpeted hall in which there is a green leather chesterfield
and a long low table. The light comes from a small chandelier suspended on a chain hanging from decorative plaster-
work on the ceiling. I say 'small chandelier' but I guess it
has about thirty or more light-bulbs on it. Bright.

I can hear music being played somewhere. Upstairs? A
radio or a record player. I call out hello? several times. No
reply. I draw out the bell-pull and hear the bell chime. Then
silence … and no reply.

Perhaps she's in the bathroom? I'll go in and wait. I can
smell perfume in the room – the vestiges of some heavy
musky perfume. She must have been here only a moment
ago. But intermingling with this is another smell and I'm
not sure what it is. It reminds me of something.

I look round the hall. There are some magazines on the
table, *Punch* and *Country Life*. There's a drinks cabinet just
to one side of the front door. It's open. Dozens of bottles of
wine and spirits. Rows of expensive-looking glasses and
tumblers on top of it. An empty ice bucket.

The carpet is a deep rich green. Classy. Looks like it has
just been vacuumed.

There are half a dozen framed paintings on the wall.

Coastal scenes. Big skies and mud flats and isolated boats. They've all been done by the same person in the same place but there's no signature or identifying panel. Each painting is surrounded by a generous expanse of white mounting board which, in turn, is engirded by a chrome metal frame. Clean looking. Antiseptic, almost. Three polished wood doors lead elsewhere but the room is focused on a wide staircase leading up to the next floor from where the music is coming.

What's up there?

'Vicky Stafford!'

My voice lingers in an echo on the stairs.

I go back out and ring the bell a couple of times.

Nobody shows. I pace about inside. Where the fuck is she? What's she doing? Am I supposed just to wait here for ever and a day until she deigns to appear? This is fucking ridiculous. I'm going. Fuck Vicky Stafford.

Then the music stops.

I stop, frozen to the spot. The silence is like a lead smog. Just hanging there. Still and engulfing.

Minutes seem to go by. I'm stuck there. Expectant.

She's waiting for me. I'm supposed to go up the stairs. That's the deal.

But why?

Why can't she come down here? I'll only find that out when I go up.

I took the stairs one tread at a time. I had to be careful. I had to do it right. And silently.

The walls on either side had more of the framed coastal scenes. Whoever did them certainly rang the changes on that place.

The stairs turned and ahead I saw a landing. Light was coming from behind a door that was just a few inches open. There I had to go. She was waiting for me.

This foot here and that foot there and one step at a time. Higher and higher and nearer and nearer.

And now I'm on the landing.

The door is about six paces in front of me. There's no turning back now. It's too late to stop.

I glance back down the stairway. It's silent. Nobody is following me. I'm all alone.

That smell again. Not the perfume, the other one. I know what it is. It's like fireworks. Like those indoor fireworks I used to have when I was kid. It's lingering here, stronger than downstairs. The fingertips of my right hand touch the door but then I pull them back suddenly. I cannot rush this. I wait. The perfume is much stronger here. A heady intoxicating perfume worthy of a beautiful odalisque.

An odalisque? Why an odalisque?

There's a feeling to this place. Yeah, that's it. Odalisques. Somewhere on the periphery of my mind I was trying to figure out what happens here. It was neither home nor office nor anything else. Homey but antiseptic. Contrived warmth, engineered domesticity, like a special kind of hotel. But not that. Some front for something. But what? A studio she said. A studio for what? Some de luxe bordello?

My fingertips touched the door again. I waited several seconds, then I moved my hand forward and the door opened. There was a bedroom. A bedroom with floor to ceiling mirrors on every wall. And a bed. A larger than king-size bed low off the floor with black sheets and pillows and what looked like a silk bedspread half hanging on the floor.

There was also an armchair with its back towards me. It was just a few feet in front of me. On the floor to the right of it was a large crystal ashtray in which sat a fat smoking four-paper joint that someone had just lit up.

I could not smell the perfume now, not even the joint, just the fireworks.

There was someone sitting in the armchair. I could see the back of his head. It was Sonny. He was just sitting there feeling really mellow, his joint at his side.

So this is what that dodgy little black bastard was into. This. But what is *this*? Some sort of class pimping ... on a heroic scale? Something *really* special for moneyed perverts?

'Sonny!'

He just sat there.

I walked forward and gently pushed him. His head started moving forward. It continued moving forward and I thought to myself, how odd that this trajectory bore no resemblance to the amount of pressure I had applied to his skull. How strange! Moving forward still. And now his shoulders and his torso are arcing forward. And then a thump as he hits the floor and he rolls over and now he's staring at the ceiling. His eyes wide open. His teeth bared. Red stuff in the corner of his mouth. And there in the middle of his forehead a perfectly neat little circular hole surrounded by black markings on the skin and a dull red semi-glistening substance that is blood. Very neat. Right in the centre of his forehead. Perfect.

I see myself reflected back and forth a million times in the mirrors. I see Sonny from as many angles. The two of us.

I kneel down and start searching through Sonny's pockets. I don't know what I'm looking for, but there may be some clue. But there's nothing. Nothing. Not a even a bus ticket or a bit of loose change. Just nothing.

There's an alabaster foot with bright red nails on the floor at the end of the bed. As I move around I see it is attached to an alabaster leg. And now in full view I see the twisted remains of what I assume is Vicky Stafford, her long blonde hair flecked with blood. Her other leg is bent underneath her. Her arms lie limp at her side. Her head is in profile. She's naked except for a slip pushed up around her hips. Her pubic hair is black. She never bleached there.

Vicky has a neat little circular hole too. It's in her right temple, just to the left of her eye.

She's frozen, just like in a photograph. Still for eternity.

Behind her is a record player. It's switched itself off at the end of a Frank Sinatra record.

The drawers in the cabinet are full of ointments,

unguents, emollients and lubricants – lots of those. There's also a couple of Pifco vibrators, loose amyl nitrate spansules, and a variety of pink latex dildoes, each one bigger than the last.

And there, beside a cabinet, languishing on the deep pile of the carpet is the device that lowered the curtains on Sonny and Vicky.

I pick it up and marvel that something so small and beautifully engineered could be so fatal. It says Walther on it and something about *fabrik* in Germany. It's not a revolver, it's a semi-automatic or whatever they are called. It's been around a few years. The blueing has aged and faded. I remembered what a newly blued pistol looks like. One of the officers at the Pistol Club in the dockyards had one. All bright and deep rich blue. But this one's old.

I hold it to my nose. That firework smell.

I sit on the bed and look at myself at a thousand different angles in the mirrors and then I look at the two corpses, the two human forms from which life has been extinguished. This has been the end of the road for them. This is it. The grand finale in a gaudy bedroom/studio/something somewhere near Shadwell.

I hope they rest in piece. It is still and quiet.

A train passes over the bridge and the building seems to vibrate. The noise is loud and would blanket out any sounds in here, whether they were human cries or gunshots.

Silence again. A heavy mournful silence.

A Walther pistol.

The mirrors.

Lubricants and dildoes on the floor at my feet.

A naked woman who, whatever she may have done, didn't deserve this. But then deserving has nothing to do with it, does it? Doesn't life teach us that it is indifferent to our values and our hopes and our dreams?

The stars in the heavens. Is their progress across the night sky affected by this?

There's that funny little poem by Stephen Crane. It's the only bit of verse I can remember aside from the opening two verses of *Sir Patrick Spens* that I learnt at school. Stephen Crane. The author of *The Red Badge of Courage*.

The poem goes:

> A Man said to the Universe,
> 'Sir, I exist!'
> 'However,' replied the Universe,
> 'That fact has not created in me
> A sense of obligation.'

And there you have it. Pithily and wittily put. I look down at the mute evidence before me that this is indeed so.

Somewhere far off over the roof tops of the East End I can hear a police bell shrieking with urgency. Far off, but getting nearer. And nearer.

I sit here transfixed, running the Crane poem through my head, oblivious to the bell getting louder.

There's more than one bell now. Two, maybe three?

Ringing. Like there's an emergency.

They're getting nearer.

And nearer.

And they now sound like they're in Caroline Street.

They must be coming here.

I race across the room and across the landing. If I go down the stairs I'm going to go bang into them, aren't I?

Where can I go?

In the dark I can see a further flight of steps going up to the floor above.

I run up them two at a time. There's a landing illuminated by street light coming through a large window.

I can hear urgent movements, running, in the street below. Pounding feet. Shouts. Cries. They're in the building.

In the dark I can make out several doors and then, ahead of me, there is a fixed ladder leading up to the ceiling. I climb up it and enter darkness. I can feel a wooden door. My hand moves round its edges. There's a bolt. I slide it and then push the door up. I take a couple more steps up the ladder and push again. The door opens and falls back over with a thud.

There above me is the vastness of the night sky.

I pull myself up and look around the roof. There's nowhere to go. I'm trapped here. I go over to the parapet and look down. There's about three police cars with flashing lights, a couple of vans, some motorbikes. Coppers milling about. Alsatians.

I run to the other side of the roof. Nothing except a 40-foot drop. I turn and see that the adjoining building is too far away for me to jump across. I'm stuck. I'll just have to sit here and wait until the Old Bill piles out on to the roof mob-handed.

And then a train thunders by over the bridge and along the viaduct. I run across to the parapet and realise that the railway is my only hope.

There's a brick wall running along the railway about two feet higher than the top of the parapet. A dark chasm about eight feet wide separating me from it. I'd never be able to jump it. Never. If I could launch myself across and up I could only hope that I'd get a grip on the top of the wall.

What if I couldn't pull myself up? What if I missed? I looked down into the darkness into which I'd plummet, perhaps a pile of bricks following me ensuring that this was the final movement of my life even if hitting the deck didn't do it. I'd be signing my own death warrant.

More police cars are arriving below. Reinforcements.

If only there was a plank or something to bridge the gap, but there's nothing up here. Nothing at all ... except the ladder. The ladder. The ladder that got me on to the roof.

I scrambled back to the roof door and got down on my knees. I could hear a lot of commotion coming from below, but the police hadn't reached the top floor yet.

The top of the ladder had solid brass hooks on either side that rested in a notched groove on the inside of the jamb. It would be simple enough to disengage them. Yes.

Then I realised I was still carrying the gun. I looked at it in horror … like it had been planted on me. What do I do with it? Without thinking I put it in my jacket pocket and started hauling the ladder up.

This wasn't easy. The ladder was made of hardwood and was about ten feet long. I puffed and wheezed as I dragged it out on to the roof and just as I got it clear I could hear coppers racing up that final flight of stairs.

I dragged the ladder over to the parapet and then realised that I didn't have the strength to feed it across the gap. The thing was just too heavy. It would fall down into the blackness.

I had a better idea. I pushed its feet against the bottom of the parapet and then moved down to the other end. I lifted it above me and then started 'walking' it upright, the other end being firmly lodged against the brickwork. When it was at an angle of about 75 degrees I took a big slow breath and pushed the ladder forward with all the strength I could muster. I looked up as sweat poured into my eyes. The ladder slowly decelerated as it approached its apogee and then it was still, as though it didn't know which way to fall. I watched it and prayed. It teetered and then moved forward, as if in slow motion.

The slow motion became fast motion as it gathered speed. I jumped back a couple of steps as the near end slid back along the ground towards me.

Fuck, I thought, I don't want it to bounce off the wall and fall! So I reached forward and grabbed the first rung as it rose towards me. It hit me in the face and I jerked my head back, but I didn't let go.

The far end crashed down on the wall and the shock travelled the length of the ladder and into my hands and arms and a dull pain made me cry out.

The ladder had come to rest. Now it was still.

I tried moving it. It seemed secure, its own weight keeping it in place. It's now or never, I guess.

I inched along the ladder on my hands and knees. My

hands on the side and my knees, or rather just below my knees on the rungs. I did it so slowly and deliberately. I mustn't rush it. Just cool and careful.

I've got all the time in the world.

I didn't look down and I didn't look back and I didn't look forward. I didn't even listen to anything other than my heartbeat. You'll soon be there and when you are you'll know.

Slowly.

Gently.

Time is on your side. My hand touched the railway wall.

Gently still. Don't rush it.

Cautiously.

I tumbled over and landed on the granite hardcore in which the railway sleepers were embedded. I stared up at the night sky and took some deep breaths and said a prayer to whoever might be out there.

I pushed myself up and peered over the wall. Light was coming from the hatch but as yet there were no coppers on the roof. I yanked the ladder forward so as to pull the far end off the parapet of Caroline House and then I let go. It started to fall.

As the ladder crashed down on to oil drums or whatever it was that was stored below at street level I was a good many yards down the railway track.

I was running hard.

Running. Along the rail tracks perched high above lost and forgotten streets. Slow broad curves as the railway sweeps through the rooftops.

Don't look back.

Keep running.

And now down an embankment and through an archipelago of bomb sites and I'm by some Stygian canal. Without stopping I take the gun from my pocket and cast it into the murky waters. It's gone. Swallowed up.

I'm running into the night, enveloped by the moonless dark of the East End.

8

Brilliant Corners

I'm just a patsy.
– Lee Harvey Oswald (1963)

SATURDAY. A slothful Saturday afternoon. Saturday, 3 August 1963. I've got the day off. Charlie and a new guy are covering me down at Modern Snax. First Saturday I've had off in a couple of months.

I've just been out and got all the papers. I've bought all the papers every day now for the last three days. All of them. I've gone through them a column at a time, scanning every last little news item and filler. But there's been nothing, not a hint or a whisper of what happened in Caroline Street. It's like it never happened … and I'm beginning to think that perhaps it didn't. There hasn't been anything on the radio or the television either. I even went down to the East End last night and picked up all the local papers I could find. I checked through them a column-inch at a time. Nothing. Not a dicky bird.

I heave today's papers across to the growing pile in front of the wardrobe. There might be something in the Sundays tomorrow, but I have a feeling there won't be. If this story was going to surface it would have by now. It's dead. It's a non-event.

But why? Do the police sometimes keep stuff under wraps? For a while anyway? They might … but why? I'll ask Nick about that some time, he might know. They often keep important evidence secret when they're on to someone, a suspect, when they don't want to tip their hand. But the thing itself? The event? I wonder.

Listen, if the Old Bill turns up on my doorstep what's the worst that's going to happen to me? I'll have a bit of explaining to do. That's the worst. A bit of explaining. I just tell them exactly what happened. They'll have to believe me. No doubt about that. Yeah, I knew Sonny ... but I hadn't seen him for a while. He was into all sorts of villainy I knew nothing about. Vicky Stafford? Never met her. Didn't know her.

Why did she want to meet you?

Don't know. That's what she was going to explain.

How'd you meet her in the first place?

I didn't. She phoned me, said we should meet. Out of the blue.

You'd never met her, didn't know who she was, and she just phoned you?

Yes. Well, she did say we met once some time ago but I couldn't remember her.

Where was this?

She said at a party or something ... with Stephen Ward.

Who did you say, sir?

Stephen Ward.

Stephen Ward, sir? Stephen Ward?

Hold on a second. I can't say that. That'll just get me deeper in the shit. No. Nothing about Stephen. I can't mention him.

No, she just phoned me out of the blue. Right out of the blue.

And you have no idea, sir, why she wanted to see you?

None whatsoever, Chief Inspector.

Anyway, I'll say if I was going down there to do something like that I'd hardly wander into the nearest pub, chat with the barmaid, say I was supposed to be meeting someone at Caroline House, and announce that I'm from Bayswater, would I?

Well, would I?

You certainly wouldn't, sir. I'm sorry to have bothered you. You're free to go. The officer here will chauffeur you home. And, here, have some petty cash for your time and trouble.

Now there's a point. An interesting little point.

The barmaid.

The barmaid I had a little chat with.

I said I was meeting someone at Caroline House. I said I was from Bayswater.

The coppers must have gone to that little pub and said: any strangers been in? You notice anything that night? Must have. They'd have got a description from her. She'd have remembered that I said Bayswater because she went there once herself. She couldn't have forgotten. Now if all that's true, why hasn't around here been swarming with coppers? Maybe it has. But then why haven't they turned up here? Are they still looking for me?

They could have got a description from her and broadcast it. They haven't. Nothing.

I don't think they're looking for me.

If anything was going to happen it would have happened by now. The show's moved on. Yeah, that's it. Moved on.

I take a half-smoked joint from the ashtray and search about for a box of matches which I eventually find over by the spluttering percolator. I light the joint and take one big draw on it until my lungs are full to bursting. I hold it in and then slowly exhale. I take another hit right away, hold it all in and let it out very slowly again. I feel so light I think I'm going to float up to the ceiling, but instead I stumble forward. I steady myself against the sink, and then my knees seem to disappear and instead of floating to the ceiling I glide to the floor.

It's comfortable down here and at least I'm not going to fall any further.

There's the joint. There still, in my left hand, smoking away and waiting for me. I crook my arm and over comes the remains of that little four-paper number. It hovers in the air above me. One last hit. There you go. Good stuff this. Strong too. Really strong. Charlie says he got it from some spades over Hoxton way. The radio: 'And here is the news.'

'Kim Philby, the "Third Man", who was granted Soviet citizenship earlier this week, said in Moscow yesterday that ... .' Another hit on the joint.

'Mr Anthony Wedgwood Benn, the former Viscount Stansgate, announced ... .'

Good dope this.

'And here is a news flash. Dr Stephen Ward, the osteopath who figured prominently in the scandal surrounding the resignation of Mr John Profumo, the Secretary of State for War, died earlier this afternoon at St Stephen's Hospital in London ... from a drugs overdose. Dr Ward had been in a coma for seventy-two hours. There will be a full report in the six o'clock news.'

Oh, my God!

'Who was Vicky Stafford, then?'

I'm sitting on a park bench in the gardens on the Embankment feeding peanuts to the pigeons. It's overcast. Might rain. My watch says ten past four. Nick Esdaille is sitting next to me with a joint in one hand and a pen in the other. His reporter's notebook is open on his lap.

He repeats the question.

'Who was Vicky Stafford, then?'

The question isn't just addressed to me. He's asking London too, the city that surrounds us.

I look across the sweep of the River Thames in front of me. Cleopatra's Needle there and Waterloo Bridge beyond it. The Royal Festival Hall on the south bank opposite. Hungerford Bridge over to the right taking the trains out of Charing Cross and across Ol' Man River, Father Thames.

Buses. Taxis. Lorries. Pigeons. And pigeon shit everywhere. Even over the fresh litter.

'Who was Vicky Stafford, then?'

'That's the third time you've asked that.'

'I know. If you keep asking a question you'll eventually get an answer.'

'Who from? These down-and-outs and winos here? The pidgins?'

'There's an answer out there somewhere.'

'Yeah, I know. But how do we get it?'

'That's another good question.'

'We've got two good questions … and this is really strong shit, man. Takes your head off.'

A worse-for-wear tabby cat ambles over to us from the bushes and frightens off the pigeons. The cat noses around for something to eat, sees it's only peanuts here, and heads off back into the greenery.

'I tell you what I think, Nick. I think that wasn't her name. It's an invented name.'

'Quite likely.'

'Very likely.'

'I wonder if she knew Wendy Davies?'

'Who's Wendy Davies?'

'Wendy Davies worked in this pub just around the corner from where Ward lived. She had a boyfriend who was a copper. Ward used to go into the pub and she got friendly with him. Sucked up to him a bit. And she spent a lot of time round at his place in the months leading up to the trial … as a police spy. She started to hawk her story about Fleet Street and then her mother stepped in and got some injunction on one of the papers and took her back to the country.'

'Where's she now?'

'Who knows, Timmy?'

Nick takes another hit and exhales slowly and deliberately with his eyes closed. Wendy Davies? What was all that about?

'There's a lot of strangeness about in the metropolis these days. Big heavy doses of strangeness.'

Nick's gnomic statement hangs in the air. He'll amplify it in a moment, after a further hit.

'There's whispers … there's rumours. There's whispers of rumours … there's rumours of whispers. You don't know what to believe … you just don't know what the fuck to believe. Real strangeness.'

Another hit.

'You hear that Rachman, the slum landlord, isn't really dead. He's alive. He worked for MI5. He worked for the KGB. He was Ward's controller. Then you hear Ward was *his* controller. Then there's the Great Train Robbery, right? A million pounds goes walkies. A million in ready cash. Who took that? Then Macmillan says that he got it all wrong in 1955, Philby was the "Third Man" after all. Sorry about that. But then who is the "Fourth Man"? Who else have the Russians got over here? Who was engineering what?

'And ain't it just so convenient to have them Russians to blame stuff on, eh? Just so very convenient. Any skuldug-gery – look for the Russians.

'Who are we not supposed to be looking at?'

I latch on to that: who are we not supposed to be looking at? There's some piece missing from all these stories. Some hidden hand. Some factor X. Something unseen. Obvious only because it's glaringly absent. The lacuna. Who are we not supposed to be looking at? Or what? It's like reading one of those official biographies of public figures where you seem to be told everything, but as you read it you keep thinking there's something missing. It doesn't hang together as it's told. It doesn't knit. Then, years later, you read that John Doe was a raving old queer who spent all his time chasing young men. You've been given the key to the biography. It now makes some kind of sense.

These news stories and events are like this. We've got everything except the driving motivation. The main point.

Who, indeed, are we not supposed to be looking at?

'I mean you read all this stuff about the Profumo Affair.

Do we really have any idea what was going on, Tim? Any idea at all? It's supposed to be about Profumo fucking the arse off Keeler while she was carrying on with the Russian naval guy at the embassy. Went on for ages. Now the security services must have known this because those Russian embassy blokes can't piss without our chaps knowing about it. So why didn't they give the word to Profumo? Why didn't they say, "Listen, old man, things could be a bit tricky here. You could get yourself in a spot of hot water"? No, they didn't say anything. Makes you wonder. Really makes you wonder.'

A final hit and Nick flicks the remains of the joint into the litter bin where it continues to smoulder.

'One thing that worries me, Tim, is those girls that Stephen used to send along for your films.'

'It worries me too.'

'It should ... but I don't know why.'

'Nor do I.'

'And that guy's wife you photographed. Bizarre.'

'I didn't photograph her. I walked out.'

'Yeah. But you were supposed to.'

'But I didn't.'

'Stephen was really strange ... wasn't he?'

'I guess so ... Nick.'

'I can't work out any of the rhyme or reason to this, particularly when I'm totally fucking loaded.'

We both laugh.

Nick stands up and totters forward. He turns and steadies himself against the bench.

'I really am fucking loaded ... and I'm hungry. Ravenously hungry.'

I push myself up and support Nick with my arm.

'Come on, I'll take you over to the café. We'll get something to eat.'

'Yeah.'

Nick looks like a drunk as I steady him along the path that leads over to Villiers Street. We take our time. We go slowly and thoughtfully, one consecutive step after another.

'I'll tell you one fucking good thing that's gonna come out of all this. One great fucking bit of good news.'

'What's that, Nick?'

'I'll tell you. Macmillan's fucking resignation. That slimy old bastard is finally going to have to go. The worst fucking Prime Minister we've had this century. That old tosser will have to go. He's fucked up on everything and the Tories will ditch him. His days are numbered. I'll be dancing in the streets when he goes.' And with that Nick's legs seem to give way and he topples back on to the grass. He's on his back, spreadeagled, pigeons wandering around him. He's lying there smiling at the sky.

'You all right?'

'Yeah. Listen, Timmy.'

'What?'

'Bill le Sage's playing at the Marquee tonight! We'll get some dope. A couple of girls. Make a really big night of it. What you say?'

'Bill le Sage? Sonny used to follow him all over London to hear him play … thought he was almost as good as Milt Jackson.'

'Sonny. Poor, poor Sonny … .'

August gave way to September and then it was my birthday. I was twenty-six years old – four years short of thirty for Chrissakes! October hurried in and Beatlemania was born – the Fab Four were a fact of life and there was no escaping them. Even Charlie was going around with a Beatle haircut and wearing collarless jackets. Nobody could avoid *She Loves You* and all those other songs.

Nick was right about Macmillan. He resigned in October, though what resign means here is anyone's guess. Nick says the Tory grandees got together and said, right mate – jump or we'll push you! Supermac jumped and then out of a hat the magic circle produced the Earl of Home (pronounced Hume). Who? the country said. Who?

Some old duffer from the Scottish borders nobody outside Westminster had ever heard of.

The Labour Party weren't the letting the grass grow under their feet. Harold Wilson was talking about the 'white heat' of the scientific revolution.

In contrast, you looked at the Earl of Home and you wondered if anyone had ever uttered the word 'science' in his presence? No, he wouldn't know what it meant. He used words like grouse, tradition, Our Great Party, the Monarchy. This guy was living in Victorian times. His one concession was to renounce his six (yes, six!) titles and henceforth he was to be known as Sir Alec Douglas-Home. Not Mr Douglas-Home. *Sir* Alec Douglas-Home.

Then the mists of November roll in and 1963 continues slowly to ebb away. Aldous Huxley's death on 22 November is completely overshadowed by another death on the same day: the assassination of John F. Kennedy. I was in the bar when the news came through on the radio. The place went silent. Some woman started crying. Nobody could believe it. This was some terrible mistake. A thing like that just couldn't happen.

I'd never been a big fan of the President yet the news knocked me for six. How could this lone nut, Lee Harvey Oswald, do something so awesome? Christ! And then two days later when this Dallas night-club owner and hoodlum shot Oswald in the basement of the police headquarters (and how many times did we watch and re-watch it on the TV?) all sorts of bells started ringing. Hold on a minute! Who was Oswald? Who was Ruby? What's really going on? How the fuck can some guy just walk up to the man who assassinated the 35th President of the United States of America and shoot him dead? How does that happen?

On the day that Ruby shot Oswald Veronica turned up in Porchester Road with her suitcases. I've moved back, she said. She stayed four weeks, until Christmas Eve. It was good while she was there. We just screwed and got stoned every night. That's all.

Later there was a note from her stuck to the mirror over the sink:

> *TIMMY,*
> *I don't think this is what*
> *either of us really want.*
> *Sorry.*
> *Luv*
> *R.*

Well, it may not have been what I really wanted but I was prepared to stay with it. She was not. I don't know where she's gone but if she needs anything she'll be in touch. That I can be certain of.

Charlie rescued me late on Christmas Eve and I spent the next couple of days with him and his enormous extended family over in Finsbury Park. There isn't a street over there that doesn't have some relative of his in it. The next two or three days were a fog of booze, dope and food: Charlie supplied the dope, his relatives the booze and food. It was one of the best Christmases I'd ever had ... what I can remember of it, that is.

It took me a couple of days back in Bayswater to sober up. I sat there hungover watching the last episode of *That Was the Week That Was*. It was supposed to go on for another thirteen weeks but the BBC chickened out and cancelled it. 1964 is going to be an election year and the politicians didn't want some bunch of satirists taking the piss out of them. No, sir. So off it came.

I opened and closed Modern Snax myself on the last two days of the year – the Monday and Tuesday.

And I went home to welcome the New Year in by myself. There was just me, a joint or two ... and Thelonious.

January started slow and cold and then gradually got slower and colder still ... but the Snax Bar takings were really up on last January. About 45 per cent up, believe it or not. There seem to be a lot more kids about with a lot more money. They buy their 'mod' clothes in Carnaby Street and don't give a toss about all the shit that clutters up this country.

I bought a hot 35mm Nikon off Charlie with half a dozen lenses in a fabulous carrying case (which I immediately dyed just in case the previous owner spotted me with it) and started getting out and about at weekends photographing anything that caught my fancy. People. Street scenes. The river. I wanted to do for London now what Brassai did for Paris all those years ago.

I was taking some shots down Old Church Street in Chelsea early one Sunday morning when I got talking to a young girl wearing a black shiny mac with long black straight hair. Well, she started talking to me. Her name was Flavia Rowley. She was a first year student at the Royal College of Art. I took her out a couple of times for a meal and to Ronnie Scott's and late in February she moved in with me. I felt a warmth and tenderness towards Flavia that I had never experienced with Veronica.

There was an intellectual zest too. We were always going to art shows and galleries and seeing every foreign film at the Academy and Paris Pullman, and she introduced me to her sister, Julia, who was a commissioning editor at Hutchinson's, the publishers. Julia commissioned me to do a book of photographs called *Secret London*. She and Flavia would write the linking text. The advance was small, only £50, but the important thing was that here was someone with confidence in my work, someone who gave me a focus for what I was doing.

Flavia had enormous dark eyes. Her skin was olive-coloured. She was tall and slim and moved like a ballet dancer. I could watch her for hours, just look at her movements and into her eyes. She would often sit in the armchair working on a pen-and-ink sketch and I'd be spread on the bed just staring at her, mesmerised. Enthralled, I guess, is the word. She'd sometimes look up at me and laugh, throwing her head back and I'd watch her long hair cascade over those shoulders and I'd want her like I've never wanted another woman. But if a new chapter opens in one's life an old one will close. And vice versa.

In mid-March Mr Calabrese handed me a large brown manila envelope. I asked him what was in it? £250, he said. What do I do with it? Put it in a bank, he said. Why? Because, Timmy, I am shutting the bar. I am an old man and the lease runs out on 25 March, Lady Day. I cannot afford to renew it.

I had worked there for nearly five years, ever since I came to London in 1959. Now it was over.

Mr Calabrese gave me a card with his new address on it – somewhere in Folkestone. His son lived down there and had a coffee bar on Tontine Street (the strange name always stuck in my mind). He and his wife had bought a little house there and he was retiring. I've had enough of London, he said, I don't recognise it any more. It has all changed. We will see you soon, I hope?

Yes. I'll come and see you soon, Mr Calabrese.

With the few hundred pounds I had in the bank and the £250 I got as a golden handshake, finding another job wasn't an immediate problem. Not an immediate problem, but a problem nonetheless.

I had no idea what I would do. What, indeed, I could do. Or, for that matter, what I wanted to do. The thought of working in some other coffee/milk bar filled me with dread. That was certainly out of the question.

As it was, I did a bit of this and a bit of that while continuing work on my book.

This was working four days a week in the clippings library at the Press Association in Fleet Street, and *that* was doing commissioned photography for a picture agency on Farringdon Street, Albion Features, who specialised in supplying material to continental magazines and papers of which there seemed to be thousands, certainly enough to keep Albion in business.

The bloke who ran the agency was an old *Express* pictures editor called Doug Maxwell.

The first thing he said to me when I met him was: 'Tim Purdom? What sort of name is that? That doesn't sound like a press photographer! That sounds like a hairdresser or, worse, an *actor*. I'm not sending out pictures credited to Tim Purdom. You, son, are going to have to get yourself a new moniker.'

'What you got in mind?'

'Umh, Harry. Good press photographers are always called Harry. You can be Harry.'

'Harry what?'

'Harry *Fleet* … after Fleet Street. That'll do a treat.'

So, Harry Fleet it was, and my name graced many pictures in dozens of lesser known continental magazines that were so lesser known, in fact, you didn't even see them in the newsagents in Old Compton Street.

I later learnt that there was another reason for Doug changing my name. I wasn't in the Union. With this Harry name, if anyone asked, Doug could always say it was one of his pseudonyms. But nobody ever did. And, anyway, couldn't he have said that if I'd used my own name?

Youth and youth culture were what the editors wanted. So I was forever traipsing round to Carnaby Street, going to rock clubs, photographing the kids on Oxford Street, the fans chasing the Beatles, and so on. Flavia and I spent the Whit weekend down in Margate and I must have shot a thousand frames or more of the Mods and the Rockers and their 'historic' battle that got the middle classes wetting themselves. It was a good weekend and I made a fair few bob out of it.

Flavia's parents, who lived up near Barton Mills, the other side of Cambridge, finally tumbled that she wasn't sharing the family flat in Old Church Street with Julia, but was living with me. An ultimatum was served early one Saturday morning (the Saturday immediately after my 27th birthday) in a sealed envelope borne by the family chauffeur: move out or get cut off.

Flavia said, 'Screw Mummy and Daddy.' And I said,

don't be so hasty, you've got your studies and your future to think of, right? Moving back to Old Church Street won't prevent us from seeing each other.

She broke down and sobbed. And then I started sobbing too and we both felt very sorry for ourselves.

At the back of my mind I thought the separation would see us slowly and inevitably drifting apart. In fact, it had the opposite effect. Our love (for that is what it was) intensified.

We were watching *Zazie dans le Métro* one evening out at the Everyman when I looked out of the corner of my eye at Flavia and saw tears rolling down her cheeks.

'You're crying. Why?' I whispered.

She turned and put her arms round me. She pulled me to her. I could feel her tears on my neck.

'I'm crying because I think I'm going to lose you.'

'I'll never leave you. Never ... ever, I promise.'

'Promise me that. Really promise me that.'

'I do.'

'I want to be your wife and I want to have your children.'

No woman had ever said that to me before. It cut me to the bone. I could feel tears in my eyes. We shared a handkerchief and missed the rest of the film.

We were going to get married.

The joy of my autumn was pierced when Charlie handed me a letter one evening that had been entrusted to him by someone I would rather have never seen again. A bloke who had turned up again like the proverbial bad penny – Desmond the slimy journalist. Desmond soddin' Raeburn. And after all this time! What the fuck did he want? Why did he want to see me *now*?

I was going to ask Charlie if he had said anything when he gave him the envelope but Charlie was now snoring on the sofa. I looked at Flavia asleep. I've never ever lied to her, but then again there's so much I've never told her ... .

Timmy,
Of utmost importance we meet. Mutual advantage. Urgent. Come
alone – Jasper's Eating House, Bourne Street. This Saturday, 9-ish.
We won't be seen there.

Desmond (Raeburn)

P.S. Phone office if you can't make it.

I lay back and put my arm around Flavia. I stared out the
window to the rooftops on the other side of Porchester
Road silhouetted against the night sky. I now feel like
there's some kind of time bomb ticking away in my life.
The seconds tick away and each one could be the last. An
odd feeling I can't seem to shake off. It's just sprung up
within me. Perhaps it's just the unfocused anxiety that
comes with age?

Saturday, 10 October 1964. Flavia and I went to see *A Hard
Day's Night* at the London Pavilion. She thought it was
funny, but I must admit it didn't do much for me ... though
it was a change to see a British film that had some energy
and humour and wasn't full of middle-class creeps like
John Mills and Kenneth More. I'd give it five out of ten,
perhaps six even. It was anarchic and I liked that.

Afterwards we wandered lazily about the West End and
had a couple of drinks in the Pillars of Hercules and at the
French (we split a bottle of pink champagne between us).
Gaston was dressed in the most splendid double-breasted
striped suit I'd ever seen. George Raft couldn't have had
anything finer in his wardrobe. In the buttonhole Gaston
sported a large red carnation. Flavia told him he looked
like the head of the Marseilles Mafia. Gaston took that as a
compliment and kissed her on both cheeks. He said he'd
just been to some French wedding. It was time to be going.

We wandered down to Shaftesbury Avenue and I
stopped a cab. I told the driver Old Church Street, Chelsea,
via Sloane Square.

Flavia snuggled up to me and the journey passed in

silence, a good warm silence. Just the two of us together in
the back, my arm tightly around her as though she'd slip
away if I let go. Flavia and me.

Now my mind was concentrating on the meeting with
Desmond I began to feel a nervous sickness in my stomach.
A semi-nauseous feeling that wouldn't go away. I leant
forward and opened the window and took some deep
breaths.

Flavia was asleep. Champagne always has that effect on
her. A couple of glasses and she's gone.

The cab passed round Hyde Park Corner and then down
Grosvenor Place, taking a right and going through some
minor Belgrave streets that bring us out on to King's Road
as it passes through all that stuccoed magnificence of Eaton
Square. Just before we got to Sloane Square I asked the
cabby to pull over.

Flavia sleepily opened her eyes.

'I get out here,' I whispered.

'Hope it all goes well.'

I had lied to her. I said I was meeting Doug Maxwell and
some of his really boring clients. I'd said she would have
found it crass and awful. OK, she had said. You go alone.
I'll wait for you down at the flat. I had lied to her. She
trusted me without question.

I held her head in my hands and gave her a long
lingering kiss. I could taste the champagne on her lips.

'I love you,' I said.

'And me you!'

I shut the door and the cabby pulled off. Flavia appeared
in the back window waving and blowing kisses in a funny
exaggerated way. I stood there until she disappeared from
sight towards the Royal Court.

The turning was Bourne Street all right. There was the
sign. One on each side of the road. I noticed on an old street
map that I have that it used to be called Westbourne Street
years ago after that lost river that runs underground now
(you can see it in a culvert above the platforms of Sloane

Street station). But, I suppose, as there were so many Westbourne *this* and Westbourne *that*, they shortened it. Now it's just Bourne Street.

And there's the restaurant ahead of me. Jasper's Eating House. Tiny and like a bistro. Real Chelsea-ish.

I push the glass-panelled door open and enter. The place is small but packed with spindly tables and chairs. It's crowded with young Chelsea-ites, talking loudly, laughing. I can smell a faint trace of dope in the air.

This isn't his sort of place at all.

A young waiter dressed in something like a coster-monger's costume (you know, striped waistcoat, collarless shirt) thrusts a large menu in my hand.

'I'm meeting someone here, actually.'

I describe Desmond as I can't readily see him.

The waiter frown. 'Oh, *that* gentleman,' and his eyes look up: 'we've put *him* in the far *corner*.'

'I'm afraid so,' I say, distancing myself swiftly from my dining companion.

The waiter waves me through to the back of the restaurant where, in a little alcove, sits Mr Grease. Desmond. Sitting there like a big self-satisfied spider. His fat sweaty nicotine-stained fingers waving a Player's Navy Cut in the air.

'Timmy, old man. Good to see you! Grab a pew.'

He's put on a lot of weight since I saw him last. His face is redder. His nose more bulbous. His hair is greasier than ever. Beads of sweat are regimented along his hairline.

That photograph they use of him in the Sunday paper must have been taken twenty or more years ago.

'Sit down. Sit down. Have a drink. Make that another large gin and tonic, waiter. No, make it another *two* large gin and tonics. I'm ready for another one. Make yourself comfortable, Tim, old man. Make yourself comfortable. The food here is supposed to be very good, or so that slut who edits our woman's page says. What would you like? The oyster and mushroom pie is supposed to be worth a nibble. We'll each have that. We'll start with that. So what have you been doing lately? What new villainies have you been getting yourself into? You know you can tell Uncle Desmond. Mum's the word if you say so. I'm the one chap on the Street of Adventure you know you can trust, aren't I? I don't have to tell you that, do I? Me, old Desmond!'

I'm being reminded of a part of my life I'd sooner not remember. My stomach is churning.

Desmond offers me a Player. I shake my head.

'Suit yourself. They're the only things that keep me going. Them and the gin!'

The waiter returns with the drinks. Desmond reaches forward like a child who thinks someone's going to steal his food. He takes the glass, pours the same again of tonic in it and downs it in one.

I sip my drink slowly. It makes me feel a little better.

'So,' says Desmond, 'the Olympic Games started in Tokyo today. I suppose you'll be following that?'

'What am I here for?'

'No need to get shirty, old man. We can get to that all in good time. Let's order first. Waiter! Two starving buggers over here. We want to order! And two more large gins – pronto! You only get decent service when you show them who's boss. Always works.'

'What am I here for?'

'Let me order first.'

I light one of my Benson & Hedges as Desmond orders the pie. I tell the waiter I'd just like a couple of bread rolls and some butter.

'I've got something to show you.'

'Show me then.'

'I can't across the table. Somebody might look over your shoulder. Come and sit here next to me for a minute.'

I move round to the empty chair next to Desmond. He smells almost like old French Joe used to smell – drink, sweat, fags, cabbage.

'I've got something rather special here, Timmy, old man. Rather special indeed.'

He produces a large stiff-backed manila envelope. Printed on the front of it at the bottom in red are the words PHOTO-GRAPHS – DO NOT BEND. All the photographers use them.

'Collecting photos, Desmond?'

'I suppose you could say that.'

He takes out a couple of dozen black-and-white 10 x 8s. He hands the top one to me. It's a grainy print of a blonde girl sitting on the edge of a bed. She's naked. Her legs are wide apart. There's another girl kneeling in front of her holding a dildo in her vagina. The kneeling girl is being fucked from behind by a spade.

'So what, Desmond?'

There's a maniacal grin on his face. He knows something I don't know. He hands me another photograph.

A brunette, late teens with large breasts, is lying on her back on a bed. She's wearing stockings and nothing else. A bloke is crouched by her head with his dick in her mouth. Another guy is kneeling between her legs fucking her. There's something very familiar here.

The third photograph is a close-up of another brunette. She's got a black cock in her mouth. Come has run out of her mouth, down her chin and over her breasts. The girl's looking into camera quizzically, as if to say: is this all right?

I recognise the photographs. Or, to be accurate, I recognise the models.

I take the rest of the pictures from Desmond and flick through them. They're familiar to me all right. They are frame enlargements from some of the films I made. I hand them back to Desmond, who is still sporting this shit-eating grin.

I go back to the seat opposite the fat bastard. What does he expect me to say? What's his angle? What's the reason for all this? Where's it leading?

I'll be nonchalant. Let him make the running. I light another cigarette, sip the gin and listen to the Supremes singing *Baby Love*, blasting out from two big black speakers at the front of the restaurant.

'Had a couple of other pictures to show you, lad, but I seem to have left that envelope back in the office. I'll tell you about those later. Now, charming set of photographs, aren't they? You certainly knew how to get a good performance out of those girls, didn't you? I suppose you got your own end away after the filming was over, eh? Director's perks?'

'Where's all this leading?'

'General election next week, Tim. General election. Who do you suppose is going to win?'

What's he going off on a tangent for? He'll answer his own question if I say nothing. And he does.

'I'll tell you who'll win. The fucking Communists! The fucking Communists will be moving into number 10 Downing Street!'

'The fucking Communists!? You're out of your mind! They only field a few candidates. They even lose their deposits!'

'I'm not talking about the Communist Party of Great Britain, you ass! I'm talking about the real communists – Harold Wilson and all those reds in the Labour Party. Wake up, son. Those are the *real* communists!'

Harold Wilson a communist? What a joke. I don't even know anyone who considers him a socialist, let alone a communist! This is laughable. Totally fucking laughable. But then we're not dealing with reason here, are we? This is Desmond and the extreme right wing of the Tory Party. Reds-under-the-beds. McCarthy. Hot warriors in the Cold War. This is the politics of paranoia. Desmond finishes his gin and shouts to the waiter for another one. His face has got even redder now. His breathing is laboured. He waves his finger at me.

'You walk around with your head up your arse. You need a course in political reality, you do!'

'Yeah, Desmond.'

'You fucking do. It's people like you who let the communists trample all over us.'

The young waiter appears and places Desmond's oyster and mushroom pie in front of him. I get some rolls.

'Will sir be requiring the wine list?'

'No sir will not. Sir requires another gin and tonic. Sir ordered it from your *boyfriend* – go and sort him out and see what's he doing with it.'

'Wiping the Vaseline off the bottle neck, I dare say,' says the waiter.

But the line went over Desmond's head. He was too busy stuffing into the pie and spluttering mouthfuls of food over the table.

'Now, Timmy, lad. Where was I?'

'Labour Party. Communists. Gin and tonics.'

'Right. Now those photographs. You recognise the girls, don't you?'

'Carry on.'

'They've all got a couple of things in common, they have. They all came to you through your good friend, the late Dr Stephen Ward who may God rest in peace. All came through him, those ones. And do you know what else they've got in common, eh? Most of them anyway … and we're working on the others.'

'Tell me.'

'They've all got connections with the Labour Party – in one way or another! But I'm not going to go into all that right now. Just take my word for it.'

'So what does this all mean?'

'I want your story for the paper.'

'*My* story?'

'Yes. I want a photograph of you on the front page and the headline: I RAN THE LABOUR PARTY BLUE FILM RACKET. You'll be paid well for your story. Give you enough to disappear off to Spain or somewhere for a few years. We'll run that for two or three weeks and then we'll drop the bombshell.'

The bombshell? What bombshell? What's he for fucking Chrissakes talking about?

'We'll save the strongest stuff for last. The bombshell will rock them. How you photographed two big buck niggers working their way through the *Kama Sutra* on Caroline Callaway ... shagging the arse off it! Great photographs. I've got them back in the office. You couldn't print them in a family newspaper though, more's the pity.'

So she had a name after all – Caroline Callaway. But who is she? Where did Desmond get the pictures from? I'm wondering how all this came together.

'Who's Caroline Callaway, then?'

'You don't know?'

'No I don't fucking know.'

'She's the wife of Dick Callaway, the Labour MP. He's aptly named, I tell you – always getting his dick away. He's always flitting over to Moscow on so-called trade deals. All a front. He had an affair with this Russian woman interpreter back in 1958. The KGB photographed him and they've been blackmailing him ever since. His wife has had a few bits on the side too. She's never been afraid of giving it away. She's seen as a security risk all right. Probably in league with him. But doing it with a couple of *niggers* ... that's a bit thick, isn't it? In more ways than one!'

I broke a roll in half and started buttering it. There would be no point in arguing anything with Desmond. No point in telling him about the circumstances of the Caroline Callaway shoot. No point at all. So what if my finger wasn't actually on the button of the camera? It seemed academic. I took the two spades around there. I organised that. Who'd listen to me with my track record if I said Stephen suckered me into it? Nobody. I'm wasting my time thinking about any of this. Let it be.

'Anyway, lad, you stand to make a lot of money for your full and frank story.'

'I haven't got a story.'

'Don't start getting tetchy. You'll do very nicely out of this. You've got a duty to tell it.'

'I haven't got any fucking duty.'

'You're an Englishman. You've got a patriotic duty to the Crown!'

Crown? What a strange choice of word. Who's he been speaking to? The Crown? Don't people say the Queen? Or the Country? Why the Crown? Odd.

'Timmy – are you going to fucking sit there and do nothing while the Communists in the Labour Party take over? There's a fucking election next week. You're just going to sit back? Wisen up. You can be patriotic and make a packet. It's here on the plate for you.'

'Stuff it, Desmond.'

'Listen, son. I've been very nice about this. The story can run without you just as well. You can be left out in the cold without a penny!'

I broke another roll in half and began buttering it. Desmond was getting a little bit desperate. The story couldn't run just as well without me. With me on the inside saying this and that the story would run pretty smoothly. There'd be nobody about to contradict me. I could virtually say what I like. But with me on the outside Desmond would be trying to make bricks without straw. I'd be sniping at him … another paper would take the story up. Desmond and his allegations would be investigated. No, Desmond needs my co-operation … or my silence.

'You've got to come in on it, Timmy, for your own good. For your country's good. For the world's good.'

The world's good? Let's not be stinting – why not the universe's good?

'These are difficult times we're living in. The Cold War could blow up any minute. How do you think President Johnson's going to feel when he's going it alone in a big way in Vietnam and he reads in the papers that the people he's fighting are now running his closest ally, Britain?'

'Harold Wilson the communist?'

'Yes. He's been a communist for years. He's been to Moscow more times than any other politician in this country!'

'That makes him a commie?'

'No that doesn't. But they've got files on him. They know all about him. He's a communist all right.'

'They have, have they?'

'Yes, they have.'

'They. I'm interested in *they*.'

'Believe me.'

'Let me ask you something, Desmond. Let me ask you a question. And let me see if you can give me a straight answer.'

'Just ask it.'

I knew full well I wouldn't get a straight answer but I was just curious what he'd say. Idly curious.

'OK. Now you, Desmond, couldn't have got a story out of Christ on the Cross, could you?'

'Steady on, old man. I've been in the street for over thirty years! And I've had my own byline for twenty!'

'So how is it that you have all this? Where did all the photographs come from? Who handed them to you? Who put the spin on the story?'

'Resourceful journalism. Thirty years' experience ferreting out the full and fearless truth!'

'Stuff that up your arse. This was all given to you. I know that. Tell me who.'

'A journalist never reveals his sources, old boy.'

'Tell me who? Tell me because I'm the centre of it.'

'I don't think … '

'Somebody walked in and gave you a great big package and said Desmond, here it is. All you've got to do is read it!'

Nick's remark starts running through my mind as though it's on an endless loop: who are we not supposed to be noticing? It's the same people we're not supposed to be noticing elsewhere.

The fearless and frank journalist is uncharacteristically quiet. He's going to shift ground and try another tack.

'Tim. You can be a very rich man if you go along with this. And you'd be making some very good friends too.'

'So you keep saying.'

'You won't know about Sonny, but perhaps I should tell you.'

Sonny! Believe it or not, I don't think I've thought of Sonny once this year. I thought about him plenty of times immediately after Caroline Street, but that was it. This year, not at all. One's mind can just block out whole areas when it wants to. Sonny!

'You won't know about Sonny, but perhaps I should tell you.' Desmond says it again.

'Let me know all about Sonny, Desmond.'

'It's like this. I can't be too specific, you know how these things are, but Sonny proved himself very useful to ... very useful ... .'

'To they ... them?'

'Yes. They found him very useful. Very pleased ... indeed.'

'And?'

'And? Well, that's why he was spirited back to the West Indies. He got a right royal amount of cash for his trouble and he lives the life of Riley out there now ... surrounded by all those other niggers.'

'He does, does he?' I want to say something more but I can't right now. Not this very minute.

'You know this about Sonny for a fact, do you, Desmond?'

'I most certainly do.'

I've got a question. A stab in the dark.

'Does the name Vicky Stafford mean anything to you?'

Desmond freezes. The forkful of oyster and mushroom pie remains fixed about six inches in front of his face. He stares at me. His eyes seem to be getting ever bigger. The name rings a bell somewhere in Desmond's polluted head.

'I'll tell you about Sonny, Desmond. Sonny is fucking dead and he's been fucking dead for a year. He was shot through the head like Vicky Stafford. I saw them. Saw them both together.'

Desmond drops the fork. He's still staring at me, food and saliva dripping from his mouth.

Let Desmond stew in that for a while. See what he's got to say for himself then.

I take another bread roll and break it in half. I reach over to the butter dish with the knife and scrape some butter. I begin to spread it on the roll when the plate seems to begin moving towards me. It starts rising. I seem to accept this initially and then I wonder *why*? Now I realise it is the table that is moving upwards and towards me, and at an angle. Slowly at first. Now faster. The table is moving. Plates, cutlery, glasses, ashtrays and oyster and mushroom pie are falling towards me. A pitcher of water flies past and smashes as it hits the floor. Glasses break. Plates smash. There's a frightening noise. A long, tortured scream as if from an animal in endless pain. I don't know where it is coming from – the sound envelops me. It comes from all directions.

I sit as a spectator. A passive member of the audience wondering what is going to happen next.

'Oh, my God. They're out of control!'

Who said that?

'They're out of control!' It's Desmond's voice.

Slowly and deliberately, as if controlled by someone else, I raise my eyes from that point where a little earlier my plate had been.

I see Desmond standing. His eyes are bloodshot and look like they will burst from their sockets. There's a frenzied maniacal look in them. Desmond is a man who has glimpsed the future and seen his own final moments. The horror is hastening him towards his terminal destination – his extinction.

Whatever unhealthy redness was in his face has now gone. It is white and pallid and wet. All colour and emotion drained. Life is leaching away from it. There is saliva foaming in the corners of his mouth – bubbling and frothing up and lazily dribbling down his chin.

'They're out of control!'

The last word is strangled in his throat.

His body begins trembling. Trembling so fast it almost becomes a blur. He screams. A screaming glissando racing ever higher in pitch until it becomes inaudible.

Colour seeps back into his face. It is a dark rich blue. Veins down his temples spring into relief, stretching the skin almost to bursting point.

Blood spurts from one of his eyes.

Desmond falls forward, staggers sideways, spurred on by physiological processes over which he no longer has control. These are his final moments. There's a lingering odour from the descending Angel of Death.

He careens through the restaurant, ricocheting from one table to another, propelled by the hastening end that is now enveloping him, spewing vomit, blood and the last vestiges of life. Women scream and try to avoid him; their boyfriends are paralysed by an inability to comprehend what they are seeing.

This is Desmond's final late edition. That wonky heart of his, after years of abuse, has now gone on strike.

I cannot remain here.

I rise from the chair. I look past Desmond towards the door.

Effortlessly and unnoticed I glide through the shadows and confusion and out of the restaurant on to the street.

I'm running now down towards Sloane Square.

Running.

I'm being watched.

Someone is following.

The feeling is persistent. I can't shake it off.

The curtain is about to come down or go up. I don't know which.

Where did it all start to go wrong?

I've got to keep going.

Can't stop now.

I've kicked a horse's skull … .

Part Three

1

Bye-ya

If the atmosphere in Britain [in the 1960s] was by no means actively nightmarish as in other parts of the world, it was certainly eerie enough.
– Christopher Booker *The Neophiliacs* (1969)

THE CURTAIN seems to come down on Timmy Purdom on Saturday, 17 October 1964. *Seems* to come down, that is. But we cannot be sure. The final chapter here could be the opening chapter elsewhere. The past is prologue.

It is hard to differentiate fact from fancy, to sort out what a witness actually saw from what his reconstructed memory *thinks* he (or she) saw. Difficult indeed.

But what about the 'tramp'? This unknown (and incongruous) figure who dogs the early hours of that Saturday morning? Am I, are *we*, seeing a connection where there is none? Is happenstance seen as design, chance as purpose?

The tramp (I'll drop the quotes) is first seen by a cab driver at around 5 a.m. lurking … no, that is a loaded term, *standing* might be better … standing in a doorway of the Royal Oak. The cabby sees him there again an hour later and this time he appears to be holding a brown paper bag to his mouth.

At around 6.35 a.m. the tramp goes into Terry's, the newsagent's opposite Timmy's house. The tramp, in an educated voice, asks for the *Telegraph* and pays for it with a threepenny bit. Terry Dixon, the eponymous newsagent, thinks there is something odd about him, that he is dressed up to *look* like a tramp. His shoes are muddied and scuffed

but the heels are hardly worn. His trousers are splattered
with what appears to be white paint and are ripped in
several places, yet they have sharp creases. His army greatcoat looks new and clean beneath the 'applied' dust and
chalk. His shirt collar is clean and freshly starched. His
hair is short under the old fedora. His skin looks clean
beneath the day's growth of stubble.

Terry wonders what's in the brown paper bag the tramp
holds against his chest with his left hand.

'But the thing that really alerted me was his manner …
his gait. All tramps have a slow sort of slouch … a shuffle
sort of thing. This geezer didn't. He just strode in and then
strode out … a bit like he was, you know, *busy*, or something.'

The tramp strode out and strode next door, to Enzio's
Rendez-Vous Café (Prop. Enzio Salandria).

Enzio is behind the counter at the far end of the café
frying eggs and bacon for himself and his brother, Franco.

The tramp strides towards him.

It is now 6.40 a.m.

The tramp is Enzio's first customer of the day. Enzio
looks at the tramp apprehensively. There are plenty of
them about here: mendicant hoboes, derelicts, winos,
dossers, down-and-outs. Paddington and Bayswater are
full of them. Enzio always dreads them coming to the café.
They beg food, upset other customers, cause a disturbance
… and smell. The tramp stops at the counter. Enzio tries to
make him out behind the glasses, within the turned-up
collar and beneath the hat, but with little success. He waits
for the figure to speak.

The tramp smiles at Enzio and looks at the menu on the
wall behind the counter.

'I would like the egg, bacon and sausages … with some
toast, marmalade and a cup of coffee … *if* you please.'

An educated voice indeed.

Enzio says nothing.

The tramp takes a wallet from inside the greatcoat,

produces a crisp £1 note and hands it to Enzio.

'Yes, sir,' says Enzio. 'Sit down ... I will bring it to your table. And your change.'

The tramp says nothing, turns and walks back to the front of the café. He sits at a table that has been placed at right angles to the plate glass of the frontage.

The inside of the glass is thick with condensation and it is not possible to see out. The first thing the tramp does is wipe the window so that he can have a clear view of the street. He remains motionless, just staring out.

Enzio delivers the breakfast and change. The tramp thanks him by nodding. Enzio notices several things: the tramp is wearing a very expensive watch, he seems to be having trouble with a hearing aid that looks quite different from any aid Enzio has ever seen before and, despite the generally dirty appearance of the man, his shirt is spotlessly clean (thereby corroborating what Terry next door had said). Enzio wonders about the hearing aid. It looks more like an ear radio receiver he remembers from his army days.

The tramp begins to eat his breakfast.

The café is slowly filling up with other people.

At 7.30 a.m. the tramp has finished eating. Enzio clears away the cup and plates and the tramp asks for a further cup of coffee.

Enzio sees a brown paper carrier bag on the tramp's lap that he has not noticed before. The tramp clutches it with one hand. An antenna-like wire projects from it.

When Enzio gets back to the counter Franco says to him that there is something very odd about this tramp.

7.45 a.m.

The tramp is now casually reading the newspaper: the *Daily Telegraph*.

A photograph of Harold Wilson dominates the front page. It measures seven inches by six inches and is positioned very nearly in the centre of the uppermost half of the page immediately below the masthead (there are

smaller pictures of George Brown and Patrick Gordon
Walker to the left). Wilson is standing in the doorway of 10
Downing Street with his left hand raised in a wave. The
caption reads:

> Mr. Wilson arriving at 10, Downing Street
> yesterday after his audience of [*sic*] the Queen.
> [Other pictures – Pp. 14 and 19.]

The Labour victory dominates the front page:

WILSON'S EARLY START
ON CABINET MAKING

MORE MINISTERS TODAY
The youngest
Premier since
Rosebery

The tramp continues reading the paper for nearly an
hour, his reading interrupted only by long stares out on to
Porchester Road.

It is now 8.55 a.m.

He continues staring across to Albert Terrace.

It is now overcast and raining steadily.

Dave Finney (19), a maintenance worker at Whitely's
store, puts a coin in the jukebox and plays the first record
of the day, the Kinks singing *You Really Got Me*.

Finney notices the tramp gazing intently out of the
window, thinks he is looking for something or somebody.
Enzio and Franco think the same thing. There's an alert-
ness he cannot disguise.

Now some conjecture.

The story as I see it.

A figure hurries up the path of No. 16, Albert Terrace,
takes a key from his pocket and lets himself into the house.
The door closes behind him.

The figure might be Tim.

The house is still.

A few moments later the light comes on in Tim's room.

Is this what the tramp was waiting for? It could well be.

But enough conjecture.

Finney sees the tramp 'whispering' something into the paper bag before he, the tramp, gets up and walks quickly out of the café. Finney is intrigued by the figure and goes to the window. He wipes the condensation away and sees the tramp getting into a white Jaguar car that then speeds northwards up Porchester Road.

Finney turns to Enzio who is at the other end of the café and shouts, 'He's got a walkie-talkie in that bag!' These are the last words Dave Finney ever utters.

Several seconds later there is a noise, like distant rumbling thunder. Distant but getting nearer. It increases in volume.

If you were standing out on the street you would now see the window-panes of Tim's room stretch and bend outwards until they suddenly fragment into a million shards of glass which arc up and over Porchester Road. Pieces of curtain rise in the air, hover momentarily and then begin falling like lazy autumn leaves.

Then the solid wooden window-frames move forward, but the solidity is illusory for they are instantly transformed into a myriad splinters, joining the triumphant arc of glass.

An engulfing ball of fire shoots forwards, rises, and dissolves, leaving in its wake an acrid pall of black smoke.

Another rumbling now. A rising rumbling that transmutes into the splitting crack of an explosion.

The outside wall of Tim's room bows out, the stucco bursts and is propelled forward.

The balcony is now disengaged from the wall.

The brickwork is becoming unbonded as the force of the explosion rips through the mortar.

The balcony tilts forward and splits vertically in half before beginning its tumbling descent.

The roof lifts slowly, hesitantly, and seems to hover. The slates rise in unison and are then shot upwards.

A blanket of dust and debris covers Porchester Road.

Masonry now smashes through the plate glass of Enzio's Rendez-Vous, propelling Dave Finney with it.

The story might now be continued through a montage of newspaper headlines:

BAYSWATER BLAST
MANY INJURED
* * *

MYSTERY EXPLOSION IN LONDON
* * *

PADDINGTON [sic] ROCKED
BY EXPLOSION
* * *

EXPLOSION IN PORCHESTER ROAD
Local residents say 'It was just like
the Blitz all over again'

The explosion made the inside pages of several of the national daily newspapers but thereafter it was left to the local west London papers and the *Standard* and *News* to pursue the story:

BAYSWATER EXPLOSION
One dead – twelve injured
* * *

PORCHESTER ROAD EXPLOSION
TWO DEAD – NINE INJURED
* * *

WEST LONDON BLAST
– THREE DEAD – MANY INJURED –

KENNETH THEODORE: I'd been with the old *Paddington Weekly Advertiser* for about six months when the story broke. My first newspaper job. Alfred Dare was the editor then. He'd been editing it for fifty years, perhaps more, and he called me in and put me on it because Cyril Reddington, the chief reporter, had had a heart attack.

I was round at Paddington Green when the copper on the case, Jim Munby, a chief inspector, announced the deaths ... and here it is, as we reported it:

George Eric Purdom, aged 27, of 16 Albert Terrace, a café worker from Kent who had lived in Porchester Road for five years, Florence Edith Dodds, 84, a widow, also of 16 Albert Terrace, and David Terence Finney, aged 19, of Harrow Road.

There was a lot of pressure on Munby to find out what caused the explosion. He had his forensic lads going over the house day and night for a week and then they disappeared into the laboratory. While they were there the *Telegraph* ran a couple of paragraphs saying the police now believed it was a build-up of gas that had caused the explosion. Munby was furious. He was the investigating officer and he hadn't made any announcements, one way or the other. I was quite pally with him by this time and he asked me to find out where the story came from (he knew I had a friend on the *Telegraph*). I got in touch with my friend there – we'd been to school together – and it turns out the story originated in an off-the-record Home Office briefing. Jim blanched when I told him. He was furious. Anyway he kept his own counsel and about two weeks later was taken off the case. He never quite got over it. You see, he was a copper of the old school. He regarded himself as a public servant and saw his job as discovering the truth and seeing that justice was done. Just a good copper, that's all. Didn't understand politics and couldn't play the game like the smoothies at Scotland Yard.

Then the Gas Board who had been doing their own investigations stepped in and announced that there was no evidence to suggest it was a gas explosion. They effectively threw a gauntlet at Scotland Yard and said, put up or shut up.

So that put paid to the gas theory.

We were all waiting for the next development … and it wasn't long in coming.

The reason Jim was taken off the case was that the forensic boffins had discovered, so Scotland Yard said, traces of gelignite in Albert Terrace. Special Branch stepped in and started their own investigations. I didn't have any 'in' with those boys so I just turned up at press conferences like any other journalist.

The fact, of course, that it was Special Branch on the case now alerted us to some 'political' dimension to the story. Rumours went around, inspired no doubt by Special Branch, that some South African blacks had been staying in Albert Terrace and were storing explosives there which they were going to use to blow up the South African Embassy in Trafalgar Square.

Don't forget, it was only a few months earlier in 1964, in April, that Nelson Mandela had been convicted of sabotage in Pretoria. Blacks and bombs were hot news.

This theory had a fair bit of plausibility going for it until I blew it out of the water. I was always proud of that. I was just turned twenty! What I found out was that the landlords in Albert Terrace – the landlords and two landladies – effectively ran a colour bar. There were plenty of blacks all over Bayswater and Paddington but none had ever kipped down in the Terrace. We made that the front-page lead story. This little old local paper shouted 'Not true!'

So, it was back to the drawing board for Special Branch! Christmas came and went and other stories elbowed out the blast in Bayswater. I got a job on the old *Evening News* and moved to Fleet Street. Then it was Churchill's funeral and that was the end of it. Nobody followed the story up. It died a death.

About ten years later I was reading Commander Melvin's memoirs. He'd been one of the top brass in the

Metropolitan Police in the sixties. He mentioned the explosion and said that the gelignite had been stored in Albert Terrace by some extremist supporters of the Campaign for Nuclear Disarmament, the 'Ban-the-Bombers', who had planned to blow up a number of top secret government fallout shelters. I believed him up to this point but when he went on to say that the police knew who was responsible but did not have sufficient evidence to bring a successful prosecution I thought to myself, pull the other one, squire! If you believe that, you'd believe anything! Not enough evidence! Not enough bloody evidence! They'd just sit back in the face of explosives and do nothing! Can you believe that? And written by one of the Yard's top bananas! Huh!

It's a mystery all right … a real mystery. And Melvin saying *that* was just part of the cover-up. We never got to the bottom of it. Just another Bayswater mystery.

BERNARD PROTHEROE: My boss, Jim [Munby] was very bitter about being taken off the case. His attitude to the force changed after that. He just wanted to serve his time and leave … and he did. He took early retirement and moved out to the coast, to Frinton, with Edna his wife. I often used to visit them there. We used to sit out on the veranda drinking and talking about old times.

The odd thing was that after Special Branch took over the case from us they never ever contacted us to ask us *anything*. It was like we were a bunch of swedes who didn't know hay from bullshit. We sent the files over as a matter of routine but that was it.

I made routine inquiries into George Eric Purdom. Established who he was and what he did and so on. Just the basic stuff. At that stage we had no reason to go any further. He wasn't a known associate of criminals, didn't have a police record or anything like that. Didn't appear to be the sort of person who stored explosives under his bed. I spoke to a couple of people in the house who told me odds and sods. I think I even went to see some girlfriend of his out down in

Kent somewhere. She was a hairdresser. Recently got married. Didn't want to say much.

And then we had the rug pulled from under us.

Now, it's funny that you should mention the tramp. Jim was convinced that there was some connection between him and the explosion. Just a hunch, that's all. But how do you investigate something like that? You don't, by and large. You rely on a tip-off. You rely on some informant coming forward ... but no one ever did. The café owner, the chap who had the newspaper shop, and a couple of others supplied good descriptions. We knew exactly what his movements were. But where do you go with it? Where does it lead you? It intrigued us. It intrigued Jim. And it led nowhere. I don't think it even made the papers. I floated it informally with one of the journalists from, I think, the *Kensington Post* and he laughed.

We're talking history now, aren't we? It's nearly thirty years ago, a third of a century ago.

NICK ESDAILLE: There was a big explosion all right, but who was blown up? Who was in the room when the gelignite (or whatever it was) went up, eh? The pathologist at the inquest said he couldn't positively identify the human remains as Timmy's or anyone else's for that matter, and I think it was the coroner who took evidence and said it must be him, Timmy. Couldn't be anyone else. But that was based entirely on circumstantial evidence.

The whisper that went round Soho was that it wasn't Timmy who went up but Charlie. Charlie was always staying over in Porchester Road in Tim's room and it could equally well have been him. Now if it was Charlie I can just see Tim being smart enough to figure out that it was him, Timmy, who was supposed to have gone up in pieces ... and then, accordingly, making himself scarce. Perhaps Tim disappeared to South America, to India, to Australia? Perhaps he's living in Aberdeen? Who knows? Perhaps he's still here in London? You tell me.

Nobody's ever seen Timmy since then, but then again nobody's seen Charlie since then either. He disappeared at exactly the same time. You tell me what's going on. Who's dead and who's disappeared? If Timmy were alive now how old would he be? Mid-fifties? Getting on for sixty or thereabouts? I wonder if I'd recognise him?

What about the photographs?

The photographs? The stills from the films? The girls? And were they indeed from the Labour Party?

These questions are academic. It doesn't matter whether the girls were or were not connected with the Labour Party. The intention is what matters. They were to be *presented* as being connected with the Labour Party. That was the important thing. Whoever was behind this had a clear intention – fuck over the Labour Party at all costs. These are the people who make Peter Wright look like a bleating liberal.

Wright admitted that he and these other MI5 officers tried to fuck over Harold Wilson and destabilise the Labour Party. He admitted it. It's a fact.

If you are going to do something about this don't go around blaming MI5 or the other intelligence-security agencies … you know, like they blame the CIA for everything in the States. That's a trap that's set for you, one you're supposed to fall into. By concentrating on MI5 or the CIA you're taking the searchlight off the real culprits.

These agencies are dogs that do their masters' bidding.

Why weren't the photographs used?

That's a rather naive question! Just because they weren't splashed all over the front page of the *News of the World* don't assume they weren't used. Do we know what went on behind all of the locked doors of the Establishment in the 1960s? Are we privy to every dirty trick of the last thirty years? Do we know about every bit of midnight leverage and dead-of-night blackmail that's come to pass since then? Of course they were used, but how and when and where we can only guess. The big thing about the recent past in Britain, the post-war period, is that our history is shifting all the while. We've got an unpredictable past. New stuff is emerging all the time and changing our understanding and perception. The more that comes out the less we seem to know.

*Coming back to what you were saying a moment ago …
who are they? The real culprits?*

Let's just say … servants of the Crown … and leave it at that. And I've put the emphasis on *servants*.
    You get my drift?

L'Envoi

Now's the Time

The drama's done. Why then here does anyone step forth?
– Herman Melville *Moby Dick* (1851)

GEORGE TREADWELL: A couple of years ago, just before Christmas, I took the grandchildren to the castle over in Rochester. It was bitterly cold and we were the only people about. We were standing by the wall looking over the Medway at the boats and things and the bridges.

I was standing there watching them play and I had this funny feeling I was being watched. I turned around and looked across the grounds towards the keep. There wasn't a soul about. All I could see was a black dog sniffing about by that house that's built into the wall. Nothing else at all.

A little later, after we had walked along the wall a bit, I had the same funny feeling. I looked back and I saw this man standing right by the keep, near the steps that lead up. He had a long raincoat on and he was standing there with his hands in his pockets. Just standing there and staring across in our direction … at me, in fact. He wasn't moving. Just like a statue. Still.

I started walking towards him and when I was about halfway across the park I glanced back at the kids to see they were all right and then when I looked back to the keep the man had gone. Just vanished.

I carried on and when I got to the keep I looked all around it and couldn't see anyone. He'd gone. Just disappeared. I couldn't make it out really because there was nowhere he could have got to without me seeing him.

Now you may not believe this, but I'll swear to the day I die that it was Tim there. It was. I know it was. Don't ask me what he was doing there because I don't know. Perhaps a little visit for old times' sake? I don't know. But it was him.

I stood there looking around but I realised he had vanished. It was very quiet. I looked across the grass and saw little Alex and Michael coming towards me, calling out.

I told my wife about this and she laughed. She reckons I imagined it or I'm going senile or something. Perhaps your mind does play tricks on you but this didn't feel like any trick.

When had I last seen Tim? It must have been about 1960 when he came down here to pick up a case I was looking after for him. Over thirty years ago.

That wasn't the last time I'd had contact with him because we spoke on the phone a few times after that. I was supposed to go up to London and stay with him some time but I never got around to it. Wish I had, but there was never the time. There wasn't much time for anything in those days, I was starting up the business and working all hours God gave.

Now another thing happened that same afternoon, about three-quarters of an hour later. I'd taken the kids for tea and scones down in the High Street and we'd come out of this place and I stopped. I just stopped and looked down the High Street to where Northgate crosses it. And then from up College Gate towards the cathedral and the castle a car appeared and silently drove across the High Street and down Northgate and out of sight. It was a Mercedes-Benz 450SEL from the late sixties or thereabouts – a nice big car, beautiful bit of design, with lots of gleaming chrome work. It looked like new, like brand new … in that lovely non-metallic gold you don't see much any more. Somebody had spent a good few bob on restoring it. Not many of them about. Very distinctive but not flashy or anything. The windows were all darkened glass so you couldn't see in. It glided across the High Street and didn't seem to make a sound.

Now, if that was Tim up by the keep ... I *know* he was also in that Merc. It was him all right. I didn't see him, but I know it was ... I just wished he'd said hello. There's so much we've got to talk about.

A NOTE ON THE TYPEFACE

This book was composed in PALATINO *– a face designed originally by Herman Zapf for the German typefounders Stempel in 1950. The roman has broad letters and strong, inclined serifs. The italic has a lightness and grace that reflects its calligraphic origins.*
MICHELANGELO *and* SISTINA
are companion titling fonts.